A
LIMITED
SEASON

Also by Fiona Bullen
PAINTED BIRDS
THE DREAM HOUSE

A LIMITED SEASON

Fiona Bullen

LITTLE, BROWN AND COMPANY

To Elizabeth,
with love

A *Little, Brown* Book

First published in Great Britain in 1993
by Little, Brown and Company

Copyright © Fiona Bullen 1993

The moral right of the author has been asserted.

A CIP catalogue record for this book
is available from the British Library.

ISBN 0 316 90328 0

Typeset by Leaper & Gard Ltd, Bristol
Printed in England by Clays Ltd, St Ives plc

Little, Brown and Company (UK) Limited
165 Great Dover Street
London SE1 4YA

Chapter One

Repulse Bay
Hong Kong, 1969
Claudia dug into the sand with small, chubby fingers, humming gently to herself. When she encountered a shell, she carefully scraped the sand away and washed it in the water, holding it up to examine it, this way and that. Next to her, Harry, dark, silky hair flopping over the smooth golden skin of his face, sat back on his heels and peered at it.

'Too many holes, Liddie,' he pronounced after a second's pause and Claudia sighed and tossed it shining and glimmering out into the green waters of the bay. Around them, rising up into high peaks, stretched a dense growth of greenery, beaded with palms and the occasional house as it cupped the bay in its shimmering grasp. A lone hawk swooped over the empty space of cloud and sky, spiralling in the thermals, peering down over the South China sea as it spread flat and winking below. It was hot in the haze-clouded sun and they both sweated in their bathing suits as they squatted on the shoreline, hunched over themselves, intent on their task.

A stray dog hovered beside them, clownishly digging in the mud-like sand and darting quick wolfish grins at them. Occasionally they looked up and threw a stick half-heartedly, the dog dashing off with enjoyment. He always returned and dropped the stick back at their feet.

It was late August, and Harry was nine that day. That morning, his mother, in her black and white amah's uniform, a cardigan thrown on untidily over it, had thrust a pair of school shoes at him for which she had paid too much of her monthly salary, and told him sharply not to get them dirty before pushing him out of the kitchen to play. He had

1

silently placed them in the bedroom he shared with his mother, sniffing the sweet, sickly fragrance of incense and his mother's particular smell made up of hair lacquer and odd fatty lotions that she bought from the local herbalist and Chinese medicine stall.

He had stood beside the small cot bed he used, for a moment, looking around him at the tiny room, the linoleum floor and tiled window, high up and barred. Then he had gone in search of Claudia. And Claudia had begged her mother to take Harry with them to the beach. It was his birthday, she had insisted, and Lucille Babcock, her mind on other matters, had given in.

But now she sat further up the curved beach, beneath the shade of several scraggy trees, watching the children with narrowed eyes. When Harry stood up, laughing and holding aloft a perfectly formed shell, Lucille's lips folded in; her rather pretty face became marred with disapproval. Claudia was spending far too much time with their amah's son, she thought crossly. She was seven now and old enough to know the difference, to know better. There were lots of other children, decent, European or American children. What made Claudia so interested in a Eurasian servant, for God's sake? Just like her father, no sense of what was right. With impatience she turned back into the group of women, her mouth still tight with annoyance as she fanned herself languidly.

'Look, Liddie, look! It's a whole one.' Harry held it out proudly and Claudia knelt beside him, the shell resting delicately on her palm. Her small face was absorbed as she looked at it, her straight dark hair pulled behind her ears. Like a wafer of pink granite, the shell was so thin that when she held it up to the light, she could see the shadows of her fingers right through it. She gasped with delight.

'Can you find me one too, Harry? Are there any more?' Carefully she handed it back to him, and peered into the hole in the sand. Her back was butter-brown where the bathing suit scooped down and her backbone stood out in a series of small, protruding knobs. Harry looked at it in silence for a moment.

2

'No. I don't think so. You have it, Liddie. It's for you,' he said, after a moment's tussle with himself. A broad smile crossed his face when she clapped her hands together and ran with it up the sand to show her mother. Another boy, taller, with fair toffee-coloured hair and a sturdy, bright face, wandered over, his foot scuffing the sand as he went, sending it in arcs out into the water. He ignored Harry, digging in the sand instead. Harry watched him.

When Claudia returned, her face carefully devoid of expression, she handed the shell back to Harry.

'I wasn't thinking. It's your birthday. You keep it, Harry. I'll find another one.' She turned away quickly, so that he wouldn't see the disappointment pulling at her mouth or the anger in her eyes. Why couldn't she accept presents from Harry? Why?

She stared moodily across at the dazzling white walls of the life-saving club where a flag flew, ruffling in a momentary breeze, and then shifted her gaze to the large statue of Tin Hau that sat stolidly in front of the club. She suppressed an obscure wish that she were Chinese too and could pray to the Goddess of Heaven to play with whomever she wanted. For a moment she felt oddly inferior and diminished by her mother's words.

There was a whoop from the fair-haired boy as he dug frantically in the sand at the water's edge, his fingers hunting desperately for something as the sea poured into the hole and the dog circled, barking delightedly. At last he held it aloft. A perfect starfish. He grinned widely. Claudia sidled closer and stared longingly at the prize in the boy's hand, breathing in deeply the smell of sea water and vegetation, warm silty sand and hot oil that rushed in laden on the breeze.

'Oh, look, Tony! Isn't it lovely?' she murmured, hesitating before putting out a finger to prod the strange shape. 'What is it?'

He laughed, puffing out his chest. 'It's a starfish, stupid! Don't poke it like that. It won't bite you, Liddie. Here.' He spoke with the arrogance of all his eleven years and pushed it into her cringing palm, laughing as she stumbled

3

backwards and held it out with a straight arm.

'Look, Harry! It's a starfish!' Claudia turned to show the younger boy who stood, face down, his own shell clenched tightly in his fist. Reluctantly he looked up and stretched out delicate fingers to take the odd-looking thing that was obviously more interesting to Liddie than his own shell. He flashed a look of resentment at the other boy, who caught it full force.

'Hey, Liddie! I didn't say you could pass it round the whole beach. Give it here.' Tony snatched the starfish before Claudia could show it, holding it possessively as he eyed the other boy. A look of mutual dislike passed between them, unthought of until now but suddenly clear as they vied for Claudia's attention. Claudia stared at Tony, taken aback for the moment and then her face became stubbornly disinterested.

'Keep it then, see if I care. Stupid old starfish! I didn't want to see it anyway. Come on, Harry.' She pulled away from Tony, running instead into the shallow water and shrieking as it lapped in small rippling waves at her body. The sand felt soft and squelchy beneath her feet. She shrieked again.

Harry followed her, after pausing to glance obliquely at the boy with the starfish. He didn't know him. He didn't know many of Liddie's or her brother's or sister's friends. They went to different schools and different parties. Different? He didn't go to any parties, neither European nor Chinese. And there was nothing in the middle. The boy stared back at Harry, coolly looking down his nose. Harry smiled then and ran into the water.

'Wait up, Liddie. I'm coming.' Harry wasn't a good swimmer. He had seldom had much practice. So he waded, splashing awkwardly through the water to where Claudia leapt and cavorted through the waves, diving under them and over them, her body gleaming slickly like a fish. They played together, laughing uproariously when the waves slapped them in the face or they pulled each other's legs from beneath them and Tony watched them from further up the shore with a hurt expression on his face.

4

He turned away, going to stand over a small Chinese child as she dug with a spade in the sand but her amah quickly descended to lay a protective hand on her head. Tony smiled uncertainly and the amah scowled. With a sigh of relief he spotted two of his cronies and gave a war-like shout, running up the beach to leap on them and throw them into the waves. The starfish lay discarded on the sand where Tony had thrown it.

'Isn't that Reginald Hsu's daughter, the little one down there?' Joanna Ingram, Tony's mother, asked as she arranged herself more comfortably on the deckchair, wiping a trickle of perspiration away from the hollow of her back. She peered short-sightedly down the beach, wondering whether she could risk a quick look with her glasses. But no, what if Reginald were around and saw her in them? He might suddenly think she was a frump, like that dreadful Lucille Babcock. Joanna smoothed the oil down her arms and shoulders, lingering on the soft swell of flesh that edged over her navy blue and white spotted bikini top. Her fingers curved backwards as they moved rhythmically against her skin. Her hair, blond like her son's, was caught back in a wide bandeau, emphasising the high cheekbones and deep blue eyes. She smiled at the child in the distance.

'Portia. Isn't that her name? So theatrical ... Portia Hsu? I wonder if the family are here?' she added and heard her husband grunt uncooperatively from beneath the *South China Morning Post* that he had draped over his face. 'Bill? Bill! Did you hear what I said?'

'What?' He grunted again and Joanna sighed.

'That bloody Babcock woman's here again,' she murmured to her husband in a lower voice. 'Kicking up a fuss because Claudia took a shell from a Eurasian boy. Honestly! The woman's too much. Can't stand her ! None of us can.'

'Why not?' Bill appeared, flushed and impatient, from beneath the paper. He snapped his fingers and his driver came running down the sand, his shoes and long socks chafing in the heat.

'Oh, you know, she's such a ghastly hick from Nowheres-ville in the Deep South and yet she's always so pleased with herself, with her husband, her lifestyle, her friends – I wonder how pleased she'd be if she knew dear old Frank had a Chinese mistress?' Joanna laughed, the sound deep and throaty. 'That'd make her run for the "bathroom" as she likes to call it! She probably wipes her hands every time she shakes hands with one of them, and her husband's actually screwing one! She'd have a fit!'

'Don't swear, darling, it's so common.' Bill glanced at his driver's immobile face. 'Besides, I quite like her, actually. She's got hidden strengths.' He accepted the gin and tonic the driver put in his hand with a brief nod of thanks, waiting for the man to leave. 'And she has a point, really. Shouldn't let the children get too chummy. I'm not being racist, but let's face it, that sort of thing doesn't work. Upsets the apple cart.' He paused and then added, 'Her husband's a bit of a fool. She's bound to hear some time or other. He'll lose her and the children. And he dotes on the youngest.'

'Claudia? Hardly surprising considering the other two. Bloody monsters! That boy is a spiteful tease and the elder girl! She's only eleven and she's already got all the boys circling, like a bitch in heat. There'll be trouble there, all right. I'll keep Tony well away from her in the future. God knows how Frank or Lucille ended up with a child like Claudia.' She also paused for a moment, considering. 'Well, I expect he'll adapt to bachelorhood again. Amazing how well most fathers do. Mothers too, I'm sure.' Her voice was acid and Bill avoided commenting. He knew she was referring to his threats to take the children away from her if she didn't curtail her own excursions. He wondered whether Reginald Hsu was one of them? Then he cleared his throat dismissively and sipped at the gin and tonic. God, that was good!

'Did you get me one too?' Joanna asked sharply, knowing he hadn't. He shook his head.

'We'll go in a minute. Sun's too hot. Don't know why we came anyway, on a Sunday in August. Dreadful place. We

6

should have gone on to South Bay or Middle Bay, the way I wanted to. Or better still, not come at all.' His face was burnt pinkly in the way that only freckled English skin burns. 'Go get Tony and the girls, will you?'

'Oh, darling, I was hoping we'd have a drink first up at the hotel.' She gestured up the beach to the Repulse Bay Hotel on the far side of the curving road, sitting placidly amongst palm trees and bougainvillea as though it had never been witness to the horrors it had seen.

Bill Ingram's father had been there, in the war. It had been the British HQ then, keeping the road open between Stanley and Aberdeen. After three days of fighting, the Japanese had overrun the place and some of the prisoners had been executed, up the hill a bit, at Eucliffe Mansion. Bill's father had been one of them, Joanna remembered belatedly. She wasn't surprised when Bill didn't answer.

'Tony!' Joanna called, her voice high and clipped. 'Tony, go and get the girls. We're going.' But the boy ignored her too, excitedly dashing through the waves to sink his friend and be sunk in turn. 'Oh, really! Why do I have to go? Can't you do something for a change, Bill?' she said in exasperation. She looked up and caught sight of Portia's father and smiled unexpectedly. Such a good-looking man! 'Oh, well, I suppose I'll have to go,' she said and levered herself easily out of her chair, a tell-tale pat to her hair informing her husband even before he saw Reginald that some quarry was in sight. With a sigh he raised the paper again and lay back.

Beneath the shade of the trees, Lucille slapped at a mosquito and applied more lotion to her pale skin. She never sat in the sun, never went swimming. It didn't agree with her fair complexion, she told the others and gestured to her auburn hair. 'I would risk it if I thought a tan would suit me, but I look like such an old hag if I stay out in the sun. I can't think how you all do it,' she added with the sort of brittle laugh that meant something entirely different. The other women smiled tightly.

'Where's Frank, then? Surely he's not working again?'

7

Another American woman, Fran Clements, newly arrived from Boston but already weary of Lucille Babcock, raised her eyebrows. Everyone knew about Frank. Everyone except Lucille.

'Yes, 'fraid so. He's just such a workaholic. Can't get him to relax for a minute. But I suppose when he's in such an important position …' Lucille sighed and shrugged her shoulders, eyes large and expressive as she quickly shooed away a coolie carrying plates of noodles, his face glistening over the steaming food.

'Not here. They're not for us. No. *Mhaih, mgoi*,' she said crossly, resorting to pidgin Cantonese. The other women looked at each other and winked.

Cecilia Hsu saw Joanna coming and smiled, waving her hand quickly and too enthusiastically, like a child seeing her best friend. Joanna forced her face into a smile, forced herself to pause, to show liking. She did like Cecilia but she was such a silly, predictable creature. Perhaps an antidote to the ferocious quality of Reginald's business, a light-hearted balm to frayed nerves? Running one of the largest Chinese trading hongs in Hong Kong couldn't be easy.

'Hello there, Cecilia. What a surprise. I thought you always went out on your junk on weekends. This place is just such a cattle market. What on earth brings you here?' She kissed the air beside the Chinese woman, admiring the jade green one-piece with a practised eye movement that gave no hint she had even noticed it. Bet that had cost a pretty penny. But then the Hsus had no money worries. Wouldn't that be nice, Joanna thought wistfully.

'Reginald insisted. I can't think why. How are you? You look beautiful! Such a nice bikini. Where did you get it?' Cecilia was transparent in her delight at seeing Joanna.

'What, this?' Joanna feigned astonishment. 'Oh, just at Stanley market, forking through things. What a sweetheart you are. How is Reginald? Oh, there you are!' She turned, in her viciously expensive bikini, bought in a boutique in the smart business area of Central, to open her eyes wide to the man who stood there, his head slightly to one side, a

8

sleepy smile on his face. He still wore glasses, even on the beach, Joanna thought, and he still looked gorgeous. Gorgeous to her, although she had once thought his mouth too large, his eyebrows too heavy and that mole on his upper lip quite off-putting. He must have northern Chinese blood in him, she thought, as he stooped down from great height to kiss her cheek, a waft of some expensive cologne catching at her senses. She sighed deeply.

'Stunning as always, Joanna. How do you manage it here of all places?' He seldom smiled, but he was smiling widely now. The sunlight winked off the steel frames of his glasses.

'Isn't it awful? If it weren't for the children clamouring, I would never bring them on a weekend. So hot, so sandy, so noisy! Repulse Bay used to be so *nice* just a few years ago. But now *everyone* comes. And we couldn't get the junk this weekend. What on earth brings you here?' They had turned away from Cecilia slightly, their shoulders coming together to shut her out. They gazed out at the graceful curve of the bay with its steeply rising hills of greenery enfolding the shimmering sea dotted with sailboats and waterskiiers. In the background a thousand radios blared and Chinese coolies called out their wares. Cecilia bit her lip and looked away.

'Don't you know?' Reginald stooped, his eyes abnormally large behind their glass lenses. He showed no hint of feeling the heat, his hair groomed back immaculately from his pale, intelligent face, his plaid swimming trunks looking almost freshly starched. As though he were about to go into a board meeting, Joanna thought, that elusive scent of power and authority never leaving him. She gave a soft laugh.

'Oh, flatterer!' But she preened herself, her hand caressing her hair again and around her, unobserved, several people gave quiet, knowing smiles to each other. Was Joanna Ingram at it again? Surely not? And they gestured to Bill beneath his paper and laughed lightly.

Lucille Babcock was not so discreet.

'My God, how does poor old Bill take it? And it's not as

9

though she's so very good-looking, either. I've never thought much of those rather showy sorts, have you?' And she sniffed, her long, thin nose perfectly suited to show her disdain. Lucille had the sort of taut body that came from years of denying herself and she concealed it beneath a well-boned floral bathing suit that could have, as the others had suggested in private, stood up entirely on its own. They shuddered at her idea of what was 'proper'. Proper in a small provincial town in the South, they laughed, but decidedly dowdy in Hong Kong. But Lucille, sublimely unaware, readjusted her straw hat and cast discontented looks at Joanna.

'Bill's so weak, letting her fool around in public like that. I'll just bet everyone, including the Governor, knows about it. That can't do his career much good, can it?'

'It can if H.E. admires her too,' Sally Freeman, an old Hong Kong hand, quipped. She liked both the governor, H.E., His Excellency, as they jokingly called him, and Joanna. They livened life up. She showed imperfect white teeth to Lucille, the chip on her left front tooth adding a piquancy to her comments that Lucille with her perfect teeth never understood. 'And he does,' Sally added.

'Well, I'd never let myself be made a fool of like that. Hasn't Bill got any pride?' Two small spots of anger flushed Lucille's cheeks.

'Bill knows how to handle his own life. He and Joanna just have a different way of sorting things out. They're very fond of each other, though. Which can't be said of a lot of other marriages,' Sally replied, her normally placid temper straining with the heat and noise.

'I still wouldn't put up with it,' Lucille replied obstinately. 'I'd leave someone who cheated on me, so fast his head would spin.' She fanned herself, wilting in the heat.

'You're very sure of that, are you, Lucille?' Fran Clements asked, her thin face quick with the delight of hidden knowledge. She nudged the others, who glanced up, beyond Lucille. They stirred, like a stand of trees through which a breeze has suddenly passed, with unexpected movements. Dismay, amusement, concern passed over their faces. Lucille frowned.

'Sure of what?' she demanded. Awkwardly, she leaned forward in her deckchair to crane behind her at what everyone else was looking at.

Frank stood there, his large, good-natured face under its short haircut looking sick. Beside him, her arm still entwined around his waist, stood his mistress.

Joanna turned from flirting with Reginald Hsu to answer an insistent tug on her arm. Tony stood there, his normally sunny face closed and stubborn.

'I thought we were going?' he said rudely.

'Well, we were, darling, but then your father went back to sleep and ...' her voice trailed off as she squinted over at where she had left her husband. He wasn't there. She shook her head. 'You know Mr Hsu, don't you, Tony? Oh, and Mrs Hsu too?' Belatedly, Joanna remembered Cecilia and turned to include her again. But Cecilia had gone to inspect Portia's sandcastle and Joanna turned back again, her smile over-bright.

'Yes, hello, sir.' Tony held out his hand and Reginald winked at Joanna as he formally shook hands with her son. The boy was stiff and awkward, his eyes only too aware as he glanced between them, his manner uncharacteristically lacking grace. He had heard the rumours before, been teased by other boys. His manner showed it.

'Dad's gone to help Mrs Babcock,' Tony added, as though that might convince his mother that they should, indeed, be going. 'There's a bit of a stink.'

They all turned to look up at the crowd beneath the trees.

From beneath two feet of cool, limpid water, Claudia surveyed her domain. There were several sets of legs, abnormally white in that strange rippling light, and acres of pale sand, rising and falling in desert-like undulations. She blew out a chain of bubbles, wishing Harry would come down there and see it too. But he insisted on keeping his head firmly above the waves and had fought her hard when

11

she had tried to pull him under. She tickled the feet nearest hers and was surprised when they leapt high in the water. A head suddenly submerged, the face curious.

Claudia rose to the surface, embarrassed.

'Sorry. I thought you were Harry,' she explained, her cheeks glowing pinkly as Tony, his hair dripping as he flicked it back from his face, frowned.

'He's gone back up on the beach. Your ma's been looking for you. I came to get you.' He looked odd, Claudia thought. Embarrassed and angry, but not with her. She nodded and he took a deep breath, continued. 'There's a bit of a scene going on. Between your ma and dad. Don't get upset. Okay?' And then he took her by the arm, leading her out of the water and through the crowds of noisy, hot, irritable beachgoers to where her mother stood beneath a tree. Tony's father was there too.

Claudia had never seen her mother cry before. She wasn't even sure if that was what she was doing, because her mother didn't look like most people did when she cried. Instead her face was very pale and blotched, a pink and white effect. But there were wet marks and her nose was running and she looked strange, Claudia thought. When her mother held out her hand, Claudia obediently took it and was surprised by the strength with which her mother held it, pulling her to her side.

'Take a good look, Frank.' Lucille's voice was high-pitched and straining harshly to make sense through the tears and disgrace that caught at her throat. 'Because it's the last time you'll see Liddie.' Which made Claudia look up and yes, there among the crowd was her father, looking unhappy and awkward. She smiled at him brilliantly.

'Hi, daddy,' she said.

Frank looked away. 'You just need to calm down a bit, Lucille. Come on, let's go home and talk about this in private, okay, honey? We don't need other people knowing our business.' He tried to smile at her but Lucille only laughed, a cracked, bitter sound that made the awkward and unwilling participants of this particular scene wish they were a hundred miles away. A few, like Fran Clements and

12

Sally Freeman, heads down, got up and strolled away down the beach.

'Everyone already knows our business, Frank. You've made sure of that. There's nothing more to talk about. Where's she gone anyway, that little bitch?' She looked around wildly, jerking Claudia with her. She didn't notice Harry's face, peering between the tall European bodies encircling her, his face blank with puzzled concern. And no one noticed the dog, pressing against the back of Harry's knees, his salt-and-pepper hair giving him a grizzled appearance, like an old man. His eyes were on Harry.

'I sent her home. Now come on, Lucille. We're adults. We can handle this. I know it's been a shock—'

Lucille shocked him even more by using a word he hadn't realised she even knew. She pulled Claudia up by the arm, hastily throwing her basket over her shoulder.

'Don't come home, Frank. I don't want ever to see you again. Let go of me, Bill. I know what I'm doing. Just let go.' She was pale and fierce as she shouldered her way through the crowd, dragging Claudia along beside her, the little girl beginning to wail in distress as she saw her father suddenly walk away in the other direction. She wasn't sure what was going on, but she knew it was bad; so bad that she knew, unerringly, that she was going to remember this day for the rest of her life. Uncertainly, Harry began to trail after them.

They were nearly at the car when Tony came dashing up, his face swallowed up in huge eyes. Awkwardly he thrust out his hand and pushed something into Claudia's hands. She looked around, looking for something, someone. Her voice called out brokenly, 'Harr-eee!' ending in a high whine. Tony stood silently while Lucille pushed the sobbing Claudia into the car and the driver quickly edged out from the kerb. The car disappeared down Repulse Bay Road, a white blur as it moved amongst the trees and then turned the bend.

Tony turned away and then stopped, his throat tightening as he saw the boy Claudia had been playing with standing there forlornly, staring after the car, the dog

13

waiting patiently a step behind. They looked at each other in silence and then the younger boy's face twisted, screwing up tightly as he fought against the tears.

'They left me?' he asked and Tony folded his mouth together, nodding awkwardly, all previous animosity forgotten in the enormity of that betrayal.

'I guess they forgot. Come on,' he said, putting a hand on the boy's shoulders. 'You better come home with us.' But the boy shrugged the hand away angrily, standing there with tears shining bright in his eyes. Before Tony could stop him, he disappeared in amongst the crowd, the dog looking around panicked for a moment, and then with a howl running frantically in circles, searching for a familiar face.

Tony felt that howl pierce right through him and he dropped to one knee, calling softly to the dog. Reluctantly, it came close and he caught it by the scruff of its neck, talking soothingly to it as he stroked it down, soothing its trembling panic. 'Shh, there's a good boy, good dog, it's okay, you can come home with us. It's okay.' And he led the dog slowly over to where his parents waited, a stubborn set to his mouth.

In the car, still sobbing, Claudia looked down at what Tony had given her. In her hand lay the starfish.

'Dear God, I didn't think she really meant it! I'd never have baited her, if I'd thought that. Everyone here's sleeping around and yes, of course, they're normally more discreet about it than Frank ...' Fran Clements looked dismayed, pushing the hair out of her face as an idle wind from the sea caught at it. She walked on slowly down the beach, keeping pace with Sally Freeman beside her.

'Like Joanna, you mean? Maybe so, but everyone still knows who she's fooling around with, no matter how discreet she might like to be. Hong Kong's too nosy a place for anyone to get away with anything for long. Besides, Lucille comes from a small town. Her morals are a shade higher than most of Hong Kong's, Fran! And she expects the same of her husband. Oh, stupid man! How could he have brought that girl to Repulse Bay – and on a Sunday!

14

What was he trying to do? Show her off to the world?' Sally was beside herself with anger and guilt that she had not prevented matters from escalating as they had.

'Exactly that, Sally. To all his male buddies, here she is, isn't she gorgeous, aren't I a stud? Why he didn't think Lucille might be there too . . .'

'She doesn't like the beach, remember? I expect he thought she was safely at home with the children. God, the look on her face – I thought she'd been turned to stone, or was going to have a stroke at the least. Poor, poor woman! Oh, whatever is she going to do?'

'And what is Frank going to do?' Fran Clements looked out at the last of the rolling surf, as it flattened out into approaching dusk.

'Probably move his mistress in to take Lucille's place,' Sally replied tartly. 'Isn't that what all the men out here do? And everyone else will go on just the same, Joanna'll start things up with that, admittedly, rather good-looking fellow, Reginald Hsu—'

'Oh, surely not. Not now! After today. She'd never risk Bill and the children.'

'Yes, she would. Joanna's the sort who always thinks she can get away with whatever she wants. And she generally does, too. She's had her eye on Reginald Hsu for some time now and, let's face it, he's rich and powerful in the Chinese hongs and he has something about him . . . a sort of, oh, I don't know, a sense of being a law unto himself, or even above the law. I can see the attraction all right.' Sally sounded abstracted, almost tempted.

'Is that why she married Bill in the first place?' Fran asked, interrupting Sally's musings.

'Oh! So it's not just me who senses there's more to Bill Ingram than he makes out?' Sally laughed lightly, giving Fran a knowing look. 'No, he's not exactly my idea of a civil servant. In fact, I wouldn't be at all surprised if Bill didn't dabble in matters that had nothing whatsoever to do with paper pushing.' Her chipped tooth gleamed as she gave an impish smile. Fran's eyebrows lifted into an exclamation point.

15

'You mean, he's a—?'

'Spy? Goodness, doesn't that sound ridiculous when it's said aloud? Perhaps it's just that he has something to do with intelligence matters. Maybe that's it?' Sally mused and then shrugged. 'I don't know. I don't suppose anyone does – or ever will.'

It was late by the time Harry found his way home, having hitched a ride with an old peasant farmer, swaying his way around the curves to Central in his wooden-framed truck, geese flapping and screeching in cages behind. He deposited Harry down by Western Docks. From there the boy walked up the side of Victoria Peak to the Mid-Levels where the Babcocks lived. And into a scene of turmoil.

Suitcases and packing boxes were littered around the floor of the main room, and his mother, kneeling on the floor, was busy wrapping tissue paper around a carved figure that used to stand on the table by the front door. She glanced up as he timidly poked his head around the door, her face relaxing into a satisfied grunt for a moment. She nodded to him, sending him back into their quarters and Harry reluctantly turned away.

He found Claudia and her brother Mark in the kitchen, sitting together on the floor, Mark's arm around the little girl. They looked up sullenly when the door swung open.

'Harry! You made it home all right! I kept telling Mama we'd left you behind but she didn't listen ...' At which point Claudia remembered why her mother hadn't listened and relapsed back into tears of misery. 'We're going away, Harry. Mama's taking us back to America.'

'Not me, she's not!' Mark ground out between firmly clenched teeth. He shook his fair hair out of his eyes and breathed in deeply. 'I'm not going. I'm staying here with Dad.'

'But Mama says—' Claudia began only to be cut off tersely.

'Mama can't make me. Dad'll want me to stay.' Mark was stubbornly determined, glancing down at his younger sister for a moment as though considering something. Then he shook his head. 'You're a girl so you have to go with mama. Peggy too. But I'm a boy. I stay with Dad.'

'But, what about Harry?' Claudia argued. 'He's a boy but he stayed with his mama.' She looked at Harry where he had squatted on the floor beside them, trying to understand what was happening to his world.

'That's different. His dad didn't want him,' Mark said brutally and Harry flinched.

'Are Harry and Ah Lin coming with us, too?' Claudia asked suddenly, her mouth parting as though a sudden, terrible fear had sucked the breath from her lungs.

She looked at him with eyes that were wide and alarmed. 'Don't be stupid, Liddie. Harry and his mother are Chinese. They stay.' Mark looked at Harry, seeing the delicate features of the boy begin to tremble, the stretched pain of those staring eyes. He cleared his throat awkwardly. 'But Ah Lin won't stay here, she says. Not with Dad if he brings his – his girlfriend here. So Harry'll go away to another house somewhere, maybe. I don't know.' Mark shrugged, as though he didn't really care that much. But he had to get up suddenly, scowling as he pushed Claudia away. 'I've got to go out,' he said abruptly and Claudia saw him brush his arm across his face angrily.

'But Mama said not to go anywhere, Mark.' Claudia's voice rose as Mark continued to walk towards the back door. 'She'll be mad if you're not here when we have to leave.'

'You tell her I'm not coming, Liddie.' Mark paused, his back to her, his voice very tight and high. 'You tell her I don't want her to be my mama any more if she's leaving Dad. Because I'm not!' And then he flung himself out of the door and let it slam behind him.

And Harry and Claudia huddled together on the floor, beneath the kitchen table, their faces twisted with a grief that they couldn't fully understand but knew that their childhood sorrows were as nothing compared to this. And when Lucille came looking for Claudia, it was Harry who clung on tightly and refused to be dislodged. Only when his mother held him back, crying and sobbing, could Lucille pick Claudia up and carry her out of the room.

And Claudia heard Harry's voice shrieking down the passageway after her. 'Don't leave me, Liddie, pleeese! Pleeese, Liddie, don't go!'

Chapter Two

Tai Chau Village
The New Territories, 1972

Harry poked several pieces of pork wrapped up in a thick vine leaf into the crevice of the stone lion he prayed to and stepped back hurriedly, glancing behind him as he did so. There was no one in sight and he gave a sigh of relief before bobbing his head quickly to the lion. From out of his pocket he drew a joss stick and a packet of matches and once again he hurriedly poked the stick into the crevice and lit it. The thin wisp of sweet smoke wavered and threaded its way past the lion's nose and disappeared in a shimmering wave of heat. With a grunt of satisfaction Harry set off down the trail, occasionally looking back over his shoulder at the lion set amongst the trees. Nothing moved.

He reached the village just as dusk set in and the lights of the fishing boats out in the bay swayed with the surge of the waves. There were long shadows across the cement channels and several dogs huddled over a package of dried fish that flavoured the air around it. If you opened your mouth, you could taste it on your tongue. Harry quickened his pace.

'Ho Li? That you?' It was the closest they could come to the sound of his European name. The old woman who squatted in the shadows beneath the window, tending to her basket hives, was bent with rheumatism. The hives swung from the eaves as she deftly removed the combs. Harry sidled past, not getting too close to the hum of indignant bees. He could make out the coolie hat netted and swathed around his grandmother's head.

'Yes, Grandmother, it's me. Look, I brought some branches back.' He lifted the stripped lower branches of the hill pines that grew up near the stone lion and showed her. She cackled with delight.

'Well, don't just stand there with them! Go and put them in the store room. And hide them. We don't want to get fined!' Everyone stole the branches for fuel for their stoves and the local policeman knew it but he had to pretend to watch out for it and would, occasionally, fine someone who flouted the law too openly. Harry nodded and sprang up the wooden steps and entered the village shop.

Behind him the buzzing of the bees died away as the noise from the shop overtook it. There were people everywhere, talking, playing mahjong, listening to the radio; a naked child was even sleeping in the rice bins. A few were actually gathering together, from the crowded supplies, spare nets, soap, torch batteries and sweet biscuits, delving amongst the pots and hanging equipment, pushing the straw and wicker baskets out of their way to reach some particularly necessary and elusive item. Harry stepped over a three year old waving his money clamorously amongst the legs of the adults grouped by the counter. He reached the store room door and paused for a moment, looking around.

A mixture of Hakka and Punti (or Cantonese as it was known in the cities) was being spoken by the various groups and Harry listened eagerly, hoping there was some news from the other side of the bay, from Hong Kong island, some news of his mother. But it was all local talk, the tides, the weather, the rice crop and how unprofitable it was now with cheap rice coming in from Thailand and China. With a sigh he turned, shying away in alarm from a boat boy not much older than himself. The boy sneered.

Harry had been with his mother's family in Tai Chau for three years now. Three years since the Babcocks had left and his mother had gone to work for someone else. Three years since she had sent him away. He kicked at the door as he went through, half to show the boat boy he wasn't frightened, half out of frustration at still finding himself there, no matter how hard he prayed to the stone lion.

He didn't like rural village life. There was no school until they could find a new master and it was too far for him to ride into one of the bigger towns. There were no shops except for his uncle's and there were no cinemas, no trams, no ice-creams, no fun. There wasn't even any electricity! Instead there was work – endless work. Tending the different vegetable crops – cabbages, eggplants, chili peppers, maize, leeks, watercress, it went on and on; helping his auntie in the store, helping his grandmother with the cooking, helping his uncle with repairing the nets and restocking the shelves.

Work and no Liddie to guiltily share it with, so it was done in half the time, no Liddie to laugh with, no Liddie to turn to when life became unbearable. With a sigh he sat down on a sack of grain and leaned against the wall, closing his eyes so that for a moment he glimpsed that dark-haired girl, smiling at him, her head to one side. But then the image faded, grew indistinct and he could not bring it back. He sighed again.

Maybe this time his prayers would be heard? Maybe his mother would want him back some time soon?

The taunts of the other boys in the village had stopped long ago. They had accepted him now as one of their kind, even though his father had been Portuguese rather than Chinese, even though he had abandoned them when Harry was born. For some reason, that acceptance almost hurt more than his earlier ostracism. He didn't want to be accepted as one of them. It was too frightening to contemplate becoming – being – one of them. He didn't want to live in a place where someone like Liddie could never fit, would never want to share it with him. He didn't want this life. He didn't want to be a Chinese peasant.

But then the old gut fear started in him again, wrenching at him, making him wonder whether he dared ever try to be something else. Half of this, half of that, but nothing whole. A European peeping out of a Chinaman's skin. Not European. He hit his hand flat against the wooden boards. Not like his father.

It was dark and musty in the store room, smelling of dry hemp and grains, the cloying scent of spices and old nets steeped in mangrove bark and pigs' blood. He hated the

21

smell but it was the only place he could go to get away from them all, their loud voices and their prying eyes, all too aware as they looked him over and whispered and nodded to themselves. The old people knew. He didn't fit. He pressed the fir branches to his nose and breathed deeply their sharp, throat-clearing scent.

It was nearly harvest time and Auntie would be cross with him for not being where she could find him, down at the stone quay or playing on the beach with the other boys and the dogs. She never understood why he crept away to be by himself; nor did his uncle, a small, bow-legged man with large ears that stood forward from his head making him resemble a good-natured troll.

Auntie was dough-faced and larger than her husband, standing firm in her black pyjama-style *siam-fu*, her face half concealed beneath the billowing black curtains that encircled her coolie hat, and her wooden, slipper-like shoes clattering loudly when she moved off across the wooden floor. In the fields she went barefoot, like all the others. But in the store she always wore shoes and a grim, rather silent expression.

The whole village was made up of one clan, the Tang clan and Harry could number his many cousins and relatives in scores. It was a small poor village, mostly one-storey houses of mud and brick with the door jambs, entrance posts and lintels made of red tiles. The floors were either of beaten earth or, in the case of the village shop, rough wooden planks.

Outside, the pavements and streets were of coarse concrete or earth, with channels cut through to let the water run away to the stream that the white-washed houses clustered around, surrounded themselves by lush green fields, hand-tended. Behind the village, a large grove of banyan trees sheltered them from wind and dust and enticed old men to sit beneath them in the heat of the day and play endless games of mahjong.

Bougainvillea splashed over walls and small ancestor shrines were set up in open doorways with sweet smoke and flowers trailing over the tatty red and gold altar coverings and often a picture of a dead grandparent propped up in pride of place. The temple was so small you could barely fit four people at a time in it, the gilt paint peeling away and the wood split from the weather.

Mangy dogs with curling tails and bright eyes slouched in the shade and there was a constant smell of hot, oily cooking permeating the air.

The Tang clan were Hakka, descendants of immigrants from the interior of China some three hundred years before, but the boat people, who shared the village with them, were Tanka or 'egg people', so called because they had once paid their taxes in eggs, instead of money. It was an uneasy alliance that had gone on for as long as anyone could remember, the Tanka preferring to live on small, bright sampans and junks in the bay, a floating community lying, lashed together with a maze of gangplanks leading from one to the other, offshore from the stone-built land people.

Harry had heard tales of the Tanka having six toes on each foot and eating strange foods that made him shudder with anticipation and dread. They didn't worship at the temple or the shrine, but at their own gods, the *tai wong ye*, on different parts of the coastline. In the old days they were forbidden to take the Imperial civil service examinations, to intermarry with land people, or even to live on land. Harry's grandmother, with her aniseed-smelling breath and heavy patchwork of wrinkled cheek, would lean against him and whisper vile things about the Tanka that made him shake with fear in the night when he had to go outside to empty the bins. He stayed far away from them, even when they came on shore to visit the shop.

His uncle didn't seem to mind them and didn't charge them for storing their winter bedding or their spare nets or rope, unlike the village itself which made them pay for grass or firewood gathered on the hillside or to bream their boats twice a month on the beach. His uncle said it was unfair but everyone knew he was too soft and let people run up credit forever.

Harry would spy on them with his cousins, trying to

count their toes as they paced to and fro examining the twine, hooks and glass globes and mantles for their purse-seine lights, and then they would be off running and shrieking with fear and exhilaration when the Tanka discovered them.

Boat children his own age or younger could do that special rowing motion called *yu loh*, skulling, using both arms with skill and ease as they flitted back and forth between the shore and their homes. Harry and his cousins watched them uneasily, full of their grandmother's malice and distrust.

Now, Harry lay back on his grain sack and tried to visualise the boat boy he had just seen. An arrogant and ugly boy, larger than him by some four inches with broad hands and feet and a bulbous nose. Harry sneered back in the safety of the dark, and thought of witty and withering things he might have said, that he would say, the next time. Then, in spite of himself, he shivered.

He lay there for some time, thinking about how good it would be when he eventually returned to Victoria, the civilised part of Hong Kong, how he would talk and talk with his mother, how he would go to school and learn to be an important man, like his father, how he would buy all the things he wanted in the shops of Wanchai and Causeway Bay. It didn't occur to him, even in his daydreams, to think of buying in Central, the business district with its expensive boutiques for Europeans and millionaires. No, he would wander along the lanes of Wanchai, staring at all the possible wares, at the clothes, the food at the *dai pai dong* stalls, the songbirds that filled the sky in their small bamboo cages ... and Liddie would be there again, come back just especially for him ... oh, it would be so good!

'Ho Li? Hoo-llee!' A distant voice called, muffled through the walls of the store room. Harry stiffened and sat up, holding his breath. The voice came closer, more strident now and the door creaked open, shading yellow light across the sacks and wooden boards. 'Ho Li! What are you doing in here? Didn't you hear me call?' There was a heavy sigh. 'I need some help. Come out immediately.' Auntie's voice was shrill with annoyance. She gestured to him with a sturdy arm that had been known to land on his backside before now. Harry scrambled to his feet.

'Sorry, Auntie. I was just thinking—'

'You're always thinking. What good is that when there is no one to help in the shop and your uncle has gone to help deliver some stores? I can't do it all on my own, you know. Your grandmother is old tonight, she says, and I now have dinner to make and cleaning to do and your cousins are helping your uncle while you sit here and dream.'

'Sorry, Auntie,' Harry replied meekly, not trying to argue further. He followed her out into the noise and confusion of the shop.

It was two days before he ran across the boat boy again and there was little point then in saying those clever and cutting words he had stored up. Because it was the Tanka boy who saved him from drowning.

He had been crossing the stream, further up in the tree-shrouded hills behind the village and the valley, up near where the stone lion that he prayed to daily for deliverance lived, when he had slipped on some wet moss and fallen, hitting his head on the sharp stepping stones that bridged the stream. The water had dragged him down, tumbling him over and over in his half-stupor and he would have been drowned like an unwanted puppy had the Tanka boy not been there, where he was not supposed to be.

The boy had fished him out with a long branch and dragged him onto shore, slapping him gently about the face as he tried to bring him to his senses. Harry coughed and retched, tasting blood. He turned his face away from the slaps, coughed again and vomited up a thin, watery bile. He glanced up through the blood and matted hair that cascaded down over his eyes and saw the broad face, the flattened nose of his nightmares, and then, much to his surprise, the amusement in the small dark eyes that were leaning over him. The Tanka boy sniffed and let his hand fall back to his side.

'You cannot swim?' It was said with arrogance but also

pity. Not to be able to swim to boat people would be not to be able to walk to a landsman. Unthinkable. Harry strained to understand the boy's garbled version of Hakka. He shook his head.

'I slipped and hit my head,' he added as though that excused his lack of skills.

The boy grunted. 'You're P'u Ch'ih's son, aren't you? From the village shop.' Tap-tap left foot, as Harry's uncle was called because of his lameness, was popular with the Tanka. Harry coughed again.

'Nephew. I'm Eurasian.' The denial was swift. He wasn't some ignorant shopkeeper's son. His father had been a lawyer, at least. Perhaps a doctor. He wasn't sure, but something important. He knew that, at least. The Tanka boy smiled, his eyes crinkling up into slits as his nose moved up and spread across his face. It was a shrewd, mocking smile.

'Ah! Eurasian! Your father pong-pan,' the boy said. Harry flushed. A pong-pan was a Westerner born in Hong Kong who had married a Chinese wife and spoke colloquial Chinese. He was generally someone in a uniformed super-visory job, subservient to the true boss, the tai-pan. Harry shook his head vehemently.

'No! My father was an important man. A very important Portuguese gentleman but he had to — to — go away. He had to go back home, to Portugal.'

'Ah! Home? Your home is here, little fish, and you must learn to swim. I have no father either. He was killed in a storm many years ago. So, we are alike. I must learn to speak Punti clearly and you must learn to swim, in the Chinese way.' The boy wrinkled his nose again, laughing.

'What do you mean, the Chinese way? Swimming is swimming.' Harry was curt. The Tanka boy shook his head and signalled with his finger, tapping his temple.

'There are all sorts of swimming. You must swim with the shoal, not against it. You are Hakka, you speak Hakka, you live with Hakka, you must learn to be Hakka or you must go away and learn to be something else, something

26

better perhaps?' He grinned, ugly broken teeth bared in a broad grimace.

'I am half-European.' It was odd how short of breath Harry felt he had become, how sick with fear. His words were barely heard, lost in his breathlessness.

'Half is not whole. Half is not good enough. You should be whole something. Whole Chinese, maybe? Not Hakka or Punti or Tanka – just Chinese. Maybe.' The boy considered Harry, his head to one side. Then he shrugged.

'And what about you? What are you? Just Tanka!' Harry said contemptuously. The boy's smile slipped.

'I am me. That is enough. You are who people think you are, but I am me, myself.' He drew himself up proudly, looking Harry straight in the eye. Harry flushed and looked away and the boy laughed.

And that was when the other boys, Harry's cousins, suddenly appeared through trees that were dim in the morning mist and dark with dew. They paused, the three of them, and hesitated, wondering who the figures were, and then, upon coming closer and seeing the blood pouring down Harry's face and the Tanka boy laughing, they ran to Harry's aid. Harry did not see them approach. He was too busy contemplating what the boy had just said. 'I am me, myself.' It was enough.

With a howl of fury and rage the Tang cousins launched themselves on the Tanka boy, beating him about the head and shoulders with the bamboo poles they used to balance their loads of firewood and kicking him, their cries of outrage becoming glee, the grunts muffled in the still, wet air. The boat boy fell to the ground and curled into a ball, holding huge hands over his head, like a clay figure of a monkey, and the boys' kicks became harder, more confident, some of that malice their grandmother had dispensed taking hold of them.

'No, no! Let him go! No!' Harry shouted, hoarse and pleading, pushing at his cousins and being jostled aside, bleary-eyed from the blood and the knock to his head. 'Stop it! Stop!' he howled. Reluctantly they stood back and looked at Harry, puzzled. Why would he defend a Tanka?

27

What were they worth? Their breath clouded up dense and close around them, their heavy pants sounding like dull, thudding heartbeats. The Tanka boy alone made no sound.

Slowly he unfurled himself, looking up at the faces above him, at the hatred and fear in three and the dismay in the fourth. They towered over him in the half-light, menacing. His eyelids fell, concealing his thoughts. He tried to stand and fell sideways and the boy, Ho Li, put out his hand to help. The boat boy knew it had been without thought, knew, if he had thought he would not have touched. They stood face to face, examining each other curiously, and then the Tanka boy did a strange thing. He dipped his finger in the blood from his cuts and then touched it to Harry's face, where the blood still ran down his cheek. And he smiled, the bulbous nose lifting and spreading, almost obscuring the small intelligent eyes.

'My name is Yee Fong Lo,' the boy said formally. 'Remember what I said, if you want. You should learn how to swim.' But there was more being said and the other boys grew uneasy, shuffling from side to side, eyeing the Tanka boy with suspicion.

'And I am Harry Braga. Thank you for not letting me drown.' Not Tang Ho Li, as he was called in the village, but Harry Braga, the name that concealed his real identity. They smiled at each other awkwardly and then, when the Tanka boy turned away, he spat at the feet of the other boys before limping down the hill, back to his territory, the water.

Harry's cousins stood angrily still, unable to retaliate since Harry had told them to leave the boy alone. They muttered amongst themselves and remembered how they had first mocked this Eurasian boy for not being one of them; how now he associated with boat people, had strange meetings in hidden-away places. Their mouths pulled down, their faces grew hard.

From then on, they looked at Harry with the same distrust they had previously reserved for the Tanka. And Harry was secretly relieved. He wasn't a shopkeeper's son, he wasn't a Chinese peasant. He was better than them because they feared him. It was nice to be feared.

Yee Fong Lo also liked to be feared. Not because he felt superior to the village boys but because he knew he was despised and cursed by them. Their fear of him was his only consolation. One day he would be feared by many people, feared and respected and obeyed. That was his dream. He spent many months explaining that to Harry, teaching the Eurasian boy that it was fear and the force to back up that fear that made people honour you, not good works. Pht! Good works were for old women!

He would gain honour by joining the Triads, Yee said again and again, until it became a chant, in the dark when they crept out of their homes to meet each other. 'Down with the Ming, up with the Ch'ing.' The Triads' *raison d'être* did not make much sense to either boy but they mouthed it over and over, rolling the syllables around in their mouths, enjoying its dearth-like intonation. They sat in the salty, pungent-smelling shelter of a breamed boat and whispered their thoughts and their ambitions to each other.

Yee was going to make it to Kowloon, to the old walled city there and join up with a Triad lodge. Maybe the 14K, *aie yah*! Or the Wo On Lok – they were smart, into high-level blackmail, kidnapping, financial crime, it was said. Plus the Thai and Malay prostitutes over in Wanchai. He grinned and dug his elbow into Harry's side, his face knowing and full of glee. Harry smiled uncertainly as Yee continued his list of delights. Maybe he would go over to Wanchai? Or best still, join the Sun Yee On. Now that would be something! He would wear smart clothes and people would tug their hair and bow to him, he would be somebody!

Yee urged Harry to run away with him. What did they have to lose? What sort of life did they have now? His mother was never going to come back for him, was she? So why not? But Harry hesitated, uneasy, not quite sure that he liked the sound of the Triads. He urged caution and then, one day, Yee was gone, slipping away in the night to walk and hitch his way over to Kowloon.

From there, he would catch the ferry across to Hong

Kong side, Harry thought, as he sat alone that night, wondering what Yee was doing at that precise moment. Was he, even now, undergoing the initiation ceremony for a Triad lodge? Or perhaps sleeping in a cardboard box in the back lanes of the dock area, around Western district? Was he missing Harry as much as Harry was missing him? Probably not. Yee was the sort who went straight ahead and never looked behind. Harry sighed.

For several long, lonely months, until his fourteenth birthday, Harry continued to be ignored by his cousins and bullied by his auntie. Dogs snapped at his heels, urged on by the boys, old people hissed and shouted, knowing he wasn't one of them, had consorted with a Tanka. Tankas sneered at him, for having stooped so low. Only his uncle continued to smile at him absent-mindedly – but no one respected his uncle. Harry learned that you had to belong to someone or something or there was nothing. You were nothing.

It was a relief when, at last, his mother came to claim him. Even though they were almost different people to the ones they remembered, she was still his mother. She was his kind. But dreams of living in the Mid-Levels of Hong Kong island, the luxurious lower slopes of Victoria Peak where the expatriate rich had their apartments, proved to be nothing more than that. His mother had given up her job as amah and married again.

They were to move, instead, to a small island called Cheung Chau, between the larger islands of Lantau and Lamma. It was nothing more than a fishing village with a few artisans who liked to imagine they were escaping from the frenzy of Hong Kong. To Harry, it was yet another dead end.

And Harry's mother was curt and abrupt these days, irritated by his clumsiness and his lack of sophistication, by the smell that clung around him of fish and rice paddy, by his lack of schooling. Harry, sullen and pained by his mother's new marriage – her first really, if he was honest, and to a flabby, balding Englishman, a *gweilo* but nothing like his father, *aie yah*! – wondered to himself whether he

30

ought not to have gone with Yee to join the Triads after all. Gone to learn the secret mysteries of that brotherhood, gone to test himself against the savagery of that calling. Gone to hang the blue lantern ...

Chapter Three

Devon, 1973

The sea was dull and sheened under the grey sky, stretching out across the mud flats into the distance, only the nearer breakers showing any movement. They curled, long purring rolls of water that hung suspended against gravity before reluctantly collapsing in on themselves, releasing the smooth silk into froth and foam, spewing out across the wide strand before sliding back again. Tony Ingram knelt on the shoreline, digging with a claw-like trowel in the wet sucking sand. Occasionally he pulled out a clam, rinsed it in the foam, and added it to the wire basket beside him.

His shirt flapped in the breeze and he paused to untie the thick guernsey from around his waist and pull it over his head. Despite it being an unexpectedly fair Easter, it was cool near the sea and the breeze had a chill to it that made him stand up and jump up and down, his rolled trousers slipping from where he had pushed them up above his knees. Otter, their black labrador, came racing along the sand from where she had been inspecting Plum's work, to leap delightedly into the air and dance with him across the sand.

'You finished yet?' He cupped his hands together and yelled into the wind, his hair ruffling and almost standing on end. Plum stood up and waved her trowel and, further away still, Hattie gave up her pretence of work and hurried towards them both. They were alone, just the three of them, on the shoreline.

'Gosh, it's chilly suddenly. Let's get back, shall we? Ma said that artist fellow was coming to tea. I expect it's nearly tea-time now,' she said, her hands red and blotched with cold. She thrust them into her pockets.

32

'Where're your clams?' Tony asked and Plum looked at Hattie sternly.

'You haven't got any, have you? All this time! Well, you shan't have any of ours, I can tell you that!' and they turned back along the sand dune path that led over into the bay on the far side, where their cottage was huddled down out of the wind, its windows shining welcomingly in the gathering dusk.

'Ma's lit the lamps already. Bet Dad's out, then. He's such a penny-pincher, he'd never let her light them yet. Bet she's got the fire going too. Just as long as she doesn't want to read any more Arthur Ransome to us. Anything but that!' They all laughed and shrugged into themselves with anticipation, small grins appearing and disappearing as they slid down the grassy slope and clambered around the rocks by the boat house, Otter splashing through the mud and then pausing to shake herself all over the children.

'I think she fancies him, actually,' Hattie said as they neared the garden gate. The others paused and looked at her.

'Who? The artist? You must be joking. He's got a beard!' Plum scoffed and Tony turned troubled eyes on his sisters.

'He isn't rich,' he added meaningfully and they both nodded.

'Well, true, but he is titled. There's something going on, I'm sure. I caught her posing in front of the mirror the other day, with a big beach hat on, saying in a silly voice "my Lady Joanna" and wiggling her hips.'

'She wouldn't be Lady Joanna, which sounds stupid anyway; she'd be Lady Staves. That's his name isn't it? Terence Staves? Trust her not to know the difference,' Plum said acidly and they all laughed.

'Does Dad know?' Tony asked but Hattie shook her head, pursed in her lips.

'No, poor darling. He thinks the holidays are going along swimmingly, just the same as always. He wants this Staves fellow to paint Ma.'

'In the nude, no doubt, if she has her way.' Plum, at sixteen, was unforgiving. Tony sighed.

33

'Come on then, let's go show him what a hideous bunch we can be. That'll make him think twice about taking Ma on.'

'We wouldn't be part of the package, Tony. Dad would never allow it and anyway, Ma wouldn't want us. She hates the fact we're all so old now, anyway. Makes her seem ancient. She'll be happy to dump us. Besides, we're mostly away at school, so she'll have that excuse.' Hattie, at fourteen, was going through her brutally frank stage. Tony, caught between his sisters, felt a moment of black fear. They loathed their mother because she was female and therefore indictable, but he still loved her, still forgave her her moments of weakness. Was she really going to leave them this time?

He raced ahead of them, the clam basket banging against his leg as he ran, Otter dodging in front of his feet, from side to side, her silly, sweet face lit up at the game. Tony cursed her.

When they burst into the cottage, it was curiously quiet. The lamps were lit, the fire blazed but there was none of the happy bustle of late afternoons, people coming and going, the kettle whistling, the sandwiches and cake being laid out on the checked oilcloth, yet another tale of Swallows and Amazons propped open to bore the girls and secretly delight Tony. Instead, their father sat in the big wing chair by the fireplace and stared into the blaze, his long, beautiful hands that everyone admired so much and that Tony wished he had inherited, clasped tightly together. Bill Ingram didn't look up at the children but seemed to shrink into himself.

Otter skidded across the rugs to nose her way into their father's hands, her rump wiggling with the excitement of the day and her joy at seeing her master. Slowly he fondled the bitch's ears.

'Good girl, good girl, shhh, calm down now, that's it, that's a good girl.' Their father quietened the dog and then, as the silence became painful, he looked up at them.

'Where's Ma?' Hattie asked baldly. The two older children looked away. He sighed, forcing a voice up out of somewhere deep inside him.

'Gone, I'm afraid, my dears. It's, ah, a bit difficult. She wants to be an artist's wife, you see. Got this yearning to be a bit bohemian, I think. I'm so sorry ... but I thought it best to tell you.' He paused, having run out of things to say but presently he rallied himself. 'Well, I expect we'll learn to manage, somehow. Make us all more self-sufficient, won't it? And you'll see your ma from time to time. She'll come back – from time to time.'

And they all stood around, looking foolish, feeling foolish that they should be the ones left, that somehow it was their fault.

'Will we still come out to you in Honkers for the long hols?' Plum asked and saw her father's face brighten at the thought. She felt a surge of passionate hate for her mother.

'Of course you will, my dears. And Easter too, if you'd rather. It gets a bit chilly here sometimes, doesn't it?' It was the first hint that he had ever given that he didn't enjoy the sailing holiday in Devon as much as they had thought. 'You'll spend Christmas with Grandma as usual, of course. She'd be so upset if you didn't. And you'll probably see your ma much more during term time. Long weekends, that sort of thing.' He was trying so hard for their sakes, Hattie thought. She glanced at Plum, mirroring the rage in her eyes. Only Tony looked completely bereft. The others had their anger or their injured pride to sustain them. Tony only felt the loss.

'Is she going to marry him? This Staves fellow?' he asked and tried not to catch his father's eyes.

'That's what she says, Tony. But we'll have to wait and see. Divorces are messy things and they take time.' Time in which he could bury himself in his work and try to forget. Thank God, his work was the demanding sort, with no time for stray thoughts, brooding ... 'Come on, let's get some tea together, shall we? Your ma said there was some shortbread in the green tin.' Her last words, in fact, he thought in wonder. 'Will you get that?' He stood up as though he had recollected his duties and was determined to follow them through although he could barely remember to light the gas under the kettle and filled the teapot before adding the tea. Hattie and Plum bustled him to one side so that he sat at the table and stared at the apples in the bowl instead. Tony sat down too.

For a moment Tony remembered that scene, several years before, at Repulse Bay. He remembered the little girl's face, the tragedy that he had read there, the unerring knowledge, even in one so young, that what had happened was irrevocable and that they could never go back to the way it was before. Liddie. That was it. And the boy, the amah's son. Forgotten – and in turn, forgetting his dog. Wolf was the only one who had survived that day well, Tony thought. He had found a home, anyway.

Tony felt a deep hard lump in his throat and fought to swallow over it. That was what trusting people did for you, he thought grimly. Trusting and – loving. He knew what his mother was but he had still loved her. And now she had betrayed him. It happened all the time, if he only looked around. He was no different.

But he felt different. He felt like only he had ever been so hurt and yet he couldn't cry because his sisters weren't crying and his father would only get upset. He squeezed the spoon that had been laid out for his tea so hard that the bead pattern appeared like a welt in the palm of his hand.

Chapter Four

Most of Judson had a comment or two to make about the Babcock's moving back home, especially the people from over near the Ridge. Not many families ever left Judson in the first place; even fewer came back after the disgrace of divorce. That made Lucille Babcock and her two daughters an object of interest and gossip. They stuck out, people said, didn't fit and didn't try to fit. And Judson was uncomfortable with people who didn't fit.

The town might have felt differently, felt more sympathy if Lucille Babcock had ever let her guard down enough to let someone see the black despair she went through, month after month, when the alimony Frank was supposed to pay never appeared. They might have judged less harshly if she had shown some of the pain she hid so valiantly behind a stiff, unyielding mask. Some people even began to feel sorry for her, in spite of herself, for the way her elder daughter, Peggy, got around. That had to be humiliating for a proud woman like that, they said.

But before much sympathy could be generated, the talk would move on to the boy who didn't come home. And that was a topic all in itself for a small town like Judson. It was thought odd that the boy stayed out there, in that foreign place. Children stayed with their mothers, no matter what, they whispered to each other, especially when it was somewhere foreign and heathen. Lord knew what he would grow up to be. More Chinese than anything else, the town critics pronounced, and there was that mother, no better than she ought to be and walking around so stiff and proud with her nose in the air, when she had left her only son out

37

there in that unchristian land. It was more than some people could take, they said, shaking their heads with grim pleasure.

There were those who found it fitting that she should have come from the better side of town down to the Ridge. It was a judgement on her, the moral community of Judson hissed quietly to itself, for her divorce, for leaving her son, for having a daughter like Peggy ... And so the comments in the Ridge would continue and Lucille would stiffen and ignore them, and Peggy wouldn't care, and Claudia was too young to really know what was said. So far.

It was a dusky, balmy evening, the shake of sprinklers spraying out water and the scrape of cicadas dampening the voices of children playing and mothers calling. Claudia plodded on by, her thoughts elsewhere, unaware of Judson peeping out through its lace curtains to muse and debate. She was too busy thinking just what Harry might be doing at that particular point in time. It would be, what? Thirteen hours later? Was that right? About eight in the morning then, and he would be at school probably, with all the hustle and bustle of Hong Kong around him. She looked around at the stillness of the evening there in Judson and sighed heavily.

Judson was a middling to small town by Texas standards, population 12,907, according to the sign that greeted you as you drove in out of the Hill Country to the west, where live oaks, scrub cedar and mesquite-clothed soft limestone outcroppings with occasional ranges, and 12,908 according to the sign that greeted you as you drove in out of the blackland farming country of cotton and sorghum to the east. No one knew which sign to believe, if either, since they never changed for all the births and deaths that regularly appeared in the *Judson Herald*.

In the middle of these two extremes, near to but not quite on the Colorado river, Judson hunkered in on itself, with its old part smugly Federal in style, the red brick and white cuppolaed courthouse and library flanking each other across the main town square, the row of clapboard and brick shop fronts overhung by shady verandahs, self-conscious in their smart Sunday paint, linking them both and continuing in either direction.

Back from Main Street, to the north and east was the newer area of town, where neat rows of suburban bungalows spread out into neat streets and neat concrete drives, intersecting with regularity, as all new subdivisions should according to accepted theory. To the south and west lay the more established suburbs and the wealthier, older families of Judson. Where the Babcocks had lived before they went to Hong Kong. And beyond the newer area lay Haskell Ridge, the border line that divided white from black, black from Hispanic, middle class from desperately poor, the Babcocks from their old lives.

Claudia walked more quickly, knowing her own mother would be looking out at the evening and seeing not the beauty of the end of the day, the paper-thin moon shafting out a watery light in the dusk, but only the beginning of the night. She skipped over a lake of puddles that had rolled down a steeply shelving driveway where someone had been washing his car, hanging back as she saw her sister appear from behind a house with her friend, Elly.

The two of them were giggling and shrill, their bottoms tight in their jeans as they ran down the garden and along the road. Peggy's hair was blonder than ever, Claudia thought, seeing it haloed briefly under a street light. It showed up the darker roots like a black gash in her head.

She trailed along behind them, wishing they would walk faster; it was dark now and they would all be in trouble when they got home. But the two girls in front sauntered along in their toe-pinching boots, examining their newly painted nails and exclaiming over the colour, laughing endlessly and uproariously over things that had been done or said in class that day.

'. . . And everyone was humming, real low, so that Miss Pickering couldn't tell where it was coming from, just this noise! God, she kept spinning round like a top trying to figure out who it was. Drove her mad and I thought I'd bust a gut trying not to laugh.' They shrilled away and then

Peggy, glancing behind them, caught sight of her sister and her face hardened.

'What're you doin' back there, sneaking along, spying on us! What're you gonna tell Mama now, tattle-tale? Did you hear anything interesting?' Her voice was loud and sharp, but there was a note of fear in it that Claudia wondered about. Reluctantly she caught them up.

'I was just walking home and you came out in front of me. What was I supposed to do? Turn around and walk back by the stadium? It isn't just your road, you know.'

'You didn't have to sneak along like some sort of creep. You could've said hi or somethin' like a normal person. God, Elly, anyone would think I've got enough to deal with, with Mama, but no, I have to have Liddie as well.' Her friend Elly laughed and ignored Claudia who walked ahead of them now, her back very straight and her jaw set.

The neat houses became more careless, the cement drives began to have weeds and splits in them. The road itself had cracks where crabgrass grew in tufts and potholes that you couldn't see until you fell in them because the street lights had all been smashed. Claudia waved to the Jimenez family who were sitting on their porch, the scent of spicy fajitas like a cloud across her path, as they ate and played bingo together, laughing and slapping down their numbers with loud, carrying voices.

She hurried on in the warm purple haze of sundown, feeling the dew damp on her skin, her clothes heavy with it. There was a smell of gasoline mixed up with sweating plantlife and ditch water, and she breathed it in deeply, liking its strange flavours, touching her tongue to her lips where it was strongest. The porch light of their own house was on, she could see, and she quickened her step still further.

Mama was in the kitchen, sitting at the little formica table where they normally had dinner so that the good table wouldn't get messed up for when they had guests. Except that they never did have guests because Mama never seemed to like the sort of people who lived just around them and the sorts she did like, their old friends from when

40

they used to live over on the nicer side of town, she didn't want to come all the way down to Haskell Ridge. Certainly not at night.

'You're late. I've been sitting here this last half hour worrying myself sick about you. Where've you been, Claudia?' Mama's mouth was pinched in and her face grey and set, Claudia thought, really old suddenly in a way she had never seen before. She held a letter in her hand that Claudia saw had been returned, unopened, from Hong Kong. Again. So, no maintenance from Daddy to help pay the bills this month, Claudia thought with a deep sigh. She averted her eyes.

'I'm sorry, Mama. I was at the library and I didn't see it had got so dark. I walked as fast as I could. It's okay, Peggy's just coming. I saw her at the end of the block.' She saw the relief, quick, on her mother's face and was guilty at letting her worry so.

'That's all you ever do, study in that library like some sort of mole when it's a lovely day and you should be out playing with your friends more, Claudia. There's time enough for all that hard work and studying when you're a bit older. And as for Peggy ...' But her mother bit off whatever she was going to say about her other daughter and looked at the clock instead.

'You'll have to fix yourselves dinner. I've got my book-keeping lesson in twenty minutes and I'll probably be late, thanks to you. Thank you very much.' She closed her eyes and sighed sharply before getting up and gathering her bag and her raincoat, even though it was a beautiful night with not a hint of rain.

'I'm sorry, Mama.' Claudia's face became stricken. 'I'll be home on time in future, I promise. Can I fix you a sandwich or something to take with you?'

'No, it's too late now and I'll just have to go without. I know you're sorry but sorry doesn't help when I sit here thinking the worst. This isn't a safe neighbourhood, Liddie, you know that. I've told you again and again and you know I want both you girls in before it gets dark.' She shook her head, as though Claudia never listened to her, was constantly ignoring her warnings instead of only having been late once in the last six months. 'Now, you make sure your homework's done and that Peggy doesn't sneak out anywhere. You tell me if she does, Claudia. I want to know. God, look at the time! As if I didn't have to rush enough all day, and now this.' She slammed the screen door on the way out and Claudia sat down at the table, chewing her lip and swinging her legs under the chair.

As if she would dare tell on Peggy! What must Mama be thinking? She started to clear the breakfast plates from the table but caught sight of the book she had been reading that morning, still open at the right page. Almost unthinking, she sat back and started to read.

The sound of the car starting up and being reversed out of the drive reassured Claudia and she settled more comfortably in her chair with a sigh, sinking into the fantasy world of elves and hobbits, Gollum and Mordor, with delight. But then the car stopped and there was the sound of voices raised in irritation, words like 'selfish' and 'nagging' being bandied around so that Claudia felt a deep sinking feeling in her chest and then the car shot off down the road, its tyres almost squealing in alarm, and the screen door slammed as though it had exploded.

Peggy came into the room, her face screwed up in fury and she shied away at the sight of her sister. 'What'd you do, Miss goody-two-shoes? What'd you tell Mama about me?' Her voice was scathing but Claudia looked up blankly.

'Nothing. I said you were coming. She was just in a bad mood 'cos she was late, that's all.'

'Well, that's nothin' new, is it? What is it this time? Is Daddy late with the maintenance again? Or has he just given up paying it completely?' Peggy frowned at the thought. 'God, I'm starving. What's for dinner?' She slung her bag on the table and Claudia sighed sharply, the urge to bury herself back in her book so strong that it was an effort to speak.

'Sandwiches, I guess. Maybe a can of soup? I dunno. What d'you want?'

'Just somethin'! Don't ask me to decide everythin', for God's sake, will you? You think of somethin' for a change, Liddie. I've got to get some work done. You're lucky you're not in ninth grade, I can tell you. It's all endless, stupid work and none of it's going to be useful in the long run. Elly's going to beauty school next year and she'll be earning a fortune six months after that. Why does Mama insist I stay on? It's so fucking stupid!'

Peggy crashed out of the room, the door hitting the wall and swinging back again, and Claudia shrugged, wondering whether she wasn't right. They had had this same argument so many times and no one ever seemed to change their minds. But school was wasted on the likes of Peggy and Elly, and Mama was just worrying about what people might think if her daughter dropped out. Mama wasn't thinking about Peggy herself. Not that anyone would really want to. She was a waste of space.

Claudia stood up and went to the larder, peering in at the rows of cans with little interest. Tomato, vegetable, chicken and sweetcorn. She took down the tomato and set about preparing dinner.

Chapter Five

Cheung Chau
1975

Harry's mother carried the steaming bowl of soup into the small living room and placed it on the table. Harry remained slouched in front of the television. His mother wiped her hands on her apron and called sharply.

'Harry! Dinner, now. Turn that thing off.' She was rough-voiced with him now, impatient, wishing he weren't there so that she could enjoy her new life with her new man. She didn't see Harry any more, just a boy, a loutish, ungracious boy who, at nearly sixteen, was more of a nuisance in the household than a help. A boy whose features she refused to recognise, the original bearer of those features too painful to remember and therefore long dead to her.

But he was her son and she couldn't turn him out. She sucked in air through her teeth, wishing once again as she had wished thousands, no, hundreds of thousands of times before, that she had never met Harry's father, never felt the strength of such dismaying emotions as love, trust, hope, never suffered beneath that devastating smile. They let you down; they always let you down. She didn't feel them any more. Not for anyone.

'Where's Jedemy? On the roof?' she asked when Harry reluctantly stood up and snapped off the television. He shrugged.

'Go see, will you? And ask your friends to go home now. Their own dinner is waiting for them. Go home.' She raised her voice, staring hostilely at the two other boys, one European, one Chinese. They smiled slow, insolent smiles. 'Go home before your mothers start to call here. Harry,' she turned and lowered her voice so that it was a still audible but clearly private communication. 'You know Jedemy doesn't like these boys. Don't bring them here again.'

Harry burned with shame, the heat flooding through him. He slouched instead, jerking his thumb towards the door for the benefit of his companions. 'See you later. Maybe around eleven at the waterfront.' They filed from the room and he turned to stare through half-closed eyes at his mother.

'Jeremy taught those guys. He should be glad to see his old pupils from time to time,' he mocked and saw his mother straighten and look at him, her face old.

'They are not to come here again. And you are not to see them. They are bad, rough, boys – thugs, Teddy boys!' She paused, unable to think of a worse insult. 'You stay away from them.'

'They work, just like me, at the factory. How can I stay away from them? Don't be stupid.'

'Then find another job. A better, worthier job. You are smart. Jedemy has taught you everything you need to get a better job.'

'But I have no qualifications. We've been through this before.'

'Then get some. Study hard and pass your A-levels.'

'How can I when I haven't got O-levels? I haven't got anything, not since fourth grade. And that's not my fault!' With an exasperated slap of his hand against his thigh, Harry turned and climbed up towards the roof. His step-father, Jeremy Law, stood in a pair of faded shorts and a string singlet tending his garden, oblivious to the voices he had heard raised below. He never got involved. It was easier that way.

'Dinner. Ma's in a froth. Better come soon,' Harry said dispassionately, eyeing the curved and dimpled buttocks of his stepfather and feeling a small shiver of distaste pass through him.

'I will be there presently, Harry. Please inform your mother.' The beautifully precise, rounded vowels and sharp consonants were no surprise. Jeremy Law gave the

45

impression of a man of breeding, long since lost to his true place in society but happy enough to make do as life saw fit. He glanced sideways at his step-son, breathed in the tiny, sculptured nostrils before flaring them once again. 'Give her these, will you? For the table.' He passed across several freshly cut sprays of dendrobium, their scent heavy and cloying. 'What's she in a froth about?'

'Me. My friends, my job, my lack of prospects, my laziness, my ingratitude.'

'Nothing new, then?'

Harry laughed. 'No. You're safe. As long as you come now.' There was a wail of sound from below and the two men flinched. 'Right now,' Harry added with meaning.

'You should go over to Hong Kong. Find a job there. There's nothing for you on a little fishing island like this.' Jeremy looked around at the score of rooftop terraces surrounding them, like patchwork fields but hard and concrete, packed with chickens in coops, children screaming, bamboo mats flapping in a cloyingly scented night breeze. 'No future. Someone like you could go far.'

'Maybe I will. Maybe I'll go be a stockbroker for Jardines. What d'you think?' Harry gave a jeering smile.

'You could be, if you tried. Work your way up. Start as an office boy. You've got all the right looks, knowledge, just no bits of paper. You'd get ahead fast.'

'I don't need your help, Jeremy. I can do it myself. Don't start on me like Ma does.'

'Suit yourself.' Jeremy turned, giving a quick, slapping brush to Harry's head as he passed him, an old schoolmaster's sort of movement that both hurt and humiliated without seeming to. Their eyes met for one furious moment and then Jeremy lowered his face so that it was no more than an inch from Harry's. He smiled and said softly, his breath sweet and foul: 'You don't know what you've got, Harry. I do, oh, by God, I do! So much! And I don't want to see you waste it.' And then, unable to help himself, he brushed his lips across Harry's.

The boy threw himself backwards, his mouth bared in

seething disgust, the creeping sensation of flesh on flesh still with him.

He drew the back of his hand across his mouth, staring at his stepfather. 'Fuck off! Just fuck off!' Harry spat out the words, as though he would spit out the disgust and rage within. With a quick lope, he took off down the stairs and out the front door. His mother, hands on her hips, stared after him.

'Where's he going then?' she demanded as her husband gingerly descended the tiled stairs.

'To hell, probably. I don't care.' But the rheumy eyes were sad and wistful. 'He'll be back.'

Chapter Six

Bill Ingram lived in a flat along the Old Peak Road now. 'Handy for work,' he would say, when people looked at the crumbling plaster or the overgrown gardens. 'Just a walk down to Government House,' when they raised their eyebrows at the mildew dotting the walls like a *trompe l'oeil.* But people liked Bill and no one really minded except when the amah threw up her hands and left to spend a week with her daughter in defiance of the kitchen conditions or when the air-conditioning went on the blink and the fans rotated as lazily as a fly about to drop. Then they simply insisted he visit them instead and matters progressed more smoothly in his absence. Life was just a matter of accommodation, Bill realised after a while, and he smiled wryly to himself at the pun.

He was saving a lot, of course. That was what it was all about, people said knowingly. Saving up for retirement after Joanna had gone off with all the family jewels. She actually asked for a settlement too! He wasn't going to go any further in the civil service, after all. Not after all that mess. He'd be going home in a few years. And Bill, aware of what people were saying but, for his own reasons, whether too indifferent or perhaps simply too bloody-minded to correct them, or perhaps for some other reason entirely, continued to live in the decaying flat with his little lizard friends and the macaw in the garden and his black labrador Otter, who wasn't the same Otter who lived with his mother-in-law in England but who offered the same unflagging devotion. Wolf was dead some years ago, a sadly

48

missed character in the household, but a relief to the amah who had never trusted a mongrel in her life.

Bill didn't really need or want people knowing what he did, after all. His was the sort of profession where the least said, the better. If they thought he was a passed-over civil servant, then that was fine. If they thought Joanna was a leech, well, he wasn't going to say otherwise. And this way he could afford to have all his children come out to him twice a year and still send them to nice schools back home. It was a fair exchange, Bill thought.

Not that Tony would be coming for much longer. Bill considered the young man sitting in the armchair by the open french windows, his forehead puckering up with a slight frown. Thinking deep thoughts? Or just wondering where he was going to eat dinner? It was hard to tell with that boy. He made an oyster look easy bait, the way he just shut it all up inside and never let anyone know what was what. Bill smiled.

A small breeze was playing across Tony's hair, ruffling it as though to tease. There wouldn't be much hair left after the Sandhurst barbers had had their go, Bill thought ruefully.

'Have you decided what you're going to do tonight? You can still come with Plum and me, you know. Sally'd love to see you. She's always complaining she doesn't get to see you enough.'

'Sally Freeman? That's only because she has a plain daughter out for the holidays, Dad, and you know it. No thanks. I'll go and see what's going on in Wanchai or perhaps over Kowloon-side instead. There're some good nightclubs over in Tsim Sha Tsui East, I hear.' Tony grinned and stretched, arching his back.

'On your head be it, then. I hear there'll be quite a bevy of beauties there, though, the lovely young Silvia amongst them ...'

'Silvia ...? Not the half-French one? I thought they'd locked her up in a convent and thrown away the key?' He showed the first stirrings of interest.

'More of an ivory tower, I think, but she descends for

chaperoned dinner parties. Mark Babcock's got his eye on her, I also hear,' his father taunted.

'Mark? He's only sixteen!' Tony protested. And pretty strange with it, Tony thought to himself. He, himself, was eighteen, finally finished with school and about to start at Sandhurst. Surely that would impress more than a sixteen year old who hadn't even started shaving yet?

'But a very worldly sixteen, wouldn't you say?' Bill was at his most ironic. 'And Silvia is only fifteen, after all. Her tastes may run to boys rather than men.' The curl to his father's lip, the gentleness of his words was infinitely mocking. Tony grinned when his father added, 'So, you might like to come?'

He hesitated. 'Who else is going to be there?'

'We-ell, I can't be sure but I think Sally mentioned two different tables, one for the young and another for us old crinklies. So I imagine there'll be quite a few people you know there. Aidan Lockhart for a start. You know he's started working for me?' They looked at each other, steadily, and Tony nodded.

'No, I didn't exactly. I heard he was going into the Civil Service.' He smiled slowly and his father coughed and cleared his throat, caught out by Tony's words. Reluctantly he smiled back.

'Yes, exactly. That's what I said.' He watched Tony, telling him things without saying a word and Tony subsided, the moment of teasing, the moment when he hoped his father might confide, passing. Bill Ingram continued on smoothly, 'Plum's quite excited about tonight, I gather.' An offhand remark calculated to draw interest. 'Perhaps you should ask her who's going to be there? Pity Hattie had to miss it but I expect Macao has its points.'

Hattie had been invited by her closest friend to spend the weekend in Macao at the legendary Lisboa Hotel and had, wisely, chosen to be indulged. Tony grinned again.

'Hattie'd only end up offending some old biddy with her views on sex and women's lib. Hope she grows out of that soon. She's bloody ugly at the moment.' Which was both true and unfair at the same time, his father thought. Hattie

50

was being boring on the subject but her ugliness was only a temporary age-related defect that would, if Bill knew anything about women and he rather fancied he did, blossom into true loveliness in the next year or two. He rather suspected that the virulent strains of feminism would become more muted as Hattie's appearance improved.

Tony, on the other hand, was very much as he would look right up until old age. A fairly compact body with clean, regular features and dark blond hair that had almost become brown in places. Grey eyes that were flecked like the dappled scales of a trout were his best feature, managing to somehow seem friendly and cool at the same time. He looked a pleasant, dependable sort, Bill thought but not chatty. Definitely not chatty. Perhaps one day he would find himself choosing a more solitary career than the army? Bill wasn't sure he wanted his son to follow in his footsteps but perhaps there was no choice in the matter. It was all mapped out at birth.

Not that there was anything wrong with being solitary. Tony had turned out well. In fact, all three had turned out well, a fact he took little pride in himself. Sensible sorts, his children. Feet very much on the ground. He smiled.

Plum was already working in London as a rather well-paid cook doing directors' lunches and she was seeing a steady, rather boring young man who worked in the City. And Hattie would shape up well too, once she was through this stage. Considering how little he had had to do with it, he had a lot to be grateful for.

'Well, let me know in the next hour if you want to come with us, Tony. I'd like to give Sally some warning on numbers, although she was good enough to say you could just turn up if you wanted. I'm going to take Otter for a turn in the gardens, if you'd like to come?' But he saw the denial even before Tony shook his head, apologetic but firm. That was Tony all over, Bill thought as he clicked his fingers for the dog. Apologetic but firm. His mother's leaving did that to him. Closed him up tight. Ah well, two out of three came out unscathed. That was something.

*

51

The Freemans had laid on an al fresco party in the grounds of their Peak bungalow, an old colonial house where servants discreetly attended the tables laid out on the York flagstones beneath towering elephants' ears and magnolia trees. The night breeze flipped and caught at the blue and white batik tablecloths but they were secured down by heavy Italian china and silver that Sally had brought with her years ago. The scent of roses wafted towards the group gathered on the terrace. They flowed and mingled, parting and regrouping in their social rounds, admiring the crystal bowls of deep pink peonies and ranunculas that were lit in all their dazzling colour by the candles that gleamed straight and steady in the glass storm lanterns.

None of it was particularly grand but it was quite exquisitely elegant and beautiful, Plum thought with a pang that mixed both envy and irritation at herself for feeling that envy. Sally Freeman was old enough to be her mother – in fact had been a good friend of her mother's – but she had such a flair for always appearing to be innovative and trend-setting, even when she was re-using old ideas, that she seemed more Plum's own age. She had – panache, Plum decided, and became, in that moment, determined to acquire some herself.

Beside her, Tony was almost completely unaware of his surroundings, glancing around casually but looking for only one person. His eyes narrowed, became focused, and his nostrils flared out as he exhaled deeply. A glorious cloud of dark hair, just peeping over the shoulder of the man in front of him, revealed the presence of the perfect Silvia Bateman. The man moved slightly and the equally glorious profile came into view, the long line of the forehead curving down into a perfectly straight nose that just dipped at the last moment in classic French hauteur, the short upper lip and the chiselled fullness of those lips above a sharp, determined chin. The profile swivelled until the pale, lettuce-green eyes were turned upon him, lingering meditatively.

Tony felt his stomach fall to somewhere around his knees and the tightness in his chest begin to deprive him of air. He looked away.

The voices around him rose and fell in swoops of laughter and animation, drawling out welcomes ...

'... Looking wonderful! How was the old place? Still standing?'

'... Best holiday in years. Can't think why we used to rush off home for the summer with hill stations like Fraser's around. Felt like I was living out my childhood all over again ...'

'... No, no, Saki! S-a-k-i! What d'you mean you've never heard of her? It's a him!'

'... Gone back to Singapore. He's with Jardines, you know. The children will start at Tanglin Trust but will probably go back home rather than go on to UWC. Rather unreliable ...'

'... Liberty's. No, no, very reasonable. Ask your daughter to send you some ...'

Tony turned and walked inside the house, making for the bathroom. He felt the green eyes following him, boring into his back, and he could barely walk, his legs unsteady and stumbling. He glanced behind him but Silvia had turned back to the man she had been talking to.

'She's too young for you, don't you think?' A voice said at his elbow and he started, swivelling around to almost collide with Mark Babcock. The younger man smiled a tight-lipped grimace that was half-tease, half-annoyance.

'Who?'

'Oh, come on, we all know who, Tony. Silvia and I are pretty much going steady, you know.'

'Going steady?' Tony raised his eyebrows, a faint twist to his cheek signifying amusement. 'That must take stamina.'

'Going out together, is that what you Brits say?' The sneer became apparent and Tony, looking Mark over, thought how little he had improved in the last year. He had become smart-mouthed and attempted to cover his insecurity with mocking bravado. It was unattractive.

'I'd assume, since Silvia is half-English that that is what she would call it, yes. Hasn't she?'

'Silvia isn't interested in you.'

'Thank you for the bulletin.'

53

'Look, you may think you're hot shit—'

'Grow up, Mark. Silvia'll tell everyone in her own good time just who she is interested in and who she's going out with. Until then, why don't you just go cool your heels?' He had half turned away when a thought struck him. 'By the way, how's your sister?'

'What?' Mark looked bewildered by the sudden change in conversation. Then, sensing condemnation, his brow furrowed. 'Peggy? None of your damned busine—'

'No. Liddie – Claudia.' There was silence while Mark thought hard, wondering what interest Tony could have in a sister he hadn't seen or spoken to in years.

'You do like them young, don't you?' He laughed and Tony shook his head and turned away. For a moment Mark hesitated and then called after him, angrily. 'She's fine, why?' It was a demand, not a query.

Tony shrugged. 'No reason. Send her my ... say hello next time you write.' And then he walked off down the hallway, wondering to himself why he had bothered to ask. She had probably become another Peggy or, worse still, loud-mouthed and swaggering, like Mark. But he couldn't quite quell the interest that wondered how she was, how she was coping. She'd be, what? ... almost fifteen by now, he thought. The same age as Silvia. The thought came as a shock, since he had always imagined her as a seven-year-old child. For a moment he saw her face again, twisted in misery. But that was all over now. Old news. He mentally shrugged.

When he returned to the party, he saw that Mark was monopolising Silvia, the younger boy's face curiously vulnerable as he laughed and flirted. There was charm there in that long, bony face, fair hair swept back off a wide brow, pale blue eyes no longer challenging but trying to engage, Tony realised. Charm, even intelligence. Or, perhaps, especially intelligence.

But it wasn't a nice face. It wasn't kind or compassionate. Not that either were prerequisites for capturing a female's attention. And it was weak. Tony watched them both for a moment, seeing the droop and lift of the edge of Silvia's eyelids as she smiled, the way the long lashes lingered over her soft cheek, the pout of her mouth as she disputed some fact. And then Silvia's head turned fractionally, her eyes caught his. She smiled.

'I wouldn't go dabbling my toes in that pond,' Plum said drily. 'Liable to get them bitten off, I'd say.' She handed her brother a small crispy ball on a toothpick, as he wrenched his gaze away, raised his eyebrows. 'Try that. Tell me what you think's in it.' Plum was always demanding they tell her what was in some food or other, her culinary interest exceeded only by her dislike of seeming to like something enough to ask for the recipe.

'Shrimp, I think. Why bitten off?'

'You're useless. It's definitely crab. But which herbs?' She looked distracted.

'Toes.' He prompted her.

'Or fingers or any other part of the anatomy for that matter.' She gave him an arch smile, the sort an older sister reserves for her younger siblings. 'She's a piranha, Tony, can't you see that? Beautiful and dainty and vicious. Don't get yourself scarred up for life, all right?'

'Plum! That's a pretty catty thing to say,' Tony said, stung. 'What makes you such an expert?'

'I went to school with Silvia for years, even if she was in a younger form. Ask Hattie, she knows her even better. The girl's got no feelings. She just takes a bite here, a bite there, samples them all but never goes any further . . .'

'She's only fifteen!'

'Going on thirty. Look, it's up to you, I'm just giving a little sisterly advice. I'm not trying to say she should go any further, obviously not, but she shouldn't dump the poor devils quite so quickly or so casually. She doesn't feel anything, you know. I hear she's a bit odd, actually. Loopy . . . has fits. Goes off to the "clinic" from time to time.' Plum circled her finger in the air, describing an uneven arc. Silvia, watching, flushed and looked back into Mark's eager face.

'What rot! God, Plum! You're always saying you hate gossip . . .'

'Fine, fine! I didn't say a thing. You do whatever you want. Just don't come crying to me when she shreds you, that's all.' Plum bit her lip, knowing that Tony would never do that no matter how badly he was mauled. He didn't discuss his hurts or woes with anyone. She looked after him worriedly when he walked off to get a drink but then an old friend claimed her and the matter slipped from her mind.

Bill, standing in the shadows, another darker figure beside him, watched them all with studied indifference. Quite predictable, he thought. They all were. Even his own children. That made his job easier really, since it became obvious to anyone who was in the slightest way observant just who didn't fit the mould. Like that young Mark Babcock. Now he was going to be an interesting little sideline, one of these days. Well worth knowing. And Reginald Hsu ... now he was more than a sideline, he was a whole avenue of thought, all to himself. Just where did all that money come from, after all?

Watching the tall, bespectacled man from Shanghai flirting with Sally Freeman, Bill knew that he was perhaps influenced by Joanna's affair with Hsu some years before. But still, there was something else there that made Bill's hackles rise. A man well worth watching, and that was, after all, what he did best. Bill murmured something to the young man beside him who smiled appreciatively.

They were seated for dinner, a cross-section of young people ranging in age from as little as the eleven-year-old Portia Hsu, her long dark hair swinging silkily down the back of an immaculately starched dress of Filipino lace and her quick eyes dark and flashing in their excitement, up to a couple of older graduates of about twenty-two or -three. Tony was amused to find that Silvia had been separated from Mark by the entire length of the table. He, on the other hand, was immediately opposite her. Had Sally Freeman been aware of just what she had done, he wondered, and, glancing up at the other table, saw her drop him a slow wink. He raised his glass to her, unable to contain the amusement that bubbled up, heady as champagne, inside him.

56

Silvia was not in a smiling mood. She had seen that circling finger of Tony's sister, known what it had meant and her heart had seemed literally to stop, freezing for several beats until she felt so faint that she had to lean on Mark's arm and let him lead her over to a chair. She had thought the rumours had died out about her. They were only occasional fits, after all, and the doctors had them under control now. What had that dreadful Plum told Tony? She had seen his face harden, the anger there and been unable to face it. Mark didn't see but she knew it wouldn't matter if he had. That was what they both had in common. Not the fits but the not fitting. They were both a little odd to other people. A little wild. She glanced around her, her light green eyes like deep water lit from below at night. When Tony smiled at her, she looked away.

The meal passed in a blur of awkward movements, little eating, crossed glances when they both flushed, glanced aside and were immediately engaged by their partners on either side. Tony was dimly aware that he was disappointing the girls beside him with his distracted answers, his inarticulate questions, but he couldn't dredge up the consideration to try harder. Plum had noticed as well. It wasn't like him, she thought. He was normally everyone's favourite companion, polite, interesting, witty even with a certain distance to his manner that always intrigued. Tonight, she thought with despair, he was a blithering idiot.

'Which regiment do you intend to join, Tony?' The young man on Silvia's right broke in, hearing some mention of Sandhurst. He was a few years older, just finished at Oxford. Tony looked up and swallowed hard over the fresh lychees in his mouth, their taste turning sour as he intercepted Silvia's eyes.

'I'm not sure yet, Aidan. Dad was Blues and Royals but I don't think I'm cut out to be cavalry. I'd quite like the Gurkhas.' He saw surprise on the boy's face and stubbornly ignored it.

'Not a lot of future there, would you say? If you want infantry, you'd be better off getting into one of the fast-moving lot. Maybe the Light Division.' The boy grinned, almost slyly, heavy pouches beneath his eyes bunching up to squeeze them shut. Tony shrugged.

'It's too early to say. I'm not particularly keen on making it all the way up to General and I doubt they'd have me anyway. Basically, I'd just like to come back out here to Hong Kong before it's too late. Find a niche. You too, I hear? The whispers are spreading.' He smiled and was not particularly bothered when Aiden gently pelted him with a bread roll. His smile broadened.

'What are you two talking about? What whispers?' Silvia asked, driven at last to try and understand what they were talking about. Why did she never understand the quick repartee of the English? She was too much like her mother, too French at heart, perhaps.

'Aidan is joining the ranks of the civil servant, Silvia. Can't you just see him with his driver and his slicked-down hair and rolled-up umbrella?' Tony teased. Aidan threw another roll.

'The junior ranks, Silvia, and I'll be catching the tram, let me tell you.'

'Oh, not with your connections, Aidan.' Tony raised his glass, laughing, and was relieved to see Aidan's face relax, his rather loose lips fasten onto the rim of his own glass, draining it back easily. Drinks like a fish, Tony thought. Must be all those pirating traders in his genes, who made the Lockhart fortune and drank their way clear of the fevers and pestilence. Aidan was just a quieter version.

'Tinker, tailor ...' Aidan mouthed. Ah yes, Tony thought. Tinker, tailor, soldier ... Civil Servant. What a nice euphemism. His father's favourite. They smiled at each other, in perfect understanding.

Silvia paused uncertainly, not quite sure what they were laughing about. She glanced down the table and saw Mark's face, thin and long, looking aggressively back at her. She sighed and saw his face soften, his smile wry and understanding.

'We're thinking of going across to the Golden Dome if any of you'd like to come.' Plum's clear voice called down the table, her own admirers already staking out their privileges, one to hold back her chair, another to help her adjust her jacket across her shoulders, a third to hold her diminutive evening bag. The older table were making jokes about the latest dance place, comparing it to a perspex fishbowl. Sally called to her own daughter not to be too late and at that mark of approval from the hostess, half of the younger table rose and, calling farewells and thanks, went out to the cars, the drivers hastily leaving a game of mahjong they had been playing on the grass and hurrying over.

There was a long and protracted argument over how many cars were needed to take them down to the Star Ferry and who should go in which car. Mark stood to one side, refusing to involve himself, and Silvia stood near him, communing instead with the flashing specks of light overhead, like glow worms on a bed of black silk.

Tony called for silence and arbitrarily ordered five apiece into two cars. He put Silvia and Mark into the second car and met Mark's look of amused contempt, his light-hearted rendition of 'We're in the army ...' with studied indifference, although he felt a surge of blinding anger engulf him for a moment, shaking him even more than the teasing spite. Silvia appeared to be in a dream world and she didn't notice him as he walked quickly away.

The cars sped down through the dark, tree-overhung loops of road, threading in and out of banks of mist, their lights picking out the dark foliage that jostled and threatened along the steep precipices, down towards the cluster of lights that were each individual but so numerous they appeared like banks of stars somehow inverted below them. It was a warm moist evening, so laden with scents of sweet rotting matter, lingering smoke, excitement, that Tony breathed it in deeply, the wind billowing and gusting in through his window beside the driver. He closed his eyes and felt the silent rushing through the dark, the edge of fear and anticipation churning at his belly that Hong Kong always provoked. He smiled in deep contentment.

Beside him, the driver glanced in his rearview mirror at the following car and stiffened, his hands clenching more tightly at the wheel, but whether out of concern or anger it was difficult to tell. Tony heard the muttered imprecations beneath the man's breath, quick and lilting in Cantonese and he opened his eyes again, turning to peer out through the back window.

Balanced on the roof of the following Mercedes, his fingers, hands, arms and legs spread so that they could adhere better to the smooth metal, was Mark Babcock. There was a look of fierce exaltation on his bared features, teeth almost snarling in a rictus of abandonment, his shirt flapping wildly in the wind. Tony recognised the feeling of exhilaration, startled that it should be Mark of all people who should share it.

The driver of the second car was slowing, carefully, his face twisted and red with a fury that would soon become sullen and uncooperative, Tony knew from experience. The car stopped and Tony signalled for the driver of the first car to stop also.

'No good here. Velly bad road here. Better soon,' the driver confided. Tony snapped at him to stop. Already, he saw two of the other men in the party climbing out and attempting to pull Mark down but he was resisting, kicking out with his feet, swearing and laughing as though he were drunk. Plum had half climbed out and Tony could see her silhouetted in the momentary beam of a following car. It was still high above them, still several loops and twists of the road back, but it would be on them soon. And then there would be no time to react, nowhere to go on that thin mountain road but the deep expanse of darkness below them.

Tony threw himself out of the car and darted back, climbing on to the bonnet of the second car and catching Mark by the scruff of the neck before anyone noticed him. He yanked him down and over the side into waiting arms that bundled him hastily back in the car, fighting and protesting, a strange gurgling laugh unsettling them all. Tony leaned in and took Mark's shirt in his hand, pulling the boy close to the window. There was a blankness to that face, the pupils pinpoints of dark in a wash of blue that

60

unnerved Tony and infuriated him at the same time.

'You do that again and I'll personally toss you out here on this road and let you walk down. Now sit down!' He felt Mark's breath on his cheek, saw the jerk of his head as he pulled away and slumped down in his seat. He gestured to the driver and walked quickly back to the lead car, climbing in with a smooth movement that pulled the door shut. Immediately the driver rolled the car forward and the convoy continued on in silence for some time. Aidan breached the strained quiet finally.

'Pity Americans don't believe in boarding school. Do that boy the world of good, I expect. I thought taxi surfing was the thing, not climbing on top of your host's car. Rather odd behaviour,' he remarked into the dark and Tony, without turning around, grimaced quietly to himself. Mark was indeed an odd creature but sometimes, just occasionally, Tony felt as though he understood him, one outsider, one onlooker to another. They were both so reserved with their emotions that he didn't feel he could condemn Mark for his occasional lapses.

'He has some sort of weird death wish, I think,' one of the girls said, greatly daring. 'He's always doing something crazy like that. His father lets him get away with just about anything. Doesn't even notice, Mummy says. She says he's going to end up in dreadful trouble, one day.' Conversation lapsed after that but Aidan's odd, rather bulbous face became thoughtful, Tony noticed, as he caught sight of it in the wing mirror. Contemplative.

They pulled up in front of the railings outside the Star Ferry ramp, climbing out in newly boisterous mood, Plum immediately beckoning them all through the turnstiles, waving a dollar bill at the ticket collector. There was a ferry about to leave and they dashed along the concrete passageways to the dock, laughing and breathless, their shoes beating a tattoo of urgency, arriving just as the coolies began to lift the wooden slatted gangway. They thundered on board, squeezing between people, pointing towards the bow and regrouping only as the small two-tiered ferry

61

churned and frothed its propellers and parted from the concrete dock.

It set off jauntily across the harbour, the smell of salt spray and joss sticks mixing sweetly with the fresh night air; several naval frigates were anchored off in the roads, lit up with charming abandon. It was only then that Tony, looking around, said blankly:

'Where're Mark and Silvia? Didn't they make it?' Everyone turned around and searched the throng of Chinese, Filipino and European faces, incurious and stoic as they crossed the dark oil-lapped waters yet again. There was no sign of the missing pair. With puzzled shrugs or looks of relief, they turned back to each other.

'Perhaps they had other plans?' someone suggested and Sally Freeman's daughter's plain face became a little plainer. Tony pressed his lips together firmly, breathing in the scent of the night and letting his mind drift away from the others and their cheerful babble.

He drank in the beauty of the dark spangled water, the fairy lights of other junks, ships anchored off shore, the way the ferry manoeuvred around a sampan that swept in front of its bows, the old woman at the tiller stoically indifferent to its path. She glanced up briefly, a withered, tanned face beneath a black scarf pulled back behind her ears, her padded jacket tight around her. He lifted a hand and she replied, her face showing no emotion as the sampan was lifted by the bow wave and hurried on its way. Contained and withdrawn, he thought, but not rude. Just not interested. Like Silvia.

The glow had gone out of the evening, the fear and anticipation he had felt on the drive down drifting away leaving him impatient that he had agreed to come with the others, irritable at the length of the evening still to run before he could decently make his excuses. He hunched forward on his forearms, leaning on the varnished rail and listened to the clatter of Kowloon drawing near.

Kowloon never slept, certainly not the neon-lit area bordered by Salisbury Road, Nathan Road and Chatham Road South. In that area of Tsim Sha Tsui, the tip of

Kowloon, there were more bars, nightclubs, and massage parlours pressed together than in the whole of London. The Golden Dome was new, owned by a syndicate who had begun to expand their business empire into leisure pursuits. It huddled between a hotel coffee shop and a tailor, only its entrance visible, the rest below ground. There were lights encased in perspex that flashed around the entrance and an expanse of red carpet down gilded stairs that offended Tony in his newly sour mood, when normally he would have been amused by its blatant vulgarity.

He followed the others downstairs, ignoring the doorman who hesitated over whether to ask them to pay or not. It was a quiet evening. They should be glad of the custom, Aidan murmured to him, reassuringly. The red plush led down to a long mahogany bar where several Thai girls sat, cross-legged on tall stools, the slits of their cheong sams discreetly revealing. They turned and smiled a welcome that barely made it to their lips before they saw Plum and the other girls in the group and they turned back to the bar.

Small tables in the back room surrounded a clear perspex dance floor beneath which, true to their parents' word, swam large koy carp, glistening in shades from amber and gold through to pure white. Tony wondered if they were in place of the traditional goldfish that every Chinese home possessed, the idea being that bad luck would find the goldfish first and be deflected from the owner. He thought wryly that it would take quite a bit of bad luck to kill a fish as big as a carp.

A few bored couples danced to disco music above the fish, reflected inversely in the concave surface of the golden dome-like roof. Hideous, Tony thought, perfectly hideous. And he was stuck with it.

They sat and ordered drinks, Tony leaning back in the too short-backed chair with resignation. He would have to stay and dance with the girls for at least an hour or two since they were now short of men. The prospect did not improve his temper.

'This is what you're so anxious to return to, Tony? To

63

join the ranks of the young, rich and bored, forever seeking a new place to replace last week's favourite? I do so like the fish, don't you?' Aidan was mocking himself as much as Tony, the latter realised and took no offence.

'Just the right touch. Can't think how nightclubs managed before.' His eyelids turned up in amusement, although the rest of his face was still sombre. He shrugged when Aidan yawned and beckoned him to lean forward.

'I shall be glad when I'm old and married and don't have to be out on the prowl anymore,' Aidan said softly and surprisingly bitterly. 'It's too bloody exhausting, these days, and the only talent is already taken.' Tony wasn't sure whether he was referring to Plum, who was almost engaged to her man in London and had let everyone know it, or to Silvia – but he didn't want to think about Silvia any more. He forced himself to sound positive.

'Oh, come on! There's more than this to Hong Kong and you know it, Aidan. We're just humouring people tonight, doing our duty.' He stressed the last word, making a joke out of it, out of the sheer awfulness of it all. 'Tomorrow we can head off to Shek O and Big Wave Beach or go sailing, grab some lunch over at one of the islands, join the Hash in the evening.' He paused, taking in Aidan's grimace at the thought of a Hash House Harry jog through the folds and crevasses of Hong Kong's peaks ... 'And finish off with dinner in some village on the other side of the island with lots of beer and good company. But tonight, if the girls want to dance ...' He drifted off, noticing a disturbance over by the bar where the waiter who had taken their orders for drinks was being jostled by two young Chinese men. Seeing the fixity of Tony's stare, Aidan swivelled in his seat and watched also.

The waiter was being pushed by the youths now, his face tight with alarm. He had signalled to the bouncers by the door but they were not responding, and the two men smiled, tight, vicious faces pushing him back further against the bottles, crowding him. The Thai girls scattered off their stools and rushed past them to the rear of the club.

'Christ, what's going on?' Tony asked and would have

risen to help the waiter but Aidan clasped a tight hand around his arm and anchored him down.

'Triad matter by the look of it. Sent in the thugs for a bit of intimidation and squeeze. Maybe the new owners don't want to pay them off so the staff are going to get roughed up a bit. Don't get involved, Tony. There's nothing you can do,' he warned. The volume of the music had been raised and most clients still seemed unaware of the ugly little scene behind the bar. The two youths had smashed a bottle now and were holding it in front of the waiter's face, waving it gently from side to side as the man's eyes followed its razor edge with sickened fascination. Tony shook Aidan's grip free and stood up.

'Don't, Tony! You'll get yourself slashed up. These guys know what they're doing. They're professionals.' Aidan had risen also but Tony was already walking towards the three behind the bar. He picked up a bottle and, without pausing to consider, landed it heavily across the back of the older youth's head just as the broken bottle touched the waiter's face, drawing blood. The second youth whirled around, startled and furious, his features unaccountably familiar despite their aggression. Tony hesitated, staring, and the boy – for he couldn't have been more than sixteen or seventeen – hit him a back-handed chop that doubled him over and made the room fade alarmingly around him.

There was a scuffle, some grunting, and by the time Tony looked up the youths were halfway up the stairs, the younger supporting the older across his shoulder. Aidan sighed and leaned down beside him.

'You all right?' he asked, taking a cigarette out of his pack and placing it between his lips. He lit it while Tony shook his head and forced himself to stand. There was something so deliberately poised about Aidan, leaning against the bar, cigarette dangling from his lip, that Tony couldn't contain the laugh that bubbled up inside him. He reached for the cigarette and took a deep drag.

'Glad you found that amusing. Maybe the army's the right place for you after all. There always have to be a few thick-witted heroes around,' Aidan drawled, lighting another cigarette. He glanced over at the waiter who was dabbing at his face with a cloth. 'Why did you hesitate like that? You could have landed them both.'

Tony paused, blowing out a cloud of smoke, his eyes narrowing as he searched his memory.

'I knew him. The second one. From somewhere ... I just can't quite—' He broke off as the face slotted into place, his own quite blank with surprise. 'My God, that was Harry!'

'Harry?' Aidan's gaze sharpened with interest.

'The Babcocks' amah son – Harry. What the hell is he doing mixed up with Triad thugs?' Tony said in dismay.

'Learning to be a big brother, I'd say, wouldn't you?' Aidan gestured to the girls who were looking across the darkened room in alarm. 'Come on, let's go reassure them you're in one piece.'

'And Harry?'

'Harry isn't your problem, is he?'

Chapter Seven

Judson, Texas
June, 1976

The day shimmered with cloudy heat, pressing down on them like a dull weight. Clouds of dust blew across the concrete play area, catching leaves and brush and pinning them against the meshed wire fence that surrounded Haskell Ridge High. Gina Fratelli wiped the perspiration that had gathered on her top lip away with her sleeve, trying not to look at the boy's shirt where large damp circles betrayed him. He didn't care, leaning in close to her, his words twanging in a Southern drawl.

'Can't you'all do something 'bout them? They're ruining the curve. We'll all get Ds 'cos of them,' Tommy Bering complained to Gina and Gina shrugged. The curve, always the curve. Why there was such a thing, she didn't know, grouping the exam results together and then raising or lowering them as necessary in order for normality to reign. And very smart people, like Claudia and Paul, now they upset everything, since if the curve was raised, Paul and Claudia's marks just went off the scale. She could see Tommy Bering's point but she wasn't about to admit it.

'You can't expect them to flunk just 'cos you can't make it. Besides, the teachers don't want us doing badly either. It makes their records look bad. I figure they just give Liddie and Paul As automatically and then grade the rest of us without curving them in. Otherwise how would any of us make any Bs?' It sounded reasonable. 'I figure the teachers have got it worked out,' Gina added confidently and Tommy shook his head.

'I dunno. Makes me feel like pushing them under a bus or somethin'. He's such a runt with those round spectacles and that squinty face. He looks like a gopher or somethin' and she's just a stringy little thing always watching silently without saying a word but you know, you just know, she's thinkin' real hard inside. Why couldn't she be like her sister, now? Huh?' He laughed, remembering what some of the other guys had said about Peggy.

He glanced back at Gina, thinking she wasn't much of a looker either, no wonder she was friends with them with her pasty-looking face and heavy eyebrows beetling over cow-like eyes. They were all oddballs, that's why they went around together.

He gave a sigh of disgust and loped back over to the basketball courts in time to snatch a ball away from another boy and dribble it quickly up the other end before taking a quick leap and slam dunking the net. He turned around with a grin, his raised hand slapping against those of his team, all thought of the impending exams gone from his mind. From the far side of the court, the cheerleaders, Kathy Toreno, Missy Hatchard and Clarice Sturming, swung their golden arms and golden hair in appreciation, practising to be Dallas Cowboy cheerleaders.

Gina, cringing into herself as she had read the thoughts in Tommy's clear blue eyes, wandered disconsolately over to where Paul and Claudia were sitting together beneath a tree, going over the dates of the French Revolution. She sat down heavily and watched them, hoping they would look up and acknowledge her. She was pleased when they did.

'Gina, hello!' Claudia smiled and shifted so that Gina could sit more comfortably beside them.

'Hi there, Gina,' Paul said, lifting his spectacles for a moment to get a better look at her. He dropped them again, almost immediately. 'You want to join in?' There was reluctance in his voice; he knew she would slow them down. He was relieved when she shook her head.

'No, I don't know them yet. I'm gonna learn them tonight, I guess. Tommy's fussing that you're gonna alter the curve so badly everyone else'll flunk out.'

'That's not hard with Tommy,' Liddie said with some asperity and Gina laughed, her plump face wobbling slightly with pleasure at being able to mock Tommy Bering in return.

'Jocks!' Paul said with contempt. 'Imagine if we complained about how bad they make us look at sport. Load of weekend cowboys,' he added witheringly and Gina smiled again, trying to think up something else to ridicule the sporty, good-looking set who made life such hell for them all, driving around in their pickup trucks after school, laughing and fooling around, whistling at the kids who weren't popular, who weren't part of the in-crowd. Why did she have to be born into a country and especially a state where being a quarterback or a cheerleader was considered more important than passing exams? She settled herself more comfortably on the grass.

Claudia looked at them both and smiled too but inside she was wishing she weren't quite so bright or quite so skinny and that she wasn't such a klutz at games. That she didn't have to be a misfit all the time. She looked all right, didn't she, in her jeans and cotton shirt, her hair pulled back into a neat plait and only a stray cowlick escaping to fall into her eyes from time to time? She shouldn't have to be with the misfits. And then she was angry with herself for her treachery.

She slipped a photograph out of her pencil holder and held it in the palm of her hand for a moment, summoning up that rush of sadness and nostalgia it always produced. A younger Harry and she looked up at her, mocking her with their bright smiles and the waving fronds of palm trees behind them. Oh, Harry ... where are you now, what are you doing now? Are you happy? She sighed. Perhaps it was only in Judson that she was a misfit and perhaps she ought to be grateful for that fact?

'What's that?' Unseen, Tommy Bering had come up behind her and he leaned down now and snatched the photograph from her hand. He held it up and gave a loud hoot of laughter.

'Hey, it's a nigger! You and a nigger boy, huh? Why d'you'all keep this, Liddie? What's so special about your nigger boy?' He was jeering so loud that one of his friends

69

came over and whipped the photo from his hand. Claudia stood up, red in the face.

'Give it back. Just give it back!'

'It ain' a nigger, Tommy, you dumb-ass, it's a Chink! Liddie's in love with a Chink!' The jeering became louder, chanting, as the boys danced away from Claudia while she tried to snatch it back, laughing and taunting at her as she grew redder and more angry by the moment.

'Liddie's in love with a Chink!' They tossed the photo from one to the other, the bright slip of paper fluttering and twisting in the wind, Claudia standing there silently staring at them, as they pranced in their coloured checked shirts and their high booted jeans, so alike she could barely tell them apart. She couldn't believe the fury she felt, nor the humiliation. There were tears burning in her eyes and she blinked them fiercely away.

'Aw, give it back, Tommy, stop playing the fool.' A louder voice commanded sharply from behind Claudia and she turned involuntarily, catching Bo Haskill's eyes and looking away again quickly. Bo Haskill who had nothing to do with Haskell Ridge for all the jokes that were made about it. He came from the nicer side of town, the son of a lawyer. Bo who, in his senior year, was the local heart-throb amongst the girls, changing them out regularly, like disposable razors, as the initial cutting edge dulled.

Tommy stopped dancing around and aggressively jerked his chin out. The other boys around him quietened down suddenly.

'Yeah? Why? Are you in love with Liddie too? You and a Chink boy? That'd be a laugh! What'd you be? Number Two Boy?' Tommy went off into a high-pitched hyena cry that a few of his friends joined in faintly before lapsing back into silence. Claudia's flush became acute and she dared not look up into Bo's eyes.

But he was quietly contemplating Tommy instead, his head slightly to one side, the red thatch of hair and sandy freckles standing out brightly in the sunshine. He was a tall, gangly boy, nearly three years senior to Tommy, widely respected for being both good at sports and bright. A real

70

all-rounder, Claudia thought painfully, wishing he would go away and let Tommy's attention span expire all on its own. But no, Bo was going to be a hero, going to stop the bullying. Most of the school figured he'd make homecoming king that year. Maybe he was collecting votes? She saw his mouth tighten as he shook his head.

'God, you can be a real jerk sometimes, Tommy Bering. Why don't you stop picking on little girls, for God's sake?' He turned his back and deliberately walked away before Tommy could think of something effective to say. He stood, flustered for a moment, his cheeks puffing out as though to spurt out his frustration while the smiles around him grew larger. Claudia winced.

'Yeah and you're a fucking prick!' Tommy shouted loudly after Bo. The window beside him was raised sharply, as though the person behind it could take no more.

'Tommy Bering. Inside, now!' The school principal slammed down the window again and there was silence. Then the titters began and Tommy, red in the face, looked around him in fury.

'There, you little weasel, there!' He held out the photo toward Claudia and deliberately ripped it into pieces that he let flutter to the ground. Claudia watched them, her mouth slightly parted as though better to bear the pain, as they fell scattered across the pavement.

'And as for you, Haskill, I'll see you later,' Tommy shouted but Bo was long gone and Tommy was secretly relieved. He slouched angrily towards the Principal's office, the others parting and moving away, their game over.

Claudia bent over the fragments of photo, picking them up slowly and putting them carefully into her hand. Why couldn't the Principal have intervened earlier, when they were taunting her? He must have heard them? Why only when Tommy swore? She closed her lids over the scratchiness in her eyes.

'Can we help?' Paul was bending down beside her now, and Gina too, searching for the last pieces. She looked at them both, her mouth tight. Well, if that's what the others thought was funny, then she was glad she was a misfit, glad she was with Paul and Gina. Paul smiled, his eyes shining sympathetically behind his spectacles.

'Nice to hear Tommy coming out with another classic line.' He smiled. 'Such a bright guy to say it so loudly right there by the window. How will we all manage with the curve he'll set us?'

And Claudia had to smile too, even over the heaviness in her chest. 'If it worked the other way, he'd send our grades into orbit. Such a prat!' She put the fragments into her pencil case, wondering if she could glue them together again.

'Gosh, that was nice of Bo, wasn't it? He's a good guy,' Gina said wistfully. Claudia looked at her in surprise. Was Gina in love with Bo? Like all the rest of the girls.

'Yeah, guess so,' she muttered but she knew if he hadn't intervened she would have got her photo back whole. Now it was in pieces, just like her former life, she thought moodily. She stood up.

'Come on, let's get back on with our studying. How else are we ever going to get out of here?'

And Paul looked at her with a crooked grin. 'Amen to that.'

'Why'd your brother never come back, then? Why'd he stay and both you girls came back?' Bo asked. He had been standing by the bus stop when she walked by and he had fallen into step beside her quite naturally, saying he was sorry about the photo. Claudia had barely looked up at him, walking on fast with her bag heavy on her shoulder, muttering that it didn't matter. But Bo knew it did and was sorry. He continued to walk beside her, puzzled by the lack of interest and the straight answers he received, not a hint of flirtation in her words or glances.

'Mark wanted to stay with Dad and I guess Mama didn't make a big fuss over it. I don't know really. She just wanted to get away. I don't know that she'd have really minded if all of us had asked to stay but I just didn't think to,' Claudia said and again Bo thought, how odd that she would say something so blunt and appallingly truthful to him.

He looked at her more carefully, at the long thin legs and the bright eyes that occasionally looked up at him and blazed with such intelligence and intensity that he felt as though he had been scorched.

'Did you want to stay too, then?' he asked, slinging his bag more comfortably across his back and darting a quick look at his watch. He had to be at basketball practice in five minutes.

'Of course! Why would I want to come back here? What has Haskell Ridge High got to offer? A jock scholarship so I can become an Aggie?' she said scornfully and then looked at him and wondered whether he intended to go to an Agricultural School on a basketball scholarship and whether she had been unforgivably tactless. But then, he had lost her the photo. Tough if she had been tactless.

'I guess not. What do you want to do then?'

'Get out of here. Go to Princeton or Harvard.' She glared at him, daring him to mock her. But he smiled instead, that long, lazy smile of his that made girls' hearts flip over, easy as a pancake on a griddle. Claudia felt a quiver herself at the way he looked at her, just at her, and then she fought it down.

'Yeah, I guess you probably could too, if you wanted to badly enough. Well, if you write to Mark, say hi from me. We used to be friends a while back. Oh, and tell Peggy it's seven-thirty, not seven and we won't wait if she's late. She knows where. See'ya.' He gave her a distracted smile and loped off down the block, his bag bouncing across his back as he ran. She saw him pause to chat to Clarice Sturming, laughing as he put his arm around her, leaned in close. Clarice giggled back at him.

And Claudia, squinting after him, seeing his red hair haloed in the afternoon sun, mocked herself for the slight tingle of excitement that threaded through her but was still obscurely pleased that he had been so casual about her ambitions. 'Yeah, I guess you probably could, if you wanted to badly enough' – badly enough! He had no idea.

But surely someone like Bo Haskill wasn't dumb enough to be getting mixed up with Peggy? After all, Peggy was half the reason Claudia wanted to get away. What was he doing meeting her at seven-thirty? And why, when the likes of Clarice Sturming were there for the taking? Or perhaps that was the problem? The Clarice Sturmings of this world only went so far; Peggy went all the way.

And what was that about, 'if she wrote to Mark'? She shook her head, wondering if all boys were mad or just plain thick? How could she write to Mark when Mama had said she didn't have a son any more? No son and no husband. Claudia sighed and walked on. But the thought continued to niggle at her from time to time. What if she did write to Mark? Would he write back?

Chapter Eight

Central, Hong Kong
October, 1976

There were three of them spaced out along Queen's Road Central, one leaning against a pillar, his loose khaki trousers, striped T-shirt and zippered jacket proclaiming him to be non-professional as much as his long dark hair falling from a side part over shaded eyes, the way he stood there in his Nike running shoes looking at his fake Rolex. He was waiting for the other two, one in dark skin-tight jeans and leather jacket, the other in blue jeans and sweat-shirt, to signal him. Aidan watched them both closely, thinking it odd that he had been chosen for this job. His finger hesitated above the walkie talkie button. Not yet, not quite yet.

They were careful not to glance at each other too much, Aidan noted. Just quick glances, as though looking around, waiting from someone. Timing the jewellery shop's employees, who went out at what time, who was still left. This was the fourth time this week they had been here, like this, keeping watch. It was going to happen today, Aidan thought. He could feel it.

What the hell was he doing there? This wasn't his side of things. But he had mentioned that boy's name – Harry – and the powers-that-be had been delighted, set it up, watched and located the boy, waited patiently and now, months later, Aidan's job was to get that boy. No one else. The others could go to hell, and so could the jewellers. They just wanted Harry. But looking at that lean body, those long legs, Aidan thought there was almost no chance. He wasn't fit enough to run that boy down.

He patted the bulge beneath his jacket, slipped a wary

hand in to check it was unclipped and ready to draw. How mundane his job had become already, he mocked himself. From the heady dreams of international espionage he was jettisoned into local police enforcement. Catch a Triad thug and make Uncle Bill's day, won't you, Aidan my boy? But the pulse of nervousness continued to beat in his stomach until he felt almost ill with waiting.

It was nearly noon, and the swirls of hurrying pedestrians became thicker as they filtered from office buildings, more clogged as they met and joined together, fighting to move along the narrow pavements with speed, spewing across the four lanes of traffic like a mass of hurtling termites intent on eating their way through the flimsy façade of Queens Road. The cooler October air was like a tonic to them, urging them on, faster, faster, where to eat, quick, get in line, quick, quick, get a table, faster, eat, quick quick, there's no time and so much to do, *aie yah*! They rushed in demented hordes from shop to shop, and still the three men somehow appeared to hold their places against the roaring tides of humanity scouring all along in their path. Aidan took a deep breath and stilled himself also.

The clock ticked around to ten past, quarter past the hour and the first two assistants left the jeweller's punctually, pausing for a moment as though to adjust to the force of the tide and then being sucked into it and lost. The one in the black leather jacket was the Triad's strongman, Aidan guessed accurately, their Red Pole or Enforcer. He gestured across to the other two. Harry moved forward slowly, slipping with an ease, through the flow, that caught and excited Aidan's admiration. Damn, he was good! The third man, in blue jeans, seemed to be the back-up, a new recruit perhaps being initiated into the lodge? He hung back, glancing warily up and down the street, his young face tight with fear.

The strongman had entered the portals of the jeweller's with Harry right behind him. Aidan pressed down on his button, murmuring a code word that made him feel faintly foolish. He pocketed the walkie talkie and pressed forward himself, appearing to window shop but moving now with considerable speed himself. The young one hadn't noticed him.

There was a police constable inside the jeweller's itself, and another three stationed along the street. The inspector was out the back with another man. Aidan felt his breath tight in his throat, the smell of the bodies pressed around him, expensive perfumes and colognes vying with the fast food noodle and hamburger joints, the pressed Peking ducks swaying from their strings, and the heavy clog of cars' exhaust fumes rising, protesting, in his gorge. He swallowed down on it and paused outside the windows of the shop, trying to see in past the expensive rows of watches, gold bracelets, jade.

When the shotgun explosion came, he almost wasn't prepared. He ducked, flinging himself down as the window shattered into a thousand flying shards beside him, hard nutty nubules of reinforced glass crumbling out. The strongman was lying across the display, his fingers outstretched as though to clasp at the flashing baubles, but the pumping red tide from his chest was as frenzied as the human tide outside, thrusting, hurrying, quick quick out of his body, lying in pools of frothing liquid glory. Aidan looked away, sickened, seeing the quick flocking of the crowd forward to devour the violence.

Harry had moved so fast, he was out and almost beyond Aidan's grasp when the older man erupted from beneath the glass fragments and threw himself forward. He couldn't hold the boy. He knew there would be no chance of that, having seen Harry chop Tony down. But he could shoot him. Stop him that way. Aidan shouted at Harry to halt. And then, almost slowly and thoughtfully, he pulled out his gun and fired.

Harry, flying past on panic, dimly heard the words being roared out, first in English, then Cantonese. But his feet propelled him forward, eating up the ground, almost free, almost ... ah, no, not free, falling down, the hard concrete of the pavement curiously soft, not nearly as bad as he had thought, quite soothing and nice the way it was all fading around him, the noise and confusion and fear, going, going, gone. He closed his eyes and lay quite still.

77

'Yes, but was it really necessary to shoot him, Aidan? It'll be at least a week before we can question him properly now.' Bill Ingram's voice was wearily patient, trying to contain the anger within him. He trusted Aidan but sometimes...

'It was only in the leg, sir. Just a clean shot straight through. The doctor's say he'll be fine, sir. We can question him this afternoon. Besides, it was either that or lose him completely, sir.' Aidan's voice was distorted by the mobile phone, sounding tinny and mocking. Perhaps he was mocking? Bill's anger mounted.

'Which we may have done anyway, now. He's hardly likely to want to cooperate with people who pump lead through him, now is he?' The exasperation came through clearly.

'I'm sorry, sir, but I didn't feel I had any other choice. At least I didn't kill him.' Aidan's tone had sharpened, reminding his superior of the other rather messy shooting that had resulted.

'That man was no use to us anyway. The constable had a right to defend the people in there.' Bill paused. 'All right. What's done is done. Let's not dwell on it.' His manner became brisk. 'At least it'll look right if he spends some time in hospital, a bit in prison and is then let loose back to his lodge brothers. They won't doubt which side he's on then, at least.' Because there won't be any doubt, Bill added to himself furiously. He tapped a pencil, lead down, on the edge of his desk.

'Just what's behind all this, sir? Why the sudden dire urgency in getting someone on the inside of a Triad lodge?' Aidan wasn't just curious. He already suspected a great deal and was waiting for confirmation. And also for trust. Bill smiled tightly. The mobile was supposed to be on a secure channel but who really knew? Who really ever knew about anything in Hong Kong? Not even the seasoned and select band of China watchers were ever sure.

'Not any old lodge, Aidan. The Thin Blades. They've a new man in charge, we hear. Very young, very aggressive.

Started out as a strongman, a Red Pole, and then took most of the younger members with him when he ousted the old Big Brother, Wong Shih Yu, and knocked off his second in command. I hear old Wong now waits for buses in the rain and has lost so much face that shopkeepers sell him only damaged goods.' Bill smiled enigmatically, wondering whether Aidan was catching on.

'So who's the new Big Brother?'

'Yee Fong Lo. Nicknamed Big Feet – probably because he kicked shit out of Wong. He's Tanka. Rather unusual, wouldn't you say?'

'Very. But I still don't grasp—'

'Harry Braga spent part of his boyhood with this Yee fellow. They know and trust each other and Harry is tipped to be the next Red Pole. You saw him in action. What do you think? Is it possible?'

Aidan shrugged to himself, looking down as he tried to recall the two brief occasions in which he had seen Harry. 'Possible, yes I suppose so. He's very good for someone so young. Only seventeen. He scares the hell out of me, for one thing. But why is this Yee so important?'

'There's word he's being backed by someone pretty high up with a lot of financial as well as political clout.' Word gleaned so very slowly and so very painstakingly, monitoring radio and TV programmes in China, putting together the snippets of regional information broadcast in Hunan or Shangsi or Tibet, rubbing careful shoulders with Communist business men at the Marco Polo Club, sifting through the colony's hints and rumours. And it all came down to "There's word" ...'

'This isn't just another Triad trying to muscle in on the prostitution racket or extortion or video piracy. There's a much bigger game going on here and I want to know what it's about and Harry Braga is my only chance of that. So you be a nice boy to him, won't you, Aidan? Because I want some answers.'

'Yes, sir. I'll do my best.'

'Oh, you'll do better than that, Aidan. I know you.' Was that another jibe at him for shooting Harry or was it genuine praise? Aidan wasn't sure.

'And I know you, sir, if I don't,' he finished drily and made his farewells. And I know, he added to himself, as he let himself out of the inspector's office and closed the door behind him, that Uncle Bill hasn't been telling me half of what's going on, has he? Oh, no!

Tishing angrily through his teeth, Aidan went out to visit Harry again.

Harry lay on his back, a pillow wedged uncomfortably beneath his neck, and stared out the grilled windows. There was little to see, a patch of sky, another building, the sun catching the window and reflecting a wavering gold light across his face, flaring like a beacon into his eyes. He forced himself not to blink.

It was the only way to control the fear. He could feel it lurking beneath his immobile calm, ready to tear and slash its way into his mind, to overrule his conscience, to betray his brothers. Anything so long as they let him go. It wasn't fear of pain, of what they might do to him. He was good where pain was concerned, had proved himself to Yee and his brothers many times over. But he couldn't bear the thought of being sent to prison, crowded into bed-like cubicles with all those other vile, petty thugs, the grey concrete cells for hour after hour, day after day, being ordered about, contained, circumscribed, the smells, the filth, the aggression. No friends, no brothers. What was the point of life like that? He couldn't bear that. He'd rather kill himself first. He was so desperately afraid. The thought revolved in his mind again and again as he forced himself not to blink.

The door of his room swung open and he forced himself not to look, not to breathe. Just lie there, immobile, dumb, inanimate. Don't look up.

But no one came close to the bed, no one made a sound and eventually, unable to help himself, Harry slowly swivelled his head and looked over at the door. The man there smiled in quiet triumph.

He was dressed in a suit, Harry noted with misgiving. Senior police? Perhaps, but he didn't quite have that look about him, too young for a start and seeming smoother and more slick somehow, his suit made for him the way it curved over those slightly hunching shoulders and didn't ride up at the back, the smooth skin of his face that looked like it never produced bristle, those slightly hooded and pouched eyes. No, not police ... but what? The fear rose closer and lapped at the edges of his mind.

'Hello, Harry. How are you feeling now? Much better, I expect.' Harry felt the fear wrench through him, twitching in his neck as the man used his name. How had he known his name? How? He watched the man look around the room and select the more comfortable of the two hardback chairs to sit on. He took out a cigarette, tapped it down on the battered silver holder and put it in his mouth. For a moment the 'No Smoking' sign seemed to catch his attention but he merely gave a flickering smile and lit up. 'The doctor says your leg will recover nicely as long as you rest it and receive all the right medications.' The man paused and Harry felt there had been a warning in his words that was more unsettling than anything else that had happened before. He didn't answer and the man blew out a lungful of smoke.

'Of course, should you not get everything you need, your leg could easily go septic. You could get a bad infection in it, you understand, that might result in it not healing right so that you walk with a limp ... or it might mean having to take the leg off completely if it were to develop gangrene. You know what gangrene is, Harry?' The man settled back into his chair and stretched out long legs across the lino-leum. Harry made no comment, but continued to stare at the man as though unable to break free.

'I know you understand English, Harry, but if you prefer I'll speak in Cantonese?' The man smiled, displaying sharp spiked teeth that were faintly discoloured from tobacco stains. Harry felt ill, forcing his mouth to remain steady when it wanted to quiver at the thought of losing his leg, being a beggar on crutches, dressed in rags, jostled by the lunchtime hordes of Central along the overhead walkways, begging, begging . . .

'How's your mother, Harry? And your step-father? Do you ever go visit them on Cheung Chau? Would you like me to call them for you? Tell them you're here? I suppose when you finally get out of prison, they'd take you back, wouldn't they? I mean, a man with only one leg and no way of supporting himself except by begging? Such a shame for a good-looking boy like you. Surely your mother and Jeremy,' a sweet smile of concern, 'would look after you, wouldn't they? Even though you had lost them so much face.' The man was silent a long time after that, quietly smoking, but he would glance across at Harry occasionally, see the sheen of perspiration on that pale skin, the way Harry's mouth had become so dry that he had to keep licking his lips.

Finally the man gave a long sigh, flicked the cigarette end onto the floor and ground it out beneath his toe. He hunched forward, his palms together, pressed between his knees.

'Do you know how I know your name, Harry? Harry Braga. Do you know how I know so much about you?' There was no movement from the boy on the bed. 'It's because we know a lot about everyone in the Triads, we know what sorts they are, petty thugs and criminals with little intelligence and no future beyond beating up frightened restaurant owners and demanding free beer. But you're not like that, are you, Harry? That's what we noticed straight away about you. You didn't look like the right sort to be mixed up with those thugs and we thought we'd keep an eye on you. How did you get mixed up with them anyway, Harry? What happened?' The man's tone had become so sympathetic, so understanding that Harry had to fight down the moan of despair that rose in the back of his throat, had to fight not to blurt out just what had happened, how he had had no choice, how only Yee had been willing to help him.

'You know your accomplice was killed, don't you? He was shot and died instantly. I could have killed you too, but

I thought it so unfair when you're only seventeen still. I thought you deserved another chance.' The man looked at Harry intently, reading something in the eyes. 'The third man? He got away. He's back with all the other thugs in Yee's bunch, telling them you're both dead. They'll be sighing with relief that you can't finger them to us. And right at the moment, no one else knows any different, do they? Just us.' A gentle, understanding smile enveloped Harry.

'What do you think would happen, Harry, if we were to treat you well and then just release you, let you out on the streets?' Another pause. 'I'd be suspicious if I were Yee, wouldn't you? I'd start thinking maybe you'd let out a few secrets, perhaps? What would happen to you then, Harry?' Aidan looked bright and interested in Harry's reply. 'Or, if you chose to be useful to us, Harry, we could help you, look after your leg properly, get you out of jail, make sure Yee never suspected you. It really is your choice, Harry. You think about it.'

The words would not be contained any longer. They burst with ragged fear from Harry's lips.

'Who the hell are you?'

Chapter Nine

Claudia cowered in her bedroom, listening to the screaming voices, the vile words of abuse on both sides, the sullen silence that, she knew, would continue for days. She had seen her mother's face when she came home, stricken beyond anything Claudia had seen before, except perhaps that time at Repulse Bay, long ago. And Peggy had been standing defiantly in the middle of the room, her lower lip pushed out in that habit she had when she was not going to be sorry. Not for anything. Claudia hadn't argued when Mama said to go to her room. She had known what it was about.

It was too late, of course, to do anything. Four months gone. Claudia, Paul and Gina had whispered about it as they sat over their books on the lawn, each adding a little knowledge to each other's meagre store.

And, looking back on it, Mama had been very brave, Claudia realised. She hadn't thrown Peggy out or publicly disowned her. She had just put her head down and stopped seeing her friends from outside Haskell Ridge and stopped saying anything to her neighbours from within Haskell Ridge, not replying to the smiling barbed enquiries of how Peggy was getting along, not answering the louder jeers from some of the boys from school. No one knew who the father was and Peggy, for once, wasn't telling.

Mama had finished her book-keeping course and had a better paid job that could feed them all, she said, even if their no-good father never sent them another cent, but there would be no extras. No chance of a new dress for Claudia, no chance of repainting the porch, definitely no

84

chance of presents at Christmas that year. Claudia sighed, watching Mama's pretty face become sharper still, the lines appearing around that pinched-in mouth. No chance.

It all went on the extra mouth that duly appeared another five months after that, Claudia knew, and tried not to begrudge the poor little thing its rights. It was so defence-less, all pink and wrinkled and ugly! Such a dear little thing. But Mama still let Peggy enrol at that wretched beauty school that she had wanted to go to so much with her friend Elly, Claudia thought bitterly and that cost a bomb. Peggy wasn't about to be chastised financially, even if everyone else was because of her folly.

But, before long, no one really remembered that Todd had been such an unwelcome surprise for them all, Peggy laughing as she bounced him on her lap, saying archly to her sister:

'Now wouldn't you just like to know who his daddy is, Liddie? Wouldn't you just roll your eyes, girl, if'n I told you 'bout Toddy's daddy. But I shan't, 'cos you wouldn't believe it, now would you? You wouldn't believe he's a college man, would you? Oh not, not Toddy's daddy.' She would boast, elaborating on the theme until Claudia could scream, knowing it was all made up. It was probably just one of the Bering boys or some of the other riff-raff she'd hung around with, but no, Peggy had to make it someone special now that she need never tell who. If she even knew! Claudia, stony-faced, would walk away and Peggy's laugh would rattle after her.

And Mama was spending most evenings cooing over her Todd despite how dim he really was, poor duck, not saying a word when Peggy started going out again in the evenings, leaving her son to anyone else's care as long as she didn't have to stay in, Claudia thought furiously. Except that everyone knew what Peggy was and that she was with a boy most nights. It didn't matter who, the saying went, just how often. And Claudia knew what the nudges from the boys as she went by were about. They were wondering if she was going to be like her sister and whether they should give it a try.

*

When Bo Haskill had got the basketball scholarship everyone had expected him to get and went off to the University of Virginia, no one was much surprised. Perhaps they had thought he would go to A&M, closer to home, or perhaps they had thought he would major in something easier than Architecture but still, he was a bright boy and a normal boy and he would come on back one day, they all thought. And at least he was still in the South.

But when Claudia got offered a scholarship to Duke and turned it down because she said she wanted to go North, everyone was astounded. And offended.

That was at the end of her junior year when she was still filling out college applications and trying to sort out with the College Prep advisor just what her limits ought to be. He knew she was bright but no one from Haskell High had ever been to Harvard, he pointed out, when she insisted on giving it a shot. And even Paul was only trying for places like the University of Massachusetts ...

'But Paul is a mathematician, Mr Pringle. He doesn't want the sort of place I want. He just wants to go and learn how to conquer quarks and electromagnetic fields and stuff like that. I want to major in English,' she said for the fifteenth time that week and heard the impatience in her voice but couldn't be bothered to conceal it any more. Her advisor sighed.

'Well, Duke has a wonderful English department and the fact that they wrote to you and offered you a place with a full scholarship and a whole year early ...! You'd be mad to turn it down, Claudia. I've spoken with your mother about it and she wants you to go.' He paused, adjusting his tie, hesitating as though he were reluctant to disappoint her, but Claudia knew him. He was enjoying it.

'Sometimes you have to learn your own limitations, Claudia, and I know it's hard and unpleasant but you can't do everything you think you can ...' Claudia felt a bubble of anger burst from her own lips.

'Yes, I can! If I want it badly enough and I'm willing to work hard enough at it. Of course I can do anything I want!

And I want to try something outside of the South.' She was outraged at his defeatism and she didn't care that he had those familiar white lines around his clenched lips that meant he was very angry indeed and she didn't care that his voice was chipped and splintered when it came out. This was her life, her one chance to get out and get on and he, some small-minded jerk who thought he was God to the other kids, wasn't going to ruin it for her.

'Well, missy, if you're so sure of yourself and your own worth, why don't you spend all the money you have for college applications on snob places like Harvard and Princeton? You do that, honey, and never mind what ole Bud Pringle has to say about it. What does he know? He's only placed about a hundred kids in his time. But don't you worry about that 'cos you know better. Right?' He shifted his bottom on the chair, looking at her, his finger absurdly wagging at her as thought he felt it was his duty to wave it.

'But jus' don't come runnin' to me or anyone else for sympathy when you get turned down or find that they can't offer you a scholarship and you can't go 'cos you haven't got the money and your mom's too busy keeping your sister's bastard chil' to spend any money on you. No, siree, I'll be too busy helping the others who want my help. And you, missy, you'll have to dig your own way out of your hole.' He smiled tightly over the beige woollen tie and matching shirt he wore, satisfaction at having found a way to include her family in his chastisement making his eyes brighten.

Claudia stood quite still and waited for him to say she could leave. He jerked his head towards the door and she stood there, one moment longer, surveying him silently from his grey shiny shoes up to his grey shiny face until he flushed with anger.

'I'll remember your words, Mr Pringle,' she said coldly. 'Every single one of them.' Then she left, closing the door quietly and with such control after her, that even the school secretary who had heard every one of those words that Claudia had promised not to forget, was surprised.

And good ole Bud Pringle who was supposed to have the same sort of client confidentiality as that of a lawyer or a doctor, let everyone in Haskell Ridge know just what that younger Babcock kid wanted, and why she wanted it.

'Guess she'd do anything to get away from that whore of a sister and that dried-up nagging prune of a mother. But she's too sure of herself by half. She's gonna take a real tumble and it'll do her a world of good ...' And the rumours spread so that soon everyone knew Claudia didn't want the South. And in a small town like Judson, that caused offence. There were comments that perhaps the South didn't want Claudia.

But then the summer arrived and most people forgot and Claudia got a job in town on Main Street in an ice-cream parlour that was all painted up in pink and white stripes like bunting for the tourists. No one there cared about where she was going to college or even thought to ask. And Claudia silently filled out the applications in the evenings, writing the essays over and over until she got just the right note for each college, carefully hoarding away a little of her money every week for the entrance fees. And she dreamed of escape.

On her way home, in the evenings, she would linger down the nicer streets just off Main and Trafford, the large clapboard or red brick houses set well back in their own gardens, so soothing and ordered after the turmoil of Haskell Ridge. She would walk by slowly, not gaping obviously but still, her eyes would flicker over the lighted windows and the glimpses of antique furniture within, the large dogs that rushed up and down the driveways greeting their families home, the flags flapping idly from their flag poles, the large, shiny cars parked next to smooth, clipped lawns. They had lived over here once, before they went to Hong Kong, her mama had told her. She didn't remember, being too young, but she sensed she had once belonged here. It was familiar.

Once she saw a group all dressed up in tuxedos and evening dresses, laughing and confident as they came out, not noticing the young girl who slid by, her hands pushed down deep in her jacket, watching them with an eagerness that was painful to see.

One day, she told herself, one day she would be a famous author and live in a big, rambling house like that, somewhere north, say Maine perhaps, and she would have big dogs and a wooden-panelled wagoneer to drive them in and lots of children running up from the beach to the house, laughing and confident like these people. And they would go out to dinner parties all dressed up and glitzy and say fascinating, witty things to each other or talk about politics and Europe and the Far East and no one would ever be rude or scream obscenities, like Peggy did, and no one would criticise and belittle, like Mama did, and no one would run off with their mistress, like daddy.

She didn't mention Mark in this liturgy because she wasn't sure yet what to make of him. Perhaps he would still come back into her life and she could be proud of some of her family? Perhaps?

She had written to Mark three or four times over the last year but never received an answering letter. And yet, there it was one evening in late July of that summer, a letter postmarked from San Francisco stuffed in amongst the junk mail and bills in the old metal letter box that made her cringe when she accidentally scraped her nails against the side.

It was addressed to Miss Claudia Babcock and she stared at it in complete astonishment, never really having seen her name written so formally before, for several long moments, before jamming the rest of the mail back into the box and slitting the envelope open. She walked back up the lawn in a daze. She didn't hear the greeting from her neighbour or see her mother's car appearing down the street. She didn't notice the way the sun disappeared behind a cloud, casting the lawn into sudden chill shadow. All her senses were bound up in the spiky, flourishing handwriting that darted across the pages like Chinese symbols, opening up a hole to the outside through which she could peer in wonder.

Mark was now studying economics and pre-law at Stanford on a partially funded scholarship from one of the bigger trading hongs in Hong Kong, he wrote, the rest being made up by his father. Frank Babcock had married his Chinese mistress, Joyce, and gone to live in Singapore, and Claudia wondered whether her father would ever consider helping her out with her schooling. Did he even remember he had any daughters to help? But no, she wouldn't even ask. She would do it herself.

And Claudia wrote about Peggy and Todd, who was a nice enough child if rather unattractive, and how old and tired Mama was looking for all she seemed to do was bustle about and make sharp, waspish comments like always. She asked about Harry, in vain, but Mark didn't know. And she wrote about her aspirations to go to Harvard and how she wanted to get a job in the publishing world in New York and Mark wrote back with sane, helpful advice that made her feel normal for the first time in a long time. He wasn't surprised or offended that she wanted to go to a good college. He just accepted it. Like Bo Haskill.

Bo was back in Judson for the summer, also working in town at the gas station in the afternoons and as a waiter at the Red Rooster at night. So many of the boys tried to get jobs on the ranches surrounding Judson, thinking they were real-life cowboys in their new Stetson hats and boots, four-inch-wide silver belt buckles holding up their jeans and most of them not knowing one end of a steer from another, but Bo shook his head when his turn came, saying he had to earn more money than that. Besides, his uncle had a ranch up in the hill country near Austin and he knew all about ranches, enough, he said with a rueful laugh, to last him a lifetime.

Sometimes, in the mornings, he would drop in and buy an ice-cream and hang around for a while 'shooting the breeze', as he put it, before setting off for work. All the other girls, especially Gina, thought he was a hunk the way he wore his blue jeans all faded and ripped, and a loose white T-shirt that still showed the tight muscles round his ribs and arms. When he smiled that open, teasing face of his at you, the girls all agreed, you could just about keel over with wanting him. But Claudia, embarrassed and uncomfortable with the giddiness Bo's presence could produce in her, pretended to be too busy to notice him, saying to Gina she

90

only thought of him as one of the few who had made it out. What made him come back for the summers, then, she wondered? He must be mad!

'Hey, Claudia, hey, Gina. You got some rocky road left just for me?' he would call, leaning in round the door and Claudia would briefly look up from her customer and give a quick smile but Gina would brighten like a firebug at night, shining out her message through dark-lashed eyes and a childish puckered mouth that would one day soon become voluptuous. Already Gina's puppy fat was dropping away and her pasty skin was taking on the dusky olive tones of her Italian forebears. Bo looked at her with interest now, flicking a glance over at the quiet Babcock girl who only occasionally seemed to remember him and smiling again at Gina.

It wasn't hard to arrange to meet Gina for a drink or two later in the evening. It wouldn't have been hard to arrange to meet Claudia either. But she wasn't even aware what he was suggesting, looking instead at her friend Gina and telling her to have a good time, that she would mind the shop. Irritated and faintly piqued, he left her alone for the moment, thinking he had a bird in hand with Gina. But she got to him, that Claudia did. Made him think of that day when she had blurted out her intentions of making it out of there, making it to the big league.

He liked that, the guts and the determination. It interested him a lot more than sweet pouting smiles and cow eyes. But Gina was willing to please him and that was all he wanted at the moment. He had no time for any more, no matter how much that Claudia got at him with her smiling indifference. Hell, she'd come round in time, he told himself; they all did, in time.

And Gina would cast languishing looks every time Bo went by, wondering if he would call her again, and Claudia would remind herself that he hadn't called Gina after he'd got what he wanted and that she would be no different. She pretended barely to notice he had gone, telling herself she dismissed him more because he had come home for the summer than because he had treated Gina like every other

91

girl in their claustrophobic little town. And then, despite herself, her eyes followed him every time he walked by.

But Bo Haskill liked the hokey small town-ness of Judson; he liked the way that everyone knew everyone else, the way people called out 'howdy' and 'Hiya, Bo' as he passed, and he liked the old shoe-shine parlours so dark you could barely see when you came in out of the sun, smelling of boot polish and tobacco. He liked the old blues bars down off Congress and Fannin where old black singers sucking on lemons to clear their throats would pluck out their melodies of bad men and worse women, of hard days gone and still to come. Yes, Bo liked Judson and Judson liked him back.

Chapter Ten

England,
1978

Grey rain drifted down, light as misting spray, on Tony's uncovered head, gently dampening and turning sodden the light-coloured hair, moulding it to his skull. He lay, mouth faintly parted, eyelids closed, his cheeks sunk in with dark fatigue, the flaking remains of camouflage cream streaking across his nose. Around him, his platoon slept also, save for the two men left on stag. They kept a wary vigil in the early dawn light.

The tanks had churned the plain to a consistency of mud soup in the night and the 1st platoon, or Hunter platoon as it was politely referred to with barely a smirk or snigger, had spent most of the night avoiding those tanks, cursing when someone at HQ issued the wrong grid reference that nearly resulted in them being churned underfoot, and generally blundering around in circles as inaccurate information was relayed to them again and again.

Their objective, in tracking down and capturing or annihilating enemy forces (a euphemism for the 2nd platoon who had spent the night comfortably dug in around the tree line) had been abandoned in the early hours of morning after their platoon commander, Lieutenant Ingram, had wearily called a halt and got on the blower to his company commander to inform him politely but with some exasperation that the particular cavalry regiment who had passed through in the night had decided to light up the area with flares and consequently made it impossible for them to proceed further.

Major Templeton smiled to himself as he heard the careful restraint Lieutenant Ingram was imposing upon his anger.

93

'Take a break, Tony. Catch a few minutes' kip and I'll try and sort it out for you,' he advised and Tony lost no time in telling the men to make themselves comfortable. There was no possibility of setting up bashers against the rain or pulling out sleeping bags to warm chill bones. Instead they slept where they fell.

Half an hour later, the radio operator shook Tony awake with the extraordinary words that most of the platoon had been desperately waiting two long weeks to hear.

'Endex, sir, Major Templeton on the horn.' Tony sat up and shook out the droplets of rain that had pooled in his eye sockets, feeling ill and dizzy with fatigue. He took the radio telephone with relief.

'Lieutenant Ingram, sir, over.'

'We've got a double booking on the training area, Tony, and I don't want another night of you dodging those great tinned cans, so we're calling a halt. Tell the boys Endex and come on in. Over.' End of exercise. Thank God.

'Will do, sir. Over and out.' And Tony closed his eyes for a moment, trying to summon the energy needed.

They always had a few days' leave after an exercise. Give them a chance to recuperate, to go out and cut a lark, his colonel would say, referring more to the men than to his officers. He knew the same would apply with the younger subalterns but he preferred not to acknowledge it.

And that was why at seven o'clock on the following day, Tony and his best friend in the battalion, Johnnie Crighton-Stewart, found themselves scrubbed and in civilian clothes, (or mufti as Johnnie tended to call it, earning derisive comments from Tony) that still bore a startling resemblance to uniform, of beige chinos, striped cotton shirts and suede brogues, driving slowly down Frith Street in London's Chinatown, looking for a place to park.

They found a space eventually, on their third circling of the block and Soho Square, and they drew up outside the Gay Hussar Restaurant with a few withering remarks about Hussars in particular and cavalry in general. Then, in good spirits, they made their way down into the back lanes where

Chinese restaurants, herbalists, cookware shops and street barrows vied for attention. It was almost dark and the streetlights were picked out in the dark puddles that gathered in the gutters. Tony breathed in the smell of incense and warm, clean laundry overlaid with wet vegetable decay and felt comfortably at home.

'What's it to be, Tony? Dinner first and then a film or the other way round? I have to tell you I'm starving, by the way.' Johnnie grinned his disclaimer.

'That's subtle.' Tony laughed. 'But you're in luck. I'm starving too. Listen, can you hear that clicking sound?' Tony held out a hand for Johnnie to pause and listen. Indistinctly a clattering, tap-tapping sound could be heard.

'What is it? Where's it coming from?'

'The basements around us. It's the sound of mahjong tiles being clicked together. When they speed up it sounds like a machine gun chattering.' He saw Johnnie's blank face and added by way of clarification, 'Illegal gambling dens. But they've started early tonight.' Tony listened a moment longer but his friend had lost interest and wandered off. Reluctantly Tony followed.

'Hope you know what all this stuff is,' Johnnie commented, standing outside Lee Ho Soon Restaurant, reading the menu in the window. 'Stir Fried Fish Rolls with Corn ... Red-Cooked Beef Slices ... Broiled Pork Slice with "Sha Cha Jiang". What the hell is that?'

'A hot shrimp and peanut sauce, I think. You won't like it. Don't worry, I'll order. Unless, of course, you want sweet and sour?'

'And if I do?' Johnnie raised his head defensively.

'Then I'll go eat next door.' Tony smiled.

'Look, just feed me, all right. Nothing sloppy, nothing slimy, nothing too hot. And if I like it tonight, I'll think about coming out to Hong Kong with you next time round. How's that?' Johnnie offered bravely.

'The conquering hero. Marco Polo had nothing on you, Johnnie. You're a regular connoisseur of the art of cultural adaptation. I'm proud of you.' But Tony's laughter stilled as they entered the dark confines of the restaurant; the bead curtain rattled noisily to warn of their approach but nothing moved.

Small lanterns on the white-clothed tables flickered in the gloom and gold and red tassles hanging from the ceiling fluttered in the breeze from overhead fans but there was no one behind the cash register, no large, fat mama-san to click her fingers at thin, nervous waiters, no waiters to rush forward and propel a customer into his seat, no customers sitting at any of the tables, although there were signs of half-eaten food having been hastily abandoned.

'Looks a bit deserted for a busy Wednesday evening, wouldn't you say, Tony? Just a bit lacking in something – like other customers, maybe?' Johnnie tried to joke but the atmosphere was oppressive in its silence.

'Hello? Hello!' Tony called and was relieved when, at last, a head appeared in the doorway to the kitchen. It was a nervous middle-aged man who wrung his hands together and shook his greying head like a puppet.

'No open! Close! Go'way! Close now! Go'way!' He shooed them with his apron, not daring to step beyond the door of the kitchen. Tony wondered just who was pulling his strings.

'What's the matter?' Tony asked in quick colloquial Cantonese, the restaurateur's eyes opening wide in surprise before he let his lips droop down again.

'Nothing. We're closed. Please go away. Come back later.'

'Your door is open. The sign says you're open. Is there something wrong. Can we help?'

'No! No, nothing's wrong. Go away. At once!' He looked so completely appalled at Tony's offer of help that Tony could think of nothing further to do. He shrugged and beckoned to Johnnie.

'Come on, we'll find somewhere else. They've got problems here, I'd say.' And raising his voice to the owner, Tony called, 'All right. We're going. Change your sign round so it reads "Closed" in future.' He led Johnnie out into the street.

'What the hell was all that about?' his friend demanded and Tony shrugged again.

'I don't know. Maybe incompetence, maybe they've got some sort of crisis. It's not our problem. He didn't want any help.' They wandered along until another restaurant caught their eye and they settled on dinner there.

But, when Tony read the next day of the fatal shooting in Soho's Lee Ho Soon restaurant of the owner's sixteen-year-old son in what was considered to be a protection-related matter, he felt sick at heart for the help he had offered and had had rejected and for his own willingness to leave it at that. It was the strong who always won, he thought bitterly, the bullies, the thugs, the criminally minded, because there was nothing beyond the law to stop them, and the law was pitifully inadequate. He felt degraded by his own lack of interest or compassion which might have, had he gone to the police and reported the matter, prevented the boy's death. Why hadn't he done more? Why?

Angry and wretched, Tony no longer felt London was the place to spend the next few days. He would take a run down to his grandmother's in Kent instead. Maybe some of that clean country air would blow the grime from his lungs?

His grandmother, Alicia Gordon, was kneeling in the garden, her knees comfortably resting on a foam mat, her back bent over a bed of herbs. The soil was damp and fresh, smelling of autumn's acid sharpness mixed with the sweet richness of summer's decay. She raised her iron-grey head quickly, the angle alert as she tried to place the sound she had heard. Otter, the fourth black labrador bitch that she had owned, bounded away from where she had been idly chewing a rawhide bone, to skid through the rhododendrons and thunder out a warning.

'Who's there?' Alicia called with that sort of high, clear, demanding voice that England's matriarchal classes produce so well. The Baskerville baying had stopped abruptly, becoming a wheezing snort of welcome and Alicia relaxed. 'Joanna, is that you?' She levered herself up and dusted down the faded and bagging tweed skirt, thinking to herself that Joanna would be appalled at the sight of her old green jumper with the moth-holes at the elbow. She hoped it wasn't Joanna.

The garden was long and narrow behind the end-of-terrace house, ending in a low wall that looked across fields of hops, tied and trained in row upon row. She had meant to try and dead-head the roses and pick some raspberries before Joanna arrived and now she was early and would catch her in a complete muddle. Oh, it really was too bad!

But it was Tony who appeared around the side of the house, being tugged along by Otter who had his guernsey firmly snagged between her teeth. Tony was trying to free himself without hurting Otter's feelings. 'Hello, gran! Thought I'd drop by and see you.' He greeted her with an affectionate kiss but she saw the shadows in his eyes.

'Tony! How lovely! Stop it, Otter. Down! Otter, drop! Stupid animal but she's only a year so I suppose she'll improve. Not like my last Otter, though. Drop, I said! Bad dog!' Alicia's voice became harsh and Otter released Tony immediately, crouching down into a prone position, her brown eyes guiltily aware of trespass.

'It's the wool. They all had a fetish for it, when they were young. Don't you remember! She'll grow out of it,' Tony said easily, as he patted Otter, rubbing her tummy when it was proffered. She gazed at him with adoration.

'Hmph!' Alicia snorted darkly. 'I suppose there are worse fetishes. Come on through and we'll sit outside and have some tea, shall we? It's a bit early I suppose but you look like you could do with some and then you can tell me what's wrong.' She moved briskly round the side of the house, Tony trailing after her.

'What makes you think there's anything wrong, gran? I just came to see you, that's all.' He attempted a laugh.

Alicia snorted again. 'Transparent, just like your mother. She's coming later, you know, with Hamish. Thought you might like to know.' She saw Tony stop in his tracks.

'Ma? Here. Oh, Lord!'

98

'Yes, quite, even though she is my daughter ... Better go change my clothes when we've had a quick chat. You know what she's like.'

'But you're gardening,' Tony protested.

'Wouldn't matter if I were sweeping out the chimneys, Joanna always expects me to look the part when Hamish comes. Why is it she's so wretchedly insecure, Tony? Did I do that to her?' There was concern in Alicia's eyes, an old sore reopening to plague her yet again.

'I don't know.' Her grandson shrugged guardedly. 'Maybe it was Dad. He didn't notice her enough. She told me that once. Made her feel like she wasn't there.'

'Funny when he notices everything else going on. Now he's not transparent, is he?' Alicia smiled suddenly, her aging beauty lit up by that smile, by the amusement in her blue eyes. 'Throw something for Otter, will you? Keep her out from under my feet until the tea tray's ready. I'll call you for it.' And she set off up the garden to the white-painted kitchen, leaving Tony to curse to himself. Ma coming here, of all days! With her new husband, not the artist fellow whom she had left soon enough, God knew, but her nice, rich, well-mannered Hamish who had to have everything wrapped up in clean linen, according to Ma, or he would leave her. God!

'He was only sixteen, gran. I don't know what it's like in Soho, how strong the Triads are, but that shouldn't have been allowed to happen. None of the police know anything. I rang them and told them what I'd seen and they weren't even interested. I didn't see who did it, so they didn't want to know. I tried to explain about the Triads to them but I just got shrugged off.' He paused, thinking how to phrase the next words carefully. His grandmother interrupted his train of thought.

'What would have happened if you had gone into the kitchen and seen the Triad men there, do you think, Tony?' Alicia took a delicate sip of tea, watching her grandson.

'I don't know,' he admitted, after a moment. 'I may have been killed, I suppose. Or someone else might have been.

But I should have done something. I should have called someone.'

'Who? The police? You just told me. They're not interested in what they see as a purely internal Chinese matter. Who else then?' she probed.

Tony sighed heavily and shook his head. 'I don't know, gran. I just—, I don't know.'

'No. There was no one for you to call and nothing that you could do. It's dreadful and things need to be changed but you, on that one particular occasion, could not have done anything.' Alicia laid her teacup down and leaned forward. 'I know you feel badly about this, Tony, but please try and keep it in proportion. You're not in the police force and you don't deal with Triads on a daily basis.'

Not yet, no, he wanted to say but the words sounded too dramatic, too immature. He was twenty years old and had twice seen the results of Triad violence at first hand but he still had another year and a half to serve in the army. Time enough later to start telling his family then what he wanted to do in life. His father, perhaps, would understand. But the others? He bit down on his tongue and said nothing.

'More tea?' his grandmother asked. She waited for him to adjust mentally, to let good manners reassert themselves over personal angst. Tony saw her waiting and realised then just why his mother was as she was. He cleared his throat.

'Yes please, gran, that would be lovely. How's the garden coming along?'

Chapter Eleven

'Come on, Peggy, we'll be late,' Claudia nagged, anxious to sample the delights of nightlife on her own for the first time. She was a Senior and seventeen now, the magical age, as far as her mother was concerned, that allowed her to ride the bus on a Saturday evening into the neighbouring town of Clayton, to go see a movie with friends, to stay out until midnight. The age where her gawkiness and braces had resolved themselves into slimness and perfect teeth, where boys had begun to notice her and wonder why they hadn't before. Not that she was interested in boys. Peggy had taught her any lessons that needed to be learned there.

And the bus was due in five minutes. They'd barely make it, even if they ran. Claudia squirmed with impatience, wishing Peggy hadn't asked to come.

'Mama didn't say you could wear that.' Peggy appeared at last, eyeing Claudia in their mother's white shirt with disfavour. Peggy's youth was already wearing thin as the rigours of motherhood and too many late nights fought to imbed deep lines of disappointment between nose and mouth. She regarded her younger sister with resentment, seeing in that trim figure a memory of herself.

'Yes she did. I asked her last night. Now come on, Peggy! We'll never make the bus if you don't move your butt. Bye, Mama. See you later!' Claudia called and started out the door.

'Shh! You'll wake Todd up. Oh hell, I guess maybe I don't wanna go after all. Not with you all fancied up like that. You didn't tell me you were going to get all dressed up. You trying to show me up?' Peggy looked down at

101

herself in jeans and T-shirt and then at her sister in her striped cotton skirt and fresh shirt, her hair pulled back from her face with a barrette. She gave a sigh from deep within her and Claudia's face dropped.

'Oh, Peggy, I'm sorry, but I told you we were going to go to a movie in the mall and then have dinner at La Cucaracha. If you want to wear jeans, that's up to you, but I wear them to school every day! You look just fine but you have to make your mind up if you're coming or not, please.' If she missed the bus, there wouldn't be another for an hour and Gina and Paul wouldn't wait that long; they'd assume she wasn't coming. Claudia gave Peggy an agonised look.

'Oh, all right, I'll come. Though, why I bother with your geek friends, I don't know.' The acceptance was sullen and Peggy flatly refused to walk faster than her usual hip-swaying saunter. Claudia bit her lip and walked sternly beside her sister, wishing she had never agreed that Peggy come with them.

It had been an impulse, seeing Peggy so down at the mouth, all her money going to support her baby, no husband and no prospects, her appeal to join them so pitiful. 'Yes, come with us,' she had said, 'we'll have some fun, forget Todd for a few hours, Mama said she'd watch him, come on, be young again.' And this was her reward, Peggy sulking along, determined to feel hard done by and make everyone else aware of it. Ohh! Claudia tightened her fist into a ball and squeezed it furiously.

The evening sun slanted into their eyes, bouncing off tin roofs and car hoods, warm and dusty with the wind from the east. There was a smell of bore water on green plants and a greasy, spicy smell of jalapeños and refried beans. They lived right along the Ridge, the dividing line in the town between the nicer, suburban areas with green lawns and sprinklers, mothers on porch swings, lemonade and barbeques and the meaner, poorer parts, the broken fences and peeling paint, the weeds and rusting cars where men in singlets sat on the porch steps and eyed you as you walked by, their comments soft and sibilant in another language to any Claudia had heard before.

Mama always insisted they walk the long way to the bus, down Armstrong Drive and looping back again by South Street so that they avoided the bad parts but there was no time to do that tonight. Not if they still wanted to catch the bus. As the street began to deteriorate, Claudia quickened her pace, her eyes down, averted. The men whistled, catcalled, and she walked faster still, Peggy reluctantly keeping pace, her blonde bangs fluffing out as she blew out her cheeks in exasperation.

'Damn it, Liddie. Don't walk so fast. I'm about worn out before we've even got there.'

'You want to linger round here? We shouldn't have come this way, Peggy. Mama'd be mad as hell if she knew.'

'Well, she isn't gonna know unless you tell her, is she? *Cayate conio!*' Peggy flicked a finger at a group of youths lounging around in front of the off-licence after a laughing reference to her '*bomberos*'. The bright neon lights of the store and the lengthening shadows made them look like prowling sub-humans, Claudia thought, long, shaggy hair and flapping clothes, the savagery in them apparent in the way they moved so restlessly along the wall.

Peggy's comment provoked louder calls and sudden interest, one of the men pushing himself off the wall, walking forward, calling in a teasing voice.

'Oh, baby, baby, come to papa,' while jackal laughs went up all round them.

'Oh, geez, shut up, Peggy. Just don't look at them and keep walking fast. Don't say anything again and don't do that!' Claudia's voice rose from exasperation to fear when Peggy turned to slap her raised arm and fist with her hand and the youths suddenly surged forward, running along-side them, a pack ready to amuse itself.

'Fucking assholes! Yeah, and up yours too!' Peggy called, not heeding her sister. Claudia looked around wildly and the youth closed in, sensing her fear. They had two blocks to go until the bus stop and suddenly she knew they weren't going to make it.

The first boy touched Peggy, laughing when she shouted

103

obscenities, a game of touch and dance back, touch again. The others crowded around, jeering, pressing in, smelling of rank bodies and beer. They began herding the girls back against the blank wall of a building that had been boarded up, Claudia falling back before their advance, looking around in terror now.

She flinched away from the hands, the thrusting faces, her arms going up defensively to her breasts.

She could hear someone screaming as they plucked at her, ripping her shirt, bruising her back and hips as they pushed her against the wall, hands groping and pushing, laughing, leering faces blocking out the setting sun. She kicked at them, slapping them away, her breath jerky and panicked and all the while she could hear this screaming coming from some old woman on the other side of the road, screeching and howling as though the men were tearing at her instead.

Her skirt was hiked up and her legs pulled apart, forced back so that her hipbones wanted to crack in two, a thrusting body between them smelling of sweat and garlic and foul breath, ripping at her underclothes. She whimpered and struggled, arching away from the pain and degradation she knew was to come.

And then she fell to the ground as they pushed away from her, a sound of scuffling feet and sharp, alarmed voices fading as the woman opposite still screamed and screamed and Claudia sat against the wall, her lips swollen and cut against her teeth, her body bruised and torn, her eyes tightly shut and the feel of the hard pavement beneath her hips.

'She-eet, you two stoopid girlies, that for sure! Wha' you doin' down here, girly? No nice girly come down here. You sure stoopid!' The face leaned over Claudia and she slowly opened her eyes, wincing as the ebbing sun seared into them. A black boy, tall and gangly, stood there, his hands on his hips and a puzzled, scornful expression on his face. He squatted down and lifted her chin with one finger, staring at the bleeding lip.

'Where's Peggy?' Claudia asked but it came out differently, sounding more like 'Whepeg?' through her swollen flesh. The boy stood back. He jerked a thumb and Claudia looked around, seeing Peggy standing sullenly to one side, her T-shirt slightly ripped but no other damage apparent. She didn't fight them, Claudia thought and then was appalled by herself, telling herself it wasn't true. But she knew it was.

Slowly and painfully, she levered herself up, the black boy making no attempt to touch her. There was sympathy in his eyes now, seeing that look pass between the sisters.

'Hell, some fucking assholes they were!' Peggy said and Claudia closed her eyes at the words, the casual acceptance of it all. 'Well, I guess we missed our bus, huh? Mama's gonna be mad about her shirt, Liddie. You okay?' She attempted to help Claudia but the younger girl pushed her away.

'Yeah, I'm okay. Thanks.' She turned and walked stiffly away, back towards Haskell Ridge, the black boy and his friends watching, the old woman silent now, her arms crossed as she surveyed Peggy. She spat.

Hong Kong,
December, 1978
Harry climbed off the bus at Stanley, milling along in the flow. Around him, the market was bustling into business, stalls opening, shutters going back, barrows being trundled along laden with imitation Adidas, Lacoste, Fila polo shirts, Gucci bags, Ray-Ban sunglasses. Later, the *dai pa dong* stalls would start to serve lunch at the small group of tables, fatty pork, glistening in large woks, noodles sizzling and sending out clouds of steam, vats of boiling offal and stomach lining, duck and green *bok choy*. Ginger jars held hundred-year eggs, aged in black mud but in reality no more than a few weeks old, and baskets of golden yolks, salted and dried in the sun, glistened like smooth amber beach pebbles.

Harry ambled slowly, his own sunglasses dark in the thin winter sunlight and his face set. He strolled down the hill, past the supermarket, and turned right along the narrow concrete alleys of shops, moving slowly, browsing, showing no interest in the people around him. Mama Lee, spruce in her pale lavender pyjama set, watched him pass her stall, her jowled face squinting after him. She nodded gently to her son and turned back to her linen wares.

Stanley was a small fishing village that had sprawled out into smart residential housing and an increasingly busy and lucrative market that attracted local Chinese, European expats and tourists alike. Half an hour round the coast from Central, it was an easy place for people to meet, an even easier place in which to explain one's presence. Harry broke out of the rabbit warren of lanes and headed along the beach, past the stylish restaurant on the corner and the less than stylish pub next to it, heading up toward the car parks. Before he reached them, he seemed to tire and found a bench to sit on in the sun. The tide was out and the fishy smell of wet sand and salt water blew lightly over him. He hunched into his leather bomber jacket. It was pleasant in the sun.

Mama Lee's son kicked a stone along the road, walking some way back from Harry. He was only fourteen but he knew how to spot a tail. He kicked the stone into the gutter and played a quick game of football with it, trying to score it into the drainage channel. At last he succeeded, looking up with obvious pleasure on his homely face. The thin youth leaning against the metal rail that edged the pavement before dropping down onto the beach, barely noticed him. The boy kicked another stone along the road, running to catch up with it, kicking it again so that it ricocheted off Harry's bench. Harry looked around.

'Watch what you're doing, you little shit,' he called in a surly tone and the boy bent to retrieve the stone from beneath the bench, his fingers chill and scrabbling ineffectually.

'Red striped shirt, blue jeans, gold medallion, Ray-Bans. Mama says in ten minutes,' the boy gabbled, ducking his head as though in apology. He backed away and blew on his fingers, threw the stone down on the road again, kicking it far up into the huddle of rubbish that lined the bend in

106

the road and pinging off the metal brazier that burned raggedly in the wind. He scampered off after it.

Harry continued to sit there another five minutes before finally stretching and yawning, levering himself up from the bench and strolling back towards the market. He paused and bought a sticky sesame seed dumpling from a street vendor and wandered on again, eating it with obvious relish. The youth trailed after him, pausing to examine unlikely wares whenever Harry stopped or turned around.

Harry smiled to himself and wiped his fingers on some tissues that he dropped carelessly in the gutter outside Mama Lee's stall. He wandered on down another alley, bending his head beneath the dangling bags and clothes suspended overhead, his feet feeling cold and hard on the wet cement channels. The youth followed him, not noticing Mama Lee spearing the tissues up with her awning pole and retreating into her back room. In that dark and stuffy room, packed with boxes of linen, Aidan sat patiently smoking.

'You wan' mo' bettah place, you no smoke here,' Mama Lee grumbled as she handed over the wad of tissues. Inside, folded neatly, was a sheet of paper. Aidan looked up at Mama Lee.

'Don't chivvy me, Mama Lee. Your room is fine for now and I pay you well,' he said indifferently, opening the sheet up. He glanced up at Mama Lee's expectant face. 'Later, Mama Lee. Go see to your shop.' It was not a request and Mama Lee recognised that, turning away with a sour expression. But she would do as she was told, Aidan knew. She had everything to gain by doing so, and everything to lose by not. He smiled to himself and studied the paper carefully.

Harry continued on down the main drag, pausing to try on some jeans, a suede jacket, to buy a fake Piaget watch. He paid no particular attention to whether the youth was following him or not. After another hour's ramble, he headed up into the back streets and sat down at a café. He ordered a beer and sat there in the sun, enjoying it. The bartender brought him the bill and Harry looked at it, slapping down the coins on the formica table and ambling off to the bus station again. The bartender swept the bill into his hand and carried the empty beer bottle inside.

Watching, the youth had no idea that Harry had just had his second communication with Aidan that morning. He wandered off after Harry and the bartender shredded the bill and flushed it down the drain.

It was a simple enough procedure. The first location mentioned would be where Harry was to make his drop, dates and times provided, the second, always an hour later, was where he would receive future information. Harry and Aidan had been playing this particularly lethal game for nearly two years, ever since Harry had been released from Lai Chi Kok jail. The judge ruled there was insufficient evidence to link Harry to the jewellery store's attempted heist. He could have been an innocent bystander, as he claimed, who ran out of fear and had already suffered a bullet wound and several months' imprisonment. The judge had been convinced, even if the jury had not, and had overruled their verdict.

But Yee still suspected something, Harry knew. There was a look in his small, shrewd eyes that assessed Harry and wondered. There was always someone following him, always someone with him on a job after that. Yee might have made Harry his strongman but Yee didn't trust him. Not one bit.

And the information Harry provided Aidan with was scant. There was someone backing Yee, there was a much larger game afoot than mere racketeering, something involving the end of the Territories' lease in 1997, but no one knew for certain what it was but Yee. And the unknown backer. For all that, Harry had made shrewd guesses that he kept entirely to himself. Aidan grew impatient but never enough so to provoke a revolt from Harry. Not quite yet, anyway.

And Harry's private bank account in Macao grew steadily in size, despite how little information he passed on and despite the risks involved. Harry was satisfied, for the moment.

Not that he intended to stay with Yee, he thought to himself as he sat on the top deck of the green double-decker that swayed and lurched around the bends back to Central. Already he had climbed as high as he ever would in the Thin Blades. Yee didn't trust him enough ever to let him closer and no one would overthrow Yee in his lifetime. Everyone knew that. So, he would have to find a way to break away from Yee, find a niche that would suit his talents and allow him to progress. And to do that, he would have to satisfy Aidan as well.

He sat and mulled over the problem as the trees flashed by and the bus scraped the edge of the cliff from time to time, provoking cries of excited alarm from its passengers. The driver was probably eating his lunch, bowl and chopsticks in hand and steering with his feet, Harry thought wearily and hoped he would finish soon.

Perhaps he ought to recruit another player? Someone who liked easy money, someone who needed it to keep his habit supplied. Someone like Mark Babcock, perhaps? For a moment, Harry thought again, as he always did, of Liddie and the quick stab of pain, like an old wound, started up. But Liddie was gone and Mark was still here. Harry had seen him, from time to time, growing taller and more scornful, more like a commanding European expat by the day, seen him buying casually, openly on the back lanes of Wanchai. Just dope so far, an occasional snort of cocaine perhaps. Nothing too bad, nothing he couldn't handle. Harry could almost hear Mark saying it. Okay, so he was away at university in America most of the time but he was back for Christmas now. Offer Mark to Yee for himself? And offer Aidan, what? The truth, or what he guessed was the truth, anyway? But no, Harry needed to keep that to himself until he really needed it. Half of the truth, then. A one-time offer. Harry smiled bitterly to himself at the thought.

Chapter Twelve

Judson
Summer, 1979

'Todd, no, don't put that in your mouth. Nasty! It'll make you sick. No, let it go, darling. Todd, do as I say.' Claudia removed the offending worm from Todd's firm grip and picked him up, swinging him, wheee, over her shoulder, his cries of frustration turning to delight, hot sweaty palms digging into Claudia's back and tangling themselves in her hair. She let him ride over her shoulder, heavy as he was, while she went to check the mailbox for the third time that morning. It was still empty.

'Bother. Where on earth is he today?' she asked Todd who gave her a sunny, crooked smile from over her shoulder.

'Who?' he demanded. At two Todd looked like finally waking up from his dream world and becoming an intelligent child, his previously odd looks, where one part of him seemed to have grown faster than the other, now resolving themselves into attractive fairness. Claudia couldn't think who the father might be. Peggy didn't have an ounce of intelligence or good looks to impart herself.

'Mr Mailman, that's who. He's late and I'm waiting for an important letter.' Just as she had been waiting every morning for the last two weeks. She had received her first college acceptance nearly two weeks ago! What on earth were Harvard playing at keeping her in suspense like this?

'From nuncle Mark?'

'No, from all the colleges I applied to.'

'You go'way? Momma said you'd go'way'n be real smart'n no come back'na boring old hole like Judson'gain.' The chirping baby voice made the words seem obscene, parroted as they were from Peggy. 'Don'go. I don'wan' you t'go!' His hands caught at her throat and she felt the fear in that tight grip.

'Oh, pooh, what does momma know? Of course I'll come back, Todd. How else would I get to see you, hmmm?' She kissed his cheek, feeling the softness of the skin against her mouth and understanding for the first time why women said silly things like 'Oh, I could just eat him up, he's so cute' about babies. His skin smelled fresh and sweet from his bath, like warm freshly baked bread.

At least Peggy had achieved one good think in life, Claudia thought, swinging him down to the grass again and holding his hand as they wandered back to the house. But how was Todd going to be affected by Peggy's marriage? It wasn't that Hank was such a bad catch, she thought, and then winced at the word 'catch'. Judson had that effect on her, she thought glumly, putting everything into quotation marks. But his family were scandalised at him marrying a 'fallen woman' and Hank, well, kind though he was, he was rigid in his thinking and could occasionally go on blinders with the best of them. He was a real Bubba at heart, a hard-drinking, hard-hitting racist whose idea of fun was either gunning down wildlife or watching pro football on TV.

Would Todd suffer with two such unpredictable, all right, say it, unreliable parents, she wondered anxiously? Or would Mama end up keeping Todd and then he would be brought up as an only child by a woman who was too old and too bitter ever to really enjoy him. Claudia ruffled his hair and worried.

'Hey there, Claudia! Hey, Todd, how's it going old man?' Bo Haskill skidded his racing bike to a halt and slid off it in one easy motion, his flaming red hair seeming almost to crackle with energy in the dry air. He propped the bike against the side of the house and high-fived Todd, going down on one jean-patched knee to do so. Claudia smiled at Todd's squeal of delight, feeling her heart lighten just at the sight of Bo. A good-time guy he might be, but she always felt better when he was around.

'Bo! You're gonna come back, aren't you, Bo? You are,

aren't you? You and Liddsy? You'll both come back, won't you? Even to an old hole?' Todd's face was screwed up in anxiety, trying to peer into Bo's eyes and winkle out the truth. What his momma had said the other day had scared him a lot and he'd been thinking about it ever since. The thought of Liddsy and Bo going away forever was like a deep black hole inside him.

Bo looked startled and glanced up, catching Claudia's briefly closed eyes and rueful expression. He grinned.

'Well, hey, of course I'm coming back, Todd, ole fella, where else would I go? But, you know, you shouldn't call Judson an old hole. It isn't polite for a start and it isn't true either.'

'Momma says it's an old hole.' Todd persisted and Bo scratched his head.

'Yeah, well, sometimes mommas get a bit fed up and they say things they don't mean.' He caught Claudia's eye again but didn't grin this time. 'You just remember that I'll be back and so will your auntie Liddsy. Okay?' He straightened up and swung Todd up and onto his shoulders, looking at Claudia steadily.

'So, how's life? You hear from any colleges yet?'

'Don't ask. I've been pacing by the mailbox every five minutes and I'm due at work in the next hour. I don't think I can bear to wait through another long day before finding out.' She laughed to lessen the frustration in her words, falling into step beside him.

'And nothing from the biggies, hmm?' There was understanding in Bo's voice. He had been through it all himself.

Todd continued to cut in with prattle about how much he wanted a bike like Bo's and what they were all doing in playschool and Bo somehow managed to answer him and still concentrate on what Claudia was saying. They walked companionably down the road, dodging the sprinklers and dogs that dashed out to bark furiously before retreating again, pride satisfied.

'Princeton accepted me but no scholarship, so that's out,' Claudia said, half torn between joy and desolation. 'And then there's been the usual pile of unsolicited offers, mostly from Kansas and Iowa,' she added with a quick smile, 'and so, of course, Mr Pringle's smiling those crocodile teeth at me, every time he sees me, telling me how he knew it would be and why didn't I accept Duke when I had the chance. Maybe I should've.'

She shrugged and Bo was silent a moment, thinking.

'Did you apply to UVA?' Now that would be nice, he thought, if she had. Make it all a lot easier for him. She didn't even glance up at him, just shaking her head.

'No. I don't think that Southern gallant style is me, you know, all those sororities and fraternities and junk? I mean, I know you probably enjoy it and all,' she gave an embarrassed laugh, 'but I'm not that sort. I just want to go and study and get on, get a good job, travel. Mark's doing so well, with a job lined up already out in Hong Kong, it really makes me feel a failure sometimes,' she said, almost in desperation. She kicked a stone in the road, watching it skip along before rejoining the other gravel, becoming indistinguishable from all the rest. Like herself. She'd skipped along for a while, being brighter than the rest of Haskell Ridge, and now she was going to find she wasn't that different or that much better and would just slip in with everyone else. Oh hell, no she wouldn't!

'Don't be stupid, Claudia. Mark's two years older than you and not totally dependent on a scholarship. You're way brighter than the rest of us and you'll get accepted somewhere good. Maybe not as good as UVA,' Bo grinned, to let her know he was teasing, 'but somewhere where you'll fit, where you won't feel you're a freak because you can think. Just don't go off forever, will you?' He unconsciously echoed Todd's fears and Claudia laughed at them both, reaching up to pat Todd's leg.

'Not when I've got my main man here,' she said with a catch in her voice and for a moment Bo wished she were talking to him. He shook his head at himself, heeding the warning signs and backing off. He liked Claudia but that was all. Definitely all. There were too many other girls out there who deserved his attention too.

'Speaking of which, I hear Peggy and Hank are going to

113

tie the knot. How are things there?' He jogged Todd on his shoulders, making the boy whine like a train's whistle being dumped down a track. They both looked delighted at the noise.

Claudia, examining Bo, thought how odd that he should get on so well with Todd – so effortlessly – while Hank was laboured and stilted, either talking down to Todd as though he were a half-wit or talking above his head so that Todd felt excluded and became painfully silent. It was a pity that Bo hadn't fancied Peggy, she thought and then was surprised at the way her mind rejected the thought vehemently. He had gone out with her a few times, sure, Claudia knew that, but nothing more. As with most of Bo's girls, there was always another waiting in the wings to replace her as soon as the edge blunted. It hadn't taken long with Peggy.

'His mother isn't happy and the mere thought of Tommy Bering as a brother-in-law is enough to send me off in a fit of the vapours, but I guess it's what Peggy wants. We'll have to see how it goes.' She sighed and was silent for a moment before rallying herself, glancing sideways up at that smiling profile as he waved at two girls passing on their bikes, and forcing her voice to sound calm. 'What about you? You've got two years under your belt now. Are you going to stay on for the whole five years or take a break at some point and go and work for a firm of architects for a year?'

'The latter, I think. I've got to get some experience and maybe a few clients who think I'm okay, that I'm reliable before I graduate. You see,' he hesitated, glancing over at her, 'I've got this plan sort've. I'm going to build houses, well ... design them and go into partnership with someone who'll build them. For lower income people, you know, people who've never owned houses before. But don't tell anyone.'

'Build houses? Here?' Claudia opened her eyes wide, knowing what the town would say, the prejudices that would appear out of the woodwork. The disputes about what sort of people were wanted in their town, the wrangles over property lines and bylaws. 'In Judson?'

'No, up North somewhere. It wouldn't work down this way. Not yet, anyway.' Bo's voice had become flat and hard. He gave her a flinty look. 'Why?'

'Oh, well nothing, that's okay then.' Claudia breathed out in relief. 'I think that's great. And they say the East Coast is going to start booming soon. They'll want lots of houses built. Yeah, I think that's really great!' She gave him a dazzling smile and he grinned too, the fear that telling her would make him change his plans, make him re-evaluate the whole idea evaporating like a puddle on a hot pavement. He smiled in relief at her.

'And I'll work as a writer for Forbes in New York and we'll get together and go out to dinner from time to time in Greenwich Village or SoHo and be wild and bohemian and nothing like boring old Judsoners.' It was a dizzying thought to Claudia, quite thrilling in its vision after the dusty confines of the Ridge.

'Yeah, why not?' Bo laughed, 'I'll have oodles of money by then and live in a loft on the West Side and we can go jogging round the Reservoir every morning.' They grinned at each other, caught up for a moment in their dreams.

Only Todd was silent, gripping tightly to Bo's collar. He refused to kiss either of them when they left for work.

Todd was waiting for Claudia when she arrived home, walking the short, direct route rather than the longer one she preferred because she wanted to see if the letter had come. Todd saw her coming up the street and he ran down the hill on small, sneakered feet to be caught up in her arms and swung around in a circle, his breath going out in a long wheezing whistle while he stuttered to make himself understood.

'Momma said uh, it came but, uh you didn't g-g-get in so now you won't g-g-go, will you, Liddsy?' He felt his aunt become very still, her arms tightening around him until they were almost painful. He squirmed but she didn't seem to notice, her face very pale and set and staring at some point in the distance. He turned to see what she was looking at.

'Momma opened my letter from Harvard, Todd? Are you sure?' She forced herself to break away from that point in infinity, to look down at him with eyes that refused to focus. His pale gold hair nodded up and down.

'S-s-sure I'm sure.' He slipped to the ground through her arms and craned up at her. 'Momma laughed. She's g-g-glad, like me, 'cos you won't g-g-go now, will you, Liddsy?'

'Momma laughed? She opened my letter from Harvard and then she laughed when I didn't get in?' Claudia's voice had become mechanical, repeating and fitting together the snippets that Todd imparted in his childish way. Todd fell silent beside her.

'Where did she put the letter, Todd? Will you run and get it for me? I don't want the others to know I'm home yet.' They would all be back now, Peggy from her hairdressing salon and Mama from her job and probably Hank too, who had simply moved in with them after the registry wedding last Saturday, instead of taking Peggy away as they had all thought would happen. Mama hadn't objected because she didn't want to lose Todd and Claudia had known she would be leaving in a few months and what did it matter? It was better for Todd this way.

But, suddenly, the thought of facing them all, the thought of the smirks on Peggy's and Hank's faces at her failure, the thought of the concern and irritation on Mama's that she had turned down Duke ... Oh, it was all too much! She felt sick at the thought, shying away from it, dulling her mind in blankness. But she had dug her own hole, as good ole Bud Pringle had said, and now she would have to work her own way out of it.

Todd appeared out of the side of the house, holding something white in his fist and he ran headlong down the slope to her, his face full of anxiety and hope. Claudia knew he was pinning his hopes on her not leaving now, but knew deep down that she would go anyway. Poor little boy, she thought painfully. How much she would like to take him with her. But she couldn't. She scooped him up and kissed him soundly.

'Well done, Todd! Did anyone see you?' She was relieved

116

when he shook his head. She set him down again and, with trembling fingers, slid the letter out of its envelope and unfolded it. The words were polite, impersonal, speaking of regret but not involved in that regret. She was just one of thousands of bright, hopeful applicants who had been turned down. She folded it up again and put it away.

'This one too, Liddsy. Momma didn't open this one.' Gravely, Todd passed over another, marked with Columbia on the outside. Claudia took it but didn't have the strength to open it. Instead she stuffed it into her pocket and forced a smile.

'Okay, thanks, Todd. Listen, I'm gonna go for a walk, okay? You go on back up to the house and I'll play with you when I get back, all right?' She squeezed his hand, looking into that troubled little face and trying to give him some of the security that she had felt at his age. But he was too quick; he saw her pain and his mouth twisted, the fist going up to knuckle at his eyes, the sobs grieving for her as much as himself. Claudia went down on her knees beside him and held him tightly.

'Aw, Todd, Toddy, don't please. It's okay. I'll still go somewhere good and I'll still come back and see you a lot. And you've got Momma and Nanna and Hank. You won't miss me so much, you'll see.'

But he continued to sob, the pace quickening into a howl of rage and rejection, odd words like 'you g-g-go' and 'B-B-Bo too' filtering through the hubbub, making Claudia ache with guilt and grief. If she could have taken anyone with her, it would have been Todd.

She took him on her lap and sat on the kerb, staring at the shimmer of heat that writhed over the tarmacadam, hearing the cicadas shrilling tightly and the gentle hum of a lawnmower in the distance. Slowly, Todd quietened down and they sat like that for a while, both spent with emotion.

'Listen, Todd, and listen good, okay? You're my favourite person, the only one who really, really matters to me. You understand?' She looked at him seriously and he nodded his head, his mouth faintly parted. 'Good. Now, I have to go away for a while to college otherwise I won't ever be any

117

good at anything. But I'll come back in the summers, just for you. And then, when you're older, maybe we can arrange for you to come and stay with me during your summers. See? And we won't ever not see each other because you're too important to me.' She smiled and was relieved when he gave a tentative smile back.

'But I'm not your momma. I wish I were, but I'm not. And your momma wants you here, with her, and so does nanna. They both love you very much too. So, we'll have to share you out, in little parcels of time. Okay?' That was how most of life worked anyway, Claudia thought grimly, little parcels of time with a shelf life of just so much happiness, so much love. She kissed Todd and he settled back into her arms with a long sigh.

'Okay, I guess. But you promised, didn't you? You and Bo too. You'll come back.'

'That's right. We promised.' She kissed his fair, shining hair and felt how warm he was, a soft, warm bundle of love and fear and need that she knew would tie her down, bring her back to the place she most wanted to escape. She rocked him in her arms.

Bo looked down at the girl at the table, his smile automatic as she fluttered her lashes at him, dimpling warm, sun-kissed cheeks that made him want to run a finger over them, just to feel that peach soft skin. He saw her glance across at her father, head bent over his menu, and then hold a folded piece of paper down beside her leg. Bo dropped his pad beside her, going down on one knee and slipping the paper from her hand as he retrieved his pad. He smiled at her knowingly before purposely looking away.

When he glanced across, out of the windows, he saw Claudia coming across the main square, her steps firm and steady enough to make him think she was fine. But he saw her face through the window of the Red Rooster as she passed by and it was tight with pain. He frowned, throwing down his napkin and pad, leaving the girl's pouting looks and her family's earnest deliberating over Knickerbocker

Glories or Banana Splits, and pushed his way through the crowd of diners to the door. He reached it just as Claudia did.

'Claudia? What is it? Here, come here a sec. Look at me.' He pulled her to one side, out of the rush of impatient families, and brushed the hair back from her face, seeing how pale her skin was and how dark the shadows beneath her eyes. There was that same steely determination in her eyes but it was there to hold back the turmoil inside, to not let it get a grip of her and whirl her away like just so much debris.

'I'm okay. I need your advice,' she said in quick, tense bursts of sound. Bo resisted the urge to fold her up in his arms and rock her like a child, to soothe her and tell her it would be all right because he was there. She didn't want sympathy at the moment. She wanted help.

'Yeah? Shoot,' he said. Behind him he heard the manager calling his name, but he focused his thoughts in on Claudia, excluding outside interference.

Claudia, looking up at that intense face with its spattering of orange freckles and its pale blue intelligent eyes, thought how nice Bo was. She smiled at him with difficulty, folding her lips firmly one over the other.

'I got turned down by Harvard.'

'Yeah, I figured that was it. Where else did you get in?'

'Columbia, Duke, Princeton – but that's out for lack of funds – and Brown.'

'Not too shoddy,' he said with irony. Claudia smiled a little less tightly at that.

'Which do you think I should accept?'

'Well, are they all full scholarships except Princeton? You don't want too much of a loan built up by the time you graduate or it slows you down for years after, paying it off. Restricts your movements.'

'Yeah, they're all okay. I can work in the evenings to pay for extras.'

'Well, then I guess it's a question of which one has the courses that suit you most. You looked at the handbooks yet?' Bo could hear his manager's voice becoming more

119

insistent, more intense. He glanced over his shoulder and caught the man's eye.

'Yes, of course I have! I just still can't decide and I have to pretty much immediately. Look, I'm sorry, I'm messing you up at work. Can I see you after you get off?'

'Bo? Bo! What the hell do you think you're doing? Tell your girlfriend to go home and get back to table eighteen. They're ready to order now.'

'Yessir, right away.' Bo glanced back at Claudia, hesitating, a wave of unaccustomed embarrassment engulfing him at the manager's assumption. But Claudia didn't even seem aware of his words, hadn't reacted to 'your girlfriend' at all. She was just looking impatient.

'You go. When do you get off?' she ordered and Bo grinned.

'Midnight. I'll see you right here, by the door. Gotta go.' And then he was gone in a swirl of white apron and striped shirt, the red of it clashing with his hair.

Claudia walked away, wondering what advice Mark would give. But there was no time to write to him and wait for a reply. And she couldn't call him; she didn't have his number. Besides, he wouldn't say anything that different to what Bo would and Bo understood her dilemma better than anyone else. Mark couldn't give her any advice that would be better than Bo's.

With that firmly resolved, she walked home through the long, darkened streets to face her family.

Only Mama was home to greet her. Todd was in bed and Peggy and Hank had gone to a barn dance, Mama said.

'A barn dance! My God, what's gotten into Peggy? All those do-ce-does and two-steps and waltzes! She hates barn dances,' Claudia blurted out without thinking and saw Mama sit up a little straighter in her chair and cross her arms. The television in the corner droned on about Foley's latest sale.

'She's trying to be a good wife and she knows Hank likes them. Don't be so snooty superior all the time, Claudia. There's nothing wrong with a barn dance.' Her face was pinched, her blue eyes faded now, like her hair. Mama had disparaged barn dances not so long ao.

Claudia sighed. 'I know there isn't, Mama. I just didn't think Peggy would go, that's all.'

'No, well, she did. And you're home late, aren't you? It's well after dark. Where've you been?'

'I, um, just walking around, I guess. Todd told me Peggy opened my letter from Harvard. She had no right to do that.' For a moment Claudia saw her mother's face soften, the faded eyes become misty in sympathy. But it passed almost immediately.

'She knew you would want to know, so she was gonna run down and tell you if it was good news. But no one had the heart when we heard it was bad. You don't wanna go getting difficult at this time, Claudia, not when we're all just trying to help. 'Course, if you'd have taken Duke, when Mr Pringle said you should ...'

'Mama! I don't want to go to Duke, can't you see that? And I'm not trying to be difficult ...' She took a deep breath. 'I'm gonna go out again later, to talk to Bo Haskill when he gets off work. He said he'd help me decide which courses would suit me best.'

'Which courses? You gotta decide on the college first, Claudia!' Mama said tartly. 'And there's nothing than can't be decided in the morning.'

'I'm working then. It's the only time we have.'

'That what he told you?' Mama gave a dry laugh. 'Well, I'll just bet he did. Don't they all? Men! And Bo Haskill especially! There's not a girl in town who hasn't heard sweet words from that boy. And more.' She peered at Claudia beadily. 'You're not going out again tonight, girl, and that's final. Now you go get yourself some dinner, will you? I left you some on the table. And, Claudia,' she paused and stretched out a hand to clasp Claudia's wrist as she passed her chair. 'I'm sorry for you, child. I really am. I know what it is to lose your most precious dream, believe it or not. I know it hurts.' And then she smiled, looking, for a moment, like the woman she had once been. Claudia was startled.

'You mean Daddy?'

121

'Him? No! He wasn't my most precious dream. He wasn't a dream at all. No, I was going to sing, once. I trained for years and I had a good voice too. But then I got these little bumps, like warts I guess, on my vocal chords and they said that was it, my singing career was over. So I married your father instead.' She snorted, as though to suggest how absurd that move had been.

Claudia squeezed her hand. 'You never told me. How come?'

'Oh, it was a long time ago now, long before you were born, and when your dreams are shattered, you don't want to talk about the pieces, now do you? You run along, child, and you talk to Bo tomorrow. He'll understand.'

Claudia paused and then leaned down to quickly kiss her mother's cheek. She walked hurriedly out of the room before Mama could see her tears.

Claudia didn't like to climb out the window in direct defiance of her mother's commands but she couldn't help it. She had asked Bo for help and she couldn't not turn up. Besides, he wasn't interested in her at all that way. Mama was just being silly.

It was eerie walking through the streets that late at night when no one and nothing moved except the odd flitting shadow of a cat or the howling of a dog chained to a wall. She walked lightly, as though any sound of her own might obscure some other sound that she should have heard, should have reacted to.

It was to her relief that the lights of Main Street began to glint through the trees and she quickened her pace until it was almost a run, trying to control the shudder that was running down her backbone, knowing that she was only just going to make it before the shadows engulfed her. She was shaking by the time she arrived at the Red Rooster.

'Whoa, what's spooked you?' Bo laughed, seeing the goosebumps on her arms, the way her eyes stared wildly and she fought to control the shivering. 'You seen some bogey man?' His smile faded and became a frown, re-membering what he had heard about Claudia's and

122

Peggy's trouble some months ago. 'You okay?'

'Yeah, fine. I just scared myself listening to the trees and imagining all sorts of things lurking in the dark. I'm just being a wimp, that's all.' But she gave a final shudder, unable to help herself. Bo draped an arm around her shoulder, chafing her arm and laughing again.

'Scaredy cat! Come on, let's go get a coffee at the Fifty-niner.' He steered her towards the all-night diner on Bascombe Street, his arm still around her and she let it stay, reassured by his warmth and solidity. Nobody was going to get her now, she thought, and then realised how childish she had been, letting her fears run away with her like that. She smiled up at him apologetically.

'Pretty stupid of me, I guess. I hate the dark sometimes. Mama said I couldn't come out, so I had to sneak out and I guess that made me nervy. Thanks for still being there.'

'You were only a little late,' Bo said dismissively, trying to pretend that his arm around her was nothing, just a friendly gesture, trying to ignore the sensations coursing back to him from that arm that made him tingle and shiver and want to lean in against her and breathe in the scent of her hair and skin, to let his mouth taste those lips that were so innocent and unaware. But the lips were going on prosaically about colleges and handbooks, courses marked and professors noted. He sighed and let her go.

'Come on, let's sit over in that booth in the corner. That way no one's likely to see you and tell your mama. I sure as anything don't want her coming down on me for corrupting her daughter.' He laughed but there was a twinge of truth to his words and Claudia heard it.

'I'm not the corruptible sort. I'm not my sister,' she said coldly and Bo flinched in surprise.

'I never said you were,' he said, after a pause. 'And I never thought it either. Don't go getting defensive on me, Claudia. I like you nice and straightforward, the way you always are.' He watched her steadily, with a faint smile in his eyes as he saw her jaw descend again slowly and her shoulders relax.

'Just checking,' she said grudgingly and he smiled more

123

widely, his freckled skin becoming taut around his large mouth. Reluctantly Claudia smiled too, feeling the odd goose-tread of emotions beating an unsteady path up and down her heart and trying desperately to subdue it.

'I'm a good guy basically, despite what mothers think about me,' he added comically and Claudia grinned and raised a hand to order two coffees and two danishes.

'Sure you are. The last of the innocents.'

'I haven't laid a hand on you, have I?'

'Not yet, no. But there aren't many girls in town who can say that, are there?' She was teasing but there was a serious note beneath it that Bo recognised.

'So I like to have a good time. So what?' He grinned, teasing her back. 'Does that cut me off your list just because I can't bear to make a few girls unhappy?' He didn't notice the couple who had just entered the door and neither did Claudia.

'Just a good guy at heart.'

'That's right.'

'And do good guys escort scaredy cats home or would that be asking too much?' she enquired. Bo looked thoughtful.

'That would all depend.'

'On what?'

'Ah,' he took her hand and raised it to his lips in mock salute, barely brushing it with his mouth. 'I'll tell you that later.' He winked as the coffee arrived and the couple in the doorway moved away, backing out into the night, Peggy's peroxide hair gleaming for a moment before disappearing into the shadows. Claudia snatched her hand away.

'You do that. Now, come on, here are the books. I've marked the relevant pages ...' She launched quickly into business, uncertain and flustered by the look in Bo's normally easy-going eyes, by the sudden awareness she had felt of him as a male and a predator rather than just a friend. She glanced up at him doubtfully, from time to time, as he pored over the college courses. Surely he wasn't going to spoil things between them, was he? Because she didn't want to lose his friendship for a quick fling. She hoped he realised that.

124

Bo was methodical, listing out the best courses and professors, weighing those against other pros and cons like cost of living, college ranking and so on, filling several pages and probing Claudia to see what she really wanted, what her gut reaction was. They drank several cups of coffee along with the danishes, the minutes ticking away into hours until Bo finally circled one name with a flourish.

'Well, looks like Columbia has it. It's a good school and you'll like the non-Ivy league collegiate atmosphere there and it has the courses you want. How about calling it a night? It's nearly two.' He smiled but there was a weary look to his face and Claudia realised, with a pang of guilt, that Bo worked two jobs every day and needed all the sleep he could get.

'Right, that's it then. Thanks, Bo, that was just what I needed. I'm sorry it took so long.'

'Important decisions can't be rushed. C'mon, let's get you home.' He rose and paid the bill without listening to her protests, and then led her out into the night, their eyes taking time to adjust so that they drove Bo's old pickup truck slowly towards Haskell Ridge in silence, each pre-occupied with their own thoughts.

It was only when they turned into Claudia's driveway and climbed out that Bo took a deep, sighing sort of breath and held out a hand to prevent Claudia going any further.

'Hold it a sec, Claudia. Look ...' He paused, wondering what it was he wanted to say. Normally the sweet, easy words flowed so effortlessly but, for once, he was tongue-tied.

'Is this when you tell me what seeing me home depended on?' Claudia's voice became wary. Bo looked at her and then smiled that engaging smile of his, so like a young boy trying to wheedle his way out of a scrape.

'Maybe. Would that be so terrible?'

'Bo, look, thanks for all of this help. I don't know what I'd do without you, sometimes. You've been terrific. And I want always to be able to turn to you and depend on you. Okay? Not just be flavour of the month.' Her face pleaded for him to understand.

He shrugged. 'Who says that's what you'd be?' He leaned closer, his breath fanning the side of her throat, hesitating for a moment as she gazed at him thoughtfully. When he put his hand on her shoulder and turned her slightly towards him, he saw her lips part, as though to protest, and he leaned in quickly to press his mouth against hers.

It was a gentle, tender kiss designed to ease her fears and kindle the desire he knew she had to feel for all she denied it. He wasn't surprised when her lips became supple and pliant, when they slid apart for a brief, tantalising moment. He breathed in her scent deeply.

Claudia had difficulty in remembering why she had held him off for so long, why she had thought him unreliable as anything more than a friend. When he pulled back, stroking his knuckles lightly down her cheek, he saw her lids were heavy and languorous over her green eyes. He smiled to himself.

'It's nice to have someone to depend on, Claudia, but it's also nice just to have some fun sometimes. Don't you think?'

'Fun?' Her tone was musing, her thoughts as disarrayed as she could ever remember. 'Maybe, I don't know ...'

'Well, when you do know, you let me know. Okay?' He smiled lightly and leaned over her, brushing her cheek with his, turning away and climbing back into his truck before she could react. He was halfway down the driveway before Claudia realised how much she wanted him to kiss her again. Regretfully, she watched him go, not seeing him digging into the pockets of his jeans for the note the girl from the restaurant had given him, not noticing him turn left, back towards town, rather than right towards his own home. Claudia was in over her head and willing to sink at long last.

Peggy was in her room when she carefully climbed back through the window, sitting in her wicker chair, her mouth sullen and tight. Claudia straightened up and looked at her.

'What's up, Peg? It's two in the morning. What're you doing in here?'

'I know what time it is! And where've you been, lady muck? Out carousing with your boyfriend? Oh, don't think we didn't see you. Little Miss goody-two-shoes who's always been the perfect young lady, who's never let a boy so much as look at her, so she says, kissing and cuddling away in public for all the world to see. And with Bo Haskill, of all people, Mr Sunshine to all the girls while he smiles at you and then gone again, as quick as you can blink. Well, last time you look down your snooty nose at me, isn't it?'

Peggy's eyes were bloodshot from too much beer and a pounding headache, the irritation she had felt at having to spend the evening at a barn dance with a man who smelt and belched and groped her when she wasn't in the mood, a man whom she had married out of desperation for her life to change in some way, curdling into rage when she saw Claudia with Bo.

She had been sitting there, in the dark, for the last two hours thinking of what she would tell her prissy little sister who was going to escape any day now, leave to go off to the good life without a thought of who she left behind. Well, Peggy thought, the least she could do was give Claudia something to think about in those long hours of freedom.

'What're you talking about, Peggy? For God's sake, it's late and I'm tired and you're drunk. Why don't you go to bed?' Claudia pushed past her sister, who had risen to block her path, and she sat down on the bed. She pulled off her shoes.

'You're mighty friendly with someone you've no business being friendly with, aren't you? That's what I'm talking about. And I'm not drunk.'

'Why shouldn't I be friendly with Bo? What's it got to do with you?' And you're a fine one to preach, Claudia thought grumpily. She undid her jeans and slipped out of them.

'Oh, it's got something to do with me, all right. Just who the hell do you think is Todd's father, then, Miss smarty pants? Or hadn't you figured that one out yet, you with your IQ of one hundred and forty and your SATs of God knows what! I did tell you he was a college boy, now didn'

I? And there aint too many of them around on the ground. I'd've thought you'd have clued in on that some time ago. Or are you just plain not bothered about sharing a man with your own sister? Nothing like being second in line, is there?'

There was a long painful silence in which all that could be heard was Peggy's heavy breathing. Claudia felt as though she had fallen from a great height and had all the wind knocked out of her. She gasped.

'You're lying! Bo and you never went together.' There was a rushing sound in Claudia's ears, like a heavy wind, buffeting and screaming. She shook her head, trembling, knowing that they had, even for a brief while. 'You're lying.'

'Yeah? Why don't you ask sweet little ole Bo, then? He might tell you, though not very happily, since he didn't want anything to do with it all at the time, what with him just going off to college'n'all. He's a real prize, Liddie. Who knows, maybe there'll be a little brother for Todd soon? Well, I guess you don't need my advice, since you know everything already. Have a fun time at Har-vard, why don' you?' And with that, Peggy lurched out of the room, leaving Claudia staring blindly after her.

'You're lying,' Claudia repeated softly to herself. 'You're lying.' She stood up, sweat beading her face and she went and knelt by the window, letting the cool night breeze blow on her face. 'You're lying,' she said again, but her voice carried no conviction, and her mind was too intent on trying to understand why it was so very important not to believe Peggy. She groaned softly. 'Oh, God, why?'

Chapter Thirteen

England
December, 1979
'It's ridiculous, Bill. He can't be allowed to do it!' Joanna's voice rose. 'Tell him that, can't you? He'll do what you say.' They were all in Alicia's small drawing room, Joanna half perched on the wing chair, her husband Hamish standing protectively behind, Bill sprawled in the easy chair near the fire, Tony and Plum and Hattie ranged along the sofa. Alicia sat on the low ottoman, her well-bred features focused on her ankles. Otter lay by her feet.

'It's unusual, perhaps. But I see nothing wrong in it, Joanna. If this is what Tony's decided . . .'

'I have,' Tony said firmly. He saw his mother's mouth pucker up in thwarted rage.

'You don't know what you want at your age. You're only twenty-two and you don't know anything. Trust your father not to back me on this, but then he's just a passed-over civil servant so why I should expect him to have any good sense over this—'

'Daddy is not passed over, Ma!' Plum cried sharply. 'Not everyone's concerned with money grabbing and climbing over other people to get it.'

'Quiet, Plum, it doesn't matter,' Bill remonstrated, but he felt a moment's pleasure in seeing his ex-wife's outrage. 'We're not getting anywhere trading insults.'

'There's nowhere for any of you to get to. I've made my decision and I've signed off. It's done,' Tony repeated stubbornly but his mother wasn't listening. He felt Hattie steal a hand into his and give it a quick squeeze.

'But what will people say?' Joanna was wailing.

'Shut up, Ma, do! No one'll say anything as long as you

129

don't. There's nothing wrong with joining the police force, especially since Tony'll be an inspector, won't you, Tone?' Plum queried.

'Yes. It's the Chinese who fill the role of constable, corporal and sergeant. There's no point in a European doing that, when the Chinese population won't speak to them and most Europeans don't speak Cantonese. Don't worry, Ma, it's not so awful. The family pride won't be shredded forever.' He was bitter and Hattie squeezed his hand again.

'It *is* so awful! It is! How could you do this to me? The Hong Kong Police force! What will all my friends think?' Joanna wailed.

'You should be glad you've got a son who wants to do something like this and isn't running round high on drugs or alcohol, like half of your wonderful friends' sons,' Hattie burst out, seeing her mother through years of tinted prejudice. 'You're so unfair! You always have been. It's always how it will affect you, not how it's going to affect Tony. It's his life, let him choose.'

'Exactly,' Alicia said with deathly quiet. Her daughter's swift retort withered on her lips. 'Bill? I think you agree with me, don't you?' She saw her son-in-law's face, quiet with hidden reserves of strength and mocking amusement. He gave a faint smile.

'Yes, Alicia, I'm afraid I do. It's Tony's decision.' He turned to look at his wife, seeing her afresh as though for the first time and able to admire her beauty but be untouched by it any more. He was grateful for that. 'Tony is a man now, Joanna, whether you like it or not and the fact that he gathered us here, to tell us, is not, in any way a request for approval before venturing further. It is a mere courtesy, I'd say, since matters seem to have advanced well beyond that stage. So, my dear, you'll just have to learn to live with it. I'm sure Hamish won't be too ashamed of the Ingram side, will you, Hamish?' He smiled, one man to another, and noted the rueful amusement in the other man's eyes. A nice fellow, perhaps even a friend under different circumstances, Bill thought.

'Not at all. Tony's a fine young man, and his decision is a sound one, as far as I'm concerned. He has my backing.' Which, of course, started Joanna off again but berating her husband's heartlessness this time and Hamish, courageously aware of what he was doing, continued to argue with her and thus deflect her annoyance from Tony.

'When are you coming out, then?' Bill asked his son.

'February. I start in March but I thought I'd come early and find my feet again. Johnnie Crighton-Stuart may come out too, for a while. He's thinking of getting a job with one of the big hongs. Is Aidan still around?' Asked lightly, knowing more of his father's real job than his mother would ever suspect, merely wondering. Bill smiled.

'Yes, yes, Aidan's still there, though he's taken to drink a bit lately. I hope you can dry him out?'

'I'll try but he always did drink like a fish.'

'That's what some of the lads call him. Fish. Seems appropriate.' Bill shrugged, not wishing to dwell on the matter. 'What about you, Plum? Are you going to disappoint us with a dreadful misalliance in the near future or has your young man had the sense to fight shy?' But he had that cajoling, teasing tone in his voice again that he reserved especially for the girls and Plum took no offence.

'You'll have to wait and see,' she retorted archly and Hattie, who was seeing a rather endearing, if woolly, young man who had expectations on his father's farm one day, blew a raspberry at Plum's coyness.

'I'll be married before you at this rate. Can't you get George up to sticking point?' she demanded and matters descended into bickering on a scale equal to their mother's and her husband's. Bill, Alicia and Tony quietly stood up, one by one, and left the room, gathering in the kitchen where, mercifully, the loudest sound was the ticking of the clock.

'You will be careful, won't you, Tony?' Alicia said after a moment, looking at her grandson with concern. 'I do hear that it's quite a dangerous life, after all.'

Tony patted her arm. 'No more so than the army, gran, and I've come out of that without a scratch. I'm the

131

plodding, wary sort, don't worry. I don't pitch headlong into things.' Which was a load of rubbish, his father thought, watching him. That was exactly what he was afraid Tony was going to do.

N.Y., New York
1979

Mark had been at college for two years by the time Claudia began at Columbia, two years in which he had learned a lot and acquired different tastes. His letters began to talk more about parties, barbecues, wild night rides along the coast roads, hash and dope, girls. Claudia struggled to read them without small town judgements but she became increasingly uneasy and found it harder and harder to reply.

She, herself, was living in drab college rooms on Eighth Avenue and W.116th Street of Harlem, near enough to the N.Y. Public Library to make the dash, late at night, to the safety of her building's locked door and still close to the Morningside Heights campus where she spent even more time in the domed Low Memorial Library, running up the pyramid of steps several times a day.

Ever since she had arrived at the Port Authority Bus Station on Eighth Avenue, and met the rush and dirt of Times Square, the deafening traffic, the defeated faces and the hucksters who ran to get her a taxi when there were taxis already there in the rank, and who shouted abusively after them when she refused to tip them, Claudia had been fighting to find any sort of charm in New York. She was working desperately to keep level with all the flashing minds and bright, knowing faces that bombarded her from morning to night.

It had unsettled her completely, on her first day, to see so many eyes looking at her, assessing rapidly, moving on to the next person, the minds behind those eyes more than her equal. Only Paul and, perhaps, Bo, had used to look and see so much, so quickly. And now they all did. It was devastating.

She settled into a tiny room adjoining another girl called

Joaney Hewitt, who wore tight black lycra trousers and huge flowing white shirts with a belt cinching them in over snake-like hips. Her hair was a long, ragged mane of strawberry-blonde hair and her eyes were made up heavily with kohl. She wasn't all that good-looking but her confidence overcame obstacles such as a large nose or a long chin.

When she bothered to look up at all, it was like coming under the beam of a searchlight, Claudia thought with uneasiness. A smoking searchlight, since there was always a cigarette dangling from those thin, scarlet lips. She came from an East Coast Brahmin family and was going through her rebellious stage, she told Claudia with a mocking smile.

Claudia, in her plaid kilts and button-down shirts, her hair pulled back neatly in a braid, looked down at herself and then back at her and they both smiled reluctantly.

'Well, since we've got little or nothing in common I guess we better be friends. I'll loosen you up and you can throw a spanner in the works when I get too out of hand. Besides, the one rule with my parents was that I lived on campus for the first year. I don't think they realise Columbia isn't a real campus school and I'm sure my mother didn't know it was in Harlem,' Joaney said with a whimsical little arch to her eyebrows and they had both laughed and set to making their rooms more comfortable, putting up posters – Joaney, of pop stars like Mick Jagger and Sting, Claudia, of stylized black and white shots of steamy railway stations and bridges over bleak rivers, a wild striped serape from Mexico across one wall, plants and books.

Joaney seemed to have unlimited funds and was happy to share her good fortune with Claudia, keeping a small fridge stocked with diet coke and yoghurt, which explained the snake hips, Claudia thought, and buying endless packets of cigarettes which she smoked until the suite of rooms was a fog of foul air and Claudia took up smoking in self-defence.

'We'll have to do something about the way you dress, maybe burn that skirt or turn it into a pillow or something,'

Joaney said after the first few weeks when she had seen the skirt worn endlessly. 'The jeans are okay, just a bit too neat, if you know what I mean? But the skirt, geez, that has to go. It makes you look about twelve, for Christ's sake!'

'Look, Joaney, it's just a skirt and I don't have enough money to buy anything to replace it. I've only got the one pair of decent jeans—'

'So, let's see the indecent ones!' Joaney broke in enthusiastically. Claudia gave her a withering look.

'I left those home for the next time I paint my bedroom. That's it, all I have. And I've got to buy some black pants now for my waitressing job, so I can't—'

'Stop saying can't, for God's sake. I always heard Texas was the "can do" state. Here, try these on. I mean, okay, I'm a lot taller than you are but we can maybe...' Joaney's voice trailed off as Claudia slipped into a pair of her lycra pants and wallowed in them like a baby elephant in too much skin. 'No, I guess not. Well, what size are you, goddam it? ... A three!' There was silence while Joaney considered the problem.

'Okay, I know what. There's a really great second-hand place over in the Village, down in one of those little lanes off Bleecker and no one else round here's going to get the size threes, so who knows what you'll find? You can get your black pants there and something a little more trendy. And pray God we can flog your skirt!' Her tone became fervent. 'Great, come on!' And Joaney barely waited for Claudia to climb into her jeans before she hustled her out the door, their bikes clunking methodically down the cement steps to the street.

They rode down to the Village, cutting down Eighth to Douglas Circle and then through the park, Joaney on her expensive racing bike, Claudia on an old clapped-out bike that she had bought in Judson just before leaving and painted black. She had put a wicker basket on the front and had the tyres patched and pumped up by Hank, and now, riding in the late autumn sunshine through the blaze of liquid ambers and flashing bronzes, the wind plucking at her hair, she felt unbelievably and gloriously free. Finally,

134

she could see why people loved New York. She breathed in the air deeply.

'What're you doing on Saturday?' Joaney yelled and Claudia smiled brilliantly, her cheeks flushed with the exercise and her eyes sparkling. Joaney took it in, saw her friend's unexpected beauty, with surprise.

'Working split-shift in Succi's from eleven to four and then again from six until midnight. Great, huh?' Claudia laughed and Joaney shook her head.

'Hell, you'll kill yourself! Just get a loan, why don't you? Pay it off after college.' But Claudia remembered Bo's advice, the last piece just about that he had given her before she had deliberately excluded him from her life, and she glanced over at Joaney, her smile stilling.

'Easy enough for you to say, when you won't have to pay anything off afterwards. I want to be able to start life unencumbered, thanks very much. Besides, I'm only going to be in New York a couple of years, I guess. Then I'm going back to Hong Kong.' And back to Harry, she thought, exhilarated by the thought. It was a long way away still but it was there, a definite goal that she could achieve. They swept past the Loch and over the path by the end of the Pool, the water ragged with wind, dark and chill.

'Hong Kong! I thought for sure you had some gorgeous Southern beau back in Hicksville who was just waiting for you to come back to his loving arms and grow babies and hayseeds together. Hong Kong!' Joaney laughed.

'Well, there isn't! And there won't ever be because I'm not interested, not in babies or hayseeds or anything else to do with small-town men. I'm going to get ahead myself and it'll be my money, my career and my decisions that matter, not some man's!' Claudia shouted fiercely and stood up on her pedals to race furiously ahead while Joaney continued to cycle along thoughtfully in her wake, skirting the Reservoir and dodging around the afternoon joggers. Now just who had done all that damage to Claudia, she wondered. And what was his name?

*

135

The shop was down a cobbled lane that stretched wet and glowing with the yellow and amber of a neon café sign out before them. The scent of freshly ground coffee wafted out from the café and across the street a small bakery vied to impose its aroma on the damp air. Loud and flamboyant, the passers-by were a sight in themselves; actors, artists, punks, tramps, a complete *mélange*. Claudia shook her head in amazement, never having realised such a place existed in Manhattan.

The shop itself was a wonderful success, with some clothes for as little as fifty cents and all sorts of possibilities available. The girls tried on shirts and pants, long flowing skirts, old Fifties style dresses, ball dresses, and endless pairs of shoes. Claudia finally settled for the black trousers she needed, although more stylish than she had ever hoped for, a pair of very faded and slightly ragged blue jeans that she cinched in with a large brown leather belt, a white linen shirt and an emerald green silk shirt and, as a final splurge, a faded leather jacket that badly needed to be patched.

'Gorgeous! Just wait till we get you home and do something with that hair of yours. Here, hold onto these a sec, will you?' And Joaney piled her own treasure-trove of a velvet and gold brocade jacket and some smart black ankle boots into her saddle-bags. 'Now let's see what the bastard makes of me,' she added, almost beneath her breath. Claudia looked at her with a frown.

'What bastard?'

'Mick the Dick,' she said obscurely and climbed onto her bike. 'Race you home.' And then she was gone and Claudia had to scramble onto her bike and pedal furiously through the wet decay and brilliant colours and scents of the Flower District, up past the tempting window displays of Macy's and through the hustle and bustle of the Garment District, to try and keep up.

It was Friday night and Claudia had to be at the restaurant, Succi's, on Broadway, by six. But, from four until five-thirty, she indulged herself by trying on her new clothes and adding make-up and jewellery for Joaney's benefit. She was astonished by the reflection that peered out at her from the mirror on the back of their cupboard door.

'Here, put these boots on. No, don't be silly, we've got the same size feet, if nothing else.'

'Which means mine are enormous for my piddling height, I suppose?' Claudia asked, looking down at long, bony feet and across at Joaney's dainty ones.

'That's right. You can't have it all your own way. There! See what another couple of inches does to you? Now let your hair out. Go on, it won't turn you into a hussy overnight, more's the pity. Ah! See!' And Claudia did see, her normally dull brown hair seeming to glow in twists of colour, like fine mahogany and walnut wood, sheened with a patina of care and craftsmanship. It rippled around her shoulders, a glint of gold in her ears, melding with the glint of gold in her hair.

'A little cherry lipstick and some mascara and pow, Claudia hits the big time! You'll knock 'em sideways,' Joaney said positively, looking at the girl before her in her faded jeans and white linen shirt, the leather jacket carelessly but oh so carefully arranged by Joaney herself, thrown on top, the boots that gave Claudia height and, with it, presence. Damn, she'd have to be careful or the girl would be snatching the men away. Which reminded her . . .

'So what was his name?' Joaney slipped a plain gold bangle onto Claudia's wrist, feeling the girl flinch beneath her touch.

'Who?' Claudia turned away to examine the black pants and flick some dust from them.

'The man who's made you hate men,' Joaney said in a maddeningly patient voice.

Claudia laughed. 'God, don't be so melodramatic, Joaney. I don't hate men. I just don't really respect them much, not after my father, and I can do perfectly well without them.'

'Name and stop fudging.'

'Ohh! Really, it was nothing, just a guy I thought was a friend who was beginning to mean something more to me and then I found out he was a real turd. It kind of surprised me and made me pretty wary, that's all.'

'What'd he try to do? Screw you?' Joaney sat down on her bed and ripped open a diet coke, offering it calmly to Claudia.

Claudia flushed and shook her head. 'No, no, nothing like that. It was just about him and someone else that I heard something pretty lousy.'

'You heard? Do you know that it's reliable information? I mean, you don't seem completely dim to me so if you thought he was an okay guy and then you just *heard*,' she stressed the word, 'that he was a shit, well, maybe you're being a bit unfair. Maybe it was all lies.'

Claudia shrugged. 'Well, I can't be sure but I can't afford to take the risk. It's all a bit difficult, kind've personal and close to home. Maybe he is innocent, but I have to assume the worst. Besides, he's pretty much of a philanderer at the best of times, one girl after another.'

'Aah! You have a sister, I take it?' Joaney saw Claudia flush crimson. 'And she claims he did something to her? Is that it?' Reluctantly, Claudia nodded.

'Sisters can be just as unreliable and bitchy as the rest of the world. Maybe more so. What's yours like?'

But Claudia was silent, wondering whether she had been unfair to Bo and if so, oh ... she couldn't bear to think about it, the way he had been so puzzled and hurt at first when she just brushed him off and then angry, so very angry, turning away when he saw her, his face tight and closed. God!

'Look,' Joaney said after the silence had become exasperating to her. 'Why don't you write to him and ask him. He's at least got a right to know what's being said about him, don't you think?'

'I couldn't.' Claudia hung her head, shaking it. 'My sister said her baby was his. No one's ever known who and then, when we, Bo and I started getting close, she told me. She said he refused to acknowledge it and she was warning me for my own good.' Now that was a laugh, Claudia thought. Peggy never did anything for anyone else's good. But Bo could have been Todd's father. The timing fitted.

'Shit! I see. Well,' Joaney floundered for a moment, thinking, Bo! What a name, like something out of *Gone with the Wind*. 'I still think he should have a right to answer any accusations. I mean, maybe he'll deny it and it really is true but what if it isn't true?'

'Then I'll have lost a good friend.' Another good friend, she amended silently, thinking of Harry and wondering whether Mark would ever bother trying to find him, as he had promised. Harry and Bo – they made quite a contrast. 'Which I have already. So there's no point, is there?' Claudia added and stood up, putting the black pants in her bag. She would change at the restaurant like the others did. There was no reason to go around looking like a waitress in the street, after all.

'And what about "Mick the Dick"!? Who's he?' Claudia asked casually. Joaney stood and and examined herself in the mirror.

'My married man, that's who. Michael Glendinning, the most gorgeous Englishman you'll ever meet. He's over here on business for the next two years and wifey-poo decided to stay in England with the kids so, why not? But he can be a bastard. Stands me up all the time, forgets to cancel things, clicks his fingers and I come running – a real dick. That's what my brother Jason calles him, Mick the Dick. He hates him.'

'I don't blame him. Why do you put up with it?' Claudia was curious, unable to see the flamboyant Joaney so passive in a relationship.

'I don't always. We have scenes, screaming, throwing, nasty scenes and the neighbours complain and I walk out and then he sends roses by the dozen and I forgive him again and it happens all over again. But I love him, so what else can I do?' She shrugged herself into the new velvet jacket, admiring the way it went with her tight black leggings. Claudia admired it too.

'But he'll go home one day and then where will you be?'

'Right where I am now – in the shit!' Joaney shrugged again but Claudia saw the fear there for a moment in her eyes. There, that was what men did to you, she reminded herself.

'I don't understand, I thought you just came to New York?'

'God, no!' Joaney turned in amazement to look at Claudia. She laughed. 'My parents live in a brownstone over on the East Side, in the mid seventies. I mean, we really come from Boston but Dad has to work here, so we always lived here mostly and would go back to Massachusetts in the vacations.' She smiled wryly. 'I could never leave New York. I'd die of boredom.'

There was a knock at the door and both girls jumped.

'Hey, Joaney, you in there? Open up, it's me, Jason. Hey, hurry up, I had to sneak past some old dragon downstairs and there are girls all over the place staring at me like I'm sort of lizard—' He broke off as the door opened in his face and a strange girl stood there staring at him.

'Oh! Wrong room, I guess ...' He was no more than average height with broad shoulders filling out an immaculately cut suit, a tanned face with dark hair, and an air of getting what he wanted in life. Most women would have thought him attractive. Claudia barely smiled.

'No, Joaney's here. I'm Claudia. We share a sort of suite together.'

'I can see that, though maybe suite is a bit of an exaggeration. Hi, I'm Jason.'

'The lizard,' Joaney added quickly, leaning past Claudia to kiss Jason's cheek and usher him in.

'Unfair. I just said they thought I was one. God,' he looked around the tiny rooms in amazement, 'how are you surviving in this dump, Joaney girl?'

'I'm incubating. This, as you already know, is Claudia who isn't even doing that much. She's in hibernation.'

'Really? Well, that must explain why I couldn't get your telephone number, which is why I had to come all the way over here in person, so would you mind terribly sharing it with me?' He was openly sarcastic. Claudia looked away.

'Number's on the phone. Help yourself.' Joaney looked down at her watch and then across at Claudia. 'Better hustle, hon, or there's gonna be some mad old manager after you. Say 'bye to Jason.' There was a teasing note in her voice that faintly puzzled Claudia. Jason seemed used to it.

"Bye Jason,' she said dutifully.

"Bye Claudia. Hope I see you again soon.' He held out his hand, leaning in to smile into her eyes, the skin crinkling up charmingly and his teeth smooth and white and polished. Like him. Claudia, snatching up her bag and throwing it over her shoulder, clasped his hand briefly.

'Yeah, hope so. Have a nice time, both of you. 'Bye!' And then she was gone, her hair flipping behind her.

'And just why in hell did you do that to me, Joaney dear?' Jason asked, raising his eyebrow slightly.

'Because she's too nice and too innocent for the likes of you, Jason. A little southern flower. I'd as soon ship her off into white slavery than let you at her.'

'You make it sound as though I've ravished half of Manhattan,' he complained, throwing himself down on Claudia's bed. He picked up her pillow and buried his nose in its softness, the faint lingering scent making him breathe in deeply.

'Haven't you – and worse?'

He grinned. 'Not yet, but I'm working on it. Speaking of which, Mummy dearest has organised a bit of a cocktail for me and mine. Thought you'd like to come? Bring Mick the Dick if you must and definitely bring the southern flower. Next Thursday.' He put the pillow back beneath his head.

'Great. It'll be nice to be civilised, even for a few hours. This place makes me appreciate en-suite bathrooms and private sitting rooms all over again. Won't Mummy be happy. She'll think she was so-oo clever sending me off like this.' She laughed and Jason, watching her, thought ah, yes, not long before Joaney begins to conform. The rebellion was wearing thin.

'That mean you're moving back home next year?'

'Hell, no! I'll get an apartment, preferably a great big loft one and move the southern flower and me into it and pay for it out of my trust fund. I'll be twenty-one by next summer.' She smiled sweetly.

'Ah, yes, the late starter in everything. How are you

finding all these babies around you?'

'Smart. I'm actually having to work my butt off. And the funny thing is, I'm really enjoying it. Nice finally to know I've got a brain and actually to use it. Besides, Claudia may by young but she's mature way beyond her years. And she's thoroughly sour on men, so you don't stand a chance, lover boy.' Joaney laughed and ruffled her brother's hair, much to his irritation.

'Oh, don't I? Want to bet?' Jason stood up and smoothed his hair back into place, smiling tightly at his sister.

'No!' Joaney snapped, her amusement dying. 'You just leave her alone, okay? And take me out to dinner or something, will you? I could do with some food for a change.' There was a plaintive note to her voice. Jason heard it with grim satisfaction.

'No can do, darling. I've got the very hungry Petula waiting for me right this minute. I just dropped in to say hi. I'll get my hubcaps ripped off if I stay much longer. Unless, of course, you want to sit on her knee all evening?'

He smiled, knowing she was without a date because she had deliberately left the evening free in the hope that Michael Glendinning would call. Stupid bitch. Well, maybe a few more evenings alone in a dump like this would make her think again about Mick the Dick. She could do a lot better for herself and he didn't like any sister of his belittling herself like that.

'Don't forget Thursday, Joaney. 'Bye.' Hs kissed her cheek and breezed out, leaving the room shoddier and meaner by his absence. Joaney kicked the bed in rage.

Chapter Fourteen

Hong Kong, 1979

Mark rolled over in bed, wrapping the sheets around him as he reached for the ashtray. It was warm and close in the room, the overhead fan barely moving as it swept a light breeze over him. Silvia didn't wake and he paused to admire her body, bereft of covering, sprawled out across the mattress, the long smooth back swelling out into perfectly paired buttocks, the graceful line of her legs ending in a dark circle of daisies around one slim ankle that was infinitely appealing. Her tattoo. He smiled at it, remembering the uproar it had caused when she had had it done.

Dark hair cascaded out around her, snaking tendrils quivering enticingly against golden skin, her breath rising and falling gently. He replaced the ashtray, turning instead to strum his fingers down her spine, to kiss the gentle curve of her breast where it was flattened out beneath her arm. He turned her over, pulling her into his arms and nestling into that cloud of dark hair where the scent of her was strongest. Silvia murmured sleepily.

'It's late, Silvia,' he whispered and she ducked away from him, squirming back under the covers. He laughed. 'No, no, it really is late. It's nearly one o'clock and your parents will be wondering where you are. Let's not blow it, okay?'

She blinked her way through layers of sleep and opened those pale green eyes to stare up at him. 'Can't we say the car broke down?' she asked plaintively.

'Not twice, no. They were suspicious enough the first time. Come on, sweetheart, up you get.' And he pulled her to the side of the bed, propping her up and dressing her clumsily in her shirt and skirt. She lay pliant in his arms. He pushed her underclothes into her jacket pocket and let

143

her rest on the bed while he dressed quickly himself. Then he led her, sleepy and protesting, out to his car.

It was as he returned, after dropping Silvia home, that he first became aware of being uneasy. The night was still and clear, without the mist that normally enveloped the Mid-Levels at that hour, and he could easily see a pair of head-lights twisting and looping down Magazine Gap Road, that didn't seem to deviate the entire way home. He pulled into the shadowed forecourt of his apartment block and glanced behind him. A car was slowly pulling in, hesitant at first and then, as though the driver had seen him, shooting forward to park behind his own car.

While Mark might have felt uneasy, he was far from alarmed and was more annoyed and curious that he had been followed so blatantly. And for what reason? Robbery? He had little to steal. He waited for the car to pull to a halt.

Two men got out, the first, the driver, tall and well-built with a pleasant, open face that seemed oddly familiar for a moment, a faint whiff of memory floating across his mind only to disappear at first touch. The second man seemed to be designed to form as great a contrast as possible, being no more than normal height for a Chinese man, but thick-set and muscular with large feet and long, almost bowed arms. His face was wizened and swarthy, the face of a peasant but the eyes that peered out were quick and clever. Mark's alarm grew.

'What is this? What do you want?' he demanded before either could speak, his Cantonese quick and aggressive. The men smiled, the shorter of the two gesturing to the taller one.

'So! You were right.' Yee Fong Lo spoke in Hakka. 'Perfect intonation. I could not have told him from an educated Cantonese. He doesn't recognise you?' He glanced at Mark, his face creased up in interest. Harry shrugged and replied in the same dialect.

'You can see for yourself. Besides, why should he? It's been years and I have grown a great deal in that time.' He swallowed tightly when Yee darted a hard, angry look at him.

144

Mark didn't know Hakka but was aware of being discussed. His irritation and also his fear grew. This was not some random hold-up. They knew him in some way; he could sense it. He repeated his question.

'What do you want? Who are you and why did you follow me?' He studied Harry, trying to place the features, a vague resemblance to someone in his past nagging at him.

'We came to discuss a deal with you.' Yee, barrel-chested and ugly in his strength, addressed Mark at last and Mark shook his head, alarm surging through him, not wanting to hear more.

'I don't do deals at two in the morning,' he snapped. 'And not ever with people I don't know.' He would have turned and walked away but Harry moved so quickly to block his path that he had no choice but to check. 'Look, what is this?' he burst out. A faint dampness had bathed his face so that the overhead light made it glisten.

'You have expensive habits, Mr Babcock, do you not?' Yee said, after a long pause, indicating the sports car in the driveway. 'But not really the funds for those habits. A man who has to support a beautiful young woman of good family, who has to be seen to mix with the best Hong Kong has to offer, who has expenses while he is away at university, who has – a need, shall we say, for certain habit-forming distractions ...' A shrug that indicated Mark's dilemma. 'We, on the other hand, have plenty of money for those who do us small favours. Favours we cannot perform for ourselves. Shall we go upstairs and discuss things further?' He smiled but it was a bland gesture, not meaning anything.

'And if I refuse?' Mark felt suddenly ill with uncertainty, seeing that smile slip quietly into implacability, the dark stoniness of Yee's eyes.

'Really, Mr Babcock, you cannot afford to refuse us. You see, we know too much about you. We know what is important to you. What needs you have that we can arrange to have denied. The street peddlers are in our pay, after all.' Another smile, a glance at Harry who was looking indifferent. The smile broadened, tinged with a knowledge that was denied to Mark. 'It would also be unfortunate if your precious Silvia were to be damaged in any way, would it not? That beautiful face scarred perhaps, or that graceful body — well, I'm sure you realise what I am suggesting could happen. Hong Kong is a dangerous place, after all.' Yee paused, looking at Mark, his tone suddenly rallying, the smile breaking out again.

'Come, don't look so dismayed. We are merely talking about unlikely consequences were you not to prove sensible. And there is so much you can profit by, in our friendship. Come, let us go upstairs and discuss this like gentlemen. It is nothing too hard, I promise you.' He gestured towards the apartment building and Mark, sick with anger and fear at the man's words, looked around him for some means of salvation. But Harry had crowded in and he began to move as directed, playing for time, desperately trying to think of a way out.

'You see how easily he is persuaded, how biddable he will become in time?' Harry murmured to Yee in Hakka. 'There is no need to harm him or the girl. He will do as you say, find it easy and profitable, gradually more and more desirable ...'

'And now I am supposed to let you go, let you walk away with all that you know, is that it, Harry?' Yee looked at him from beneath heavy tortoise-like lids. 'How can I trust you to do that?'

'You don't trust me to begin with Yee. So let me go once and for all,' Harry said stubbornly. 'I've given you a replacement and you have others to fill my role in the lodge. I would never betray my brothers.' He licked his lips and then was angry at himself for betraying his nervousness to Yee.

'Ah, but no one can replace you, Harry.' Yee smiled and the wrinkles on his face crowded in, unpleasant and odd in one still so young. Harry shivered.

'You'll learn,' he muttered but Yee had already turned away.

146

'It'll be fun, Claudia. We'll get you something suitable to wear and you'll have a great time. I don't know why you're so nervous. This is what you said you've always wanted!' Joaney said in exasperation. It was the third time Claudia had said she wasn't going to Jason's cocktail party. Said it stubbornly and without clarification, her mouth set and her nose buried in a book. Joaney waited for an answer but none came.

'Is there some dark secret in your past that makes it impossible to go to smart parties? Why are you so sure you'll hate it when you've never tried one before? God give me patience!' Joaney exclaimed, unconsciously echoing one of her mother's favourite sayings.

Claudia looked up. 'I'd make a fool of myself. I don't know how to chit-chat with people, I don't know what to do in society, I have a hick southern voice and I don't have anything to wear. Isn't that enough?' She turned back into her book, wishing she could go, wishing she could be smart and sophisticated and confident like she had always dreamed of being. But she wasn't.

'Oh, God ... Look, let's take that one at a time. You can chit-chat with me all right, can't you? So what's different with other people, they're just the same as me, talk about the same sort of shit, they take a crap just like us. They're no different.

'As for what you do at a cocktail party, it's simple. You say hello to the host and hostess. You stick by my side, accept a drink from a waiter who's circling around with a silver tray full of probably champagne, knowing Mummy, and you chit-chat.

'Sometimes, you can wander over to the buffet table and pick up a toothpick and help yourself to some little savoury nonsense and then you put the toothpick down in an ashtray and smile at anyone who looks at you. That's it. I'll be right by your side the whole time and if you can't think of something to say, I'll say it for you. And people will love your accent, it sounds so buttery and syrupy and sexy. Now, what is your problem?'

147

'Clothes,' Claudia said sullenly.

'Village.' Joaney cocked her head to one side. 'Or are you too chicken to even try?'

'I can't afford it after the last splurge.'

'My treat. It's my cocktail and I'm dragging you there, so the dress or whatever is my treat. No argument, no anything. You are coming to this thing, Claudia, if it's the last thing I get you to do. You are going to learn to be comfortable with the sort of people you need to get to know if you want a job in publishing, and you are going to learn to enjoy smart company because I, for one, have no intention of living with an inverted snob with a chip on both shoulders. Got it?' There was a grim line to Joaney's mouth and Claudia recognised it and gave in. So, she would make a fool of herself. It was only one evening and not worth losing Joaney's company for.

'Got it,' she said and Joaney smiled.

'Michael's coming.' It was a casual, throw-away remark but Claudia opened her eyes wide. There had been no sign of the elusive married man in the last week except for the occasional telephone call late at night, at which Joaney would creep from her bed, dress and disappear out the door. And Claudia would watch her go through half-closed eyes and think again and again to herself how men messed up women's lives and how she didn't need them.

'Do your parents approve?'

'Not entirely but they don't know everything. They think we're just friends, or rather, they pretend to think we're just friends because they don't want to have to think anything else. They'll be polite to him.'

'And Jason? Will he?'

'He invited him. Why wouldn't he be polite?'

'Because you said he hates Mick the Dick's guts, that's why. Don't be naïve, Joaney. Why on earth would he invite your man along if he hates him?'

Joaney paused, thinking about it. 'I don't know,' she confessed at last. 'I did wonder myself. But it's too late now. Michael's been dying to go to one of my family's big dos for ages and I can't uninvite him now, can I?'

'Well, no, not really. Oh, probably your brother just said it to make you happy and he intends to ignore Michael all evening. That's probably it, don't you think?'

'Jason's never done anything to make me happy in my entire life,' Joaney said drily. 'Shit, now I'm going to worry all the way through it in case Jason does something unforgivable.'

'Such as?'

'I don't know. That's the problem with Jason. You can just never tell ...'

It was six-thirty before Claudia was ready and Joaney was still burrowing through her clothes, trying on different jackets, necklaces, her hair up, her hair down while Claudia sat on the bed and smoked, watching her. Thursdays weren't normally her night off at Succi's but she had swapped with another girl and now she was sitting there in her new clothes, slugging back a large glass of wine for courage and smoking tensely. Why had she agreed to this? Why?

She stood up and examined herself in the mirror again, admiring the smooth sweep of cream wool, so thin it was almost like silk, the way it wrapped across her breasts and fastened at the waist, the large leather belt cinching in the skirt so that when she moved a long glimpse of leg was revealed. She still had enough of the summer's golden tan to make the dress stand out vividly against her skin and the heavy gold chain around her neck and the baroque pearl and gold earrings glinting beneath her loose hair were reassuringly sophisticated. She looked great but how would she behave?

'Damn, I'm just going to wear what I know suits me and none of this correct bullshit. You think I look good in this?' Joaney turned around, wearing the velvet and brocade jacket and black lycra trousers that they had both admired so much only a few days before. Infinitely more sexy and stylish than herself, Claudia thought with a sigh, but then Joaney had the confidence to carry it off.

'I think it looks wonderful but you should wear your hair

up, twisted at the back the way you had it before with the long dangly earrings. Yeah, like that. That looks great.' They grinned at each other and both took large swallows from their drinks.

'Right, let's go then.'

The party was already overflowing by the time they arrived. Claudia gaped at the size of the chic townhouse on East 73rd Street, rising four storeys into the velvet dusk, light spilling from the open windows where stylish window-boxes of dark glossy ivy and white-petalled flowers gleamed against the dark brown brick. There were faint strains of Vivaldi's *Four Seasons* lilting across the hubbub of conversation and they stood poised outside the immaculately gleaming dark green painted door and heavy brass knocker, drawing breath. They smiled nervously at each other.

Claudia glanced down and along at the stately beauty of the brownstones and the expensive, impeccably groomed people who passed by. This was what she had always imagined she would love to be doing, she reminded herself sharply, fighting the urge to run. Going to smart parties in beautiful clothes and saying witty things to important people. And this was her chance. Now was no time to get a fit of nerves. She took a deep breath and turned back to Joaney who was buzzing again insistently and grumbling about the cold wind buffeting down the street.

A middle-aged woman in an immaculate white apron over a grey and white striped dress opened the door finally and smiled at Joaney.

'Why, Miss Joan, how nice to see you! Mrs Hewitt didn't mention you would be coming tonight. How's college? Oh, it is so nice to see you again.' She stood back as Joaney entered, dropping a quick kiss on the older woman's cheek, and depositing her coat over her arm.

'Hi, Prudey, it's great to see you too. College is wonderful, can't think why I took so long to go. Oh, this is my friend, Claudia Babcock. We share rooms together at Columbia. Is Mr Glendinning here yet?' Joaney barely gave Prudey time to answer in the affirmative before dragging Claudia forward, while she was still trying to smile and shake hands with the housekeeper and take off her coat at the same time. Prudey shut the door behind them.

'You don't need to shake hands with Prudey. Just smile and say hello, make some chit-chat. That's all. Okay?' Joaney whispered fiercely and Claudia swallowed in dismay. Oh, God, had she disgraced herself already? She was so intent on this social disaster that she didn't have time to notice the throng of well-dressed people circling the rooms which all seemed to lead one into another. The decor was old East Coast federal in style, with lots of walnut panelling, chinoiserie wallpaper, gilt eagled convex mirrors, Chinese porcelain lamps, oriental rugs and antiques. Claudia passed it by without seeing it, slipping along nervously in Joaney's wake.

'Those are my parents by the door over there. Mr and Mrs Hewitt, okay? We'll go say hi and then when that's over you can relax and drool over the men. If there are any, that is. Most of them look like they came with their pocket computers and mobile phone implants. Or worse still, their boyfriends. Come on.' And Joaney grasped her arm again and pulled her along quickly behind her long-legged stride.

'Joaney, darling, how lovely to see you. Goodness, what a – a dashing outfit. A lovely jacket.' Mrs Hewitt tried hard to still the irritation she always felt at seeing Joaney, kissing the air beside her daughter's cheek instead. Claudia, watching them together, was amused for the first time that night. They were so incredibly similar, both pretending to be utterly different.

She tried to conceal her smile but, looking up, saw that it was being shrewdly observed by a large man with greying hair around his temples, a high, lined forehead and the sort of weatherbeaten skin and pale eyes that sailors so often have. He winked.

'Daddy! Hello! Have you missed me? Do I get a big kiss?' Joaney slipped past her mother to fling her arms around her father's neck. He hugged her soundly.

'Hello, peach, what're you wearing for God's sake? And

151

who's your friend?' His voice was brisk and affectionate and Joaney twined her arm in his and ushered Claudia forward.

'Mummy, Daddy, this is Claudia Babcock who's my room-mate at Columbia. She's from Texas.'

'And aren't all Texan girls known for being beauties?' Mr Hewitt asked rhetorically and extended a warm hand that engulfed Claudia's like a baseball mitt. He shook quickly and lightly, releasing her to his wife.

'Hello, nice to meet you, sir, Mrs Hewitt. It's very kind of you to invite me tonight,' Claudia said, her back held very straight, her chin tilted slightly upwards, trying to remember desperately to seem dignified and not too in-gratiating. Mrs Hewitt beamed.

'Oh, what a darling accent. And what lovely, lovely manners. It always comes as such a surprise these days when a young person has nice manners. Such a lovely change! How are you, Claudia? How're you enjoying sharing with Joaney?'

Claudia flushed slightly and Joaney looked mocking.

'That's a loaded question, Claudia. Let's see how good a diplomat you are,' she whispered.

'I'm having a wonderful time, thank you, Mrs Hewitt. I don't know what I'd do without Joaney to show me around and lecture me about what not to do and where not to go. I'm from a small town, myself. I'd probably have been mugged on the first day here if it hadn't been for her.'

'Good heavens, a sensible Joaney giving sensible advice! The mind boggles!' Mrs Hewitt said with a trilling laugh and turned away as someone claimed her attention. Mr Hewitt winked again.

'Glad to know there's a nice girl around for Joaney too. Have a good time tonight, Claudia. Nice to meet you.' And then she was dismissed, Joaney smiling impishly as she steered her towards the drinks.

'Well done, southern flower! Now they'll lay off me for a bit. "Such a nice girl", "so well mannered",' she mimicked and went off into a peel of laughter. Claudia flushed again.

'What did you want me to say? I had to be polite, they're your parents,' she muttered and Joaney checked and looked at Claudia, her head to one side in her most annoying manner.

'But you were perfect. I'm not giving you a hard time. Come on, drink this and stop sulking. You do sulk a lot, you know. Oh, look, Claudia, over there, talking to that woman in the red dress, the man with the dark grey suit on and the green tie. That's Michael.'

Claudia turned to look and then suffered the most extraordinary jolt. Not only did the man Joaney had pointed out look amazingly similar to Joaney's own father, but, more importantly as far as Claudia was concerned, right beside the man's elbow was a familiar figure with a bright mop of hair that was clashing with the woman's red dress. What on earth had brought Bo to New York and by what bizarre fate had he found his way to the Hewitt party? Joaney didn't notice her look of dismay, but grasped her arm reassuringly and said quickly, 'I'll be back in just a sec hon, but I have to go see him and warn that old trout off him. Look at the way she's encroaching and nearly thirty, if she's a day, for God's sake!' And he's nearly forty, Claudia thought absently as Joaney abandoned her, if not older, but very charming, very elegant. She could see the attraction.

'Daddy complex, wouldn't you say?' A smooth voice drawled in her ear and Claudia, turning, recognised Jason. She shrugged.

'Each to their own particular poison. Isn't that the way it goes?'

'Oh, yes, indeed it is. And what's yours, Claudia? Not men, I hear.' Jason smiled but there was a taunting suggestion to his words that made Claudia stiffen.

'And not females either, if that's what you're suggesting. I guess my poison is my work. Gets to be addictive.' She eyed him steadily, daring him to mock her. And daring the figure over her shoulder to intrude on her thoughts, to send her determination spinning down to the ground in pieces.

'Don't I know? Most of the girls I see always complain that my first mistress is my work. I'm glad finally to meet a woman who understands that.' Jason was surprised by her answer and gratified. He took another look at the girl before him, so immaculately groomed with those long, slender legs that he particularly liked in a girl, so very attractive, and then he saw that determination in her eyes, not hidden in any way by the intelligence that assessed him as coolly as he assessed her. He felt a flutter of excitement.

'Well, we only get just so much time down here on earth and it seems a real shame the way most people waste half of that getting themselves in and out of romantic tangles that take up far too much of their energy. I don't need that.' There was a drawl to her voice that he found infinitely appealing after the harshness of New York accents.

'Romantic tangles? That's a nice way of phrasing it. Mostly it isn't nearly so attractive,' Jason murmured, acknowledging the first real interest he had felt in a girl for a long time. And so young. The very young were still pliable, still malleable. He was looking for someone to shape. 'So, what are you studying? Joaney said something about you wanting to go into publishing when you graduate?' He led her over to the far side of the room, away from Joaney and away from the interesting group that surrounded her. With a pang, Claudia allowed herself to be led away.

Bo, stunned at seeing the dark head laughing up at the man beside her, the way she was transformed from a schoolgirl into a lovely young woman, tried to focus his thoughts on the conversation around him. Watching Claudia out of the corner of his eye, he felt the most appalling anger he had ever known sweep over him, a desire to smash his glass on the parquet floor, to roar out his disgust, to sweep the posturing, prattling people before him out of his way and to claim Claudia back from the smooth, knowing and far too good-looking man who had her.

What the hell was he doing there, anyway, making polite noises to people he didn't give a damn about, toadying for a job in the architectural firm of his choice? They had said, come with us tonight, meet one of our major clients, John Hewitt, see whether you think this sort of life will suit you. And he had come and been impressed, been flattered by their attention until he had seen Claudia, seen the way she looked, the way she had changed. And how did he feel about it all now? God!

'Joaney, have you met Bo Haskill? He's up in town to see whether he wants a job with Purvis and Clinton. Quite one of their bright young things, I gather, from John. Architecture isn't my line really, can't stand most of the monstrosities going up these days, but evidently Bo's got a whole new line on things. Haven't you, Bo?' Michael Glendinning smiled easily, his manner charming and interested and Bo couldn't quite help himself liking the man, knowing he wasn't being patronised for a change.

'Not really new, Mr Glendinning—'

'Michael, please.'

'Well, Michael, then. Most of my work is to do with reviving the older style towns, or better still, building new ones that work on the same principles as the old.' He smiled awkwardly at Joaney, taking in the sultry looks, the pouting mouth and seeing instantly the unsure young girl beneath it. 'But it's pretty boring to people who aren't architects. Besides, it's more a case of whether Purvis and Clinton want me than the reverse.'

'I'm surprised anyone's willing to back that sort of thing, these days,' Joaney said, thinking, Bo? Now where do I know that name from? Bo?

'So am I, quite frankly, but Purvis and Clinton seem to like it – at least, they're thinking of offering me a job for my filler year before I go back and finish my degree.' He took a sip from his drink, wishing it were stronger, would burn as it went down his throat, not just bubble sourly. He had never liked champagne overly.

'Oh! You're still at college then? I didn't realise. Where're you from, Bo?' Joaney saw Michael slipping away to get another drink but she was so intent on sorting out the puzzle of where she had heard Bo mentioned before, that she let him go.

'Judson, Texas. I'd have thought you could tell from my accent.' Bo smiled and Joaney thought, wow, that is devastating. Don't get too close to him or you'll fry up in all that electricity he gives out with that smile. She regarded him

155

sleepily, a quizzical look on her face.

'Bo from Judson, Texas. Ah, of course! I don't know why I didn't recognise that accent myself, seeing as I'm living with someone else from Judson, Texas. Someone who, I think, knows you. The name Claudia ring any bells?'

She saw the smile wipe from his face, shutting down the watts like a blackout. He swallowed. 'Yes, I used to know her. How is she?'

'Fine, I think. Missing Todd, her little nephew, and a bit obsessed about a certain fella, I think, but other than that great. She's ploughing her way through the work like there's no tomorrow. Defence mechanism, I figure.' There was a teasing, knowing look to Joaney's face that Bo didn't like. He took another drink, coughed, cleared his throat.

'Yeah, well that sounds like Claudia. She always was single-minded. Tell her Todd's fine. I saw him at half-term.' His voice was rasping, harsh when he said her name, trying to block Joaney's words from his mind. "A bit obsessed with a certain fella." No guesses about who that was. The smooth looking piranha in the Wall Street suit. He nodded to Joaney.

'Nice to meet you. I've got to be going. Goodnight.' And then he had turned away into the crowd, not slipping through them but buffeting his way as he made for the door, as though desperate for air. Joaney watched him go in dismay.

'Oh, Joaney, there you are! What an age you've been. I thought you promised not to abandon me?' Claudia reached Joaney's side with a laugh, following the direction of her glance and deliberately turning her back.

'I thought you were with Jason and quite happy?'

'I was but he suddenly broke off in mid-sentence a couple of minutes ago and just walked away. I couldn't believe it. He didn't explain or say anything, just walked off.' Was it something she had said, Claudia wondered idly. But only idly. She didn't really care. Something about Jason bothered her. She couldn't quite put her finger on it but it was there.

'Something probably came up. Jason can also be very

156

single-minded,' Joaney said, as though finishing her conversation with Bo. She blinked belatedly and tried to cover up her slip. 'Oh, and, speaking of things coming up ...' she launched into her tale of meeting Bo and Claudia tried hard to feign surprise and indifference. She flushed at the mention of Todd.

'Guess that's not good, is it?' Joaney said, wincing. 'Him going to visit Todd even when you're not there?'

'Guess not.' Claudia's voice became dull and mechanical. 'Oh well, that's that. No change.' And they both, by mutual consent, changed the subject.

By the time Bo had taken leave of his hosts, explaining to several people who tried to claim him that he really had to go, and had reached the door, he saw that the Wall Street suit and Michael Glendinning were there before him. They were standing on the outside steps, deep in conversation.

Bo started to slip past them when suddenly their voices rose, sharp and angry and then Jason pushed Michael Glendinning in a short, violent action that caused the older man to topple sideways, lose his balance and fall onto the stone steps. He rolled down them into the gutter and lay quite still.

Jason glanced quickly at Bo, seeing his appalled face, the way he started down the steps after Michael to help, and gave him an irritated, distracted jerk of his chin. His message was obvious. Clear off. He turned back to Michael.

'And that's where you belong, shit-head, not in here. You remember that. And you leave my sister alone.' He turned on his heel and re-entered the house, slamming the door loudly on the two men outside.

'Michael! Christ!' Bo leapt down the steps two at a time and knelt beside the older man, gently lifting his head. He was relieved to see Michael open his eyes and wince.

'Charmingly hospitable as always, wasn't he?' he murmured and Bo sighed.

'He was certainly thorough in seeing you out, if that's what you mean. Well, good to see you're still alive, at least. I thought you'd stoved your head in for a minute. He sure

157

didn't care enough to hang around and check. Listen, hold still and I'll get help.' Bo began to get up.

'No! No, you help me.' Michael grasped Bo's sleeve, holding onto it with surprising strength. 'I can't afford a scandal. Not yet. You help me, Bo, can't you?'

Bo was surprised but he slipped his arm under Michael's shoulders without protest and lifted him slowly, exploring the hurt. It seemed to be minor.

'Just bruised and a bit wobbly, I think. Help me up, will you?' And Bo supported Michael, letting him lean against him for a few moments, raising an arm and a whistle to a yellow cab, passing on Lexington. He helped Michael into the taxi and climbed in himself when he saw Michael close his eyes in pain and relief.

'What's the matter wid' him? Drunk?' The driver looked in the rear-view mirror with disapproval, his Bronx accent as thick as the bullet-proof glass that separated them. The cab smelt sour from disinfectant and smoke.

'No, he slipped down the steps and nearly knocked himself out. Michael, hey Michael, where do you want to go? What's your address?'

They were no more than a few blocks from Michael's apartment on First and 96th, close to the bend in the shoreline where FDR Drive cupped into a bay and Mill Rock stood off in the East River like a dark sentinel. Bo wondered what the view was like from the penthouse. He paid the taxi off and helped Michael upstairs to the foyer of his apartment block. The doorman looked up in consternation.

'Mr Glendinning! Sir! What have you done to yourself? Do you want me to call a doctor?'

'No, don't worry, Sam, I'm all right. Just slipped on some steps. My friend here'll help me upstairs and there's nothing wrong with me that a bath and a stiff whiskey won't help.' And then they were in the lift and going up to the tenth floor, before Sam could say another word.

'I really appreciate this, Bo. You didn't have to go out of your way like this,' Michael said as he unlocked the door and Bo helped him in and over to the sofa. Bo straightened

158

and glanced for a moment out the huge plate-glass windows at the dark river and the lights of Queens beyond. He turned back to Michael and sighed.

'No trouble. I don't like the shit who did this to you, any more than you do.'

'Jason Hewitt?'

'That his name? Regular little Mussolini type, isn't he?' Bo tried to control his jealousy without success, the taste of it new and unexpectedly unpleasant. Was this what he inflicted on girls, without thought, moving on and leaving the rank taste behind? He felt unexpectedly ashamed of himself.

'Yes, I'm afraid so. I don't think his father entirely realises it yet, though he has his doubts about the boy, I think. But the mother dotes on him. Only Joaney sees him for what he really is.' Michael grimaced and Bo looked at him sharply, understanding dawning on his face.

'Oh, Joaney's a Hewitt, yeah, of course ... and your girlfriend. That explains it.'

'What? Me being kicked down the steps?'

'Yeah, that and other things too. Hold on, I'll get you that whiskey.'

'Help yourself while you're at it.'

'Thanks. I could do with one.'

'Because of Jason? Why do you hate him?'

'Oh, there are reasons.'

'And they're personal, is that what you're saying?' Michael massaged his scalp. He looked across at Bo and smiled, accepted the whiskey with a nod, his manner civilised and restrained. Bo admired him for it.

'Just not that interesting, really. Besides, I don't think I'll be taking that job after all. I don't think I care for the whole set-up.' Bo swallowed his own whiskey, flinging it back to glow satisfyingly down his throat. He sat down heavily in a chair opposite and closed his eyes. Michael heard him sigh again.

'Don't be a fool, Bo.' His voice was quiet but it held conviction. Bo opened his eyes and regarded the older man steadily.

'How do you figure that?' he asked mildly.

'I know New York, and I know the way things work. Purvis and Clinton can give you the start you need and there are few other firms around that would be even interested in your work, let alone prestigious enough to make your whole career like this. Don't throw that away over a petty brawl with a client's son.'

'I haven't brawled with Jason Hewitt – yet. You were the one doing that.'

'Then don't. You keep your head safely screwed on your neck and facing the right way. Don't mess up your whole life for a fellow who's going to end up on the wrong end of a prison sentence one day, or worse. John Hewitt's a charming, intelligent man. Don't judge him by his son.' He paused and glanced slyly at Bo again. 'So what'd he do to you?'

'Jason? Nothing. I just don't like him. What does he do, anyway?'

'Fund manager for Hudson Carmine. He's a rising young star in the financial markets, snapping his power braces as he goes, though God knows why he needs them, the way his suits are cut. But I hear he's good – very good,' Michael drawled. He gave an amused smile, more for his own benefit than anyone else's. He looked over at the young man who had helped him and liked what he saw.

'Yeah? Reminds me of a piranha. I'll keep away from him, don't worry. What're you going to do about Joaney? I mean, you are married, aren't you? So, this is all a bit ... unethical, I guess.' Not that he was anyone to be pointing fingers, he thought wryly. Not with his track record. 'Maybe Jason thinks he has a point?' Bo was embarrassed but his voice remained steady. Michael shrugged.

'Yup, guess he has at that. It was all meant to be just a bit of a lark at first. Joaney didn't look like the type of girl to get hurt and my wife doesn't care what I do just as long as she's got the house. She loves that house. More than me, more than the children, more than the dogs even. And she's not willing to give it up, no matter how many times I fool around.' His smile was twisted, as though he couldn't

160

explain it even to himself. Bo frowned.

'What made you think Joaney wouldn't get hurt? She's just a kid herself. And, in case you hadn't noticed, you look a bit like Hewitt Senior. Without being too overtly Freudian, I'm sure you must have worked that one out.'

'Of course I have. And so has Joaney. She knows she's got a thing about her father and that she constantly competes with her mother for his attention but she says I'm her escape valve. She doesn't mind any more, can actually look at it all and understand what's going on, just as long as she has me to herself.'

'But she doesn't! You have a wife and children. Aren't you worried about them?' Bo sounded exasperated, heard it himself and turned to look out at the window. So what if Michael was playing around on his wife? So what?

'The children are away at school, caught up in their lives and their friends and they have blissful holidays and I barely ever see them. My wife has her charities and her social life and her dogs and, of course, the house. She doesn't need me either. We'd have divorced years ago if either of us had been particularly unhappy with the way things were, but we just never thought about it, never had the time to think about it . . .'

'And now?'

'Now? Now, I don't know any more. Maybe I want more than that. Maybe I'd like to try starting again but I'm scared to and, as you say, Joaney's just a kid. What right have I to cradle-snatch her? My own daughter's only five years younger than Joaney.' Michael sighed and leaned back on the sofa, his head making an indent in the cushions. He held out his glass.

'More?' Bo asked, as he took it from Michael's hand.

'No, no thanks, Bo. I think I'll just order a pizza and veg out in front of the telly. Good expression that, don't you think? I like America. They cut through the bullshit.'

'And then wrap it up again in bureaucratic red tape and business-speak,' Bo replied with a laugh. 'Well, I guess I'd better be off, Michael. Thanks for the advice. I'll think about it.'

161

'Do. And come to dinner with Joaney and me some time, when you're next up here. Tell me what I should do. God knows I don't have any idea myself.' There was a crack of laughter, amused and bitter at the same time.

No, and neither do I, Bo thought. Neither do I.

'He did what? My God, is Michael hurt?' Claudia sat up on her bed, staring at Joaney, at the fury in her face and the tell-tale mascara smudges that hinted at tears shed.

'Not badly. The bruises are pretty awful. Your friend Bo helped him. Michael thinks he's a good guy,' Joaney said ironically.

'You didn't tell him . . .'

'No, what's the point?'

'Oh, well, good.' Claudia settled back. 'Have you spoken to Jason about it yet? Heard his version?'

'No, the shit! You were right. He hates Michael. You watch yourself around him, won't you?' Joaney sat down, staring at herself in the mirror. She rubbed at her mascara.

'I'm not going to be around him. He's your brother. What's that got to do with me?' said Claudia positively. Joaney stopped rubbing her eyes and looked at Claudia's reflection in the mirror.

'He's taken with you. And he always gets what he wants.'

'Then he's due a disappointment, isn't he?'

'Not Jason.' Joaney shivered. 'He doesn't know the meaning of disappointment. So you be careful.' She took a deep breath as though to shake herself out of her depression, smiling her quick smile that said it's okay, I'm all right now, don't worry. But Claudia did worry.

'You heard from your brother lately? How's he doing?' Joaney hunted for a cigarette and sat back.

'Mark? Fine, I guess. I wrote back at mid-semester but he hasn't replied. He's getting a bit caught up in all that free spirit, drink and drugs scene I think. Maybe he'll grow out of it when he gets back to Hong Kong.'

'Yeah, guess so.' They smiled tentatively at each other. 'Brothers. God knows why they were invented,' Joaney added.

'Better than sisters,' Claudia contradicted. 'I'll have to write a novel about them all one day. Maybe it'll hit an answering chord with a lot of people and it'll become a smash bestseller and I'll be rich.'

'Rich and lonely?'

'Rich and self-fulfilled. I don't need a man, Joaney, not Bo, not your brother, not anyone. Okay?' But she wondered idly whether that was true. Mark had written to say he had seen Harry again. Just that, nothing else. A name mentioned in passing. But for Claudia it had been like a life-line, just knowing he was there, still alive, still in Hong Kong. Maybe even still waiting for her. She laughed when Joaney pulled a face.

'Sure, sure, just like I don't need Michael. Ah, hell, roll on Christmas!' But Joaney's hand shook at the thought of Michael going back to England to spend five long days with his wife and family. Five days could be all it needed, particularly after Jason's stunt. Awkwardly, she cleared her throat, thinking God, I'm a wreck, I'm shaking all over. 'Is Mark going home to you for Christmas?'

'Mark? No! Of course not! Mama refuses to even mention his name. She knows I'm in contact with him but she just shuts me up if I try and tell her what he's doing, cuts right across me with her classic line. You know, "I don't have a son, no husband and no son." God! I'm so sick of hearing it.' Claudia punched at her pillow, settling it behind her neck.

'So where's he going? To your dad?'

'Yeah, Dad and Joyce. They're going to the Philippines. Nice, huh?' Claudia tossed her lighter to Joaney who was still checking her pockets, the cigarette dangling from her mouth.

'Well, at least you're going home to see Todd.' Joaney lit the cigarette, took a deep drag and sighed with relief.

'That's right. Todd, my main man!' They both smiled painfully at each other.

163

Chapter Fifteen

The stench was unbearable. Tony fought to control his nausea, turning pale and sweating in the shadowed entrance of the godown, a warehouse at the Government Dockyard Transit Centre. Beyond, in the reeking, fetid shadows, writhed hundreds of dark figures, seating in a heat that had become a solid object. It hit him over the head with heavy blows, adding to the wretched plight of the refugees. In that godown, despite how hard they tried to stay clean, how hard they attempted not to press against each other, their lives became a stinking misery.

They sprawled out across the floor for as far as his eye could see and then further, squatting on straw mats, lying apathetic, children screaming, the sound of someone retching in a corner, apprehensive stares straining faces into masks of fear. Families had made pathetic attempts to segregate themselves by stringing washing along lines, others just leaned against the corrugated-iron walls and focused sullenly into the distance.

Sergeant Chu glanced slyly at Tony's pale face, at the sweat slicking down his cheeks.

'Like go see mo bettah, sir?' he asked with a grin. Tony frowned and fought to swallow. 'I told you to speak to me in Cantonese, Sergeant!' he snapped. 'There's no point in speaking pidgin to me. And no, I don't want to see more, but we've got no choice.' He took off his peaked hat and wiped an arm across his damp forehead, pushing back wet tendrils of hair. There were times, like this, when he wondered why he had joined the police force. To endure bad pay and bad hours, lousy jobs like this ... but then,

164

someone had to do it, didn't they, he reminded himself. And he was the fool who volunteered. Then he replaced the hat and stepped forward into the godown, one of many that had become home to several thousand Chinese refugees from Vietnam while they waited to move on to the UN camps.

He concentrated on his irritation with his sergeant, his breathing slowly adjusting to the smell and trapped heat of the air. Chu was a problem, refusing to acknowledge that Tony spoke Cantonese as fluently as he did himself, neglecting to pass on important information, watching and waiting with mocking spite for Tony to fall flat on his face. The sergeant resented his inexperience, Tony realised, and he resented the fact that Tony, green as he was, was superior in rank. But Tony had served three years in the army and he knew enough about handling bolshie NCOs as the next man. His patience had worn thin. Chu was due some aggravation in return.

'Spread the men out across the warehouse and make sure each of them has a photograph of Wong Yip-nan. Move slowly, in a line, and check every face here, Sergeant – and that includes you.' He caught his sergeant's eye and held it steadily until the man lowered his gaze. Then he turned and looked back at the tangle of humanity with deep pity and anger that such degradation should be allowed. He damned the Vietnamese and their policy of ridding Vietnam of their Chinese ethnic minority in such a brutal way. Send them to sea and charge them for the privilege of probably drowning on the way. It was unbelievable in its callousness.

'Velly difficult, sir. No space. Too many peoples,' Chu said stubbornly, his eyes sullen as they stared at the ground, and Tony rounded on him in fury.

'The next time you disobey a direct order from me by speaking to me in pidgin instead of Cantonese, I will have you broken down in rank, Sergeant. Now take the men and search for this man. Do you understand me? Now!' He roared the final word, bitterly furious, and Chu, seeing he had badly overstepped the mark, turned and hurried over

165

to his men. The search began and Tony paced up and down the central aisle himself, grimly silent.

Wong Yip-nan had been found floating alone aboard an old leaking wooden boat, riddled with rot, with stained, tattered sails, offshore from Macao. He was from Quang Yen, in Northern Vietnam, he said, and had set off alone to sail the 2,600 miles through the Gulf of Tonkin, the Straits of Hainan and across the South China Sea to Hong Kong. The Coast Guard had been suspicious that he managed the journey alone but had towed him into Discovery Bay, to await rehousing on shore. He had been brought to the Government Dockyard Transit Centre only two days ago.

And yesterday, another boatload of refugees from Quang Yen had been brought in, one man aboard telling a grisly tale of piracy and murder at the hands of a certain Wong Yip-nan. They had found him floating in a small row-boat, in the Gulf of Tonkin and had taken him aboard. For a few days, as they cleared the straits and were blown north with the winds, he had been too seasick to cause much trouble. There was enough in just keeping that old barque afloat, shipping seawater with every swell, the rats climbing over sleeping babies to escape it, short of food and water. But as they grew closer to their destination, he became better and began to question them about their futures, about how they would afford to live. And they, unsuspecting, had told him how much money they had brought with them to start a new life.

In the night, as they lay wallowing in light winds, Wong quietly slit the throats of those who slept and then leapt upon the last two men who sailed the frail boat. One had died and the last had thrown himself overboard into the shark-infested waters of the South China Sea. Wong had thrown the other bodies overboard and sailed on with their small hoard of a few thousand dong. The last surviving man had, against all odds, kept himself afloat in the water for nearly fourteen hours before being picked up by another boatload of refugees.

It was an old tale, that had, Tony knew, probably been repeated more often than anyone cared to know. But Wong

166

had been unlucky – particularly so when the matter was handed over to Tony himself. Because, no matter how hard he tried to stop the feeling, no matter how hard he tried to become as tough and seasoned to the violence his job entailed as the other officers, Tony could never rid himself of the need to protect and defend the ones everyone else trod on without thought. It embarrassed him to be so boy-scoutish in nature but there was nothing he could do about it. It was his nature and he had to live with it. And so did Wong.

They found him on the fourth, agonisingly slow, sweep of the godown, Sergeant Chu protesting that it was a waste of time and Tony telling him quietly but implacably that they would search until Wong was found. Sergeant Chu shrugged with grudging respect when Wong Yip-nan was brought forward, the other anxious faces around them softening with relief as they realised they had nothing to fear. Tony led them out into the hazy afternoon sun that seemed suddenly cool and fresh after the hell of the go-down.

'Is that it, then, sir?' Chu asked in Cantonese, rubbing his face clear of sweat. Both of them had pounding head-aches from the long hours in the warehouse and the sergeant was aware that Tony had not had to stay in there himself while the search was completed. Another officer wouldn't have. But he had.

Tony gave a half-smile.

'For now, Chu. Well done.' And they both regarded each other warily until Chu reluctantly smiled too.

'Okay, boss,' he said lightly and walked back to his men. And Tony stared after him with a quizzical smile that held more than a touch of relief. Chu had accepted him. Chalk another small victory up to that day.

In the bar of Scottie's, at the back of Lan Kwai Fong, Aidan Lockhart poured a quick two fingers of Irish whiskey (smoother, he said), down his throat and thought carefully over what Uncle Bill had said to him that night. As used as he was now to the unpleasantness his job entailed, he was loathe to agree to Bill Ingram's suggestion about pretending to resign from the 'Civil Service' and becoming a lush. Already it was difficult feigning a heavy drinking problem, pretending to a nightly intoxication he rarely felt, and the thought of doing that for real, of actually descending into the foul world of drink and drug addiction ... and all for Uncle Bill and his information-gathering mania. It was too much to ask.

He gazed at the empty glass in his hand, hesitated, and then set it down firmly. No, to hell with Bill Ingram and to hell with all of them. He wasn't going to do it. No reward later would be worth that sort of hell.

He pushed himself away from the bar rail. His friends called to him to stay but he forced a smile and waved, beating a deliberately wavering path to the door and out into the cobbled street. He turned left, crossed over Pedder Street and headed up Wyndham Street to where he had left his car.

Afterwards, several people testified to how much he had had to drink that night and how his steps had been uneven as he left but none of them had thought to stop him. No one had realised he intended to drive.

Aidan climbed into his car and switched on the lights, taking time to light a cigarette with steady hands before releasing the hand brake and rolling forward down the hill. The car gathered speed quickly, sliding towards the blur of lights of Queen's Road Central, at the bottom. He eased his foot onto the brake and pumped it gently, looking blank for a moment and then swearing harshly as his descent continued unchecked. He pumped the brake harder, sweat breaking out in a cold prickle over his face.

He had meant to make the sharp turn into Ice House Lane, he said at the hearing, but his brakes had failed. He had fought to slow the car by crashing down through his gears but the bend had been too sudden. Eyewitnesses said he had been swerving all over the road, even before he came to the bend, fighting the car's descent.

The child had run out blindly into the road, Aidan said, brokenly. There was nothing he could do. Nothing. And his voice had whispered and become hoarse, repeating that word over and over.

Witnesses, bitter with an old cankering distrust of Europeans, or *gweilos* as they called them in contempt, said she had been standing on the pavement and that the car had mounted the kerb and hit her before swerving violently away and ploughing into a wall just near the Foreign Correspondents' Club.

The child had died later, in hospital, the court was told and Aidan had wept huge, fat tears as he stood there in the dock, his face pale and ill, his dark eyes staring out at a figure in the crowded courtroom, never blinking or wavering. And Bill Ingram had stared back.

Somehow Aidan had avoided prosecution, and there was talk of a large bribe being paid by the Lockhart family, of strings being pulled, of high-up government officials being corrupted, of shameful deals being made in the Civil Service, but no one ever really knew quite what happened. Only that Aidan had suddenly found the charges withdrawn. He resigned his job the next day and there were sighs of relief within the ministry that he had been persuaded to go so easily.

They weren't to know that Aidan had been given no choice, either play along with Uncle Bill's suggestions or face prosecution unaided. Only Aidan and Uncle Bill knew that. And only Uncle Bill knew for sure who had tampered with Aidan's brakes. His own fault, Aidan was told. He had been clumsy, let Yee see him. And he had paid the consequences, that dry, measured voice of Bill Ingram's had said.

But was it really Yee, Aidan wondered, late at night, seeing that child's face swelling larger in his windscreen, rushing forward, hitting ... Was it Yee? Or was Bill willing to sacrifice any pawns as long as the eventual game went to him?

The drinking continued after that, harder and longer now, old friends like Tony, who tried to reason with him, finding themselves avoided, and new friends, who were happy to drink with someone who would pay for them, being embraced. Aidan began the long slow slide into oblivion. Uncle Bill had thrown him to the wolves.

Judson
December, 1980

Claudia, travelling home by Greyhound bus, swore to herself as the hours droned by and the freeways stretched out into the distance that she would never do it again. As she always did. But it was cheap and she couldn't have made it any other way. And she had promised Todd.

She had only eight days to spend with her family and most of that was passed cleaning the house for her mother, putting up decorations that Peggy couldn't be bothered with, mowing the lawn that Hank had neglected, and keeping an eye on Todd. She saw Bo occasionally, passing by on his way home, but she always stepped away from the windows, distracting Todd's attention. And Bo never stopped anyway.

On Christmas Eve, Claudia started the cooking for the big day, baking pies and glazing hams under instruction from her mother who sat at the kitchen table directing operations. Peggy was too busy, she said, not having had time off before to do any Christmas shopping.

'It's all right for ladies of leisure who have plenty of time to get their presents,' Peggy remarked sharply to Claudia, when the latter complained, 'but some of us work for a living.' And there was no answering that, was there, even knowing that the malls were open until late, even knowing she worked longer hours at Succi's than Peggy did at the shop. Not without a show-down and Claudia flinched from the thought, from the ugliness, the noise. She breathed deeply and shrugged away her irritation.

Claudia and Todd iced the gingerbread men and hung them from the Christmas tree. They spun sugar and glazed toffee apples, and nuts, they painted home-made Christmas cards and sent them to Todd's friends. It was Claudia who took Todd out to listen to the carol singing down in the main town square, huffing and puffing out clouds of warm,

170

steaming breath into the chill night as they watched the Christmas tree lights being lit and Todd called out in awe and delight. And it was Claudia who listened to Todd's prayers and tucked him into bed at night.

Peggy was increasingly distant with her son, barely remembering to see whether he had been fed, or asking what he had done that day, before she rushed out again with her friend Elly. It was Mama, Claudia realised, who was bringing Todd up. Poor Mama. She was looking old and weary with it all, though she couldn't be more than fifty, surely?

Hank had reverted to his bachelor state, going out from work straight to a bar and staying with his buddies until late. He used his home as nothing more than a bed and breakfast place, Claudia muttered to herself, and the words 'redneck' and 'Bubba' sprang to mind when she thought of him. He barely spoke to Peggy or she to him.

'I don't think it's going to work, do you, Mama?' Claudia asked, as they both sat in the kitchen peering at recipe books. 'Peggy and Hank, I mean.' She looked up at her mother, seeing the stubborn lines around her mouth, the way she set her chin, a moment of doubt in those faded eyes.

'It's just fine. Don't you go getting interested in other people's business, Claudia. You're only here a few days. What do you know?'

'I know what I see, Mama. Maybe you can't see it because you're here all the time and it's just begun to slip, little by little. But I see it straight away when I come back.' She closed the book and leaned her folded arms on it, looking at her mother in exasperation.

'Oh? So now that you've been away in New York you're suddenly an expert on us all, is that it?' Mama snorted. 'Well, maybe you come back and see everything all clearly, and maybe you fuss over Todd and make him think you're the best auntie there ever was, but I'm the one who's here all the time. I'm the one who pays the bills and gets Todd to school in the morning and who picks him up in the evening, who feeds him and puts him to bed. I'm the one

171

who's here with Peggy and Hank all the time and I don't think you have any business trying to tell us how to run our lives when you're just going to waltz off again in a few days to your fancy life up in New York. So don't patronise us, Claudia.'

It was a long harangue from her mother and Claudia was hurt and offended by it, not seeing until later that it was her mother's way of coping with what was happening. If she could deny it, then it might not happen. But it caused a rift between them that refused to be healed.

Peggy was delighted, her eyes laughing and provoking, whispering to Claudia that now she knew what it was like to not be mama's pet. Claudia ignored them all except Todd, counting the days until she was free and could return to New York and Joaney.

On Christmas Day, Claudia was woken by Todd climbing onto her bed and shaking her, his small face alight with anticipation at the packages that were grouped underneath the tree.

'Oh, Toddy, not yet. It's only six. Come and snuggle in with me for a bit, okay?' Claudia mumbled, half asleep, her hair mussed over her face and eyes barely open.

'No, no, it's Chrismus, Liddsy! Come and look at all the presents. Liddsy? Hey, Liddsy! Wake up.' He pushed and pulled at her, kneading the bedclothes around her as she laughed and tried to cling onto them.

'Just another five minutes, Todd, please! Just go and look at them again and count how many are for you, okay?' She thought she had convinced him when he suddenly let go of the sheet he had been trying to pull back, and scrambled down from the bed. There was the sound of footsteps retreating and then a sharp sliding noise followed by cold air.

'Todd, close the window! It's cold!' Claudia pulled the covers over her head and burrowed down into the soft warmth, content for a few moments. She could hear whispering, Todd's childish voice barely lowered, and then a lower, quieter voice. Reluctantly she peered out.

Bo was sitting on the window-ledge, his arm round Todd

and a package in his hand. His face was flushed with the cold morning air and the brisk bicycle ride, eyes bright and dancing like some elf's, Claudia thought. He was hunched into a jeans jacket with an old battered suede collar, his hair gleaming in the morning light. It didn't seem respectable or fair that a man with such lousy morals could look so clean-cut and honest. Claudia sat up sharply.

'What the hell do you think you're doing, Bo Haskill?' she demanded.

Bo looked up, giving her a quiet, assessing look. 'I'm wishing Todd a Merry Christmas and giving him my present.'

'Really? Well, isn't that just mighty keen of you!' Claudia remarked sarcastically.

'And just what is that meant to mean? Come on, Claudia, why don't you just tell me what it is that's on your mind.' Bo, irked finally beyond endurance by Claudia's attitude, decided he was willing to risk hearing whatever it was that had gone wrong between them, if only to have the satisfaction of letting off a little steam at Claudia himself.

Claudia grew still, looking over at Bo's angry face and then at Todd. 'Not now. I'll see you later.'

'When and where later?' He pressed and she saw he meant to find out. She swallowed hard.

'All right, maybe we should have this out. How about the Fiftynine diner, later today, around five?' She saw his face pull tight, and she wished she had chosen anywhere but there, but it was done.

'I'll see you there. And Merry Christmas to you too, Claudia,' he added drily as he gave Todd a squeeze before stepping back out of the window and lowering it quietly. Todd watched him go reluctantly.

'And Merry Christmas to you too, Bo, you philandering bastard! And you can damned well stay away from Todd from now on,' Claudia whispered through gritted teeth, lying back down and pulling the covers over her. Todd continued to watch through the window as Bo climbed on his bicycle and rode away.

*

173

Bo sat in the back of the Fiftynine Diner, in the same booth where he had sat with Claudia that night they had gone over her college acceptances. It seemed like years ago and Bo felt he had soured in the intervening time, like milk left too long in the refrigerator. He felt jaded, fed up with life and girls, Claudia ... and especially himself. But he couldn't quite keep the quiver in his stomach from erupting as he saw her appear in the doorway. He waved half-heartedly and let his hand fall back to his side when he saw her approach, no smile on her face.

'Hi,' he said flatly as she slid into the booth opposite him.

'Hi.' Just that. A quick bitten-off greeting that held no warmth. She looked around for the waitress and ordered a coffee.

The silence stretched out between them, neither of them knowing how to break it. The waitress returned with a coffee for Claudia, refilling Bo's mug at the same time and then retreating, quickly and efficiently.

'Thanks for coming,' Claudia said finally, taking a sip of the coffee. She glanced at him over the rim.

'So what's this all about?' He was nervous, fiddling with the salt and pepper shakers, glancing at her defensively. Claudia felt the fear in her stomach begin to subside, weary acceptance taking over.

'We need to talk about things,' she paused, shrugging, looking up at him again.

'Yeah? What about?'

'About you and Peggy. About Todd.' Her voice was almost gentle and, hearing it, Bo wondered suddenly what any of it had been worth, all the laughs and adulation and admiring glances from the other guys, all the sighs and giggles and quick, easy passion from the girls. He felt numb, scoured out, looking into Claudia's face.

'What about us?' he forced himself to say.

'Oh, come on, Bo. Can't you at least be honest with me? There's no one listening, there's no one judging. And I'm not going to say anything, point fingers, demand things from you. I just want to know the truth.' She sounded tired and sad, but not surprised and that hurt almost more than

174

anything else, Bo thought. She wasn't surprised. He breathed out heavily.

'You want to know whether Peggy and I slept together? The answer is yes. I'm sure she's told you that already,' he said slowly. He shrugged, looked away from those eyes that held pity, understanding, and something else – regret. For what might have been but never would be now. There was no point in lying to her. She knew better. 'You want to know whether Todd is my son? I don't know. Peggy accused half the guys in my year of being the father. How the hell am I supposed to know, one way or the other?' He sighed and wrinkled up his brow, squeezing his eyes shut at her continued silence.

'I know, I know. I can hear you thinking it, but I just didn't know what to do when she first told me. I was – stunned, I suppose. I thought she was, you know, on something. And then I guess I panicked and just wanted to get away and clear my head, think about things. So I told her I didn't want to hear it and I walked away. But I felt lousy and I'd just about got the courage together to tell my father, to try and sort things out properly and then I heard all the other guys talking about it, laughing and accusing each other. And then I realised Peggy didn't know for sure, she'd just accused me along with every other guy she'd ever slept with.' He glanced up at her, seeing the outrage in her face.

'Oh, and you think badly of her for that, don't you, Bo? She's a slut for sleeping around, isn't that what you think?' Claudia whispered fiercely and Bo looked away, shrugged, not saying anything. She saw the weakness in his face, the willingness to let someone – anyone – else shoulder the burden just as long as he didn't have to. He was still a good guy, the guy Judson loved to love. And any feeling she had ever hidden, deep inside her, for him, died a quiet painful little death in that instant. She shook her head.

'And what does that make you, Bo? How many times have you slept around? But that's okay, isn't it, because you're a man and that just makes you a stud,' she continued coldly. Bo didn't reply and they both sat there in

175

silence for a long time. And then Claudia gave a laugh that held no humour in it.

'This is just great, isn't it? I used to think you were such a good guy, such a nice guy. A real friend. You even have the nerve to start coming onto me and all the time, all the time you knew!' she said bitterly.

Bo breathed out sharply. 'I didn't know anything. Not for sure,' he said harshly. 'What do you want me to do, Claudia? I see Todd as much as I can, and the chances are he's not my kid in the first place. But I like him, so I try and make a point of seeing him. What else do you want from me?'

'I don't know, Bo. I guess maybe I don't want anything from you any more.' She made as though to stand but he reached out and caught her arm, holding her back.

'Look, I'm sorry, Claudia. Don't you know that? Don't you think I'd do anything to change things? You're the only girl I've ever known who's meant anything more than an easy lay, a one night stand – yeah, ugly isn't it, when you say it out loud, but I wasn't thinking like that when I did it. It was all just light-hearted fun. Or it seemed like it.' He paused, releasing her, seeing he had her attention. 'If I'd known how it would turn out, well … but that's history now and I can't change things. We just have to live with it the way it is.'

'What do you think, Bo? That I'm going to line up and be another number? Peggy is my sister, little though I may like it. You don't do that to people. Not to her and especially not to me. Besides,' she paused, her tone wondering, 'why would you think I still care about you? Maybe I had a bit of a schoolgirl crush on you once, like every other girl in town, but that was all, nothing more. I might have thought it was more than that but I guess I was wrong or it wouldn't have just faded away looking at the guilt in your eyes.' He heard the ring of truth in her words and flinched angrily.

'You think I don't know that? But at least I feel guilty, which is more than most of the other guys who went with Peggy. I know I did wrong but it's done, over and finished

176

with, Claudia. There's nothing I can do to fix it. Or do you want me to pay for it for the rest of my life?' He closed his eyes, covering his face with his hands as he leaned on the table.

Claudia sat there, feeling empty, knowing he was right, it was over now, all her giddy, surreptitious thoughts about Bo and herself, all the doubts that she had hushed, pushed to one side, meaning to find out one day but in the meantime she was sure it couldn't really be so. Bo wouldn't act that shabbily, she was sure of it. He was a nice guy. Everyone said so. Wasn't that the way her mind had been playing tricks with her, all this last year? And deep down, right inside her, the voice that had been saying things she hadn't wanted to hear, had been right.

She looked at him and sighed again, hesitating and then reaching out to squeeze his arm.

'Bo, I'm sorry about this too,' she began tentatively, gently. 'I know it isn't just your fault. I know Peggy has a lot of the blame on her side, but she's paying for it all right. Don't worry, I'm not going to say anything. There's no point, is there?'

He lowered his hands and Claudia saw the way they trembled slightly before he controlled them. His eyes were bloodshot and bleary. He shook his head.

'No, I guess there isn't.' He sounded hoarse but there was relief there, just below the surface. 'What do you want me to do, about Todd, I mean?'

'Nothing. You do whatever you want, or nothing if you want. Todd's always going to stay with us anyway and we're always going to love him.' She wondered whether she could continue for much longer keeping her voice calm, trying to ease some of the pain for him while her own eddied around inside, churning her up, making her feel sick. Not because she couldn't have him, but because he wasn't worth having. The disillusionment was by far the more painful of the two.

'And you don't want anything from me, is that it?' He sounded almost eager.

'Nothing you don't want to give. Maybe we can be friends again, some time. Not just now but – in time.' She

177

stood up again and this time he didn't attempt to stop her.

'I'm sorry, Claudia.'

'Yeah, so am I.' She tried to smile but there was nothing left in her to ease his burden and her lips would not cooperate. 'Seeya,' she said, digging into her pocket for change and letting it dribble across the table finally to land in a clattering heap. And then she walked away.

Chapter Sixteen

Hong Kong
August, 1981

'Hey, boss, you want to come put the squeeze on old man Ching Yip? He's selling again. You bring the whole gang and I'll go talk to him?' Corporal Poon hadn't worked with Tony before. He assumed the old ways would still be in force, even in the Triad Bureau. Go scare someone breaking the law, squeeze some money out of them, and then look the other way. Everyone stayed happy that way. He smiled slyly and familiarly into his new boss's face.

'Ching Yip is selling? Did you know that, Chu?' Tony turned to his sergeant who was watching Tony warily.

'No, boss,' he said with a rueful smile.

'Why not, Chu?'

'He's been clean for some time. I guess he's just started again.' Chu shrugged.

'Then how did you come to know so quickly, Corporal Poon? You must have good sources on the street?' Tony's voice was mild, only half interested and Poon smiled again, nodding. He failed to see Chu's wink of derision.

'Sure, boss. I always have good sources. I hear things before they've even happened.' His gold tooth glinted in the afternoon light, proof of such a claim.

'Really? You know anything about a certain lodge called the Thin Blades? They're becoming an interesting pastime of mine, just lately, aren't they, Chu?' Tony smiled blandly and then added, 'You know a fellow called "Big Foot", Yee Fong Lo? I expect you've heard of him, haven't you? And about who's backing them?' It seemed an idle question, Tony looking down at his desk, doodling with a pen. But Poon froze.

'No, boss. Never heard of him.' Perspiration along the man's hairline glinted under the fluorescent lights and Chu smiled with satisfaction as Tony looked up at last, a look of quiet fury in his eyes.

'No? Oh, come now, Poon, surely you do when you have such good sources on the street? Of course you know. Doesn't he, Chu?' Tony's lips thinned into a harsh smile. 'Which lodge do you belong to, Poon?'

Poon shook his head. 'No boss, you got me wrong.'

'No, it's you who's got me wrong, Poon. And not just you. You go ahead and spread the word, Poon. You tell them I don't take bribes and I don't give up. You tell Yee that and you tell any of your other good sources. And you get the hell out of my office, right now.' His voice was like a lash and Poon stumbled backwards, cannoning off the chair as he made his way to the door. Tony watched him go.

And Sergeant Chu nodded to himself quietly. That was his boss, he told himself proudly, and soon they'd all know about him. They'd know he meant business and they'd curse his name.

Mark wondered whether he ought to have started work earlier than September. His boss had been good about letting him have the summer off, once he had graduated, but he was getting short of money and tired of having to explain to Silvia that they couldn't afford to eat at Restaurant 97, or any of the trendier restaurants in Central, every night. Wiping the perspiration from his face, he leaned forward over the bills, fingering through them uneasily. There were far too many of them. She never offered to pay, now did she, he thought in irritation as he looked through his bank statement. And the money had to come from somewhere now that his father had cut him off. Maybe it was time for another trip down to Manila? He could call Yee tomorrow. Maybe.

There was a quick, rapid knocking at the door and, glad of the distraction, he levered himself up. Padding across the tiled floor in nothing more than a pair of boxer shorts, he opened the door wide. His thin face lit up with relief.

180

'Hey, Harry! Just the man I was thinking of.' He unlocked the metal grille and stepped back to allow Harry in. Harry, catching sight of the bills, held up his hands quickly.

'Oh, no! Not my side of things any more, Mark, and you know it. You call Yee if you want something. I'm out of the business, remember?' He threw himself down on the rattan sofa and helped himself to Mark's beer, his T-shirt prickling damply against his skin. 'Damn, it's hot!'

Mark shrugged. 'It's August, what do you expect?' With difficulty he smothered the irritation he felt at Harry's refusal to help. Harry looked at him steadily.

'I don't see Yee anymore, Mark. I have a good job and I'm clear of all that trouble now. Don't try and ruin things for me, okay?' He tried to smile, to make a joke out of it and Mark nodded.

'Yeah, yeah, I know, you're about to become Hong Kong's latest DJ, right?' he mocked, and then, as though suddenly lightening in mood, went to the kitchen to collect a couple of cold beers from the refrigerator. The hell with the money. He'd sort something out. He returned in time to hear Harry say:

'That's right. The two to four a.m. slot. It's only taken a year of being the backroom boy, running this way and that to please my masters. Want to offer me some congratulations?' Harry laughed, finishing the old, warm beer and reaching for a fresh, cold one. Mark stared at him.

'You kidding me?'

'Nope, it's for real. I just heard. Thought I'd spread the word.'

'Hey, that's great! I'm really impressed. Way to go!' Mark held out his beer and clinked the bottle against Harry's, his enthusiasm as genuine as their odd friendship had proven to be. 'Have they upped your salary too?'

'Not yet.' Harry shrugged. 'If it works out, then they say I'll get another two thousand dollars a month. Not much but better than a kick in the teeth. And it is going to work out, let me tell you that. I'm going to be the best damned DJ Hong Kong's ever known.'

181

'Which isn't saying much!' Mark remarked and they both laughed again. 'Well, here's to both our new jobs and a lot more money coming in.'

'And to girls, too,' Harry added impulsively. 'Smooth, supple, golden girls to tie up in knots.' He stopped. 'Oh, I forgot. You're pretty much sold on Silvia, aren't you? Well, here's to lots of girls for me, then. All the more, in fact.'

Mark had felt a moment of exhilaration when Harry had mentioned girls and he found himself irritated and – yes, maybe even bored – with the thought of seeing Silvia again that night. He had gone through lots of girls at university, things were so different over there, everyone seemed so free and uninhibited and willing to let each other breathe. No stifling relationships. God, he'd really like to try out some Chinese girls, he thought. They understood about him having a bit of dope every now and then, or maybe a snort of cocaine. And it didn't matter if they didn't, because he could just tell them to piss off. He really wanted to go out with Harry and just have a good time, no worries, just enjoy life.

He glanced up at Harry, smiling awkwardly. 'I've got to see her tonight. I said I would. I couldn't really stand her up.'

Harry shrugged. 'No, well, it doesn't matter. I've got to meet a friend later, anyway.'

'Who?'

'Oh, an old buddy who's going through a bit of a rough time right now. I owe him one, I guess. His name's Aidan. Aidan Lockhart.'

'Oh, yeah. The Fish. I know him a bit. Heard he's drinking himself into an early grave after killing that child. It's a real shame. So, where're you going?'

'Somewhere cheap over in Kowloon. Aidan says he knows a great dive where the girls come and sit on your lap and don't expect you to order them anything more than a coke. You want to come?'

'I ...' Mark hesitated, the urge to escape Silvia, to indulge in bawdy, cheap, masculine fun more appealing than ever before. 'Yeah, why not? Why the hell not? I'll put

182

Silvia off.' And they clinked their beer bottles together again, celebrating a new era.

'Tony, I don't believe it! Where've you been hiding yourself this age? And look at that tan! I don't believe you've been working at all, or you'd be pale and pasty-faced instead of all bronzed like that.' There was a lingering warmth to the words, almost like a caress, and Tony fought the wariness in him that wanted to return a non-committal remark and walk away. He forced himself to smile at Sally Freeman's daughter, as plain as ever and growing desperate, it was said. He saw the anxiety there in her eyes, the fear that he would walk away and leave her standing there looking foolish, and he put his arm around her and gave her a squeeze.

'Hello, pumpkin, how are you?' He used her old nickname, silly and endearing, and her face lit up.

'Much better for seeing you. How's life in the police force? I hear you're an inspector now.'

'Just a dogsbody in uniform. Nothing glamorous. What about you, what are you doing lately?'

'Looking for a husband.' She winked at him and he almost choked on his laughter, knowing she had read his thoughts.

'Touché. I'd forgotten how much of your mother's sharp wit you have.'

'Just not her looks.' There was a long pained sigh.

'Come on, let's go get something to drink.' He smiled easily, pulling her arm through his and escorting her out into the garden.

Across the room, Sally, talking with Fran Clements, Reginald Hsu and Silvia Bateman's father, paused and smiled wistfully.

'How like Tony,' she murmured, 'such a kind, *nice* boy.' She stressed 'nice' so that Reginald glanced across at the fair-haired young man and then back at Sally again. He raised his eyebrows.

'Oh, no, nothing like that, unfortunately.' Sally shook her head in regret. 'If Tony ever had a yen for anyone, it was

Silvia, but he doesn't get much time for socialising any more. And, quite frankly, I don't think he ever got over Joanna walking out on them.' She glanced quickly up at Reginald, judging his expression. He smiled pleasantly but his eyes had become still behind his glasses. 'It's made the poor boy very wary where females are concerned, I think.'

'He doesn't look like a "poor boy" to me,' Reginald said calmly enough. 'Looks rather a capable young man, in fact. The sort to have his life very much in order.'

'In order, yes,' Fran cut in, 'but that's not everything in life, now is it? Sometimes things ought to be just a little disordered. Particularly at Tony's age, wouldn't you say?' They all glanced at him again, seeing him chatting easily, good-naturedly. It was Sally who put her finger on it.

'He's uninvolved. As though he's a spectator, who has no intention of getting mixed up in the game going on,' she observed shrewdly and Silvia Bateman's father stirred and nodded his head.

'He's Bill's son, isn't he?' It was not a question, more of an observation.

'Is he? He's grown up.' Reginald Hsu opened his eyes a fraction wider and glanced more thoughtfully at Tony, seeing the calm good humour, the firm chin, the unflappable nature of the young man who was going out of his way to please what seemed, to Reginald's eyes, a dull, ordinary girl. 'Bill never bothers with people,' he said shortly.

'No. And Tony bothers too much. He doesn't like to be unkind,' Fran said, her smile becoming distracted. 'He shouldn't bother so much, you know. He always seems to feel like he should carry all the weight on his shoulders, to make up for other people's neglect or cruelty. But he does it for anyone, friends, strangers, it doesn't matter.'

'That's because he doesn't allow anyone to get closer than that to him. It's a sort of blanket kindness but you better beware trying to get any closer to him than that. I've got no expectations there with my daughter – or anyone else's, for that matter. Besides, with a job like that . . .' Sally trailed off and glanced at Reginald.

184

'Like what?'

'Oh, Reginald!' Fran protested. 'I thought you knew everything about everyone. How can you not know Tony's in the police force?' Her lips curled.

'Should I?' He looked down from his great height with indifference.

Fran's eyes narrowed but she allowed her voice to remain light. 'Tony's very good at his job, I understand. All sorts of people who thought they were above the law or could bribe their way out of things are finding out they were wrong when it comes to Tony. Causing quite a thorn in the side of the drug lords, so rumour has it.' She raised her eyebrows, examining Reginald Hsu carefully. He smiled politely but coldly and Fran continued in a musing tone. 'You know, I always think it was Joanna's affairs that made Tony so worried about hurting people – and so wary of being hurt at the same time. And that's what makes him so single-minded about his job. Rather ironic, don't you think, Reginald?' There was an uncomfortable silence.

'The sins of the parents shall be visited upon their children, or however it goes?' Reginald laughed. 'I think it's the other way around with my daughter. Portia's busy sending me grey instead.' Reluctantly, they glanced across at Portia who, at fifteen, was distractingly lovely and precociously aware of it. Since neither Fran's nor Sally's daughters were anything more than passable, Reginald Hsu could be considered to have scored a point in return.

A group of young men surrounded her and she tossed back her long gleaming mane of dark hair with a practised flip of her head. There was a knowing look to her eye that Sally Freeman didn't like at all.

'Oh, I wouldn't worry about Portia,' she smiled sweetly at Reginald Hsu. 'She's well equipped to deal with life, I'd say. If she can't twist it round her little finger, she'll bludgeon it into shape.' Her eyes danced up at Reginald. 'Just like her father.' And he laughed again but this time there was no humour in the sound. For a moment his eyes glanced back, across the room, at Tony. He pushed his steel-rimmed glasses firmly into place, his mouth compressed together tightly.

New York, 1981
Claudia saw Jason from time to time, when he dropped in to see them or, less often, when Joaney and she were invited to dinner at the Hewitts. She had almost forgotten that he had been capable of pushing Michael down the steps. After all, she hadn't seen it herself and the whole thing could have been exaggerated, surely? He seemed so very normal, so charming when he turned and talked to her, telling her the latest scandals and *on dits* in New York or Westchester society, or explaining the financial politics of Wall Street, that she had quite forgotten that she had once thought him odd. He had his life in order and he knew where he was going and that was attractive to her lately. She began to look forward to seeing him.

Their newest acquisition, along with the apartment over on the West side on Amsterdam Avenue with views out over the Hudson and New Jersey beyond, was a sinuous slip of grey fur that Michael had brought over to Joaney soon after they had moved in. It was one of the litter that a friend of his was trying to find homes for, the mother cat being pedigree Burmese, the father wholly unknown. They named the kitten Bundle and watched, delighted, as he grew from a skittering ball of fluff into a lanky adolescent who liked to sleep with them by night and who demanded affection loudly by day.

And life continued in its day-to-day rush of papers due, classes to attend, exams to pass so that neither of them realised when they passed the halfway mark until November of their third year. Claudia continued to work at Succi's, cycling furiously through the clogged, belching traffic and on and off the rubbish-strewn sidewalks, dodging around wild Rastas, their plaited hair flying, around dumpy Italian matrons calling, 'Ecco, Stasi, ecco!' to oblivious children, past neat pinstriped businessmen and jeans-clad designers, their portfolios carried like badges of

186

merit. There were more ethnic mixtures in New York, she thought, than all America, all talking and walking fast in a lively, quick pulsed beat, so smart, so savvy – so alive!

She found an excuse not to return for Christmas and made up for her guilt by sending expensive presents that cost almost more than she earned during the holiday period. But she was keeping pace with the college fees and her living expenses and that was something to be proud of. Bo would have been proud of her, she thought involuntarily, and then mocked herself.

It was during the Spring term of Claudia's third year that Michael asked Joaney to marry him. And Joaney accepted.

'Marry? But he's already married!' The protest had sprung from Claudia's lips before she could think better of it. Joaney, sprawled out on the expensive leather sofa that bore marks of Bundle's claws already, stiffened. Her face fell.

'You're not happy? I thought you would be. You know how much he means to me, Claudia, how can you not be happy for us? He'll get a divorce, I'll finish my degree and we'll get married. What's so terrible about that? Why're you looking like the Ides of Doom, for Christ's sake?' She stood up, moving nervously across the floor, hopping from one patch of sunlight to another, staring out at the pale shimmer of the Hudson that could be seen from the balcony. Bundle followed, tapping at her ankles in a game of feline tag. For a moment Claudia watched him, stalling, thinking hard.

'Ides of Doom?'

'Oh, well, you know what I mean. Can't you be happy for me?' Joaney lit a cigarette, puffing quickly.

'Oh, Joaney, I am happy! Of course I am! I'm just a bit taken aback, that's all. I didn't expect this.' And worried, she added to herself, thinking of all the questions she really wanted to ask aloud instead. Like, how's his family going to react? How long is this divorce going to take? What are you going to do twenty years from now when you'll be forty and he'll be nearly seventy? But Claudia smiled instead, holding open her arms and Joaney gave a cry and hugged her soundly.

'Oh, you're such a good friend, Claudia. I mean, I know you think there are problems, but we can deal with them, can't we? I mean, we love each other, so everything else can be sorted out. Okay? You have to support me through this, Claudia, I need your help. Michael and I both need your help.' She let go of Claudia and collapsed backwards onto one of the sofas, curling up into a tight ball. Bundle jumped onto her lap and wheedled his way into the space between her and the sofa arm, singing contentedly a deep rumbling song while Joaney massaged under his chin.

'Well, of course I'll help. I'll always be right here for you.' Just don't ask me to break the news to Jason, that's all, Claudia thought to herself. Anything but that. She looked around the apartment, wondering what else she should say. It all seemed a bit flat. 'Um, shouldn't we celebrate, or something? Crack open some champagne?'

She saw Joaney's woebegone face brighten, the suspicious moisture in her eyes evaporate.

'There's some in the refrigerator. My mother gave it to me last time I saw her. She'd gag if she knew what we were using it to toast!'

'Then let's go for it. What about Michael? Where's he gone?' Claudia retrieved the bottle from the refrigerator and handed it to Joaney to open.

'To see his boss and to call his lawyer. Evidently he talked to his wife at Christmas and told her she could stay in the house – it's some ancestral pile or something and she's scared she'll be turfed out if they split – and that the eldest boy will get the house eventually, so she can relax. And she was fine about it. Agreed to say they'd been separated for over three years already, so the divorce'll go through smooth as silk. No problem.' Joaney was dismissive, waving the wife and her problems away with a waft of her slim young hand. Claudia felt her mouth tighten.

'And what about the kids? How were they about it all?' she asked and saw Joaney dip her eyes, concentrating on the cork as she expertly eased it out.

'Oh, they'll be fine. They're a bit confused and upset at the moment, naturally, but when they see how much

188

happier Michael is with me and they see that their lives won't change, that there'll be plenty of money for them, well ...' She trailed off, relegating the children to the back of her mind. 'Now, where are the glasses? Okay, here, now let's drink to Michael and me, to our happiness and to my parents not cutting off my trust fund.' She laughed gaily, but Claudia could hear the edge of hysteria in her voice.

'Can they do that?'

'No, no they can't. It's from my grandmother and she's dead, so my parents can't touch it. It was just a feeble joke. Tell you what, though,' Joaney added, as she stroked Bundle and stretched out on the sofa, 'let's not tell my family just yet. Let's wait until the divorce comes through, right? Then we can begin to work on them first, bring them round to it slowly and gently and not just drop it on them like a bombshell. What d'you think?' She looked up at Claudia eagerly.

'Yeah, I think that's a good idea.' Claudia smiled and sipped at her champagne, trying to control the nausea in her stomach. 'Why don't you have your parents to dinner here sometimes, just the four of you or maybe with Jason and me too? Get them used to seeing you as an adult with your own place and your own way of doing things. That might help, don't you think?' About as much as waving a stop sign in front of a herd of charging elephants, Claudia thought privately but she tried to be optimistic for Joaney's sake.

'Great idea! I'll ask them round on Friday night. And you can work on Jason, can't you? He's completely smitten by you, for all you give him the cold shoulder all the time. Can't you be a bit nicer to him, for my sake, and wrap him round your little finger? Hmm? Come on, Claudia, just for me? Pleeese!'

And that was how she began to find herself going out to tea and string music in the Palm Court of the Plaza Hotel, dinner at the 21 Club, to exhibitions of the modern at the Guggenheim, riding the elevator to the top and walking down the sloping gallery, to exhibitions of the old at the Museum of Metropolitan Art, to Verdi's *Aïda* on its opening night at the Metropolitan Opera or to see *West Side Story* on Broadway. It was so easy to fall in with such plans, to delight in savouring a side of New York she had not been able to afford, to happily see Jason Hewitt on a more regular basis, smiling at his witticisms, enjoying his polished company despite her own strict rules about not getting involved. And Jason began to have high hopes, although he repeated over and over to himself as he brought her home each time, don't rush it, don't rush it or you'll blow it. With things that he really wanted, Jason could be a patient man.

Which was why he made no demur when Claudia returned home again for her third summer, kissing her lightly on the lips, lingering for just a moment so that he saw her sway slightly, with her eyes closed, stepping away and saying he would miss her. He didn't offer to call her or write to her. He knew she wouldn't value him if he seemed eager.

And Claudia, delighted with his tact and humour, his air of always knowing how something should be done and of letting her in on the inside joke, wondered whether she should consider him seriously. True, she only saw him every other week at the moment and it was still difficult to fit even that in with all her work and Succi's as well, but, he was special ... And she didn't think special men grew on trees. But he would expect something more from her next year. Naïve as she was, even she knew that.

Chapter Seventeen

'Sweet boy, sweet dreams,' Aidan crooned to himself, rocking his head gently from side to side. 'Daddy's gone a hunting, keep still, my precious, shhh, gone to catch a rabbit skin,' he trailed off, humming sadly now, the thoughts spilling round the chaos of his clouded head. Mark nudged him with his foot but Aidan didn't look up, his neck cricked at an angle as he stared down at his hands. The humming continued, 'Poor baby, poor little girl gone away, Daddy's caught a rabbit skin to wrap poor baby bunting in . . .'

'He goes on a blinder every now and then, mixes everything up. Booze, drugs, uppers, downers, even Chinese herbal remedies, you name it. He can't forget killing that child, he's forever mooning on about it in some cracked fashion.'

Harry leaned over Aidan, pulling a face at the sour smell of him, at the foul breath that fogged that dim, dark space. He slapped his face lightly but Aidan didn't respond.

'Maybe he should get away for a while. Go visit some friends abroad, or something, go to a clinic and dry out,' Mark said, as they lifted him between them and carried him out of the low cot, Mark hitting his head against the metal bunk above it and cursing. The owner of the opium den smiled with relief, gold teeth winking in the gloom of sweet smoke.

'Tak' way! Dis time, no come back quick quick, no payee. Tak' way!' He scolded Aidan's recumbent form, a slack smile and glazed eyes showing no hint of hearing. Mark threw Aidan's dead weight up, so he could get a

191

better grip, and Harry skidded on some damp mess on the floor, almost falling. The lighting was dim but he could see several other bunks were occupied, the brooding dribble of opium pipes sucking away. He coughed and backed out into the tenement hall, gagging as the smell hit him, trying to remember that not so long ago he, too, had lived like this. It was a sobering thought.

'Drape him along the back seat and try and stuff his arms and legs in,' Mark ordered as they fought their way clear of the tenement and out into the street where his small sports car was parked. With a final grunt of exertion, they deposited Aidan in place and stood back, gasping.

'Shit, this is the second time this month, Harry. He's not gonna make it to the end of the year at this rate.' Mark sighed heavily. 'Where do we take him?'

'Beats me. His parents don't want to know any more and no one else'll take him. Your place or mine, I guess. But I'm on the air in less than an hour, so if it's all right with you, you better take him for the moment. I'll come by when I get off, take care of him then.' Harry saw the look on Mark's face and held up his hands. 'Okay, so what's your idea, then?'

'I don't have one, just yet. I guess I'll take him for a drive, let the fresh air get at him. You come and get him later, okay? Call me first.' He climbed into the car, raising a hand at Harry who shrugged.

'Okay, see you later.' Harry turned and began walking along Cheung Sha Wan Road towards the MTR underground station at Kowloon's Sham Shui Po. It was the quickest way he could make it to Commercial Radio on Hong Kong side before his new evening programme started at eight o'clock. He watched Mark reverse the car and head off down the street with an irritated squeal of tyres.

Aidan had hit rock bottom this time, Harry thought with the same guilty feeling of triumph that he always suppressed and felt deeply ashamed of. But it was there, and he knew it was his nature to be glad he had not someone else's destiny, that he was coming up in the world as others were going down, others with far more of a start than he had ever been given. Maybe it was all due to Yin and Yang, the two complementary halves of life, he thought, the way his mother had always said? How he had mocked her, with her old beliefs, and yet, perhaps, she had been right.

Aidan was Yin, a dark, negative force, and he, himself, was Yang, light, positive. He had his own programme and a loyal following that was increasing in numbers nightly. The producers thought he was hot and Harry gave them what they wanted, good music, good guest interviews, good tips on the 'in' places to eat and be seen.

So what if Aidan had given him that start, helped him find a job with prospects? He had done the rest himself and there was nothing more he could do for Aidan. Not now. There always had to be a Yin for there to be a Yang. You couldn't have one without the other, he reassured himself. It was just the way life worked.

Once, he might have thought of telling Aidan the truth about what Yee was up to. As much as he knew of it and more that he suspected. But there was no point now. Who would Aidan tell? And who would believe him? Besides, Harry was clear of all that side of things now and not about to involve himself again. Not when there was so much at stake, his whole future, the sort of people he would choose to spend his life with, like Liddie, when she finally came back ... He wasn't about to give up the dream for a vague nag of guilt.

He ducked down the tiled stairs into the MTR station.

Mark, driving fast down the neon flashing lights of Waterloo Road, across the interchange into Princess Margaret Road, down through Hong Chong Road and into the dim roar of the Harbour Tunnel, barely gave Aidan a thought. He was late to meet Yee. He drove with concentrated ferocity, meeting the mêlée of cars that spilled out of the tunnel and thrusting ahead so that he turned left along Victoria Park. Yee had said he would meet him at the Tin Hau Temple. It was barely dusk, the street lights forcing the shadows to hurry along before the violet mantle of night could settle. He drove more slowly now, unsure of his way.

Normally, Yee never came to see him in person but sent a junior member to give him his ticket and papers, to explain where to go. But Yee had requested a meeting in person this time and Mark didn't want to be late. Not when he already owed the money he would earn from this trip. He needed Yee. Uneasily, he wondered if it had been seven, he was supposed to meet Yee – or eight? For a moment he was uncertain. No, no, it had been seven, surely?

He skirted around the back of the park onto Causeway Road, hesitating when he reached King's Road and found it was one way and against him. He looped right, back onto Tin Hau Temple Road and passed the temple before he could find somewhere to park, cursing in his frustration. He was late, damn, he was late!

The streets were thronged with evening shoppers, stall sellers, hawkers with their wares spread out on newspaper across the pavement, old women urging him to buy shards of jade or soapstone to protect him. Fortune tellers were doing a steady trade, the clattering spill of sticks adding to his sense of disorientation. In a far corner, on a raised platform, he could hear the piercing shrieks and howls of an outdoor opera, the cymbals and tambourines beating in time as the crowd swayed and gasped at the painted figures prancing about. An old man, his wares balanced in two straw baskets, buffeted past him and Mark grunted with annoyance as he was hit behind the knees.

The temple, in contrast, was a shadowed oasis of still quiet. He hurried along the street to it, passing by the carved portals and immediately a hush descended, the soft, slippered sound of bare feet and the faint murmur of chanting from a great distance all that disturbed that calm. A few worshippers were bent over candles in the corner and he wandered past, turning through this passageway and that, increasingly anxious as he could find no sign of Yee.

It was deep in the fifth chamber he came to, coiling amber incense spirals clustering along the ceiling like baskets and spilling sweet, choking smoke in trails down over the stone floor, that he found Yee. He paused in the shadows, glimpsing something odd that made him hesitate before revealing himself.

There were no other worshippers this far back in the temple's labyrinth of rooms, opening one on the other, the occasional garden allowing a dim light to filter through. The braziers glowed redly, like jewels in the dark sweet thickness of air, catching the lacquered gold and red of a buddha-like statue in its gleam.

Mark fingered the camera he had slipped in his pocket, determined to catch a shot of Yee if ever the chance arose, just for insurance sake. He now felt it heavy and burdensome against him, a liability, perhaps worse. He considered hiding it, throwing it away. But still, it would be good to have something on Yee. He hesitated.

Yee was not alone. There were two figures with him, one, whom Mark did not recognise, a middle-aged man, heavy featured and greying. The other was partially concealed by the shadows and Mark could not see him clearly.

He waited, unwilling to break in on them, hearing their voices murmuring together. Strangely, Yee did not seem to be the one in charge. He was deferring to both men, particularly the one in deep shadow. Mark felt a prickle of fear where the perspiration ran down his temple and his throat grew dry.

Something odd, something, he knew instinctively, that he should not be watching, was taking place. A package was passed to the middle-aged man who took it and hid it in the folds of his jacket. There were more murmurs, as though a deal were being struck. Mark drew back into the deep shadows of a pillar and waited, his back pressed against the stone, trying to disappear into it. If Yee knew he were watching ... Mark swallowed bitter bile, his breath rising into a pant. He wanted to turn and run but he knew that would be fatal. Better to hide, say nothing, pretend it had never been witnessed. The camera pressed, sharp, into his leg.

It was as they were leaving, their voices rising for a moment as they moved apart from each other, that Mark ventured to lean forward and look again. They moved to

195

skirt the courtyard and, for a moment, all three became visible. Almost without thinking, Mark raised his camera and snapped the shot. It snicked, appallingly loud, in the confines of that chamber and Mark drew back immediately, pressing himself to the wall, fumbling along it until he found an embrasure into which to fit the camera. The men paused, looking around warily, but there was no further sound and they turned and hurried away, each through a separate door.

A figure brushed by, close to Mark, and he saw the tall, squared shoulders, the arrogant tilt to the head, the glint of steel-rimmed glasses and knew who the third man had been.

For long minutes of silence, he continued to cower in the shadows and then, finally, he peered out. There was no one there.

Shaking, he withdrew from the chamber, and turned back the way he had come. He reached the outer courtyard unchallenged and sat himself down on a stone bench, letting his heart quiet and his breathing return to normal. Fumbling for his handkerchief, he wiped his face carefully, sitting still and emptying his mind. Finally, he stood up and went out to the entrance of the temple. Night had fallen and the opera was meandering into its third act. He leaned against the pillar and watched the time slowly tick away until eight.

A hand touched his shoulder and he turned, calm and in control, looking into Yee's eyes with innocence.

When his meeting with Yee was completed successfully and he had the tickets and destination carefully put away in his pocket, Mark returned to his car. Aidan was gone. He shrugged, wondering where he would turn up next and then, weary with the release of fear, he climbed in and began the long drive home. His mind whirled with the dull pain of a tension headache that he knew would soon build into a migraine. But his thoughts would not be quiet. They pricked and jabbed at him as he drove. What on earth had Yee been doing with those particular two men? What the

196

hell was going on? And the consequences of what he had seen, and what it might mean if he were discovered, made him swallow tightly on a dry throat.

It was still some days before Mark could return for the camera he had hidden in the embrasure, and several more before he could discover who the second man, the greying, middle-aged one, was. But when he did, he sat putty-faced with fear, long into the night, wondering what the hell he was going to do.

New York
September, 1982
The phone rang again and Claudia sighed heavily as Bundle jumped to the ground and made off in a huff, his tail straight as a quiff in the air. She pushed her books to one side, turned Rod down, crooning away about Maggie on the stereo, and picked up the phone.

'Hello? Excuse me, what? You're a friend of who?' She sat down on the sofa, squinting as she tried to hear the faint voice. There were background noises, tinny tannoyed voices, whistles blowing, an empty cavernous sound.

'Mark. Your brother.' It came through fragmented.

'Mark? Where are you calling from?' She flicked her hand angrily at Bundle who was using her inattention as an excuse to exercise his claws on the furniture. Bundle continued, ignoring her, but his grey eyes slanted with mischief.

'Grand Central Station. He gave me a package for you. I didn't want to come all the way over there if you weren't home. You going to be in for a while?' the disembodied voice said and Claudia strained to work out its gender.

'Uh, yes, I guess. But you could just mail it to me if you wanted. I mean, you're right the other side of town and it's miserably hot. If it's a bit of a hassle for you—'

'If Mark had wanted it posted, he'd have done that himself. I'll bring it over.' The line clicked dead in her hand and Claudia slowly replaced the receiver, feeling unpleasantly soiled, as though she had come up against something repellent.

Who was this friend of Mark's? What was he or she? She wrinkled her face in distaste and turned up the music again, wishing Joaney would come home and keep her company.

For the next twenty minutes she alternated between restless pacing up and down the length of the living room, chasing Bundle around the room as he again savaged the furniture to get her attention, and blank staring out the window at the mud-slabbed doldrums of the river. The books, lying open on the sofa, that she needed to read for her next lecture, were forgotten.

Her mind focused instead on the strange letters Mark had sent her during the summer, rambling, sometimes incoherent letters about himself and Harry, how their friendship had cemented itself from an unlikely beginning that he never quite explained to her. She smiled at the thought of Harry and Mark being friends now, drawing in a deep sigh of nostalgia for the boys she had once known. But it was an uncomfortable nostalgia, wondering which of the two had changed so much that they could now be friends.

And it was obvious there was more that Mark wasn't telling her, veering off into rhapsodies about the East that she barely remembered, hiding what was really on his mind. He wrote about how he belonged there, in the East, how it breathed the same air as he did, about how it only truly understood his needs. His needs? What exactly were those, for God's sake? And what had he sent her?

Eventually, and far sooner than she had hoped, the intercom sounded. She hesitated and then made up her mind.

'Hello? Yes, come up, fourth floor, four B.' And then she sped across the room to the telephone and snatched it up, punching in the numbers.

'Hello, Jason? Yes, just now ... listen, Jason, I'll tell you all about that later but I need you to come over here right now ..., no there's this guy, I think it's a guy ... oh, Lord, he's at the door now. Look, can you just come quickly? You could be here in five minutes on a Sunday night ... I don't know! I just feel uneasy ... okay, thanks, 'bye.' She

198

replaced the receiver, wondering whether she was being foolish, whether it had been a sensible move to involve Jason. But it was done now.

'Hold on! I'm coming. I just have to put the dog in the other room. He doesn't like strangers.' She waited a couple more minutes and then opened the door on the chain.

A young man stood there, around six feet tall, dark haired, dark eyed with pouchy cheeks, a line of stubble over his chin and the sort of grey skin that only comes from leading a nocturnal existence. He was dressed in a dark raincoat and jeans despite it being September and still swelteringly hot. For all his seediness, there was an air of indefinable elegance in his movements, the way he tilted his head. Hamlet, down on the skids, Claudia thought to herself. She had never liked Hamlet much.

'Yes?' Her eyes took in all the necessary details and produced a warning sounding away deep inside her.

He smiled. 'Aren't you even going to let me in? I came all this way ...' A look of deep interest sparked from those dark circled eyes, at odds with his appearance, as he looked her over.

Claudia hesitated. 'I'm sorry, but exactly who are you?'

'I told you, I'm a friend of Mark's.' Stressed patiently. 'And I have something for you but I'm not going to hand it over out here. Look, I've come a long way to do this favour for Mark, so do you want it or not?' His voice was high and faintly wheezing, pretending to an amusement he didn't feel.

Claudia paused, unsure what to do. 'I'm sorry, I don't mean to seem rude or anything, but I don't know you at all and this is New York. Have you got something you could show me that would prove you're a friend of Mark's? What's your name?'

She sensed his irritation from the way he stepped from side to side, shaking his head while he searched in his pockets. He glanced up at her, a quick look of disquieting intelligence.

'I'm Fish – Aidan Lockhart but everyone calls me Fish. No guesses why!' When he smiled, his lips thinned so that

199

they seemed to disappear inside his mouth. Fatigue had made bruised sockets of his eyes.

Claudia smiled tentatively and shook her head. 'I don't ... no, not really. Why?'

'Ah, well, if you don't know the cliché, never mind. Here, this is a letter to you from Mark that goes with the package. Will that satisfy you?' He passed it to her with thin, elegant fingers.

Claudia slit the letter open, quickly scanning its contents, the words 'Fish' and 'package' jumping out at her. She smiled awkwardly at the man.

'Sorry. I'll just ...' She closed the door, released the safety chain and opened the door wide. 'Come in.' She gestured for him to enter and he stepped over the lintel, glancing around himself silently, his face making no signals. Bundle, perched on the dresser in the corner, watched the stranger with narrow-eyed interest.

'I guess I get a bit paranoid sometimes. Sorry.' She shrugged and he gave her another sharp look. Claudia had the oddest feeling that he was nothing at all like the figure he projected. It was merely a useful disguise. Was he playing some role for her sole benefit or was it for everyone's consumption?

'Never hurts. Nice place. You must be doing very well here. Are you and Mark doing business together or something?' He sat down, still in his raincoat.

Claudia shook her head, puzzled. 'Doing business together? No, I haven't seen Mark since I was seven. Why? What sort of business?' She felt as uneasy as she had when she first heard this man's strange, high-pitched voice. English, cultured but odd. 'What are you talking about?'

The man shrugged. 'Just wondered. You being a student. Mark told me you were on a scholarship. I just wondered how you afforded a place like this.' They both looked around the large, sun-filled room, Claudia seeing afresh the expensive simplicity of the golden floorboards, the pale earth-coloured furniture, the kilims and pottery, the large-leafed, glossy green of ficus trees in wicker pots. Yes, it was quite a place.

200

'Oh, I see. It's not mine. A friend owns it and I just pay a minimal rent.'

'Nice if you can get it. Is he home?' Again the dark eyes darted around.

'She and no, she's not. But I am expecting her brother to turn up any moment so perhaps you better give me this precious package right now. Would you like some coffee?' She walked around the counter that separated the kitchen from the living room, irritated by his probing. It wasn't quite rude, but near enough.

'Yes, that'd be great. Unless, of course, you've got a beer instead?' He glanced up at her and suddenly the loose pouchy flesh, the name 'Fish', made sense to her.

'No, sorry,' she said firmly and put the kettle on. 'Let me just read this letter. You make yourself comfortable, okay?' She called and unfolded the letter again.

'Yes, fine. So, what type of dog do you have?'

'A pit bull.' Claudia smiled sweetly and turned back to the letter.

Dear Claudia,

I'm taking the chance to send you this package via a friend of mine, Aidan Lockhart (Fish to most of us), who is passing through. Be nice to him, will you? He drinks a bit but is basically a good guy going through a rough time.

['A good guy?' Claudia thought to herself in dismay. What was wrong with Mark's judgement. A good guy! She read on quickly.]

'Don't try and open the package, just put it away carefully for me. I don't trust anyone here to look after it for me. It's my insurance, sort of. I can't really explain and I must rush to get this off. Don't get too nosy, Liddie, just trust me and keep it safe. Believe me, it's important.

Lots of love, Mark

Claudia folded up the letter and looked at Fish again. He smiled tightly back at her.

'All understood now? You want the package?' He

reached into his raincoat pocket.

'About as clear as mud but I guess if Mark wants me to look after it, then I will. You don't have any idea what's in it?' She reluctantly came forward and took the paper-wrapped box from Fish's outstretched hand, examining the wax seal with interest.

'Me? No. Mark just used me as a courier. I don't know what's in it. I thought you did. I thought you knew all about it, in fact.' For all the laziness of his posture, sprawled across the sofa, his eyes were quick, following her every thought and mood. Claudia bit back on a retort.

'No, I don't know anything about it. He just wants me to keep it safe. He called it his insurance ...' She broke the seal and undid the paper wrapping, revealing a small carved wooden box, of the sort that were sold in endless gimcrack Oriental stores south of Canal Street. There did not appear to be any way of opening it for all Mark had asked her not to try.

'Well, nice little Nancy Drew mystery, isn't it?' She laughed drily. 'Shall I shake it?' She did but nothing rustled or rattled inside.

'You aren't going to open it?' The interest was unsettling. But then, he had been the courier. It was understandable to be intrigued, she reminded herself. She looked at him and shrugged.

'No. I can't. I don't know how and Mark asked me not to. Just to put it away safe somewhere. One of his less amusing teases, I imagine.' She sighed and put it down on the table. 'The kettle's boiling.' She walked back into the kitchen leaving the box, and was not surprised to see Fish pick it up and examine it closely. Then he put it down again abruptly and stood up.

'Well,' he smiled but there was deep disappointment there in his eyes, in his controlled movements, as though the fatigue had suddenly become too much. 'I guess I better be going. I didn't realise how late it is and I have a plane to catch. I'll give him your regards, shall I?'

'Yes, do. But ... aren't you going to have your coffee first? I thought we could have a nice, long gossip and you could tell me all about Mark and Harry and everyone ...' Claudia was startled. 'You're not flying back right this minute, are you?'

'No, I have another friend to see first in DC. Thanks, but I can't stay for the coffee or the chat. Perhaps another time. 'Bye.' And then he marched across the room and out the door, his raincoat flapping as he went. He almost collided with someone in the hall, sharp words being exchanged, and then the door opened and Jason walked in.

'Oh, hi.' Claudia felt foolish suddenly, seeing Jason. He looked dishevelled and pale, his normally immaculate hair ruffled by the wind, the Wall Street suit replaced by worn jeans and a sweat shirt. He looked like he had been asleep and had been woken by a bad dream. He halted, blowing out his cheeks in a long sigh.

'That the guy? The one who just cannoned into me in the hall?' He jerked his thumb towards the door. 'You okay? He didn't do anything?'

She smiled shyly, pleased at his concern. 'No, no, I'm fine but thanks for rushing over. It was really good of you. He was definitely odd. I invented a pit bull in the bedroom, would you believe?' She came forward to kiss his cheek and was startled when he wrapped his arms around her, hugging her soundly and giving a shaky laugh. He kissed her full on the mouth and she felt a stirring of something inside her, sort of quivering and warm and definitely nice. He broke away finally and laughed again.

'Maybe I ought to get you a pit bull for real instead of that mangy cat. Look, I'm illegally parked. I better go do something with it. You want to go out tonight? See a movie, grab a meal somewhere?' He was back in control, casual and friendly. Claudia nodded.

'Yes, I'd love to. Hold on while I just sort Bundle out with some milk and he is not a mangy cat, so keep your rude remarks about him to yourself!' she protested. 'Can you grab my bag for me? It's on the table.'

'Okay. You can tell me all about your odd visitor over a drink. Say, this is new, isn't it? What is it, a cigarette box?' Jason held the box aloft, turning it this way and that.

Claudia shrugged. 'Something my brother sent me for safe keeping. He called it his "insurance". That guy just dropped it off. Come on, let's go or you'll get towed.' And she watched him put it down on the table.

'All the way from Hong Kong? Must be important insurance. What's in it?' He eyed it again, speculatively.

'No idea.' She frowned. 'Mark said not to get nosy ... Oh, wait, I need a new cheque book.' She dashed into the bedroom and rummaged in her wardrobe, calling, 'Just one of his little jokes, I expect. He can be a dreadful tease. I guess he thinks I'm going to spend days and nights trying to figure out how to open it and all there'll be inside will be an April Fool's note. Definitely Mark's style.' She laughed.

'Look, Claudia, I'll be down in the car, okay. Come on down when you're ready.' She heard Jason call and she straightened and frowned as she heard the door slam after him. His precious car, she thought with amusement. Then she pulled open drawer after drawer until she found the cheque book. Slipping it quickly into her bag, she followed Jason out into the hall, locking the door carefully behind her.

Later, when she re-entered the apartment, she didn't notice that the box was missing. It wasn't for some weeks that she thought of it at all and by then she assumed it had been put away somewhere and would re-emerge at some point. She had assured Mark by letter that she had it safe and she was sure she did, somewhere. And, besides, there were more important things on her mind by then. Like Jason.

He had been attentive for the last few weeks, relaxing with her in a way that he had never seemed able to do before, turning up in jeans, with a pizza in hand, late at night, or suggesting bike rides along the winding lanes of Westchester or long walks in Central Park on the weekend instead of the theatre or expensive lunches that had previously occupied them.

Occasionally he drove her out of Manhattan for the day, to the yacht club at City Island, fresh and preppy like a New England fishing village, or to Southampton or Fire

Island, to walk along the almost deserted shoreline now that it was getting closer to winter, enjoying the thundering crash of grey flumed waves and the wind that whipped through their hair. And they talked and talked, huddling close together for warmth, occasionally kissing or hugging, but nothing more. Never anything more.

Until the weekend he suggested she come with him to Newport. And Claudia knew that the time had come to make a choice.

They set off on a Friday night, driving out through the late-evening rush hour, Claudia tense and uncomfortable beside Jason. For once she was unable to enjoy the plushness of his BMW or the beauty of the city lit up and glittering around her as it reflected in the puddles on the street or was obscured by rushing geysers of steam from some basement source. She was silent for some time, listening to the endless classical tapes of Mahler that Jason liked to play, cocooned in her own thoughts.

Once they were clear of the New York sprawl and coasting down the New Jersey turnpike, the woods a brilliant splash of copper, bronze, and topaz in the headlights, Jason leaned over and took her hand in his. It was cold and stiff. He released it without comment.

It was nearly midnight by the time they arrived at the inn, coyly named 'The Pilgrim's Pleasure' and nestled in amongst larch and conifers, the white picket fence gleaming as Jason drew the car into the driveway and scrunched to a stop on the gravel. Claudia could feel her heart hammering in her chest, her hands cold and clammy with nerves. She risked a glance at Jason.

'Have you been here before?' she ventured and saw his brows contract. She thought she heard him sigh.

'Meaning, have I brought other girls here before? No, Claudia, I haven't,' he said steadily.

Claudia flushed. 'I didn't mean that at all, actually. I just wondered whether the hotel was better than its name.' She climbed out of the car, feeling stiff and irritable.

The night was chill and thin, and Claudia huddled into herself and walked towards the front porch. She didn't wait

205

for Jason but ran lightly up the steps and through the front door. Immediately the wind died and the atmosphere changed into one of warmth and snugness, the glow of parchment lampshades and a roaring fire lighting the mellow panelled walls and the curtains drawn tightly against the raw night. Only one man was on duty, sitting reading behind the mahogany deskfront. He looked up and smiled.

'You must be the Hewitt party? Is Mr Hewitt outside still? Ah, no, here he is. You go and get yourself warm by the fire. It's a cold'un tonight, isn't it? Winter's on the way.' He nodded firmly, as though that point were settled and took the two overnight cases from Jason.

Claudia glanced at him. 'I'm tired. I'd like to go straight up ...'

'Well, miss, that's just what I thought. You'll want to go straight up. Your rooms have both got fires lit and the beds have been turned down.' The desk clerk led the way.

Claudia's room was large and comfortable, an iron four-poster bed with a patchwork quilt and white cotton pillow-cases all plumped and ready for her, a wing-chair by the fireplace, and rag rugs on polished boards. A prim Puritan mother looked down in disapproval from above the mantel-piece. Claudia sighed with relief when the desk clerk deposited her bag on a folding stand and bade her a brief goodnight.

Jason, who had remained outside the room, followed the man without a word to her, and she sat on the bed, feeling it spring lightly beneath her. She wondered whether Jason was tense too. But no, why should he be? This was no novelty to him; he knew exactly what to expect. Reluct-antly, she turned to unpack her bag.

It didn't take her long. She waited for a while, thinking he might come and say goodnight. But when he didn't return, she undressed quickly and pulled on her night-gown. It was a long slip of ivory satin that she had been given by Joaney for her last birthday and had been saving for a special occasion, she thought with a laugh that was almost despair.

Angrily she brushed out her hair, stared at herself in the mirror, at the smooth curves and glides of silk that encased her body, and then she looked around the room. All set for the seduction scene, she mocked herself, just no seducer.

She turned the light off and settled herself comfortably into the soft warmth of the bed. It took no more than five minutes for her to drift off into sleep.

She was woken by the bed rocking beneath her and the warm slide of a hand down her hip. She stiffened and a soft kiss was planted behind her ear, a body curving itself into her, the warmth and firmness disturbing. She breathed out slowly.

'Jason?'

'Yes, it's me. Don't worry, don't be frightened.'

'I'm not frightened,' she lied, trying to ease the stiffness in her back. 'I'm just sorry about earlier. I guess I got a bit uptight.' She felt an arm encircle her, pulling her in tight against him, her buttocks fitting neatly into his lap. A hand gently cupped her breast, feeling her through the sheer silk and becoming bolder as she did not resist.

'I know. It's all right. You're still so very young, it's all new and strange to you. It's normal to get scared.' He hesitated, assessing her. 'You know I love you, don't you?' He knew he had been right when he felt her relax in his arms, settling against him. He kissed her shoulder and up her neck into her hair, and Claudia leaned against him, enjoying the explorations of his hands, the way they slid down her belly, lingering between her legs, the silk smooth and sensuous against her skin.

'Do you?' she murmured, pleased and faintly breathless with relief. 'I thought you'd prefer women to be experienced and sophisticated.' She heard him laugh softly.

'Women, yes. But not you. I want you young and untouched and all mine,' he whispered, and she felt a shiver of both pleasure and unease at his words. He rolled her onto her back and lay half across her, kissing her deeply, his tongue probing aggressively now, his manner changing.

'You are mine, aren't you, Claudia? There isn't anyone else?' he asked, his voice troubled and Claudia shook her head.

207

'No one else, Jason,' she breathed, telling herself it was true. Harry was a mere figment of her imagination, a childhood friend who would, almost certainly, turn out to be nothing like the boy she remembered. And Bo ... he was the disillusioned past. There was no one else now. No reason to hold back ... And Jason loved her.

He pulled at the straps of her nightgown, pushing it down to her waist as he kissed her throat and his hands clasped her small breasts, feeling their light weight, revelling in their smoothness, their defencelessness, the long curve down to her tiny waist.

'Put your arms above your head. That's it,' he ordered her and he slid the nightgown up over her thighs so that it barely skimmed her buttocks. Claudia felt weak-bellied beneath his hard hands, the way his fingers dug into her flesh, his mouth moving wetly over her breasts, up to her throat again, kissing her mouth again deeply as he held her arms up hard above her. He twisted her hands in amongst the railings of the bedhead, jamming them in place with a pillow and Claudia realised dimly that he wanted to hold her down.

She struggled, protesting, but he kissed her again and she relaxed against him, surrendering herself to the hard caresses, the way he had pushed her legs apart and was feeling between her legs now, oh, so gently, probing and exciting, touching the slick wetness of her most private parts, toying with her, so that she had to draw in her breath to conceal the gasp of pleasure that finger had produced.

He teased and touched, raising her excitement to almost frenzy pitch and then letting it damp down again as he returned to her breasts, kissing between them, holding them tight against his face. He never once looked at her to see her reactions, merely taking it for granted that she was enjoying his manipulations of her body. And she was, she thought in dazed surprise, the aching emptiness between her legs beginning to overpower her. She tried to lower her arms to caress him but he held them down with the pillow, pushing himself onto her and between her legs. She stiffened as she felt the hardness pressing against her.

'Don't tense up, darling. Just lie quiet and wrap your legs around me. It may hurt a bit. I can't help that.' And it's about time you felt that hurt, he thought savagely, his pulse hammering in his throat, his patience at an end as his control began to slip. He thrust up smoothly and deeply into her, feeling the barrier swept away as he plunged into the tight wet warmth. He heard her cry out dimly but he was too busy living out his fantasy, the fantasy that had kept him awake night after night, of mastering her, of pushing her legs apart and pumping into her again and again while he held her down and she resisted ...

When at last he came, he cried out deeply and collapsed onto her, his fingers digging into her breasts, his mouth sucking the skin of her neck until an angry red welt appeared. His mark, he thought. He would like to brand her, right there on her shoulder. Property of Jason Hewitt. Hell, maybe he would, too. His crest? A tattoo. Something so that she and everyone else knew who she belonged to.

He slid out of her and rolled her over, kissing her face for all she tried to turn it this way and that to escape him, feeling his desire building again but holding it in check. Not yet, not just yet, let her sleep a bit and then he would do it to her again.

'Shh, don't fight me, baby. I'm sorry if I hurt you but that's the way it goes, the first time. You'll enjoy it more when you get better at it and learn to relax.' And he held her in his arms, not letting her struggle away from him. 'Shh, baby, the next time will be better. And I'll be gentler. I just wanted you for so long, I couldn't help it. Shh, darling, shh.' And, finally, she lay still in his arms, her bottom tucked into his lap as before except that now it was damp from him and he held her in place with a hand through her legs, laying claim to all that lay beneath his touch. And Claudia lay there aching and battered, hoping he never touched her again.

But he was so kind and understanding again when he woke, holding her so tenderly, stroking her face with his fingers and marvelling at her beauty, that she wondered

209

whether she had imagined his brutality the night before. Maybe it had been her fear and her tenseness that had made it seem so harsh, so domineering. And he hadn't tried to make love to her again, content to cradle her in his arms, occasionally kissing her, whispering endearments.

By first light she was convinced she had over-reacted. He might have been a bit hasty, a bit more physical than he needed to be but he had held himself back for nearly two years. It wouldn't happen again.

'I'm going to go back to my room now, darling. I ordered breakfast in bed for you and I don't want the maid to find me here,' he whispered, kissing her shoulder and climbing out of bed, his body compact and muscular as he slipped into his robe.

'But, why not?' she protested, wanting to enjoy the morning, the cuddling in bed, the shared breakfast. 'It's the eighties, for God's sake, Jason! No one's going to care in the slightest.' But his face was stubborn and faintly patronising, as though she couldn't possibly understand.

'But I care. About your reputation and about doing this right. Besides, I like to read the paper undisturbed in the mornings. You enjoy your breakfast, sweetheart.' And he kissed her tenderly on her bruised mouth, his eyes darkening as he took in her dishevelled state, the way the sheet had slipped revealing her breasts, pink-tipped against translucent skin. It was with an effort that he pushed himself away. She wasn't ready yet.

For the next few weeks, Claudia didn't know what to make of Jason, or of herself. She enjoyed his company still, his gentleness when he caressed her, his protectiveness when they went out to the endless cocktails that he now seemed to expect her to attend. She even enjoyed most of their lovemaking, when he was considerate and careful. But every now and then, as if a black mood had descended on him, he would become brutal and masterful, forcing her to do things that left her tearful and bruised, shaking with anger and a sick fear that she couldn't explain to anyone. She wasn't sure if she was the one who was inadequate or whether there really was something wrong with Jason. If only she had someone she could talk to, ask. But Joaney was his sister. She couldn't ask her. And she wasn't close enough to anyone else.

And so she hid her bruises and her shaking hands, forcing herself to smile and act as though nothing had happened and Jason would gradually let himself off his tight leash more often. Claudia, numbed with the way everyone was assuming that she was blissfully happy and slyly asking when she would start wearing a ring, continued to smile even when Jason started demanding she give up her job at Succi's, that she forget about graduating. What did she need a career for now that she was to be his wife, he demanded? But Claudia shook her head and said she couldn't think about marriage until she graduated and she wouldn't take any money from him until they had a formal understanding.

It was her one defiance, her one absolutely adamant condition and Jason, sensing that he had pushed her as far as he could, backed down. She could have until next June. But then she was his.

Chapter Eighteen

Hong Kong
Chinese New Year, 1983

It was the Year of the Pig. A huge, glistening boar, lit up in a thousand flashing lights, hung suspended over Chater Road in Kowloon, illuminating briefly the people who scurried below it. A woman, her young face straining beneath the weight of heavy bags, paused to readjust the baby she carried on her back. It lay sleeping quietly, its dark, silky head leaning against her, its fat cheeks pink in the chill wind from the harbour, and eyelashes quivering. She drew the flaps of his quilted hat tighter under his chin and slung him on her back again.

Beside her, a man carrying a small kumquat tree that was just about to blossom, a symbol of hoped-for bounty in the new year, tripped over her bags, sending their contents sprawling. He didn't stop, stumbling over the food and cheap market clothes, to hasten home to his new bride. The woman cursed and bent to scoop her shopping together. Another woman, old and huddled into a silk padded jacket, bent to help her.

There was a squeal of tyres, horns blaring and screams. Both women looked up, their mouths opening to cry out, their hands going up as though flimsily to protect them as the mudguard of the lorry smashed into them, picking the woman with the baby up and pinning her for a moment against its bumper. It crashed through into a shop before coming to a halt against the counter. The woman was flung to the far side of the shop, landing on a red banner that proclaimed '*Kung Hei Fat Choy!* May you be blessed with prosperity!' Neither woman nor child moved.

Outside, the smeared remains of the older woman were

drawing a fascinated crowd. A young man, a small tree still clutched in his hands, looked down in disbelief at the remains of what had once been his leg. In chalked pallor, he pleaded for someone to help him, his bloody hands letting the tree slip from his grasp to lie stickily coated in the thick red gore that began below his knee. His voice rose into a keening shriek.

By the time Tony arrived, the older woman's husband had wandered down the street, wondering where his wife could be when she had only gone out for a chicken. He didn't recognise her, seeing only her jacket, and faltering, his face which had seemed mildly preoccupied a moment before becoming quite still. Tony saw him totter to one side, grasping at the rear fender of the lorry. He lowered himself to his knees beside the remains of what had only a few minutes before been his wife.

Tony looked at his corporal, gesturing to the old man.

'Help him. Find out his name and hers, if you can. Then take him home. Ng, I want you to cordon off the area, get these people back, make sure there's no looting. Get names and addresses of any witnesses.' He turned away from the pain he saw in the old man's face, trying not to let it touch him and thus cloud his mind, hamper his actions.

'That's the ambulance now, Chu. I want that injured man attended to first. The woman is past it anyway. Then join me inside.'

He stepped over the smashed remains of the shop front, peering beneath the wheels of the lorry. A pair of legs protruded, twisted and caught by the display case. They were male and didn't move. He searched in amongst the wrecked cab of the lorry but there was no one trapped in there. Sighing, he turned back to the two shopgirls who huddled, dazed and crying in the back. And then he saw them.

The woman and her baby lay close together, the little one's mouth opened wide as though in surprise, his hat still pulled tightly around his pink cheeks. His mother lay on her side, arms sprawled out and fingers clenched in the sharp debris beside her, her face almost obscured beneath her long, dark hair.

213

They were neatly skewered together by a particularly long metal rod that appeared to have come from the window awning. It glistened slickly, changing colour with the hues of a string of lights suspended from the ceiling, from gold to green to bright, fiery red.

'Oh, dear God ...' Tony murmured and for a moment closed his eyes, trying to summon the strength to remain calm, to not rail and scream and vent the corroding anger inside. He stood quite still, shaking with the force of that control, until he knew he could manage it.

Slowly, he covered them with a coat that still hung from a hook by the door. He felt ill with pity and rage churning deep in the pit of his stomach but he forced it down. He had seen enough of such butchery in the last few weeks. This was just another, he told himself. And he tried not to see the baby's face when he gently closed its eyes.

He turned back to the girls, noticing that one of them had vomited down herself. It steamed in the chill air.

'Are you all right? Are you hurt?' he asked but the girls continued to sob hysterically.

Sergeant Chu put his head through the smashed shop front. 'Where's the driver gone, sir?' he asked.

'I don't know yet. These girls must have seen him but they're too shaken up right now. There's another three dead in here,' Tony replied, answering in the same Cantonese. Chu peered under the lorry and sighed.

'He – he ran away. He was wearing a crash helmet, like on a motorcycle, you know, with a dark visor, and black leather all over him and he climbed down and ran out through the back, that way,' one of the girls said suddenly, her tear-stained face ugly in its horror.

'How long ago?'

'Five, maybe ten minutes. He's gone.'

'Right. Check the papers, Chu, and radio in the registration. Track down who owns the lorry.' But Tony already knew they would find it stolen. It was the third case of a car or lorry being driven through a shop front that month. The owners refused to pay up their protection money and this was the warning to all the others who were considering resisting. It made people's minds up fast.

'The man under the lorry, that's the shop owner?' Tony asked and both girls nodded their heads. 'He's no connection of yours, is he?' They shook their heads. 'Well, I'd like you both to come down to the station, if you will? Give a statement of what you saw,' Tony said gently, seeing the fear spring back into the first girl's eyes. Her companion continued to sob. Sergeant Chu watched Tony, wondering if he knew what he was asking.

The first girl shook her head again. 'No, no, I didn't see anything. I was mistaken.' She stared defiantly at the ground and Sergeant Chu heard Tony sigh.

'It's all right. We know what happened here. You can't identify anyone so you'll just be telling us the bare details—'

'No! No, I can't! It would be more than my life is worth, to be seen to go with you. Don't you see?' she shrieked and Tony leaned forward and held her tightly in his arms, feeling that frail body shuddering with terror. He soothed her, looking in distress at his sergeant, who shrugged.

'She's right, sir.'

'I can't!' The girl wailed again and Tony held her tightly in silence. He looked around the smashed shop, the lumped-up coat that concealed the mother and child, the blood splashed across the counters. Something inside him became quite still.

'Yes,' he murmured, finally. 'I see.'

New York, 1983

Michael Glendinning's divorce came through in the spring of 1983 and Joaney and he were married quietly, a few days later in a civil ceremony, with only Claudia and a couple of close friends present. They planned a small celebration party at which to launch the news on the Hewitt family and their friends.

Claudia argued repeatedly against such an idea, but they were sure it was the best way. The Hewitts were such an old guard family, they would never make a fuss in front of

215

friends and relatives and besides, they seemed to like Michael now, having often met him at Joaney's side. They were treating him like a trusted friend. Why would they object, they argued and Claudia closed her eyes in exasperation.

'It's not your parents I'm worried about,' she had said but they had overridden her objections, sending out invitations for cocktails on Saturday night.

On Friday night, sensing that it would be better if Jason knew in advance, she attempted to bring up Michael's name, forcing herself to sound light-hearted as she strolled from the window.

'It's such lovely weather at the moment.' She glanced across at Jason as he sat staring at the television. 'Michael says it's just like London in the spring, all the daffodils and the trees with fresh new leaves ...' She wandered over to him, curling up on the sofa beside him.

'Then why doesn't he go back and see it for himself? Do us all a favour,' Jason remarked coldly. He continued to watch the screen, without turning around.

Claudia bit her lip. 'Oh, I rather think he's putting down roots here, maybe going to stay permanently. That'd be nice for Joaney, wouldn't it?' she pressed and heard Jason sigh sharply in irritation. 'I mean, they're so fond—'

'Oh, for Christ's sake, Claudia.' He cut across her with a bored drawl. 'Michael's a fortune-seeking bastard who's got Joaney so twisted round his little finger that she can't think straight. I may have to deal with him myself,' he added ominously, 'but he certainly isn't anything you should bother yourself about. Just put him out of your mind.'

He began to caress her then, idle fingers digging into her flesh as he thought of Michael, until Claudia sprang up with a cry of fear and irritation. Walking away from the sofa, her arms wrapped tightly around her, she wondered what on earth she was doing there, why she was letting things just drag on when she knew she couldn't go through with it, couldn't marry Jason.

He was engulfing her, swallowing her whole, forcing her into his mould of the perfect woman. No matter how much

216

she liked the way he was so strong, so positive about where he was going in life, she knew she still didn't love him and lately, she didn't even like him. His charm had only been surface deep and she now feared what lay beneath that surface. He wouldn't take his dismissal easily and the thought of telling him was becoming a nightmare to her.

'What's the matter with you, for Christ's sake?' He looked astounded that she could pull away from those painful fingers. 'Come back here, Claudia. Tell me what's wrong.' She quivered at his tone, her mind suddenly made up.

'I have to go, Jason. I'll see you tomorrow, okay. I've got a paper and endless work I haven't caught up on yet and my exams aren't that far off. I have to go.' She turned and pushed past him, when he rose to block her path, reaching the door.

'Claudia, come back here and explain yourself. You're acting pretty strangely, if you don't mind me saying.' Jason was trying to sound amused but the anger was emerging clearly, like rocks beneath gleaming waves. Claudia turned and looked at him, stilling the shake in her hands by clasping them together.

'Yes, I do mind you saying. And I don't think it's *my* behaviour that's the strange one round here, if you really want to know,' she retorted, and had the satisfaction of seeing his face become quite mottled in hue. 'I'll see you tomorrow. Goodnight.' And then she walked out the door, closing it quietly behind her. She didn't wait for the lift but ran head-long down the stairs and out into the street, hailing the first cab she saw. Flinging herself into it, she dared at last to look around. Jason was watching her from the front steps of the apartment building. She slunk down in her seat and told the driver where to go.

The flat was filled with spring flowers, freesias and narcissi, white hyacinth and yellow jonquils all perfuming the air, candles placed cunningly to highlight small areas of the room where delicate edibles had been arranged. Champagne flutes were waiting on silver trays and the two

217

waitresses she had hired were busy uncorking the first bottles of Veuve Cliquot, Michael's favourite. Thank God for caterers, Joaney thought as she lit the last thin tapers and stood back to survey the scene.

Claudia, applying warm shades of blusher to her pale face, looked up when Joaney poked her head in the door.

'All set. It's going to go great, don't you think?' Joaney said nervously, dressed conventionally, for once, in a black silk dress, the emerald-cut diamond on her finger glinting against it. Claudia gave a forced smile.

'Don't worry, darling, it doesn't really matter how it goes as long as you two are happy. But yes, I'm sure it will go well.' She put her arms around Joaney's tense figure and gave her a hug.

'Well, it'll be your turn next,' Joaney said with a nervous laugh only to feel Claudia stiffen and break away. There was an awkward silence in which Joaney waited for Claudia to agree. 'Claudia? You okay?'

Claudia avoided Joaney's eyes, clipping on large pewter and cut-glass earrings instead. She was wearing a pale grey dress that clung to her figure without a ripple. She gave a long, deep sigh.

'Look, Joaney, I'm sorry, but – I'm breaking up with Jason.' Holding up her hands, she added, 'Don't worry, not tonight. But probably tomorrow. I thought you should know, so you can keep out of the firing line.' She grimaced, as she took in Joaney's shocked face. 'At least that'll take the heat off you and Michael. You should be grateful.'

'But why?' Joaney sounded more uneasy than surprised, Claudia thought. Perhaps she already suspected what her brother was capable of. But she was rushing on, breathlessly and Claudia heard her out with difficulty. 'It's nothing to do with Bo again, is it? I mean, I thought that was all over?'

'It is over, Joaney.' Claudia gave a painful smile. 'Believe me, that's all in the past. Long gone and long forgotten.' She was silent a moment, trying to organise her thoughts. 'I guess I never really loved Jason in the first place. I started going out with him because you wanted him on your side

218

and I guess I liked all the trappings, the way he made me feel special, especially after I found out about Bo. I wasn't second with him, just another girl in line. Jason made me feel like I was everything he ever wanted in life. And he seemed so strong after Bo's weakness. I thought that's what I wanted.' She paused and Joaney nodded.

'But now it's all different? The thrill and glamour's worn a bit thin?'

'Yes ... I suppose. And Jason's changed too. He smothers me. He won't give me any freedom. I can't talk to other men now without him getting angry, I can't work late or go shopping without telling him, I can't choose my own clothes even. And he ...' She faltered, unable to tell Joaney the full truth. 'I'm sorry.'

But Joaney closed her eyes for a moment, nodding. 'I know what else. I just thought things were different with you. I'm the one who's sorry. You poor girl!' She hugged Claudia again while Claudia struggled to keep back the tears and then thought how absurd, I'm free! How wonderful!

'Well, let's not stand here snivelling,' she laughed, breaking free of Joaney's hold. 'It's your big night and my big escape, so let's celebrate.' And they both smiled brilliantly, Claudia picking up Bundle who had been twining sinuously around and between her feet, begging for attention. She scratched his ears.

'I think he loves you more than me, these days. Maybe you should keep him?' Joaney offered generously as they stroked the soft grey fur and Bundle allowed himself to be carried through into the living room on Claudia's shoulder.

'No, Michael gave him to you. But I'll have him if you ever go away on holiday. He can visit me.' She caressed his sleek sides, rubbed his whiskers and then let him escape to explore the goodies on offer in the kitchen.

And then Michael and the first guests began to arrive and they were kept busy introducing people to each other and making sure they were all enjoying themselves. The Hewitts were late and by then the party was in full swing, the hum of voices rising by the minute as the champagne

219

and canapés were consumed, giving evidence of a successful evening.

Jason arrived in his most ruthless mood, his grey suit so dark it appeared black against the snowy-white shirt. It matched his hair and eyes and heart, Claudia thought sourly watching him from a safe corner.

He saw her and forced his way through the crowd to her side. She turned to intercept him with her coldest smile.

But, just at that moment, Michael chose to call for quiet, shushing the crowd until they all looked around expectantly, smiling at Joaney, sensing something momentous was about to happen. Jason, his hand tightly clenching Claudia's wrist, for all she tried to shake it off, muttered to himself as Michael began to speak.

'I want to thank you all for coming tonight, for being our friends, for consuming enormous amounts of our champagne' – titters of laughter at this, Michael smiling broadly – 'for always being there for Joaney and me when we needed support through the last two rather difficult years. And now, tonight, we particularly need your good will and wishes because we have an announcement to make.' He took Joaney's hand in his, squeezing it to give her courage.

'Many of you will know that a couple of weeks ago my divorce finally came through and so, not being a complete fool, though many of you may have thought so in the past' – even more laughter, people hushing and drawing in breath expectantly – 'I want to ask John and Pattie Hewitt for their blessing, since Joaney and I were married three days ago.' There was deathly hush while people absorbed the news and then a thunderous roar of approval and clapping, cheering, the fifty-odd friends more than making up for the silence of the Hewitt three. Finally the crowd fell silent and John Hewitt, his hand holding his wife's tightly in case she should say something unforgivable, edged forward.

'Well,' he cleared his throat, rubbed a finger along one side of his nose, 'this has obviously come as a surprise. We knew you two were very fond of each other' – laughter again, – 'but we had no idea just how much. And we wish

220

you both the very best.' He was a kind and good man, very fond of his daughter for all she seemed to rub against his wife so much, and he opened his arms and enfolded Joaney in them, hugging her soundly. With a frosty smile, Pattie Hewitt kissed Michael's cheeks.

Beside her, Claudia heard the breath rattle out of Jason, his face dulling with rage. He seemed oblivious to the rest of the room's cheers and laughter, his features creased with what looked like pain. Dropping Claudia's wrist, he pushed his way towards his sister.

Only Claudia saw what was happening. She moved after him rapidly but before she could reach him he had wrenched Joaney out of his mother's tepid embrace and backhanded her across the room. He didn't wait to see where she fell but turned on Michael, roaring with rage and disgust.

A cousin, closer than Claudia, took him down in a flying tackle from behind and, as they struggled and thrashed on the floor, several other men rushed forward to restrain him, while sobs and screams from Pattie Hewitt shrilled above them, demanding they let him go.

Michael was bending over Joaney, holding her in his arms, soothing her and stroking the large red welt across her cheekbone and John Hewitt was standing torn between the two. Finally, he turned towards his son, his face tight with anger.

'How dare you? Who do you think you are? Get out of here, right now, Jason. I'll speak to you later. Get out!' he repeated, his voice hoarse, when Jason appeared to hesitate. Contemptuously, Jason shrugged off the restraining hands and stood up, adjusting his tie and jacket. He smoothed back his hair, looking around, his eyes fastening on Claudia.

'Come on, let's go. I'll be sick if I stay here any longer.' He held out his hand peremptorily but Claudia slowly shook her head. His face became still.

'I said, "come on, Claudia,"' he repeated and made a move as though to take her by force but she stepped backwards abruptly.

221

'No, Jason, not this time. Or any time again,' she said hoarsely.

'What do you mean?' Jason's face was blank with shock and Claudia was relieved when a cool, drawling voice behind her backed her up.

'Claudia doesn't want to come with you and, as you've already heard, you're not welcome here, so why don't you just leave?'

Jason turned quickly, recognising Michael's voice. His lips tightened. 'Yeah? And what makes it any of your business? Just fuck off!'

'Jason!' John Hewitt cried but Jason had already begun to swing at Michael. Michael ducked and caught Jason's arm as it continued its swing, holding it awkwardly behind him. He enunciated carefully and slowly, as though Jason were incapable of understanding.

'Claudia's not for the likes of you, Jason. Now get the hell out of here.' Carefully, Michael steered Jason towards the door, releasing him only as they reached it. He stood back warily as the shorter man massaged his arm painfully, darting quick, dark looks about him, glaring into Michael's face as though he would gladly do permanent damage there.

He glanced across the hushed and shocked party to his sister, crying on their father's shoulder. The open window beside him blew his hair awry. He felt a pressure against his lower leg. Looking down, he saw Bundle's small body and he half smiled, relief creasing his stiff mouth as he repeated Michael's words in his mind, again and again, swirling them around in bitter despair. 'Claudia's not for the likes of you.' Oh, really, he thought? Was that so?

'Well, this is so you remember your fucking goddamn mistake, Joaney. And you too, Claudia. A lesson to both of you.'

Before anyone could stop him he bent quickly, lifting Bundle high in his hand so that the cat squirmed above his head. Claudia took a step forward.

'Don't Jason! Oh, God, please—' Her hands beseeched the air and Jason smiled again.

222

And then he tossed the cat so slowly, so carefully out of the window, Bundle howling frantically as he disappeared from sight, that no one moved, the guests around him merely sucking in their breath in shock.

'No! Oh, God, no!' Claudia shrieked, her hand flying to her mouth. 'No-ooo!'

Joaney slid down to the floor on her knees, her voice keening hysterically as her father bent over her and Jason smiled tightly at Michael before turning and walking out the door.

And Claudia, sick with horror and the knowledge that she had known what Jason was like and yet had not had the courage to stand up to him, forced herself to walk over to the window and look out.

She turned away, ashen and shaking, and went into her bedroom, closing the door after her.

Chapter Nineteen

Judson, 1985

'I'm not going to be poor forever, Mama.' Two years later, Claudia sat basking in the sun on the outside porch swing, Todd sitting curled up asleep beside her. She smiled tenderly as he grumbled something in his sleep. Her mother sat in a chair opposite.

'Well, twenty thousand dollars a year isn't exactly going to feed you on caviar, now is it?' They spoke in hushed voices, trying not to wake Todd. 'Besides, I like Todd with me. He's happy at school here, he's grown up here and everything's familiar.'

'Well, I know that, Mama. I'm not talking of having him to stay permanently, just for the summer holidays. You too, if you'd like, in your holidays. I just can't give up my job to come and spend enough time here any more and Todd's growing up without me, so I thought ...' Claudia's voice became wistful.

'You need a man of your own and children of your own, Claudia. Todd and I'll come and see you when we can but you need to get on with your own life. What you need—'

'Mama!' Claudia gazed at her mother in wonder, sitting there so calmly with her palely luminous skin beginning to wrinkle and her pale faded eyes still not seeing any joke in her words. 'I've got a good job and my first novel on the way and ... and I own my own apartment now. Why would I need a man, especially after the way you got treated?'

She stroked Todd's fair hair, looking up at her mother with determination, knowing that her mother was never going to think she had succeeded. It was just beyond her to think of Claudia as anything other than her daughter, a badly paid writer who was quite pretty but nothing special.

Never mind that Claudia had just had her first novel accepted for publication or had had one of New York's most eligible bachelors on a string for two years. Never mind that she had graduated from Columbia *magna cum laude* and landed a job with a prestigious business magazine in their San Francisco office. In her mother's eyes Claudia wasn't anything much because she didn't have anyone. No man. God!

'Because you do, whether you like it or not. The way I got treated is neither here nor there. Not all men are like that. I know Gina's done her best with you, introducing you to lots of nice young men, and Joaney's brother, well that's all over now, but he can't have been a bad catch ...' She sniffed, and Claudia looked around her, unable to believe her ears. She had told her mother all about Jason and this was her reply?

'Can't have been a bad catch? Mama, his father had him sent to Tokyo to get him away from Joaney and me. The guy's a certified psychopath! I'll just bet he's loving all those submissive Japanese women kow-towing to him and his kinky little games.'

'Please, Claudia! I don't want to hear about such things,' Mama protested.

'No, and neither do I, Mama. So cut out cracks about what I've missed out on. What about Peggy? She certainly hasn't missed out on any man who's ever come within whistling distance of her, and look how that's turned out,' she snapped and her mother sighed heavily, acknowledging the truth.

'All right, have it your own way. But you're not going to use Todd as a buffer between you and men, making him the reason you don't want to find anyone. That's not fair on either of you.'

'I wasn't going to!' Claudia protested, but an uneasy honesty deep inside her made her wonder. She squirmed away from the thought. She shifted abruptly, waking Todd. He shook his head and sat up, smiling at both of them.

'What's up? Gosh, I'm hungry. Can I have a peanut butter sandwich, Nanna? I'll get it myself,' he added as he saw Claudia's face. At eight, he was drawing out more into small adulthood rather than babyhood anymore. Claudia felt her loss keenly when she saw him grow like this. She sighed and ruffled his hair.

'I wasn't mad at you, Todd, don't look so worried.'

'You're not mad at Nanna, are you?' He stared at her accusingly and Claudia forced a wry smile.

'No, Todd, not Nanna either. I'm just a bit grumpy right now, that's all. Don't you worry.'

'Aren't you happy?' he persisted. Claudia glanced across at her mother's face, seeing a shrewd understanding there that was uncomfortably certain. She hesitated.

'I'm just a bit unsettled right now, Todd, that's all. I miss you both when I'm over there in California and I guess I don't really belong there ...'

'Or here,' Mama said, standing up. She smoothed down her dress and held out her hand for Todd. 'There's nothing here for you any more, Claudia, is there?' She paused, seeing Claudia's uncertainty, the pain of loss in her eyes and would have done anything to help. But Claudia had to sort it out on her own.

'No.' Claudia shook her head slowly. 'I guess not. Where *do* I belong, Mama? Where am I supposed to fit?'

But inside she felt a growing certainty. Just another couple of years and she would be able to afford it, maybe. Have enough experience to get another job that paid well. She felt a shiver of anticipation as she thought of Hong Kong, of Mark, of Harry ...

'That's not for me to tell you. You were always battling so hard to get away, to be different. And now you are. No, you gotta sort that one out for yourself. But you can't do that hiding behind props.' Mama glanced down significantly at Todd and Claudia dropped her eyes.

'No. Maybe not.' But her tone was not entirely in agreement. What she needed now was to work hard and get ahead. What she didn't need was men.

And then one of Todd's friends rode by, calling out to Todd to come and play, and he leapt from the porch without a look behind him. Claudia and her mother

226

watched him go with smiles that were more similar than either knew, happy for him and slightly pained that he could go so easily.

'See what I mean? He's got his life here and he's content. It's hard to be content in life, Claudia, and when you are, you should grab onto it hard and not let anyone sway your mind.' Claudia's mother crossed her arms and squinted out into the sun.

'What about you, Mama? Are you content now?' Claudia looked at her mother quickly. Her mother took a long time in answering, seeming to consult inside herself first. Finally she turned and glanced down at her daughter.

'Just about.' She smiled. 'Just about.'

Hong Kong, 1987

Tony sat at the oblong bar in California, watching a video idly out of the corner of his eye. It was *Ben Hur* and Charlton Heston was battling his chariot around the course in silent motion, his noble brow sweating with exertion, his mouth grim. Tony swirled his whiskey between his hands, deep in thought.

Beside him, perched neatly on her bar stool, Portia Hsu watched Tony's firm profile, the obvious distraction there, and sipped quickly at her banana daquiri. From time to time she flicked a glance over at him, assessing the clothes he wore, casual chinos and shirt, the short fair crop of his hair, the square, blunt fingers that massaged the glass he held. She leaned over slightly and a clean, masculine smell of soap and aftershave lingered about him. A shiver of anticipation threaded through her.

The evening crowd was gathering around the bar, spreading across to the tables and banquettes as drinkers became diners, a queue forming outside the most popular bar and restaurant in Lan Kwai Fong. It was being controlled rigidly by an elegant young woman with a clip-board in hand. The sound level was still muted, happy, light-hearted with the release of the day's tension but Tony was obstinately silent. Portia flipped her dark curtain of hair

227

back from her face and breathed in tightly.

'Can you give me a hint?' she asked, finally. Tony started, glancing across at her, his face puzzled and enquiring.

'Sorry ... what?'

'About what's got you so deep in thought ... You do remember me, don't you, Tony? Portia Hsu?' He took in the trim, lovely figure in hip-hugging black jeans and expensive white linen shirt, the long dark hair pulled back in a tortoishell hairband, the creamy pearl earrings in soft, ivory skin and he nodded, a faint feeling of surprise and pleasure surfacing through his dark thoughts. He smiled.

'Yes, of course I remember you, Portia. I just didn't know you'd grown up. How are you?' He glanced at that sulky, pouting mouth and had to force himself not to watch, mesmerised, as she said:

'Bored. I was waiting for a friend to turn up. Will you keep me company?' There was a disquieting gleam to her dark eyes, the smooth sweep of eyebrow arching just a fraction. Tony's eyes lingered across her face, sensing a moment of doubt. He smiled again.

'I'd love to. I'm also supposed to be waiting for a friend but he's so late, I was about to give up. Aren't you supposed to be at university somewhere in the States now, or so I'd heard?'

'Have you heard things about me?' She laughed, pleased. 'How nice to know I'm being discussed ...' The dark eyes laughed also. 'Yes, I'm studying business at UCLA. Daddy wants me to go into the family business after I graduate. I'm just home for a week or so.' She looked content at the thought.

'How is your father?' Tony's voice became dry and Portia glanced at him quickly.

'Are you still smarting over that?'

'Over what?' He frowned.

'Your mother and my father.' She laughed when she saw Tony flush angrily. 'Oh, Tony, it was years ago! Mummy's just like you, can't really forget. But it wasn't anything important, you know. Just a fling.' She saw his lips compress into a line that told another tale.

'Yes, I suppose ... I'm surprised you know anything about it. It was a long time ago, you were just a baby.' He looked at her with interest, wondering just what sort of relationship she had with her father. Reginald Hsu. Now there was a man who made Tony's mouth sour at the mere thought of him. There wasn't much that Reginald Hsu wouldn't help himself to, if he wanted it. And Tony wasn't thinking of women.

'Daddy and I are very close.' She read him easily, her face becoming still, even determined. 'There's nothing we don't share with each other. Well, almost nothing.' Her smile came back, dimpling into easy intimacy. 'So, what were you brooding over, a few moments ago?'

'Was I brooding?' He forced himself to laugh, shrug his shoulders. 'I didn't realise. I was just thinking about work, that's all.'

'Oh, yes, the big Triad buster, aren't you?' She teased and saw him lower his eyelids, hiding his thoughts from her even as he smiled easily.

'No, the small tadpole at the Triad Society Bureau, that's all.'

'That's not what I hear ...' her voice lingered and she leaned in towards him, whispering. 'Detective inspector, and I hear you're supposed to be incorruptible, too. Whiter than white.' She opened her eyes wide. 'Is there such a thing, Tony?' And she smiled again, intimate and mocking.

'Why? Are you offering to bribe me, Portia?' He looked at her with amusement, wondering even as he said it whether that wasn't exactly what was on her mind. He watched her pout and laugh, shaking that silky dark hair, tapping her drink with a polished red nail.

'Do I have to bribe you to get another drink?'

'No. Or dinner either, if you'd like?' For a moment Tony wondered whether he was making the running or whether he was being manipulated more thoroughly than he suspected. Did Portia really think the fact that their parents had had an affair, would have no effect on them becoming involved? He wasn't sure whether he was amused or not when she put her hand on his arm.

'Dinner? What a nice idea. But not here. Let's go somewhere quieter, shall we?' Her voice dropped even lower, caressing. She was not surprised when Tony agreed. But her smile was rueful as she turned back to the dining room. She glimpsed her father between the tables, his gaze steady as he watched them leave. Daddy was due a disappointment, she thought to herself, a moment's regret passing through her as she smiled at Tony holding the door for her. You're not interested, are you, Tony? Not in me or anything I have to offer. And then she set her chin firmly and walked out into the night.

From a dark corner in Scottie's bar, propped up in a booth, Aidan stared morosely out of the window as he watched Tony and Portia pass.

Chapter Twenty

Kyoto, Japan
January, 1989

Jason sat, cross-legged on the floor, eyeing the intricately carved box in his hands with an abstracted air. It held no mysteries for him. He had long ago discovered how to work the series of sliding panels to open the lid mechanism. But it had held only a photograph of three men, none of whom he recognised. He had replaced the photograph, thinking that perhaps, one day, he might find it profitable, and put it away.

And now, some six years later, he glanced between the photograph in his hand and the image on the television screen in front of him. A middle-aged Chinese man, greying and partially bald, in regulation Party issue of matching grey pyjama suit, sat at a podium in some equally grey conference room, conferring with elder statesmen and the British delegation sent over to resolve certain nagging issues on the end of the lease of the New Territories. He was, perhaps, plumper than he appeared in the photograph and less easy to distinguish from his countrymen when they all wore the same clothing, instead of the suit he wore in the photograph. But Jason was sure it was the same man.

A surge of interest flowed through him, unthought of until now, but suddenly compelling as he wondered how Claudia's brother came to have a photograph of a senior official of the Chinese People's Republic in his possession. And who were the other two men? Equally important officials? What was the significance of their meeting, the package being passed between them? Jason kneaded his forehead with broad, spatulate fingers that had once dug so

231

easily into Claudia's soft skin. He pursed his lips, thinking hard.

Perhaps he ought to have the photograph copied? Put it away somewhere safe, against any possible problems he might encounter while he sought the identity of the other two men. And then worked out how much it would be worth to any of them to recover the photograph. He smiled, thinking, there might indeed be quite a market for such a photograph, depending upon where it was taken and why. And that was what he would have to find out, wouldn't he?

He stood up and walked quickly over to the telephone, picking it up and dialling. A voice answered, 'Japan Airlines,' and Jason told her what he wanted.

Hong Kong
April, 1989
Claudia settled back into her seat, stretching her legs out beneath the one in front and encountering an obstruction. A briefcase? An overnight bag? It didn't make much difference, really, she thought with a twinge of annoyance. Because unless she was willing to make a fuss, to have the stewardess ask the man in front of her to remove it, there was nothing she could do. She crossed her legs in the cramped confines of her seat instead and stared out the window at the heavy cloud engulfing them.

They were less than an hour from Hong Kong now and she felt no desire to confront the leg-room issue. She had had enough confrontation in the past few weeks to last her a lifetime, she thought with a sigh. Firstly the telephone call from Mark, with him sounding so strange, agitated, unsure, his voice almost cracking under the strain when he asked her about the box. His insurance, he had repeated, when she hadn't known what he meant. And she had had to admit that she didn't know where it was any more, how could she after all this time? It was years since he sent it to her, a good five or six at least, and she had moved twice in that time, she had protested guiltily as he became aggressive.

232

Sitting in her window seat, somewhere over the South China Sea, she winced at the memory of how abusive he had been. What sort of fear could produce a rage like that, she wondered uneasily? And why?

But then he had called back, a few days later, and apologised, saying he had counted on her still having the box and it had been a blow to find out otherwise. His voice had been hearty, hale, full of good cheer that Claudia didn't believe for an instant. But she had been circumspect that time, playing along with his casual air, pretending surprise when he suddenly suggested she might like to come out to Hong Kong and visit. She had heard the need in his voice, the undertones of panic. And she had said yes.

Her editor had been sympathetic to the idea, offered to fund expenses in return for her reporting on Hong King's economic future in the run up to 1997. It had all seemed so easy suddenly, all those years of planning, trying to save up, meaning to go, one day ... and then it was for real.

She shook her head, remembering what Mama had had to say about it. For real! For a moment a groan escaped her, thinking of that dreadful scene with Mama accusing her of betrayal, saying those awful lines about not having a husband or a son any more, over and over, like a broken record and herself lashing back, accusing Mama of bearing unfair grudges. She closed her eyes, trying to stifle the memory, but it sat heavy in her chest, like a meal that refused to be digested and was causing heartburn. Too late now, Mama, she thought, with a grimace. There's no way round it now.

The cabin staff had begun to clear away breakfast, chatting and laughing with passengers who seemed excited by the thought of landing soon, and by the time the seat belt sign had been illuminated and the fussy precision of landing positions achieved, Claudia had little time left to brood. For the first time she felt a surge of exhilaration at the thought of Hong Kong. In just a few minutes, she would be on the ground, back with Mark, back ... home? She wasn't sure. She would have to wait and see.

*

Her brother was very like the photographs he had sent her over the years and yet subtly different. The photographs didn't convey the intelligence nor the insecurity that he masked behind an air of indifference. They didn't convey the shy delight that he tried not to show when he saw her, nor the impatience that that long jutting chin of his should have warned her about, having seen it in Jason. They didn't convey his almost complete lack of common sense nor the devil-may-care charm he could occasionally show flashes of to close friends. Claudia liked him enormously but she sensed he was not a man to depend on.

When she rolled her trolley down that steep concourse, seeing the hordes of people waiting to greet loved ones, clamouring noisily and holding up hand-made signs, Claudia saw Mark immediately. He was so much taller, for a start, and fair in a sea of small, dark bobbing heads. And he stood aloof from the others, somehow managing not to be jostled and to retain some small area of space around him. He looked up, seeing her, and his face had been known territory. There was so much of herself in him, she thought with surprise. She rolled to a halt beside him and tentatively held out her cheek to be kissed. Only then did she notice there was someone with him.

Someone who looked at her with eyes that hungrily devoured every inch of her, who stood almost stunned beside Mark and who didn't smile. Claudia felt uneasily aware that she should know who he was, that she should recognise the golden skin and dark hair, the eyes that held both knowledge and pain. He was judging her, comparing her to something or someone, she sensed.

'Mark? Hi, how are you? It was good of you to come out and meet me.' Her voice sounded stiff and uneasy, even to herself.

Mark smiled. 'Claudia! Wow, you've really changed, huh? I mean, even more than I could see in your photos. Um, you remember Harry, don't you? I brought him along to welcome you back.' He sounded as uneasy as she did. Claudia's eyes swivelled back to the dark-haired man, her mouth parting in surprise, almost anguish that this should

234

be Harry, whom she had missed for so many years, and yet she hadn't recognised him. She gave a gasp.

'Harry? My God, Harry!' She saw the pain lessen in those eyes and a deep delight fill them. He held out his arms and she stepped into them, allowing him to hug her tightly to him.

'Liddie! It is you. I wasn't sure at first, I kept staring to see if I could see you in this grown-up, polished-looking woman and all I could see was my memory of you.' He hugged her, laughing and she smelt his scent again, feeling buffeted by memories of that sharp citrus tang and something else, something she never could place but that meant Harry to her. In his fashionable clothes stretched out over a tall, well-built body, he could have been any other good-looking stranger. But that scent placed him as the boy she had known.

'It's me all right. Oh God, look at you both! Was someone feeding you extra Wheaties or something. How come you both grew so tall and I'm still a titch?' She laughed, including Mark in her greeting, seeing and being unsettled for a moment by the displeasure she sensed in him when he watched her embrace Harry. 'Oh, it's good to be back!'

They gathered her bags together and walked, talking and laughing, cutting across each other and over each other, outside to the car park. The smell of the East, sweet spices mixed with wet, dusty heat and the coppery tang of smog, an odd musky smell that came from drains and rotting vegetation, washed over Claudia and she breathed it in deeply, savouring it for the moment before her nose could adjust to it. It was so totally different to America and yet, felt instantly at home.

They loaded her bags into the car and she sat on Harry's lap, squashed into a corner and feeling the warm wind from the east blowing over her and the arms of someone whom she had once loved dearly, holding her tight as Mark took the corners with wild abandon.

It was hot and confusing in the late afternoon sun, looking around at the streets thronged with tourists and

Chinese alike, Chinese signs and banners, fading paint and peeling plaster giving way to shiny skyscrapers, and buses belching out grey clouds of grime, the cars honking and manoeuvring around each other.

Claudia sat there stunned almost into silence by the noise that beat in on her from all sides, the thump-ta-thump of a pile driver, the clattering of a tram, whistles and sirens, car horns, people yelling to each other, calling out their wares. She felt numb and unprepared for the pace with which it all swirled by her. Harry, sensing some of her confusion, simply held her and let her absorb it in silence. And Mark, when his concentration could allow even a moment's distraction, looked over at them both uneasily, his eyes glancing down to where Harry's hands encircled Claudia's waist.

He drove through the Harbour Tunnel and along Gloucester Road, pointing out the sights, the new Bank of China building under construction, the Bond Centre at Admiralty and HMS *Tamar* opposite before cutting up, through the confusion of new road works, into Cotton Tree Drive and they began to climb clear of the slick concrete skyscrapers of Central district and up into an older area of the Mid-Levels where apartment blocks were obscured behind enormous overhanging trees and greenery, their walls looking faded and in need of paint. They passed the point where the Peak tram began and the road wound more steeply beside botanical gardens and fern-encrusted overpasses. Mark had shifted down into second gear as they followed an overladen green and yellow bus that crept up the slope, belching and shuddering with the effort.

Where Cotton Tree Drive merged into Magazine Gap road, which led all the way to the top of Victoria Peak and became Peak Road, Mark pulled in to the left into the forecourt of three blocks of apartments, almost hidden away in their shelter of trees. There was a road that led on from the apartments, meandering into the dense foliage and Claudia thought for a moment that they would follow it. But Mark pulled in at the last apartment block and squeezed the tiny car between two others. He turned off the engine.

Even in that sheltered spot, high above the turmoil of the business and entertainment districts below, Claudia could hear noise. Traffic grinding up the steep gradient in low gear, church bells ringing distantly somewhere, a radio turned up too loudly in an apartment above them, penetrating voices raised in either amusement or anger, she couldn't tell which. The sun beat down on her head and she continued to sit there, dazed, until Mark smiled and leapt over the side of the car without opening the door.

'This is it, Liddie, or are you planning on going somewhere else?' he teased. Almost at once, she became aware of the sensation of flesh beneath her, warm and firm, an arm encircling her, a hard shoulder in her back. She turned and looked at Harry apologetically, unnerved by that close proximity and the feel of him. She levered her legs out and across the gear box, climbing onto Mark's seat and sliding across the back of the car in one swift movement.

Mark had removed her bags from the trunk and Harry climbed out too, the three of them awkward all over again with each other.

'Does it ever get quiet here? Is there anywhere you can go to get away from all this noise?' she asked, realising immediately how it sounded and feeling tense down in her belly, an unsureness that encompassed everything and everyone. She saw Harry and Mark glance at each other and shrug.

'Up on the Peak, sure, it's quiet up there. Nothing but cloud and sky and maybe a couple of hawks circling around. Or over on the other side of the island, Deep Water Bay or Shek O. It's quiet out there. But not here, Liddie. This is Victoria,' Mark said, as though she were asking too much.

Harry tried to soften Mark's words. 'It's not so bad when you've been here a while, you'll get used to it and not even hear it. You'll just filter it out, like you used to before. You'll fit right back in, before you know it.' He smiled, eyeing her cautiously, as though urging her to like Hong Kong, to feel

237

she had come home. Claudia smiled and shrugged, unnerved by that pressure. She did like Hong Kong, she just wasn't sure yet whether she wanted to stay.

She saw Harry glance at his watch. 'Come on, we should get a move on. I have to leave in an hour.' He turned, picking up a bag and Claudia watched his figure, tall and loose, powerful in a way that disturbed her. He had changed more than she had thought.

'Harry's got this great radio show going, Liddie. Half of Hong Kong switches over to listen to the Harry Braga programme. You're looking at a celebrity here!' Mark laughed, glancing between them, feeling his unease increase and wondering why he had panicked and asked Claudia to come. What could she do? Nothing.

He shook his head, leading them through into the stairwell, his laughter floating back to her so that she glanced in surprise at Harry again.

Harry smiled. 'Beats working at a real job and I get better paid.' But he was pleased and trying not to show it, Claudia thought.

'We'll have to sit and listen to it then. How on earth did you get into something like that?' she asked, and as they climbed to the third floor, Harry quickly sketched in how Aidan had helped him. Claudia, remembering Fish for the first time in a long time, was surprised.

'I thought he was a bit of a lush. How did he get you the job?'

'He didn't always used to be a bum. He had a good job in the Civil Service and he comes from an old Hong Kong family with lots of clout. He knew all the right strings back then.'

'But not now?'

'Now? Now, he doesn't know what he is. And neither do I,' Harry replied obscurely, almost talking to himself, and then Mark cursed above them as they reached the landing of his apartment and found it filled with furniture. The door to the apartment opposite was open and the loud voices could be heard coming from within.

'Hey, Mrs Tsao, what's going on here? I can't get my

grille door open. You'll have to move some of this stuff,' he shouted and Claudia saw with surprise the way he almost shook with anger, his fingers gripping tightly onto the back of the chair. He was barely holding himself in check, she thought with dismay. Or was it anger? Maybe, just maybe it was fear?

A stout matron appeared, dressed in Western clothes, her dark hair polished into a high French roll. She smelled of hair lacquer and heavy perfume. She smiled broadly, but there was a blandness there that spoke of indifference, even contempt.

'Balance all wrong, not in harmony, so we call *fung shui* man, rearrange things for better flow of good luck in, bad luck out,' she announced and Claudia heard Mark groan.

'But you had that done only a few months ago. What difference in the wind and water balance had made you want to rearrange your furniture all over again?'

'Goldfish die,' she beamed. 'Bad luck hit goldfish, not us, so it die. Lucky, huh?' It came out as a grunt from her ample diaphragm. 'Last *fung shui* man no good, not get balance right or goldfish not get hit by bad luck at all. See? This man better, get better luck, no more goldfish die, no more bad luck for us. Wait, we move furniture.' And she called sharply into the interior of her apartment and two young men appeared and carried the chair that was blocking Mark's apartment door, out of the way. Mrs Tsao peered at Mark's pale, sweating face and then shrewdly at Claudia.

'You need *fung shui* man come visit you? You in better balance, maybe you sleep better, not play music all night long? Not put so many bottles out in rubbish.' A hard glitter from her eyes pursued him. 'Not get visitors in middle of night with loud, shouting voices. You want?' She seemed oblivious to Harry's quick intake of breath, staring only at Mark.

'No, thank you, Mrs Tsao, not at the moment,' Mark said, biting down on the words as though determined not to lose his temper, but Claudia saw the shake had come loose again, like a palsy. 'I have my sister come to stay with me.

239

That is enough good luck.' A tight smile accompanied his words.

'You need goldfish, catch bad luck, warn you of trouble in your life, not sister,' she replied sharply, nodding quickly to Claudia and ignoring Harry completely. 'You have plenty bad luck, you not careful.' She disappeared back into her apartment.

'What I need are new neighbours,' Mark said loudly and unlocked the grille door and then the interior, wooden one. He led them in and quickly shut the door on Mrs Tsao's voice, leaning for a moment against the door. Harry watched him steadily, as though willing him to get a grip on himself, and Claudia, standing back and watching them both, was appalled. What was going on? Why was Mark just about coming apart at the seams? And Harry? What was there about him that seemed so still, so very much in control? Claudia shook her head, looking away.

'What was all that about? Wind and water and fung something?' She collapsed onto the rattan sofa, forcing her voice to sound light as she kicked off her shoes. It was hot in the apartment, stifling. Neither Mark nor Harry seemed to notice.

'Oh, that!' Mark gave a laugh, unsteady at first but gradually forcing himself to be calm. 'Everything in Chinese life has to be in harmony with nature, with the prevailing winds and the location of running water.' He waved his arm around, indicating the trees outside the window, rustling in the late afternoon breeze.

'They believe certain men, *fung shui* men, understand this sort of mystical science and can tell them where to buy a house, how to place the furniture, where to bury a loved one, even the position of doorways in new buildings so that the good luck doesn't fall out of the doors or windows. You remember all that, don't you?'

'You're joking? I was seven when I left, Mark. And people believe in this?'

'Sure. Just look around and you'll find, sometimes, a mirror positioned in a window or in the entrance of a door, to reflect back the bad luck that is trying to enter. It's all

240

superstitious nonsense, of course, but I promise they really do believe in it.' He sounded easier as he carried her bags through to her bedroom and Claudia didn't press him. There was time later, when he was more relaxed, when he trusted her more. 'Ask Harry. He'll tell you,' Mark added, but there was a sharpness to his words, a spitefulness that Claudia remembered from childhood. She looked at Harry, puzzled.

But Harry shrugged it away, indifferently. 'It's just a mix of mysticism and old wives' tales. You'll find more of those here than anywhere else in the world. I mean, my mother used to believe all sorts of nonsense, everything from the colour of the clothes you wore to the food you ate. She had goldfish too, just to be on the safe side. Like carrying a canary into a mine, it gets hit by any gas first and serves as a warning. It's all nonsense, none of it changed anything, she just thought it did.'

'So you don't have any goldfish or canaries or believe in any of that stuff?' She was teasing, smiling but he stiffened.

'No, none of it. Why should I? Why should I? I'm more European than Chinese in thinking. The way I figure it, you make your own luck.' He smiled at her then, looking down into her face, about to say something but then hesitating. Claudia smiled up into his eyes for a long moment.

'Harry just hangs blue lanterns for his luck, don't you, Harry?' Mark's face had become watchful, seeing the old bond between Claudia and Harry quivering there, trying to reassert itself. He smiled knowingly as Harry paused, glancing across the room.

'No, Mark,' Harry said slowly, the anger there, just below the surface. 'I've worked for it. And I've paid my dues.' They stared at each other and Claudia swallowed, not knowing what was meant but sensing the issue was herself.

'Not all of them, Harry,' Mark said quietly and sat down beside Claudia.

Harry's forehead gleamed with perspiration as he stood there, silently. Then he turned his back to them, walking away into the kitchen. 'Beer do for you?'

241

'Yes, fine,' Claudia said quickly, sensing now was not the time to confront them. She paused, calling, 'So, are you Christian, Harry, or Buddhist or what?'

'Nothing. I don't believe in any of that crap. And neither does Mark, do you?' He reappeared with three bottles and an opener. Claudia glanced at Mark.

'No. Why, do you, Liddie?' Mark sounded surprised and amused, as though he had just discovered his sister was a country yokel. She shrugged, caught between their glances.

'I'm not sure. I guess I'm Christian. Mama still goes to church every Sunday and I go with her when I'm home.'

'And Dad's become a Buddhist and wanders around their bungalow in a sarong, but that doesn't mean I believe in it,' Mark retorted and then relented, smiling lazily. 'But don't worry, I don't care what you believe. Just as long as you don't try to convert me. I'm a true sinner and I enjoy life that way, so don't try and save me, Liddie, for God's or Buddah's or anyone else's sake.' He laughed and she joined in awkwardly, uncomfortably certain that Mark had just found a way of telling her to mind her own business where his life was concerned. She glanced at Harry and saw him smile too but there was no message for her in those dark eyes of his.

It was odd that she could feel like a stranger in the midst a man who was her brother and a man who she had long thought of as her closest friend. But she didn't know either of them any more, did she, she thought painfully. They were complete strangers.

By the end of the first week, a week in which she ate in a different restaurant every night and drank more than she had ever done in her life, and met more people, casual friends of Mark's and Harry's out on the town, Claudia felt she knew little more than she did when she arrived.

Yes, she had explored Central and Wanchai, had been to the Peak and looked down over the huddled cluster of skyscrapers below her as they jostled for position on the narrow strip on land. She had looked across the shimmering harbour to Kowloon and the New Territories

242

beyond. She knew which trams went where, she had been down to the markets along Western district and into the alleys off Queen's Road where clothes were sold off barrows and the antique lanes off Wyndham and Cat Street.

Like a tourist she had paid her mite to ride the Star Ferry across to Kowloon and browse down the shopping streets of Nathan and Chatham Road, to explore the Ocean Terminal with its small shops selling jewellery and clothes. She had learned a few meagre words of Cantonese, enough to get her around and to thank someone, but she didn't feel she had really begun to understand Hong Kong. Not what was beneath the gleaming surface that smiled at the casual visitor and gave nothing away.

After work, she would meet Mark for a drink in the Admiral's Bar and they would wander out for the evening, playing it very much as it came. He seemed pleased to have her with him, to introduce her as his sister. He liked the company, he said. But he never became intimate with his thoughts. It was easier to have another drink, keep going from one bar or nightclub to another until they were so weary they rolled home to bed. And in the morning he was gone before she awoke.

Nor had she penetrated the stony armour that Harry had built up around him that protested his Western origins and denied his Chinese. He held her aloof when she probed into his past, into the intervening years since she had left, only allowing her to enjoy his charm when she accepted the portrait of him that he showed her: the successful celebrity, the Portuguese background, the social animal who was greeted and fawned over wherever they went. There was little or no delving allowed into how that image had been formed, and even that was carefully censored.

By the time she had been there a month, no matter how much he tried to hide it, it had become obvious that Mark had problems and she became increasingly anxious and frustrated about him, the more she discovered. He drank too much, he smoked dope incessantly, and he was frightened about something, for all he tried to hide it. Mrs Tsao was right. He didn't sleep.

243

And he jumped at loud noises, backfires in the street, people yelling. Jumped and looked around ... terrified, just for a moment, before he laughed and relaxed. She tried not to pry, knew he would only become angry and deny it, but it became clear there was something very wrong and that the box he had sent her had something to do with it. His insurance, he had said. She cursed herself for having lost it.

When they did talk, they fought. About his lifestyle, about her inability to enjoy life, about Harry.

And Claudia saw the jealousy there, in her brother's eyes, and she saw the fear. But she didn't realise it wasn't just for himself.

On a Saturday evening, in early May, she found herself more frustrated than usual. Mark had been purposely obtuse, purposely blank all day, but she sensed the problem was coming to a head and that he was badly frightened by it. But there was nothing she could do, nothing he would let her do. She would go out before worse could be said between them, she decided. Angrily, she shrugged herself into fresh clothes, picked up her satchel which was slowly growing heavy with material for her next article, and threw her cigarette butt in the ashtray. Mark watched her with an uneasy mixture of emotions, part irritation, part concern.

'See you,' she called, poking her head around his bedroom door, where he lay sprawled across the bed in a fog of sweet smoke.

'You off then? Going to find the story of the decade that'll make your bosses love you and give you a big fat raise?' He teased, eyes narrowing against a stray wisp of smoke, and he then paused. 'Or maybe you're just going off looking for Harry ...? Don't, Liddie.' Mark's eyes swam back into focus for a moment, clearing the way the ripples on a pool of water suddenly still and let you see through to the bottom beneath.

'Don't what? See Harry?' She looked astonished that he should say such a thing and he fumbled for the right words.

'Stay away from him at the moment. Harry's not for you. Just let it be, okay? I don't want to see you getting mixed up in any of this.' His face became serious, revealing his concern and his eyes narrowed as they saw the obstinate tightening to her mouth.

'Getting mixed up in what, for God's sake, Mark? If you won't tell me, maybe Harry will.' She hesitated. 'Won't you please tell me?' When he was silent, she added with a softer tone, 'What, Mark? What is it? What's wrong?'

He sat up on one elbow and pinched the embers out of his joint with his fingers, ignoring her plea, for all he wanted to cry for her help, let her save him. What would she do, if she knew they were under sentence, he and Harry? For something they hadn't done but couldn't convince Yee otherwise. They were to pay, Yee had said. Sometime, somewhere, they were to pay. For what? He didn't know. And neither did Harry.

He looked into Claudia's eyes, seeing the hazel flecks swimming in their sea of dark green, the pain there that would do anything to help, if she could. But what could she do? Nothing. And it was safer that way.

'Nothing's wrong, I'm just trying to give some good advice, Liddie. You listen to me. There are things here — problems, different arrangements — that you don't know about and you don't want to get mixed up with. Harry's trying to get clear of them but, as far as I can see, it isn't doing him one damned bit of good. He was your childhood playmate, okay, great. But he's different now. You haven't known him for twenty years and he's different. Can't you see that?'

'I'm not a fool, Mark. Of course I can see he's different. He's twenty-nine, not nine. An adult. Just like you. But he's still the same person inside.' But even as she said it, she wondered. Was he really? There were so many blank spaces she couldn't fill in and he wouldn't let her. But he was still Harry. 'And I like that person. And I want to help.'

'You hated me as a child,' Mark said slyly but there was humour in the eyes, a teasing quirk to his mouth.

Claudia smiled reluctantly. 'And I like you now, yes, I know ... and I just want to help you.' She ruffled Mark's hair, much like she would ruffle Todd's. She grimaced

245

when he pulled away. 'Look, I'm going down to Lan Kwai Fong,' she said, her mind suddenly made up. She shifted her satchel up on her shoulder.

'Who're you meeting? Silvia?' Mark looked up and she smiled to herself, hearing the note of interest in his voice despite himself.

'Yes, want to come? I said I'd meet her at Graffiti around seven. Come and keep me company. I know she'd love to see you. I told her you'd probably come,' she coaxed.

'Maybe ... maybe, later.' He nodded, offhand, his thoughts wandering. 'I've got to wait for someone first.'

'Who?'

'Oh, just someone. He's coming round here. You better hurry, it's nearly seven now.' He glanced at his watch and stood up, scratching his chest. Claudia turned away, a small nag of anxiety refusing to be stilled. Someone. Someone with more – something – to sell?

She saw the ribs clearly beneath his skin, the paleness of his irises, and bit her lip, wondering whether she dared bring it up again, decided against it and then surprised herself when the words blurted out of their own accord.

'Who got you onto that stuff? Fish?' Who had turned up like a bad penny, still smiling and still watching, still making her shudder with distaste. It was easy for him to smile his way through life, a partially defunct personality who occasionally revived enough to do his job, editing for a second-rate paper. But what about his friends? How were they supposed to cope? Harry, Mark and Fish. They made a dangerous trio. Mark stared through her with closed thoughts.

'Maybe. Who was your first lover, Liddie? Was he good? How many have there been? Are you on the pill? Have you ever been pregnant?' He paused, when he saw the shuttered outrage on her face. 'See? No one likes being asked impertinent questions. Especially not me. I told you that right in the beginning. Now you better get going. I'll see you later.' He almost pushed her to the door, opening it onto the grille work door and then the ugly cement steps of the hallway, the smell of several apartments' cooking mixing with that of cold tiles that had been washed down and left to pool with disinfectant.

'Come with me, Mark, please. Don't stay here,' she begged, unable to explain why she felt so tense, her emotions and thoughts jumbled up and throbbing away in the pit of her stomach. But he just shook his head as though in disbelief.

'You never give it up, do you? I don't know, maybe you should start thinking of getting a place of your own. This isn't going to work if you won't mind your own business.' He spoke harshly and she flinched at the words. She turned, hearing the click of Mrs Tsao's door open a crack and then close again. But when she turned back to Mark, he had already shut the door behind her. She stared at the blank wood and then she hurried down the stairs. The bus would be by any minute.

Chapter Twenty-One

Saturday night

Bill Ingram's grip on the telephone tightened as he listened to the voice murmuring quietly to him.

'You've got it, then?' he asked sharply, when there was a pause. The voice murmured again and he drew in his breath with a sort of exasperated sigh that made Tony, watching him from across the room, frown. Something had upset his father and he was a man who rarely showed emotion.

'Then get the paperwork sorted out and get that bank to open it up,' Bill snapped and hung up abruptly. Tony picked up the two glasses of whiskey and handed one to his father without comment.

'Ah, thanks, Tony.' Bill swallowed half of it in one easy movement of his throat, sitting back in his favourite easy chair. Otter twitched her paws out of his way, before settling back with a grumbling sigh. 'Bloody bureaucrats, these Japanese,' Bill muttered and Tony smiled faintly.

'As opposed to whom?' he asked ironically and his father's mouth twitched in agreement. 'Anything serious?' Tony added casually, knowing his father would probably not tell him. He was all the more surprised then, when his father replied incautiously, the anger still there in his tone.

'It might be. Might bloody well be. Something we've been trying to work out for a long time. But we won't know for sure until we can get into—' He broke off, suddenly realising his slip. He smiled at his son's bland expression.

'Don't bother saying it.' Tony swallowed his own drink, knowing his father would anyway, knowing they both knew Tony would never mention a word that was inadvertently let slip to anyone else.

'You're wasted in your profession, Tony,' his father said suddenly, surprising Tony even more. 'Time you made a move, don't you think?' There was an amused, gauging look in his father's eyes that Tony met steadily.

'No, not yet. Maybe not ever,' he added mildly and Bill Ingram laughed.

'You have to grow a thicker hide, Tony. There's always a greater good to serve.'

'Is that your explanation for Aidan's little tumble?' Tony asked, wondering and seeing, not a guilty look in his father's eyes, but a satisfied one that was quickly covered over. 'Or has Aidan been more of an acrobat than any of us suspected?' His gaze narrowed as he saw his father stand abruptly and turn away.

'Sad business that,' was his father's only comment. He poured himself another scotch.

'Very.' Tony's voice was dry. 'Anything I should know, Dad? Anything that's likely to have any bearing on my work?' He always asked and occasionally he received a titbit, a hint, mostly nothing. But he was a patient man and he knew his father's restrictions, for all that it was never mentioned between them.

'Possibly. I can't say just yet. Depends, rather, on which way we want things to go.' Bill looked at his son, knowing he couldn't possibly understand and reluctant to leave him totally in the dark when Yee was growing strong and impatient – and dangerous. If that mess in Japan was anything to go by, very dangerous. It was unfair to keep blocking Tony's investigations where Yee was concerned, but he had no choice at the moment. Yee was useful.

'I'd keep an eye on Harry Braga if I were you. And Mark Babcock too. You know he's got his sister, Claudia, out with him, now, don't you?' Bill Ingram saw an unexpected expression pass over his son's face. Surprise? Anticipation? Was that it?

'No, I didn't. I don't see much of Mark or his set any more. Does this visit have any bearing on anything or is it just bad timing?' Tony fought down the excitement inside him, wondering even as he did so, why Claudia's return

249

should affect him in any way. He cleared his throat, waiting for his father to explain further. He was disappointed.

'Rather more your province than mine, surely?' Bill smiled, his eyes creasing up as he saw Tony bite on the failure to draw him further.

'I don't know, that's what I was asking you. I guess you've told me, anyway.' Tony smiled evenly, feeling as though a tiny gleam of light had been focused on an impenetrably dark hole that had plagued him for some time. 'I'll watch Harry and Mark, though. Thanks for the tip.' And he smiled at his father, knowing it was the best he could do.

Saturday night
Lan Kwai Fong
The street where the young and stylish Hong Kong professionals went to drink, eat and be seen was busy at 7.30 on a Saturday night. Claudia eased herself through the traffic of Wyndham Street and down the back lane that led to D'Aguilar Street, ignoring the whistles and catcalls from the occasional sailor who had strayed too far from Wanchai. Graffiti had a queue blocking the doorway but she slipped past them with a familiar wave to the barman who pointed to the rear of the restaurant. Without much surprise, she saw Silvia Bateman sitting at a booth holding court to several men at surrounding tables.

'Hi, Claudia. Where's Mark — I thought you were going to bring him?' A slight crease appeared between the other girl's eyebrows, the light dimmed slightly in those clear green eyes.

'He might come on here in a bit, he said. Had to see someone,' Claudia added, shrugging, her own confrontation with Mark leaving her too shaky to want to discuss more.

Silvia sighed deeply and sat back. 'Ah! Of course. His weekly supply. God knows how he affords it all. There's rumours going 'round about it, Claudia. Better do something.' Her tone was chiding and Claudia felt uncertain.

She sometimes suspected Silvia was only interested in her as a friend because of who her brother was. Mark, the eligible bachelor – the semi-alcoholic druggie. Damn! What was she *supposed* to do?

'You make him sound like a heroin addict, for God's sake, Silvia! Everyone smokes a bit of grass from time to time.' She kept her tone light.

'From time to time, yes. But not all night, every night. And not just grass.' Silvia paused and then shrugged it off, laughing. 'Ohh, anyway, it doesn't seem to be doing his brain any harm. I heard he's been made Overseas Fund Manager. Not bad for his age. Lucky his boss decided to go and manage the Treasury for Tobago.' It wasn't Tobago but that wouldn't have been alliterative and Silvia cared little for details.

Claudia nodded. 'Umm, guess so. He's only on probation though. To see if he can handle it. But it's good news. He'll be on full expat pay and he'll have to work harder, so there won't be time for all the extras.' She emphasised the last word meaningfully.

'And just when he can finally afford them. No more insider dealing, then?' It was a joke, Silvia's tone said. But her eyes were watchful.

Claudia looked at her oddly. 'You don't really think . . .?'

'No, no I don't. But he has to have something else going, on the side. There's no other way . . .' Silvia bit her tongue, looking guilty. 'I'm sorry, Claudia. I didn't mean to intrude or to suggest things. I'm just worried about Mark, that's all.'

'It's just a bit of grass, from time to time, Silvia. Don't make a big deal out of it.' Claudia heard the fear in her own voice and was angry at herself for not supporting Mark better. But how could she, when she disagreed so much with what he was doing to his life?

'It's no secret grass is more expensive here and harder to find. People wonder how he affords it, that's all. Okay, okay, I won't say another word.' Silvia held up her hands, relinquishing responsibility to Claudia. Or passing the buck, Claudia thought.

251

She was fretful tonight, not in the mood for Silvia's concern nor yet in the mood to be alone. It had been Mark, she decided. He had been acting strange all day. Up and down in wild mood swings. That was the drugs, of course. But, there was something more, something of despair almost in his eyes.

'Did Portia drop by to see you? She said she was going to,' Silvia asked, breaking in on her thoughts.

'Portia Hsu? No, she didn't. Why?'

'Oh, nothing really. She said she had a message for Harry but she couldn't get hold of him, so she'd tell Mark to pass it on. I couldn't get her to tell me what it was all about. She was in a bit of a state, actually. I wondered whether you knew anything about it?' Silvia's light green eyes had the ability to cloud up, like milky jade, when she was worried.

'No-oo. What sort of state?'

'Jumpy, upset, shrill. But Portia can be like that for no reason at all, except that Hong Kong's governing power is less than perfect or her father's employees want, God forbid, to form a union!' Silvia's voice mocked Portia's own manner of speech. 'You know what she's like,' she added and they both smiled, thinking of Portia's vehemence.

'She's still young,' Claudia said, excusing her. Secretly, she wondered whether it wasn't better to feel strongly about things, about important issues in life. But with Portia it always seemed like histrionics.

'Twenty-three isn't young in Hong Kong,' Silvia said shortly. 'By the way, there's a party at the Hsus' next Friday, if you'd like to go.'

'Is Mark invited too?'

'But, of course! Is there anywhere Mark isn't invited? If only the crinklies knew what he gets up to in his spare time, I'm sure there'd be a lot less uncritical admiration and match-making going on. I mean, my mother thinks he's wonderful!'

'Well, he is!' Claudia said firmly and was amused by Silvia's pout. 'And I know you think so too, so stop pulling the tough act. Why you two can't get it together ...' She broke off as she noticed Silvia flush and look away. 'Silvia?'

'I thought you knew.' Dark eyebrows met over troubled eyes. 'About us,' Silvia said. 'I thought Mark had told you.' The girl smoothed her dress down over her thighs, tossed back dark, curling hair, green eyes defiant.

'No. Nothing. But he doesn't like me prying about his personal life. We had a row about it this evening, actually, and he pretty much told me to keep my nose out.' Claudia had a sinking feeling when she thought about it. 'So, what's going on?' She watched the other girl with a quizzical expression, wondering how much else was being concealed from her. How little she really knew about what was going on.

'It was all a long time ago now. We'd known each other for years, been in and out of each other's houses for parties and well, you know, we just started going out together. It was all very hot and heavy for a while and then he just cooled right off, when he came back from university and started work. He told me he wasn't interested any more, said something about not liking Western girls – you know, the usual thing you hear about us being shallow and pushy – and that was it. Funny thing is, though, I always thought he didn't mean it, that he still cared just as much as I did, and he was just, I don't know, playing some sort of silly game. Odd, really.' Silvia turned away, not looking at Claudia, fumbling for her cigarettes.

So, one small part of the jigsaw falls into place, Claudia thought. And ninety-nine other pieces are still in disarray.

'I'm sorry, I didn't realise. You must have been very hurt,' she said tentatively.

Silvia shrugged and struck a match. 'Mark doesn't care who he hurts just as long as he doesn't have to take any responsibility in life.' She paused, and then sighed. 'And now I'm sorry. I shouldn't have said that.' Except that it was true and they both knew it.

Claudia shrugged too and signalled to a waiter. 'A spritzer please. What about you, Silvia?'

'No, no, I'm fine.' Silvia was fiddling with the small radio she had brought along, adjusting the earphone. And she still had half of her drink left. Claudia smiled at the waiter and let him escape.

'What's that for?'

'Harry's programme. It's already started. He's doing a phone-in tonight, with people's views on 1997. He wanted us all to call in, get the ball rolling. I just wondered if anyone we know is on.' She adjusted it finally and plugged it in, handing the other earphone to Claudia. They sat at the table, doodling with crayons on the paper cloth and smiling painfully at some of the more inept comments.

It was the third caller who made them both sit back and signal quickly to each other. It was Mark. Harry's smooth voice sharpened slightly.

'And what is your name?'

'Mark.'

'Mark what?'

'Mark Anthony.' Titters from the studio crew. Harry didn't respond.

'Well, Mark, and what do you think about the future of Hong Kong after 1997? Do you think the Chinese government is going to honour the fifty-year adjustment period?'

'How long do you think Deng will last? He made the bargain. That's about how long it's good for.' Claudia saw Silvia nod, as though in agreement.

'But you think it'll last that long? You don't think there'll be a crackdown earlier?'

'Not if everyone keeps their noses clean and the money keeps pouring in from the joint ventures on the mainland. You know the old saying, don't rock the boat. China needs Hong Kong, for the moment at least.'

'And the Basic Law document? How important is that, do you think, to the people of Hong Kong? Not the bankers and big money people, but the little people, the man in the street?'

'More than the British want to admit. But that still won't give a universal franchise for another three years and as for direct elections, well, I wouldn't expect the Chinese government to welcome that idea with open arms, would you? Look, hold on a second. There's someone at the door. Just hold on.'

254

The interview ended abruptly and Harry's voice, sounding amused and confident, called out to Mark that they were going to have to leave him there, that they were going to pick up on the next caller.

And then the screams started.

Agonised, tearing screams, sounding as though Mark was crying out in such terror and pain that it made death seem like a sweet release, shrieking, 'No, oh God, no-oo!' over and over. For several long unbearable seconds the gasping, howling horror went on before abruptly being cut off.

There was an even longer moment of silence and then music, soothing and banal flowed down the airwaves.

Claudia ripped the earphone from her ear and stared, ashen-faced, at Silvia. Silvia was shaking, ugly, juddering wrenches to her body, her head bobbing about on her neck like a puppet's. Her mouth was open, the lips slack and quivering in their red lipstick. Claudia pushed past her, towards the telephone at the back of the restaurant. It wasn't Mark. It was some joke, some studio prank. It wasn't Mark screaming, she told herself fiercely, through the wretched shaking misery that had enveloped her. But she knew it was. Even now she could hear the screaming. What was happening, Oh God, what!

The telephone rang and rang. Finally, Claudia hung up and with shaking fingers dialled Commercial Radio. But the lines were jammed with callers, trying to find out what had been happening. She hung up and leaned, suddenly ill and weak, against the wall, the tears seeping out beneath her closed lashes. Was it still going on, was he still screaming? Or had it stopped finally? She took a deep breath, wiping away the tears and holding her arm over her face, as though to shield it from peering eyes. And then she dialled 999.

The drive up to the Mid-Levels was slow; Claudia, slouched in the rear seat of a taxi that groaned up the steep gradient, hugging herself tightly to warm the chill that had crept through her. Her chest felt like an ice cavity. She

255

peered out fearfully as the taxi swept into the forecourt of the apartments and came to a halt. There was flashing lights and uniformed police roping off the area, an ambulance sitting uselessly, its siren turned off, its light revolving slowly and spasmodically, as though resigned to having lost this one before it even started.

Claudia climbed out slowly and stood staring up at the apartment window. A face peered out at her. Not Mark. She shouldered her way through the crowd, catching at the arm of a policeman. He didn't have the red stripe beneath his pips. He didn't speak English.

Claudia spoke only the shakiest of Cantonese, a mixture of phrases memorised for their usefulness in the back streets of Kowloon. She pointed upwards.

'*Cheng mahn bou ging?*' May I report to the police? She saw the incomprehension on the man's face and realised she had mispronounced it. 'Police. I must see. Please! *Mgoi!*' She shook his arm and pointed upwards again and then at herself. The man shook her off and pushed her back.

'No, let her through. Bring her here.' A European policeman, in plain clothes, gestured from the steps of the building. He was impatient and kept scrubbing at his eyes, trying to erase what he had seen. Claudia reached him with relief, glancing at him, at his sturdy fairness, at the dependability she read there in his face.

'It's my brother. I called. My brother Mark. He was the one screaming . . .' She trailed off as she saw the man stiffen, his eyes, that had been so detached a moment before, suddenly softening in sympathy. Claudia knew, right then, in that moment of unwelcome pity, that Mark was dead.

He took her by the arm, leading her over to a police car and sitting her in it. He squatted beside her, holding her hand and she could only stare at him, her face as pale as a true *gweilo*'s should be, pale ghost.

'Miss Babcock, Claudia? I'm sorry. I'm Detective Inspector Ingram. You wouldn't remember me but we knew each other a long time ago.' His voice was soothing and calm. There was a quality of infinite patience to him.

Claudia closed her eyes. 'He's dead, isn't he? Mark's dead?'

He didn't hesitate, he didn't draw it out, prolong the worst out of distaste at having to be the one to tell her. He nodded and answered her immediately.

'Yes. I'm sorry.' He paused, waiting a moment for her to absorb the news. 'When you're over the shock, we'll have to ask you some questions, but right now I think you'd better go to a friend's place. Is there someone I can call for you?'

She hesitated for a moment, trying to think clearly. When she spoke her voice was dull, her manner withdrawn.

'How? Was he murdered?' She covered her face with one hand but there were no tears. She felt dry and parched inside.

'He was stabbed,' Tony said, again so calmly that it almost slid by her, almost evaded her comprehension. His face was closed, the grey eyes revealing nothing more.

Claudia looked up at him. 'By whom? Why? Didn't anyone see anything? They must have heard him. You can hear everything through those walls. Someone must have seen or heard something? Mrs Tsao opposite. She would know, she always knows. He was screaming, over and over, in agony!'

He glanced away, breathed in tightly, felt inadequate to her loss. If only his father had mentioned Mark sooner, a day, even hours sooner, there might have been something he could have done. Not now.

'We're still trying to find that out, Miss Babcock.'

'You called me Claudia – you said we knew each other....when? What's your name again?'

'Ingram. Tony Ingram. I was the same age as your older sister, Peggy. We all used to play together when we were little. I don't suppose you remember. Mark and I saw each other a bit, over the years. It's all right. I've identified him. You don't need to do that.' He still held her hand and she looked down at the square bluntness of the fingers and back at the man himself, a small frown puckering her forehead.

'You gave me a starfish. The day – that day at Repulse Bay. I remember.' She tried to fit the man to the boy she

257

had once known. The hair was a shade darker, a sun-bleached brown, like caramel, and there were lines of experience on the face now, a broad, steady face with intelligent grey eyes and a faintly crooked nose. Not exactly handsome but reassuringly attractive. She dropped his hand.

'I want to see him.'

'That's not a good idea. You'll only upset yourself unnecessarily. Try and remember him the way he was, not the way he looks now, in death. It won't help.'

'I want to see him.'

'Claudia. Please. You're still in shock.' He made some signal behind her back and she stared up at him, unblinking.

'I have a right. There's no one else here who's family. He was my *brother*!' She pushed past him, walking back to the apartment block. Ahead of her, going up the stairs, were two men in white uniforms. They were carrying a stretcher between them. She looked back at Tony who shrugged and ordered the men to let her pass.

He followed her up, talking quietly to the men at the door, taking her arm before she could step past them.

'Claudia, you have to prepare yourself. He's been badly slashed. I wish you wouldn't do this.'

She looked into his eyes for a moment, remembering them that day at the beach, when he had run after her to hand her the starfish. They had been huge then, flecked with dark like the tiger stripe of a tabby cat, imprisoned in clear glass. Mirroring her own tragedy. As they were now. She grasped his hand tightly and then stepped past him.

The flat hadn't changed. It wasn't strewn with furniture and clothes. There had been no robbery and very little struggle. But the walls were splashed and sprayed with red and the tiled floor was pooled in dark, congealing bubbles of blood. Claudia flinched, even before she saw Mark. They had covered his body with a sheet but the blood had soaked through in streaks of clashing colour. His face was oddly calm in the midst of such violence. Eyes shut, mouth firmly pressed together, it gave no impression of the horror it had suffered. Nor had it yet lost its colour. Claudia crouched down beside her brother and gently reached out a hand to stroke the hair back from his forehead. The skin was still warm against her fingers and his hair was still soft to touch. A deep ache began in her chest, pulling her down.

'Oh, Mark, why didn't you come with me? Why?' Her voice was little more than a whisper. The face didn't move. It was so smooth and pale, so very beautiful in its severity that she almost couldn't bear to look at it. She made no attempt to see beneath the sheet or to look further at the apartment. Instead she knelt beside the body and studied the face, trying to imprint it for one last time on her mind. She had known him so briefly as an adult. She didn't want his memory to just slip away.

'Claudia?' Tony Ingram's voice floated down to her, as though through layers of thick water. She heard it blurred and distorted over the distance. Dimly, she looked up.

'Who did this? Why?'

'We'll find out. Or we'll try, anyway.'

'Try?' Her eyes seemed huge in the pale face.

'This looks like a ritual killing – Triad justice. Normally it's to do with betraying the Triad oath-taking ceremony, but that's not the reason here. They don't have *gweilos* in the Triads. Not in Hong Kong.' He leaned down and pulled Claudia to her feet, letting her lean against him as her strength began to fail, the warmth of his body welcome after the chill of the floor.

'Come outside. There's nothing more you can do.' And this time, Claudia did not resist. She let him lead her downstairs and back to the car, seating her once more inside it. Then he climbed in the front seat and snapped an order to the driver.

The car pulled away as the first of the newspaper hounds arrived, baying for blood and gore, for sensationalism. This time they would have it.

'Where do you want to go? Which friends?' Tony Ingram asked but Claudia shook her head mutely, too drained to think of anyone. Not Silvia, not Harry – they were too close to the pain. Not any of the more casual 'friends' she had

259

made in the last month. She closed her eyes.

'I don't know. I don't care really. Just somewhere.'

The driver received a few terse instructions and swung the car down towards Cotton Tree Drive, right onto Queensway and through onto Hennessy Road in Wanchai. The traffic was light and the car moved quickly and skilfully through the other cars, pulling up barely fifteen minutes later outside a building on Hennessy Road. Tony Ingram got out and opened the door for Claudia, lifting her firmly and steering her inside the building.

There were two lifts. One for the odd floors, one for the even. Tony swung the grille doors to one side, helping her into them when it looked as though she might slide, instead, to the floor. There was a smell of boiled cabbage and incense and some other, sweet, slightly sickly smell that lingered in the linoleum and the scarred walls of the elevator. They rode up to the fifth floor in silence.

Tony had keys to the apartment and he let them both in, gesturing for Claudia to sit down. She followed his directions and sat on the rough linen sofa, her vision narrowed to nothing more than the wall in front of her. A black and white photograph of three children, blown up and framed in a plain silver and glass covering, stared back at her.

'Here, drink this.' He handed her a heavy balloon of brandy and she cradled it between her hands, sitting at it, feeling the first quivers of shock ripple through her.

'This is your place?' she asked at last.

'Yes. Just me, so don't worry, there won't be any prying flat-mates turning up later. There's a pull-down sofa in the spare room. You can stay as long as you need.' He wasn't being particularly solicitous, his tone wasn't overly sympathetic but there was something about him that made Claudia's throat ache to release the misery that had built up like a hard ball inside her. She knew he wouldn't be offended, wouldn't be upset. She knew he would understand and help, if he could. But she swallowed hard instead.

'I need to call my mother. I have to let her know.' Her voice was harsh.

'Tomorrow. You're not fit to manage someone else's grief. You need a stiff drink, a bite to eat, and bed.'

'There won't be any grief,' she said and Tony turned to look at her, his face becoming still, wary. Claudia shrugged, feeling ill. 'My mother couldn't give a damn about Mark. He chose to stay with my father when the break-up happened. She never forgave him for that. We had a huge argument when I decided to come out here.' Another long, warming sip of brandy slid down her throat and she glanced at him, shrugged again. 'But I have to tell her anyway. She'll know how to contact my father. He'll care.'

There was a long pause in which Tony wondered to himself about Claudia, about whether she had cared, and if so, how badly. But he didn't feel he could ask her that yet. He saw the shock pulling at her face, making it taut, saw the way her eyelashes flicked uneasily over her thoughts.

Finally she broke the silence, tentatively at first, but growing surer as he listened quietly, and the horror of the last few hours urged her to confidences she would never normally have betrayed. Tony watched her steadily, asking questions from time to time.

'I always missed Mark. For years, even though he had been a rotten brother, bullied and teased and ... but I missed him. We wrote, from time to time, but that doesn't really work. I only got to know him for a month, this time round. Not very long. And we argued tonight, before I went out.' Her voice broke. 'Oh God, I just can't believe he's gone, that's it, and I'll never see him again. Never.' The misery ground out in her voice.

'Do you know who might have killed him? Or why?'

'No, no-oo, I really don't. But he was scared about something, all the time, like he was on the verge of panic.' She looked up. 'He was smoking a lot of dope but that's not all that unusual out here, is it? He drank a lot too, and he could be – difficult – when he was stoned ... but not really, not enough to kill him for. He said someone was coming over to see him this evening. I assumed it was a dealer. You should ask Fish or Harry. They'd have a better idea.'

She pushed the hair back from her face, feeling suddenly

and violently ill, her skin breaking out in a pale sweat and her stomach heaving. Tony took the glass from her hand and manhandled her quickly towards the small bathroom, holding her head over the lavatory. He was businesslike and brisk, but his hands were gentle when he wiped her face with a wet flannel afterwards and led her back to the sofa. There was a steadiness about him that was more soothing than words of sympathy. She lay back gratefully against the pillows and let him put her feet up.

'Sorry about that.' If she had felt better, she would have been more embarrassed. She closed her eyes instead.

'It's normal. You'll feel rough for a couple of days. Just take it easy. You mentioned Aidan Lockhart, is that right? Fish?'

'Yes, you know him?'

'Yes. At least, I used to. And "Harry" is Harry Braga, I take it?'

'Yes.' Harry, whom she desperately wanted to talk to, but didn't dare for fear of what she might hear, what he might know. Harry who had secrets.

'How well do you know Harry, Claudia? And how much of his past do you know?' Tony almost seemed to read her thoughts. She flinched, seeing him taking that in as well.

'Oh, bits, I guess, not much more. He was our amah's son. Eurasian. He was with me that day at the beach. You remember him?'

Tony cast his mind back and the small dark-haired boy who had stared after the car in such misery floated back to him. He nodded at the memory. 'Yes. What happened to him after you left?'

'I only know a little. Harry won't talk about it or keeps it so brief I have to guess. He went and stayed with relatives for a while and when his mother remarried, he went back to live with her. Then there's a blank bit that he just doesn't talk about until he started work at Commercial Radio. I don't know what happened in there. Does that help at all?'

'I don't know. Maybe.'

'Harry didn't have anything to do with Mark's death.' Claudia looked at Tony steadily and he gave a brief smile.

'I didn't say he did.' But he was silent for a long time, remembering the boy who had hit him at that nightclub, who had wielded a knife with a practised air.

'How did you become a cop? I mean, wasn't your dad something pretty senior in the Civil Service here? What made you want to be a cop?' Claudia broke in on his reverie and he glanced at her, a smile flickering for a moment over his lips. She had curled herself up on the sofa, her arms loosely wrapped around her knees, the silky shorts she wore flowing loosely over her legs. Good legs, nice slim body with all the curves in the right places but unremarkable until you looked in those dark eyes. All her attraction was centred in those eyes; those contained, elusive thoughts, he realised. He watched her for a moment but she didn't smile.

'I guess I never grew up. I liked playing cops and robbers, and what better place to play than Hong Kong? I didn't want to sit in front of a desk all day long.'

'I suppose you have to speak Cantonese? That must be a prerequisite.'

'No. It helps but I know most of the more senior Europeans don't speak more than a pidgin version. I was in the army first.' He seemed amused by her surprise.

'As what?'

'A lieutenant, for the most part. I left just after I had made captain and went travelling for a bit, through Europe and the States. I got on well with Americans, they're so open and friendly. It makes a nice change. Then I came out here and started with the RHKPD.'

'Do you specialise in anything or are you just a general sort of cop?'

'Well, at first I was just a regular cop but now I "specialise" – if that's what you want to call it – in Triads. I'm with the Triad Society Bureau. We were set up to counter the Triad threat. Sometimes I wonder just who's really countering who.' There was a resigned expression that made his face seem weary. Claudia noted it with misgiving and he shrugged. 'There've been a few corruption problems,' he admitted stiffly.

263

'Why Triads? I mean, why them especially? Why do they get their own bureau?'

'Because they're the fastest growing and probably the most dangerous criminal element in the world and almost no one knows anything about them or will even admit they exist and almost no one has ever penetrated one of their lodges.' He paused and looked at her. 'Do you really want to know?'

She nodded, wondering why she did, what was the point when Mark was dead. But she had to know.

'Well, Hong Kong is the main base, now, though God knows they're everywhere. You name a place and if there are Chinese there, I'll guarantee there'll be a Triad lodge of some sort. Vancouver, Amsterdam, London, Sydney, San Francisco, New York and endless more. Maybe it's a legitimate, self-help sort of organisation, maybe an un-official trade union of sorts, but there'll be something and before long they'll be "hanging the blue lantern" and putting on the squeeze and the drug racketeering and protectionism will start and off we go, yet again.' He sounded tired and disillusioned and Claudia wondered what had happened to make him like that.

'What's that mean, "hanging the blue lantern"?' Some-thing tickled at her memory, something Mark had said. Her eyes narrowed with concentration but she couldn't remember the context. It hadn't made sense at the time.

'Some people say it means the initiation ceremony but from what I understand it's more like a provisional driving licence. You're on probation and if you pass, then you go through the full ceremony and become a blood-brother, become a proper Triad. But you have to earn the respect first, show you're worth hanging a lantern for. And then there's no way out, bar death. Once a Triad, always a Triad.'

'Is that why you were at Mark's? You said then it was some sort of ritual killing. How do you know?'

'Yeah, they called me in because ... look, it's ... not pleasant.'

'Tell me. I want to know.' She was so determined, her chin jutting forward, that he knew there was no point in stalling.

'"Dying by myriads of swords" describes how the victim is slashed, many times, with a butcher's knife or a meat cleaver, across all the main muscles. Here, here,' he demonstrated with slicing movements across his forearms and biceps and then across his calves and thighs, keeping his voice impersonal, factual. 'Sometimes the scalp also. It's an effective sort of warning against anyone else breaking any of the thirty-six oaths they swear to. That or being killed by five thunderbolts.'

'Five thunderbolts? What's that? A gun?' She looked at him for confirmation, her face pale and ill but he shrugged instead. 'And that's how Mark died, this myriads of swords thing?' She felt as though she might have to be sick again but she forced it down. 'How do you know about these oaths and things if no one's ever lived to tell the tale? I mean, Mark didn't take any oath ...'

'No, he wouldn't have. We know that much from what we've found when we've broken up a lodge. Lists of rules, that sort of thing. And they wouldn't have let Mark join, that's for certain.' Tony's forehead creased with thought. 'But it may be that he knew something and was going to tell, or did tell it to someone else. Or it may be that he saw something that he wasn't supposed to. Or, most likely, they were using him and he cheated them. As I said before, it was a warning. I know that much, at least.' He saw how pale and clammy her skin was and he cursed beneath his breath. 'I'm sorry.'

She shook her head. 'No, I asked. I wanted – needed, really – to know. But I just don't understand! Why would he have got mixed up with all that?' She closed her eyes. 'It's so unfair. He just got promoted and I just got here and everything should have been just great. I mean, he asked me to come out, so he must have wanted me here. But he was scared about something, said he didn't want me getting involved, and then he would just close up. More and more, just lately, really frightening me. Maybe it was my fault for losing that box. I don't know ...' She shook her head, her voice an indistinct blur.

'What box?' Tony looked up, frowning.

She told him briefly about it, ending with Mark's fury and fear when she had to admit that it was missing. But Tony only shrugged, barely seemed to take any notice, setting another glass of water and a couple of pills down on the table in front of her.

'None of it was your fault, so don't try and start blaming yourself. You should take these. They'll dull everything down and make it easier to bear. You take them and then get yourself to bed. I've put a duvet and a pillow on the pull-down bed and there's fresh sheets already on the mattress.' He paused and stroked the hair back from her face, noting how young she looked now that the make-up had gone. The last time he had seen her, she had been in misery and now, twenty years later, the same again. He wondered how anyone could ever think life was fair, that it evened out in the end.

'Claudia, I'm really sorry about Mark. I'll do my best to find out what happened, what it was all about. But no one can ever guarantee anything with the Triads.' He looked down at his watch. 'Now, I have to go out again and I want you to go to bed and get some sleep. All right?' She gripped his hand tightly and he knelt down beside her.

Awkwardly, she smiled through her tears. 'Do you have to go out? Can't it wait until morning?' She shivered again and he squeezed her hand more tightly.

'No. It can't. But you'll be safe here. I'll have some clothes brought over for you tomorrow, from the flat. Now you get some sleep and try not to think too much – not about anything. We can talk again in the morning.' He stood up and kissed her briefly on the top of her head before releasing her hand. 'And don't open the door. Okay? I've got my keys and no one else needs to come in. See you later.' He gave her a quick smile and let himself out through the front door. Claudia heard him locking it from the outside.

Chapter Twenty-Two

Harry Braga sat in his leather swivel chair and contemplated his own death. Long and slow and infinitely painful, he thought, with a pursed mouth. Yee would insist on nothing less. Not for a strongman, a 'Red Pole'. He wasn't particularly afraid of death. But he didn't like the thought of that pain. Once, long ago, he had thought he could handle the pain, but not the incarceration. Now he knew he couldn't handle either. At least Mark's had been quick. Relatively. His lips compressed again in anger and disgust.

Would Mark have got involved anyway, without his help, Harry wondered and would have liked to believe it, to lessen the guilt that sat like a hard, painful lump in his gut. But he had never lied to himself. There was no point.

It was dark outside now. Nearly eleven. And he had finished his shift at nine. There were no more excuses for delaying. Already the others – the back-up crew, the production staff, the news editorial bunch – already they were looking at him sideways, wondering how much longer he was going to go on sitting there.

With a sigh, he stood up. Perhaps it was a little game that Yee was playing with him? A warning to toe the line, to do as Yee asked – no, demanded. Nothing more. They would pay, Yee had said, Mark and he would pay, some time, somewhere. And now Mark was dead and perhaps that was it? Or perhaps it was to let him sweat before his own death, to let him die a thousand imaginary deaths before finally enduring the real one. Subtle. A faint curve to his lips would have seemed like amusement, had anyone seen it.

He wondered where Claudia was. Perhaps at Silvia's? When he got home, he would call her. If he got home. He pulled on his jacket, a lightweight linen one that was blessedly dark, and threw his satchel over his shoulder. His notes for tomorrow's programme. What did that matter any more? They weren't going to let him go. All those years when he had thought he was free of Yee, only to find he had been playing him, like a puppet, in an unknown role. Harry waved a hand to the late-night crew, endured a few painful jokes, and walked stiff-backed from the studio. He walked with a slight limp, unable to bend and flow, his muscles tightened as though they sensed the slashing blows and were tensed in readiness. No one noticed him in the street; he was just one more body pushing along in the evening crowds. He climbed aboard the tram and sat hunched over on the narrow wooden seats as they rattled and swayed in the neon night.

He lived in Happy Valley, in a top-floor flat near the race course that was larger and more spacious than most of his contemporaries'. But then, he knew how to get what he wanted. Yee had taught him that.

What if he hadn't run away, all those years ago? Would he have still made it to where he was now? Or would he still be some peasant boy, living with his amah mother and her new *gweilo* husband on Cheung Chau, still listening to the screaming babies and scolding wives and blaring radios of their apartment block, still working in the fishball factory, still smelling of oil and fish and grease, still flinching beneath the too soft, too lingering touch of his step-father? He closed his eyes to the rushing lights of Wanchai, blurring by in the darkness, almost nodding off to sleep before jerking awake and looking around. He reached up and pulled the cord.

He paid his fare and quickly slid off the tram as it pulled away from the stop. No one following him would have had time to jump off. He looked around but no one paid him any attention. This was one stop earlier than his normal one, and the shop sellers didn't know him, didn't call out their usual nightly greeting. He padded on down Wong Na Chung Road, almost running in places, cutting across Sports Road and the fast-moving traffic to edge onto

268

Queen's Road East. Nothing unusual appeared behind or ahead of him, despite his careful deceits of circling around the lanes and appearing each time near his apartment block from a different direction.

If they wanted him, they would be waiting inside. That's how he would have done it. Bribed or threatened the old woman who acted as caretaker, let himself into the flat and waited in the dark. That's how they would do it, if they wanted him. He looked carefully at the old woman but she was eating and not interested. As the lift door closed, her eyes slowly raised themselves over her bowl, watching the red floor lights. There was interest now, sharp and still, when the lift stopped two floors early. Slowly the old woman smiled.

Yee would send some fool first, some lightweight thug in training for the role of Red Pole for the Thin Blades. Someone expendable to see how alert Harry was, someone to lull him into a false sense of security with how easily he was dealt with. Harry knew how Yee's mind worked, even now, years later. No one but a fool would expect him to come in through the front door.

The man was a fool. Harry saw him, long before he had slipped through the glass doors from the patio and slid into the shadows of the room. It had been so easy to go up the stairs to the roof and then drop down onto his own patio. The man should have seen that. But he didn't because he was a fool and expendable. Harry cursed Yee.

Now what did he do? Kill the man? Or just hurt him and send him home in disgrace? Either way, the man would die. But Harry didn't want the blood on his hands; no more blood, not ever. He had spilled too much as it was. And anyway, it was only a boy, barely twenty, long-haired, thin and scrawny in his fake designer jeans and his loud designer shirt. Hadn't anyone even thought to tell the boy to dress in black at night?

Harry would have sighed out loud but he knew the boy couldn't be that bad. A narrow, vicious face that was frightened in the gleam of moonlight that fell on it, made Harry impossibly sad, achingly, desperately sad. That had been him ten years ago. And he hadn't really survived it either.

He had circled the boy by now, slipping through the shadows, knowing the layout of the room in his sleep. There were no awkward bumps, no tinkling windchimes, no scrapes set off by an unwary presence. He was less than three feet from the boy now. And still his assailant hadn't thought to turn around, to check the shadows with his nervous gaze. A fool.

It was hard to think of the boy as a murderer, an assassin. He was just a scared boy knowing he had been sent against a former Red Pole, a master assassin. The boy knew he was outclassed. He knew that even as he felt the pain shoot along his thumb, along his arm that was held out and up, the agony spreading so fast, so frighteningly that he couldn't move, just pant and swear into a floor that had risen unaccountably towards him. He squealed in rage and pain, but mostly pain.

Harry pulled the thumb up harder in a sudden, leftward movement that produced a thin shriek from the boy and an unpleasant snapping sound from the arm, like bamboo broken across a knee. The boy slumped down and didn't move. And, suddenly, Harry knew that he had been the fool, not this boy. Because it hadn't occurred to him that there would be two of them, a game inside a game, a trap more delicate than either the unwary boy or he had known. Yee was to be congratulated.

It was the breath of wind on his cheek that warned him, the rush of air from a fast-moving object. He rolled as the sliver of light arced through the night, tracing his path in blurred moonlight as he came to his feet again a few paces distant. But already the light was slashing down towards him, faster than he had anticipated. It left a warm burning sensation along his forearm.

This man was not a fool. He made no sound, no exultation, no laboured breathing, nothing to pinpoint his position as he danced back into the shadows. The speed and silence were terrifying.

Harry crouched low, easing himself towards the wall and

the bookcase, his breathing beginning to sound loud in his throat, in his ears as he fought to control it. The boy would have had a knife, a stiletto, a thin blade of some sort but he couldn't risk crossing to him. That would take him out into the moonlight. Grimly he felt in the gloom for wood, sucking in with relief as his fingers filled with splinters.

The man came again, rushing forward to slice with precision, a blow to Harry's leg, a quick gouging motion along the thigh and gone again, a will-o'-the-wisp in the night. Harry gasped and groped again with his hand, his fingers touching the object he sought. He relaxed, drew himself in for a moment, and then moved gently along the bookcase. There would be another attack soon, before he could reach the far wall, he knew. A more serious, more wounding flash of light, the blade cold and hot and infinitely sharp as it entered warm buttery skin. And he couldn't risk being incapacitated, couldn't risk having to seek medical attention afterwards. He needed to kill the man fast.

It didn't occur to Harry that he might be the one to die. Earlier, yes, when his mind had time to dwell on such fates, but not now, not in the midst of the attack. He only thought how to kill, not how to fear death.

As the rush began, he curled his left arm around the bookcase, embracing the objects to him and thrusting them out furiously into the path of the man. There was a quick feint, a stumble and the man disappeared again. No sound. The man was very good.

But Harry had already reached the end of the bookcase and his fingers curled around the small plastic object, hesitated for a moment, and then flicked it up. The room sprang into dazzling light around him even as the man came at him again. Harry raised his right arm and squeezed his index finger twice, soft, breathy plops of sound halting the man, spinning him around and gently laying him down on the ground. Harry smiled.

'Nice gun, huh?' he asked conversationally, but his legs were beginning to tremble, and his vision was blurred. He walked forward and knelt near the man, took aim and squeezed another bullet into the man's face. Then he walked past him into the bathroom and stripped a towel from the rail to wrap around his thigh.

No one could have heard the shots, not with the silencer. He took another towel and limped back into the sitting room, leaning down over the man's body. Swiftly he wrapped the head in the towel, sopping up the blood. He had tiled floors, easy to slide the body along, easier still to clean up afterwards. The patio doors were pushed back, the body dragged over to the far side. Harry looked down on the alley, silent and dark. With a grunt of effort he pulled the body upright, holding it to him as though in a macabre sort of dance, unwrapped the towel and then pushed it backwards, over the edge. It landed with a solid thump some ten floors below. A dog went skittering away, howling as it ran.

The boy was gone by the time he returned to the sitting room, running for his life, perhaps to offer excuses where none would be found acceptable. Or perhaps just running. Good, Harry thought. One less to deal with. He put the dead bolt across the door and leaned over it for a moment, gasping. Then he mopped up the tiles and carried the towels back to the bathroom, thrusting them and the clothes he wore quickly into the washing machine and setting it on a cold wash. The clothes would have to be dumped somewhere later, but not with blood on them. That would attract attention.

He stood naked on the cold tiles and eased his arm under the running water. It stang but he saw it was not a deep cut. He dried it with tissues and bound some gauze and sticking plaster over it. The leg was worse, a slab of flesh flensed from his thigh so that it hung obscenely. It needed stitches. Tomorrow he would find someone to take care of it. He washed, dried and bandaged it, swallowed a couple of ibuprofin tablets and flushed the tissues down the lavatory. Then he retraced his steps, examining the room through the eyes of the suspicious. There was nothing to give him away. Nothing but a dead body down in the alley below. And that could have come from anywhere.

The gun was already dismantled, the pieces wiped clean and either thrown from the balcony or pushed down the drainpipe. He had another gun, of a different make, hidden in the flat. With luck no one would find that either. Not unless they took the place to pieces and then they would find everything. With a sigh of deep exhaustion, Harry secured the iron grille onto the patio doors, switched off the lights and climbed into bed.

He was asleep when the police banged on the door.

The sheets were cool but Claudia still tossed and kicked herself into a tangle. She pushed them to one side and sat up, feeling stuffy in the small room. The moonlight shafted in brightly between the slatted blinds and she stood up, going to peer out through the window at the dark alleys and washing below, her naked body striped by the shadows and light.

Tony, sitting in the dark, could see her through her partially open door. He drew in on his cigarette, inhaling deeply. He didn't bother to look at the clock on the wall. He knew it was after three. He had been back nearly an hour, sitting smoking silently, thinking. Letting his mind drift, wondering about the girl. She didn't know anything; he was sure about that, at least. Nothing that she knew she knew. He smiled in the dark at himself, at his convoluted thinking. He was becoming more Chinese than the Chinese.

'You want a drink?' he called, regretting the impulse almost immediately as she disappeared from view. He stood up and went to stand by her door. 'Claudia?'

'How long have you been there?' Her voice was quiet. Tony shrugged. 'About an hour. What's the matter? Can't you sleep?' He moved into the room, sitting beside her on the bed. She tucked the sheet in more tightly around herself.

'It's hot. I couldn't breathe. But the windows are already open.'

'Here.' He leaned across her and snapped on a switch. The ceiling fan began to rotate slowly. Claudia shivered in its breeze.

'Where've you been? It's late.'

'Oh, asking questions, filling in reports. Deaths make a lot of work.'

'Murders, you mean. Did you see Harry?' Immediately she knew she had asked the wrong question. He continued to smoke, quietly, but there was a tension in his body that hadn't been there before.

'Yes. He says he doesn't know anything. Has no idea why Mark was scared.' But his pyjama pants were red with blood and Tony didn't think he was the sort who wore pyjamas much in the first place. And there was a dead body that had fallen a long distance in the alley below his place. Two dead bodies in one night. And Harry seemed to be involved in them both. Tony chewed on his lip for a moment, stubbing out the cigarette.

'And Fish?'

'Soaking it up at Scottie's. He's been there all evening, from before Mark was killed. Plenty of witnesses. He didn't know and he was too drunk to care.'

'Oh.' It was a small sound but Tony heard the contempt.

'Have you decided what you're going to do? Stay here or go back to America?' She looked at him then, her eyes large and unreadable. He wished he could understand her better, but she had always been contained, even as a child.

'Not yet. I don't want to go yet. I guess I'll find somewhere to stay. Silvia wants to move out of her parents' place. Maybe we'll get a flat together.'

'Silvia? I don't think her parents will care for that. You can stay here as long as you want, you know.' He didn't feel odd making the offer to a girl he barely knew. Somehow he felt he had always known Claudia.

But he flushed when she eyed him carefully, her face still. 'Can I? That's very kind of you. But I'll move as soon as possible. I guess you live alone for a reason.' Her shoulders were thin, the collar bones hollowed by shadows. He would have liked to lean forward and touch that bare skin, rub his fingers over it. Instead he lay down on the bed, one arm raised over his face.

'My hours aren't very sociable. Sharing doesn't work too well. Not in the long run.'

'Not with anyone? Don't you have any lovers? Don't you ever want to get married? Or doesn't that fit in with police work either?' They lay companionably, side by side, and Tony closed his eyes, seeing that tiger-striped body, the bumps of hips and breasts, again in his mind. It had been some time since his last lover, he thought with surprise, and then was even more surprised by how badly he wanted the girl beside him. He shook the thought away.

'One day, maybe. But I haven't met her yet,' he said after a momentary silence. Beside him, Claudia felt a twinge of disappointment and then smiled to herself, at her foolishness. But it would have felt good to have his reassuring arms around her now, she thought, with a pang.

'Are your sisters married?' They had been either side of Tony in age, she remembered. Plum and Hattie, infinitely sure of themselves, lively and laughing, sometimes silly but always charmingly so. They had drawn people to them from an early age, Claudia thought, effortlessly.

'Yes, of course. It's what they both wanted. What my father wanted for them.'

'And your mother?'

'She ... she ran off with some man, can't remember who now, quite frankly. She dropped him pretty quickly though and started up with the man she's now married to. Hamish Sheridan. Nice man, actually. We tend to see them both at weddings or funerals. Not much in between.'

Cool and careless but not entirely convincing, Claudia thought. There had been a lot of pain over that rejection, once. Maybe still.

'Like my father. He remarried too. Joyce, her name is. They live in Singapore now.'

'Chinese?'

'Yes. He liked – likes – Chinese women, I gather. Their trimness, or their agreeableness – is there such a word?' She paused, considering. 'Mark did too.'

'What about your sister – Peggy? She must be married by now.'

275

'Yes.' There was a dryness to her tone that spoke of matters unwelcome and unbecoming. She turned on her side to face him, the valley between her small breasts deepening. He forced himself not to look, not out of tact but rather out of a feeling that it would be unfair when she was still vulnerable.

'But not you. How old are you now? Twenty-five?'

'Twenty-seven. And I'm not in any hurry, if ever. From what I've seen, marriage isn't all that great.'

'No.' He cleared his throat. 'You write – what? For a newspaper, a magazine?'

'Business issues for a quarterly journal. That's how I wangled my way out here. Everyone wants to know what's happening in Hong Kong in the run up to 'ninety-seven.'

'Nothing else? No budding novels trying to escape?' He was teasing but again her quiet watchfulness made him uneasy. Perhaps he had trodden on delicate feelings? He had no way of knowing if she didn't choose to tell him.

'Yes, a few. But no best sellers. Maybe I'll make that breakthrough when I'm old and full of malicious amusement at everyone else's foibles.' She grinned.

'More fun to live them first,' he said mildly but there was a curve to his lips that Claudia enjoyed. She was increasingly enjoying Tony altogether, despite the sudden black moments, as though a fast flying cloud had shut off the sun, that reminded her why she was there, when her voice rattled to a shaky halt and the pain twisted inside.

'Of course. How else can you write about them with full understanding? It must be wonderful to have been a complete disgrace during your earlier lifetime and then age into a figure of awe and respect by the next generation.'

'Not the next. The one after that. The next would be too busy condemning.'

'True. I hadn't thought of that.'

'Is that why you condemn Peggy?' Tony wondered whether the question would annoy her. He lowered his arm and watched her. She had withdrawn again.

'Peggy? I don't condemn her. I just ...' she paused, considering whether the truth were acceptable or not, 'dislike her, really. She's stupid. She doesn't have a wild affair because the man is forbidden but dashing. No, she just has any man, every man, endless men. No discrimination.' She twisted her mouth together. 'I guess she can't help it, really. But it doesn't make me like her. You must have sensed it about her, even when she was eleven. Other boys did.'

He shrugged but he knew he had, knew that the fascination had been that there was so much allure, so much awareness of sexuality and yet none of it had been explored. No wonder his mother had kept him away.

'You have it too. No, not the wantonness,' he amended as he saw her flinch. 'But the allure. Toned down but it's there. You must know that.'

'Umm, but I'm not my sister. I don't want to get trapped with a child before I've had a chance to live my own life. Not that Todd isn't almost worth it. He's a good kid. He deserves better than Peggy.' Their voices were hushed in the darkness, whispering words they wouldn't have said in the more revealing light of day.

'And Mark? How was he? Like Peggy, or you?'

'More Peggy, I guess, but he's – was – a man, so he didn't get condemned for it. You know, I think he even had trouble remembering, sometimes, that I was his sister. I'd see him watching me and then he'd get this puzzled, guilty look on his face and he'd turn away. Hard for him to think of me as a sister when he hadn't seen me since I was seven.'

For a moment, Tony felt a blinding surge of anger and disgust at the dead Mark. But Claudia was so matter-of-fact, so unmoved by her remark that he forced himself to reconsider it objectively, seeing it as she did.

'Did you? Have difficulty thinking of Mark as your brother, I mean.' He sensed the shake of head, the amusement.

'No. He wasn't my type. I like a little more . . .' What? A little more dependability, trustworthiness, tenderness? She'd never found all three of those at once, so how could she know? Tony noticed the omission but did not press.

'But you were his. The trimness, perhaps?'

'Not the agreeableness, anyway.' She laughed soundlessly and he couldn't stop himself from trying to kiss her. He tasted salt on her cheeks.

'Are you sad?' he asked gently. She nodded and allowed him to fold his arms around her, holding her in close. He held her like that until it became impossible to hide his reaction. Equally gently, he disengaged himself.

Claudia sighed, wishing he would continue just to lie there and hold her like that. But it was too much to ask without offering more. She saw him hesitate, and she wondered whether he was considering trying. But he was too wise for that. He shook his head, smiled and kissed her cheek, forcing himself away.

Not now, it wouldn't be right, he thought. Later, perhaps, if things turn out that way. But it wouldn't be fair now.

He stood up, leaning down lightly to brush his lips across hers, smelling of ink and car fumes, sweat and his own maleness but it was a good smell and she breathed it in deeply, liking him for his reserve, his control. He was — trustworthy. Yes, that was it. And that was something rare enough to value.

'Goodnight, Liddie,' he said as he padded on bare feet from the room. She turned on her side, her hip meeting the springs from the bed. Her body felt long and flat, virginal, beneath her hand as she stroked it down and over herself.

'Goodnight, Tony, sweet dreams,' she called, and Tony, standing naked by his bed, his body protesting, cursed swiftly and silently to himself.

Chapter Twenty-Three

Sunday morning

Claudia woke with such an intense feeling of relief that she stood up immediately, slipped a shirt over her head, and went to Tony's door, calling out delightedly: 'It's all right. It was all a mistake, Tony, you got it wrong. Mark's fine ...' But even as the words left her lips, the reality began to shred, the dream-like quality became more apparent and she faltered. Surely, surely, it had been real? She had held him in her arms, his hair so soft and his flesh warm and hard beneath her hands, and the nurse, whoever she had been, had smiled and said, 'No, no, he isn't dead. How silly, it was all a mistake, he's been here all along.' And she had been so sure.

But now, like a deep, frightening darkness creeping over her, she realised her mistake. Mark was dead and there was nothing that could bring him back, nothing that could be done to have made his last few days, few minutes better. She stood by the doorway, clutching at her shirt tails, flattening the cotton across her hip bones and inside her mind howled with pain.

Tony hadn't woken but lay on his back, his mouth faintly parted, his breathing slow and heavy but his hand plucked at the sheet, twining it tightly around his fingers. Claudia looked at him for a long time, wanting to free those fingers from the sheet, to smooth the lines that puckered across his face as the dream gripped him. Instead she forced herself away.

She saw the apartment was smaller than she had thought the night before, plain white-painted brick walls dotted with paintings and photographs of laughing people clowning around in smart-looking places. She went from

279

one to another, absorbing them, absorbing Tony's background, his private self, trying to block out the despair that seemed so much worse for her temporary and mistaken relief. Then she turned to examine the room itself, the sofa in a dun-coloured rough linen, sagging and comfortable with pillows, the old rug on the wooden boards that made her smile wryly, so much a part of the photographs and smart people as it was, even in its threadbare state. But the rest was functional, a glass table, a few chairs, books. Nothing to really worry about should he be gone for some time.

No emotional luggage – that's what she had tried to say to Mark, to explain about herself, when he had accused her of going to look for Harry; she wasn't looking to drag around any emotional luggage, neither human nor material. But that wasn't true any more and she could feel her need more strongly now than ever before, someone to make things right, someone to cling to in all the pain and bleak despair, some place to call home and spend hours prettifying, nesting, a safe hole to burrow into. Well, there was no one but there was somewhere.

That was what she should do. She looked around, stronger suddenly for the conviction in her – get a place of her own, right now, today. Fran Clements, her parents' old friend who had been much like a mother to Mark after his own had left, had offered to rent her their 'boathouse' when she first arrived and she had been unsure about Mark's reception. It was only a tiny place, a sort of servant's quarters down near the water from their house, the garden that so many people would have paid so much for, nonchalantly stretching between. They had bought it when they first arrived, over twenty years ago, when Stanley hadn't been so stylish nor so easily commutable. And now they sat there in their splendour, smiling benignly at those with less forethought who were caught in the spiralling rent rises that constantly sought to outstrip their expatriate packages.

It was an old place and would need work, Fran had said, but the rent was ridiculously low and the setting quite without equal. That was what she needed; she would ring Fran today, ring her now, yes, why not? And she hurried in her oversized shirt, bare legs peeping out in her haste, to the telephone, picked it up, called, now, before she could change her mind. Keep going, keep moving, don't think. That was the answer.

By the time Tony woke and appeared from his room, rubbing hard fingers into his scalp, his hair standing on end, Claudia was dressed and ready to go. She looked around, startled and faintly guilty, as though she were running out.

'Going already?' He stilled, his hand falling back to his side, his eyes going through a phase of transparent emotions, surprise, puzzlement, regret, relief. That last hurt but Claudia smiled through it, thinking to herself, it doesn't matter, he's just a man, basically kind, basically uninvolved, getting on with his own life, his own work. As she should be. She liked him, but no more. She wouldn't allow more.

'Yes, I've found somewhere to rent. I've left the address and telephone number over there. I guess, when you hear something about Mark, you'll let me know? I mean, about the body – we'll have to do something about that, won't we? Cremate it, I guess. He once said bodies were a waste of space and money and that he'd rather be cremated any day.' She paused, tucked her hair behind her ears, looked up, shrugged, trying to hide the shake in her voice. 'Well, I guess, that's what we'll do. I'll get my father to come over. That'd probably be best, don't you think?'

'I'll call him, if you like. I can get his number pretty easily.' Tony heard the shake, wanting to go to her and fold her up in his arms, to work things out for her. But she wasn't the sort to accept it.

'Oh, no, no. Mama should do that, I think. I'll sort it out, don't worry. But thanks, thanks for everything.' She smiled tightly, embarrassed by his presence in his bathrobe, remembering last night when things might have happened had they been allowed to, had either of them been different. They had been so close then, their thoughts so intimate,

281

sharing private feelings and now he was just a stranger again, a familiar stranger perhaps but nothing more. It was odd and made her feel unbalanced, uneasy.

'I have to go. I said I'd be there by nine. Fran has to go out later and she wants to show me the place, give me the keys,' she rushed on.

'Fran? Fran Clements? Oh yes, she was a friend of your mother's long ago, wasn't she? Newly arrived and pretty nervous, I remember. We kids used to make fun.' He smiled at the memory, his eyes kind. 'She's a nice woman, though. Good, well, I'm glad you're sorted out. I'll be in touch.'

There it was, the dismissal, quick and impersonal, a friendly smile, the door held open. Claudia smiled too and hurried out, pressing the button for the elevator, waiting endlessly for it to arrive while he politely stood in the doorway. And then it came and she disappeared with a wave into it, the doors sliding shut.

Tony turned back into his flat, standing barefoot on a patch of wooden floor where the sunlight lay in a large rectangular slab. It was warm and smooth. He stood there, without thinking, for some time.

Claudia caught the bus from outside the Star Ferry to Stanley, getting off at the bus station and walking along parallel to the village, but higher up until she came to the beach. There were people out windsurfing already, enjoying their Sunday as energetically as they passed their week, not a moment wasted. She watched a boy in his early teens as he executed a racing turn with precision and went speeding back out towards the point. It was drowsily warm, the sort of morning where you felt like ambling along, doing nothing in particular, Claudia thought. A good day to put her mind into low gear, just to drift.

The Clements' house was beyond the beach, along a leafy residential road, locked away behind a high wall and an iron gate. She rang the bell and the amah came running out, Claudia trying hard to remember her name as she smiled and was welcomed in.

'Dorothea, hello, how are you?' With relief, the name

282

sprang to her lips and the Filipina ducked her head shyly, pleased that she had been remembered.

'Well, thank you, mem. Miz Clements is down in the boathouse. I'll show you down.' The accent was American- ised and lilting. Claudia followed Dorothea down the side path that skirted through banyan and hibiscus in a leafy grove, the grass worn away beneath her feet into a rough earthen track. Outside the small stone building she was approaching were dragon jars of trained bougainvillea and the dry, dusty smell of wicker furniture propped haphaz- ardly across weed-encrusted flagstones.

'Claudia!' Fran Clements emerged from the boathouse, dusting her hands down tennis whites without thinking and leaving a trail of dirt. 'You've caught me red-handed. I can't think how we intended to let this place to you. Look at it! It's a wreck. You'll have to stay with Mark a bit longer, honey, while we get it fixed up for you.' Her hair was chin- length and iron-grey now, her face weathered and wrinkled like a tanned hide, but her Boston accent was still strong. She smiled uncertainly when Claudia paled and shook her head.

'Why, what's wrong, honey? Is Mark throwing you out or something?'

'I thought you knew. I was sure ... well, so much for the Hong Kong grapevine.' A brief, harsh laugh made Claudia stop abruptly, a hand to her mouth, as though to trap any further sound.

'Knew what? What is it, Claudia? Is it Mark? What's wrong?' They both looked up to see Fran's husband, Jack hurrying down the lawn. He slowed when he saw Claudia, his normally amused air dimmed into concern.

'Claudia, darling, I just heard. Tony Ingram called and told me. My God, I'm so sorry.'

It took them some time to understand and digest the news, to fret and cluck over Claudia, finally to agree that she would move in at once. They were so sorry, so truly upset that Claudia was reminded yet again that they had known Mark better than she had herself. Fran Clements had been so good to Mark, helping Frank out when Lucille left, helping Mark out when Frank left. She was the more shattered of the two of them, Claudia thought, more in need of the care she was trying to give.

'Leave me to it, please. It's just what I want, just what I need. I'll clean it up and paint it, make it nice. It's only fair considering the rent is so little ...' she protested and gently bullied, pushing them away and they, bewildered and in pain, left her alone in her nest. That was how she thought of it. Her nest.

A cool, dank, tiled floor and dark walls, the windows grimed and overgrown with bougainvillea and other creeping greenery, the two rooms littered with broken or old furniture, no longer wanted in the big house, gardening tools, rubbish, leaves greeted her. She looked around in grim delight.

She dragged the windows open, chipping at the woodwork where it was swollen with a chisel she found amongst the tools, and she hacked back the plants until the light streamed in. Then she started tossing the rubbish outside onto the flagstones, piling it neatly. The boatboy had once lived there, when they had had boatboys, and there were all the basic requirements once she looked. An iron bed, although the mattress would have to be replaced, some old furniture that could be slip-covered, a table with one leg shorter than the others, a dresser.

The bathroom, such as it was, would have to be worked on but Jack had said he had been meaning to do that for some time. They wanted it for when their own daughter came back from college in America. But she was only a Sophomore, so it was years yet.

She set to scrubbing and washing, sweeping and brushing in a fury of energy until the house was as clean as she could make it and her arms had begun to shake with fatigue. Her shorts were filthy, unrecoverable, but she didn't want ever to wear them again anyway. They were part of the memory that she wanted to scour from her mind like the dirt from the kitchen. Mark was dead and one part of her was grieving and howling out its dirge, but the other part was secretly thrilled with her new house and feeling

284

shamed and guilty that such an emotion was possible when Mark was dead only the night before. She flinched away from the thought.

Jack came down at lunchtime with a tray of food and a jug of lemonade which he set down on the stone wall leading down to the bay. He inspected her work and promised paint and a new mattress immediately, hurrying off back up to the main house with a look of relief that he could at last do something positive. And, as promised, despite it being Sunday, the paint and mattress arrived a mere two hours later. Hong Kong at its finest, Claudia thought.

With little or no regard to priming the walls or sand-papering the woodwork, Claudia splashed the warm, creamy liquid around the room liberally, wiping it off the tiles when she spilled it, her main aim to lighten and brighten as fast as possible. Dorothea brought down floor polish for the tiles and promised to buff them when the painting was finished.

It was dusk before Claudia looked around enough to see the shadows creeping across the floor, the deep orange of the sky blending with the darker sea through the windows that now shone with their pristine and cleaned glass. She switched on the lights and looked around with quiet satisfaction.

'Have you rung your parents yet?' Tony, his fair hair gleaming under the light, frowned. He was leaning in the doorway, seemed removed from her delight, disapproving. Claudia started.

'Oh, God, no, I haven't. I'd better ask Fran if I can phone from her place. I meant to and then they were so upset and I was so busy trying to make this place liveable ...' She glanced at him, seeing the reserve that had reappeared in his eyes.

'There's no need to make excuses.' But she had been lowered in his estimation, she thought, looking at him.

'I wasn't,' she said abruptly. 'Not to you. Perhaps to myself. What brings you out here, Tony?'

'These,' he said steadily enough as he held up her suitcase and overnight bag. But he had heard her clipped tone. Just what had really brought him out there? He could have sent a constable. 'I brought everything that I could think of that didn't have to stay in the flat.' He paused, forcing himself to continue in a calm, businesslike tone. This was a professional issue, nothing more. At most, he was just helping out a friend. 'What about the car? You going to keep that?'

'I don't know. I don't know if Mark had a Will. It may all go to my father, or to a friend.' She sounded flustered, he thought, and wondered why. And then he was less than amused at himself, at his probing. She had every right to be flustered. He reminded her of it all.

'He didn't have one. I checked. Nothing's been filed here in Hong Kong, anyway. Maybe abroad but it's unlikely. In which case, far as the law's concerned, you're free to take what you want.' He raised an eyebrow, his tone almost questioning. 'I'm sure the rest of your family won't contest it.'

'No, no probably not.' She glanced at him, glanced away. 'Oh, well, I don't really want any of it. Not after what happened there. The car, maybe, yes, I guess that would be useful. But the rest ...' She shuddered at the thought of that blood sprayed up the walls, across the chairs. Tony saw that shudder, forced himself to ignore it.

'I'll arrange for it to be sold then.' That was it, just the right tone of professional indifference. He swallowed tightly. 'You can have the money. Probably more useful.'

He was brusque, his attitude different to before, to last night, she thought with dismay. She felt awkward, a nuisance, when he sighed and said, 'Look, Claudia, you can't keep putting this off. Mark's dead and people have to be told. Why don't I call your father? It's over twenty-four hours now and things need to be arranged. I know you don't want to deal with that. I'll sort it out, all right?' He looked at her, his grey eyes darker and more deliberate.

She nodded. 'Yes, all right. You're right, I should have done it.' But if people didn't know, then she could almost deny it had happened. The thought sprang guiltily into her

286

mind and she shook it away. 'You sort it out, will you, Tony?' She turned away, looking around at her new home, aching to begin work on it again, to forget the ugliness. She didn't want to talk to her mother, to hear the pain as she denied yet again that she had a son, she didn't want to speak to her father who hadn't seen fit to call his daughter in twenty years. She didn't want to think of Mark dead and needing to be buried. She just wanted to forget. If only Tony, and the look in his eyes that was almost but not quite accusing, would go away.

'Here you are then. I'll be in touch.' He read her thoughts, pushed the bags further into the room and turned on his heel before she could thank him, or say goodbye. His footfalls, retreating, were fast and without pause.

She stood there, angry at herself and angry at him for making her feel that way. Miserable. And then she picked up her paint roller again and set to work.

And Tony, picking his way, surefooted, through the dark tangle of garden, snatched at a dead flower as he passed, breaking it free with a hard, cracking snap.

Chapter Twenty-Four

Sunday night

It was night, full and dark, before Claudia finished painting and laid the roller down in some turpentine by the door. Wiping her hands on a rag, she looked around.

The interior glowed with warmth from the two lamps in their wicker shades, catching the fierce red of the bougainvillea she had collected, and splashing it against the white of the walls. For a moment it looked like the blood in Mark's apartment, sprayed up the plaster and she flinched, almost crying out. She felt edgy, seeing the darkness beyond the windows, hearing the wind gathering force outside, wishing Tony had stayed.

Someone out there had been callous, vicious – no, she had to be honest with herself, *evil* enough to slash Mark into shreds, to gaze unflinching into his fear and pain, to hear his voice screaming and still to rip and tear at him until he was dead. And she had no idea why or even whether they might come looking for her. She stared out at that blackness, dimly seeing the trees thrash against the night sea air and she was unable to control the shiver that rippled through her.

She shook her head, turning away to make the bed up with the linen that Dorothea had brought down. There was still no sign of Fran but perhaps she would appear again in the morning.

When that was done and the dinner things were washed up and neatly put away, Claudia stepped into the bathroom and tentatively turned on the tap of the shower. A thin spray of cold water appeared grudgingly but, after a few coughs and grunts, it became a steady stream of hot water. She peeled off her clothes and stepped beneath the spray.

She slicked her hair back wetly, letting the water run down hot and hard on her face, trying to block out her thoughts. Thoughts that questioned and worried around her brain, hinting, suggesting and then being fiercely denied. Mark's death couldn't have had anything to do with Harry, could it? Could it? And if so, why hadn't Harry done something, anything, to stop it? Tony didn't like Harry. The thought sprang into her mind, fully formed, and she stood quite still. Didn't like and didn't trust. And if that were the case, did she dare trust Harry herself?

It was the steady knocking on the outside door that finally penetrated her reverie and she reluctantly left the soothing wrath of the water to wrap a robe around her and pad out to answer the door.

'Fran, is that you?' Even to herself, her voice sounded tense, squeezed out from too thin an opening.

'It's me, Harry. Let me in, Claudia, for God's sake!' For a moment Claudia closed her eyes, fighting the urge to tell him to go away. She didn't want him here, she didn't want to have to ask him those questions that frightened her so much. She certainly didn't want to hear his answers.

The knocking continued and she sighed, her fingers beating a nervous tattoo on the lock. No, this was Harry, she told herself sternly. He had been abandoned once by her, though she had had no choice as a child; she couldn't let that happen again now that she could choose.

'Harry, hold on.' She fumbled with the lock, twisting it with difficulty where it had stuck, and then pushed the door outwards. Harry slid past her and pulled the door shut behind him.

'Harry? What brings you out here? In fact, how did you even know where I was?' She tried to cover her reluctance with questions.

'Just let me in first. Christ, no curtains? Turn off the damned light, will you?' He was sharp in his commands and Claudia obliged him without protest. The room sank into blue moonlight and shadows, the swaying darkness of outside becoming focused again. He stood silhouetted against that background for a moment and then collapsed backwards onto the sofa with a deep sigh.

'Sit down, Liddie, and tell me what's going on. Why the hell didn't you call me? Let me know where you were? I've been ringing round half of Hong Kong trying to track you down.' He sounded exasperated – and hurt.

'So how did you find out?' Claudia perched herself on a low stool, wrapping her arms around her legs and hugging herself tightly.

'Silvia's gone to pieces,' he continued, not heeding her question. 'She's just howling and screeching away in her room. Her parents don't know what to do. They finally called the doctor and I guess maybe she'll be shipped off to a clinic again. You talk to her yet?'

'No. No, I haven't talked to anyone. How did you find me?' she repeated.

'Not through Ingram – he said he would pass on any messages, if I wanted. Said you needed some time on your own. Bastard!' He spat the word out and Claudia blinked, taking in the force of emotion behind it. 'Portia told me. Her mother knew from Sally Freeman – who knew from Fran. It would have been easier if you'd let me know yourself.' He stretched back on the sofa, grunting with the release of tension.

He hated the dark, hated being out in it when he knew there were other people out there too. In some ways he was like a cat, content to roam as long as the night was fine and still, but wanting to curl up inside safely when there was bad weather. He watched Claudia carefully.

'Sorry,' she said and stood up, going into the kitchen to put the kettle on to boil. She kicked the gas bottle with her bare toes and cursed under her breath. There was silence for a moment.

'You're safe, Liddie. They won't come after you,' Harry said finally. His voice was flat and certain and she fought the sense of release it brought her.

'It never occurred to me they would,' she lied, trying to sound indifferent, 'and how do you know anyway?' She returned to stand in front of him.

290

'Because they want me.' He noticed the way she moved abruptly, denying what he was saying in her mind.

'They? Who's they?'

'Yee, really.' He watched her, saw the blankness in her face and relaxed, his voice becoming gentler. 'He's the one who wants me – he's getting ambitious. The rest, well, it's just a small Triad lodge. They take their orders from Yee. And he's trying to branch out.'

'Why? What's it all about? What do you have to do with Triads?' She sounded odd, wary. As though she didn't want to hear his answer.

He shrugged. 'I got mixed up in all that, a long time ago. When I was young and scared and didn't have anywhere else to turn. But I've been clean for years now, Liddie, I promise you that.'

'Then why did they kill Mark?' Her voice was harsh and low. Harry took her hand and pulled her down beside him, putting an arm around her. He didn't want her looking into his face, reading him as clearly as she always had. For his sake, and her own, she needed to believe what he told her, a version of the truth, his version.

'Because he tried to pull a fast one on them. They used him as a courier. All those trips of his down to the Philippines or Thailand. How do you think he afforded those? And all the hash?' She shook her head and he gave a quizzical smile. 'You knew. You had to have. Don't shake your head at me, Liddie. You're not a fool.'

'He only went once since I arrived and I thought that was unusual. He didn't act as though it were run of the mill. He was nervous and excited. I thought it was because he hadn't been for years, not since he went with my father one Christmas.'

'Well, he had.' Harry contradicted her baldly. 'Many times. But he'd been holding back on them. Just small amounts, enough to stack up over several trips so he could eke out his own habit.'

'But – he only smoked grass. He wasn't a junkie. He didn't have any tracks on his arms. I looked. He wasn't taking heroin.' She looked aghast, her denial sounding

291

tentative to her own ears. She had wondered, oh yes, she had wondered.

'Ever heard of chasing the dragon, Liddie? You take a piece of aluminium foil and heat the powder over it and then you inhale it through a pipe or even just a rolled-up piece of paper. It's not as effective as injecting it but it doesn't show. It's the latest thing now.' He lit a cigarette and breathed in deeply, as though demonstrating how it was done. 'There are other methods as well. Mark was on a greased path and he couldn't get off it. He kept protesting he wasn't hooked but he knew he was.'

'He said that about you. You were trying to get yourself out of something and it wasn't working. Something like that.' She didn't mean to accuse but he became still.

'Maybe. But I'm not dead.' He looked away, out the windows at the bay glinting in the moonlight, cold and unimpressed by any small problems they might have.

'But they're after you. Why? Do you deal in drugs too?' She put her head slightly to one side, regarding him, trying not to show him how much it hurt her to have to ask that.

'No! No, I don't,' he denied sharply. 'Not any more. I didn't have any choice back then, when I worked for Yee, but I got myself out of all that. I worked my way up in Commercial Radio the hard way, Liddie, just like everyone else there. No Triad backing, no pulling strings, nothing.' He breathed in quickly, wondering whether that was really true, or whether Yee had known just how valuable Harry could be to him. He tried to blank out the thought before it could corrode his confidence.

'Now, just when I thought I was clear of all that, they're coming at me again, wanting favours. I said no.' And was that what sealed Mark's fate, he wondered? Or was there more to it than that? Yee's anger had been so savage, telling them that they must pay, that he had seemed more scared than anything. What could Yee have been scared of? Harry leaned his head back on the sofa, closing his eyes.

'What sort of favours? Courier services?' she asked and he laughed, looking down at her, his mouth still puckered up in amusement but there was none in his eyes.

292

'No, I was a courier when I was sixteen, Claudia. Not any more. They want different favours now. I can't say what. I don't think they'd have killed Mark even if he had been sampling the wares a little, if they hadn't wanted it to be a warning to me. He was useful to them.'

'Useful! Dear God, Harry! Is that all you can say? Mark's dead. You didn't see what they did to him but I did. He's dead because he wasn't "useful" any more and they wanted him to serve as a warning to you? Is that all you think he was worth?' Her voice lashed him, hard with pain and horror.

'I didn't mean it to sound like that, Liddie. No, that wasn't all he was worth. Not to me. But they don't work that way.' He squeezed her tightly against him, feeling the shudders running through her. Gradually they subsided and she swallowed tightly, her voice grating at his guilt.

'So, you've had your warning. Will they still try and kill you now or give you another chance?' She was quick, Harry had to admit, thinking hard.

She realised killing him was no real use, if they wanted him to do them favours. Favours! Propaganda against the mainland. Like signing a death warrant against himself that would come due in 1997 when the Communists came to power. If Yee didn't get him first.

But, maybe Yee had recovered from whatever had made him that angry, that scared, that he had lashed out with fury at Mark and himself? Maybe Mark did something wrong and Yee figured it out? Christ, he hoped it was that. He hoped Yee knew there was no point in killing him too, not unless he was going to go to the police. Which was why bloody Ingram turning up last night was like waving a red rag, here I am, come and get me. But Ingram was no fool either. He had known that and hadn't cared. Or perhaps had done it to see what ants would crawl out of this particular hole once he had poked it with his stick.

'I don't know,' Harry said in all honesty. 'Hopefully, give me another chance. Things are brewing over in China; they want me around for that.' Claudia wasn't sure what he meant by that, it was so cryptic. Because he could influence

293

the news, in his job? Was that the favour they wanted?

'I thought Triads were criminal societies only, not mixed up in politics.' She saw him smile, a quick flash of white teeth in the dark.

'Bright girl. But there's always an overlap, a good reason to have political turmoil. Look at the riots of 'fifty-six. They were supposed to be between Nationalists and Communists but they were Triad-backed so they could loot and rampage, have a go at the cops. People are worried the same thing's going to happen now.'

'Is it?' Claudia swallowed with difficulty.

'Something's going to happen. Mark was wrong, you know. What he said on the radio last night. They're not going to just let things roll along. There's going to be trouble, maybe even anarchy before the end,' Harry said quietly but he sounded very sure. Claudia felt a coldness begin inside her.

'Who's not? Can't you be a little clearer for once, Harry? You're always talking about "they" as though it covers a multitude of sinners.'

'Well, it does.' He shrugged.

'And you're not going to get any more specific.'

'Ah, I keep forgetting you're a journalist. Facts, that's what you want, isn't it? Going to make a story out of your brother's murder? Make a little hay over all that blood and guts, maybe mention me too. That'll get me sorted out for sure.' He was suddenly at his most hurtful and sarcastic and Claudia slid away from him, going to answer the insistent whistle of the kettle.

'Why did you come here, Harry?' she said at last, once she had controlled the shaking of her hands. 'You want something? Is that it?'

He stood up and walked over to her, leaning against the wall and stubbing out his cigarette in a saucer. He looked at her deliberately and she faced him, each of them gauging the other, trying to remember the children they had once been, clinging to each other in sorrow.

'I came to see you were all right,' he said flatly.

'And, I am. Is that it?' She forced herself to sound calm.

'You can be cold sometimes, Liddie. Hard.' He made it sound like a casual remark, made in passing, but he caught her look of dismay and anger.

'That, coming from you, is good. The last of the inscrutables. Trying to be Chinese today?'

'I am Chinese.'

'Half,' she taunted, trying to hurt him the way his casual words had slashed into her. Cold, hard. Was that what she was?

'That's right.' He took her by the arms, shook her. 'Half this, half that and getting blamed for being both. There are no prizes going for being Eurasian. It's not a help. It's not something I would choose.' He stopped shaking her, seeing the fear for a moment in her eyes replaced by sudden understanding.

'And which would you choose?' she asked softly. He released her and moved away, kicking something beneath his feet with a vicious thrust.

'Don't ask. I don't have the choice.' He sat down heavily on the sofa.

'I'm sorry, Harry. I shouldn't have baited you.' She had gone to stand beside him and now she leaned down and wrapped her arms around his chest, resting her cheek against his, her hair still damp where it draped over his skin. 'You hurt me with what you said – the journalist thing. I was lashing out at you, I guess. I'm sorry.' She kissed his cheek and would have withdrawn but he pulled her round so that she sat across his legs and they hugged each other tightly. After a while Harry sighed.

'It's difficult sometimes, seeing things the same way when we're all coming from different places. Take Portia. I mean, she knew Mark well, as well as Silvia, much better than you and she's not really taken it in that he's dead yet; she thinks it's some sort of exciting and a bit frightening game. That's what comes from having such a protected upbringing. She can't recognise reality – ugly, dirty reality.' He paused.

'And then, there's you. You recognise it all right and you don't want anything to do with it, do you? You're running away from it as fast as you can. You cared about Mark but you're not sure you cared enough to try and find out who killed him. You don't want to get involved. That's about it, isn't it, Liddie?' When there was no reply, he continued. 'Do you run from everything unpleasant, refuse to confront it and pretend it's not there? What's made you like that? You and me, we're both like that a bit. But I learned it the hard way. What about you?'

He felt her shift in his arms, pulling away and he let her go.

'And Silvia? How do you equate her reaction to Mark's murder? Is she over-emotional or is she normal?' he continued, his voice growing harsh. 'Personally, I think she's the only one round here who's done what she should. Grieved. Really howled her head off that Mark has been stopped dead, there's nothing more there. He's gone and everything, all those years, all that effort that went into making him, that's gone too. Just,' he snapped his fingers, 'like that. So I'm glad Silvia's howling. I just wish I could too.' They were silent then, for some time, Claudia returning to make the tea and set it out on the table with two cups. Harry watched her, his mouth tight with wanting to tell her how much he cared about Mark too, but unable to do it.

'Did you introduce Mark to "them" – the Triads, Yee? Did you get him involved, Harry?' It was a very quiet question but there was a balance being struck and Harry knew it, had expected the question. And he could lie with the best when he had to. He shook his head.

'No. They approached him. He was on a trip some-where, I can't remember where now and there was a slip of paper in his bedroom when he got back. They're very official now, do everything right by the book, sign here on the dotted line, give your passport number, the whole bit. They even warn you, in nice official jargonese that you're for the high jump if you let them down. And that's it, once you sign, you're with them forever.

'Mark told me about it only a few months ago and I went to Yee and tried to get it sorted out, tried to get it stopped.

296

But instead Yee remembered I was alive and tried to put the squeeze on me. Ironic, isn't it? Mark might be alive if I hadn't tried to help him. Well, it amuses me, anyway,' he said bitterly when Claudia hadn't laughed. He watched her carefully, wondering whether he had convinced her, but it was impossible to tell.

And what else could he say? Yes, I did involve Mark but it was either him or me and I never thought it would turn out like this. Mark was already a junkie back then, I didn't think we would become friends, that I would like him so much. I'm sorry, Liddie ... No, he could never tell her that. She just wouldn't understand. He wasn't sure he did any more.

'Is there anything we can do?'

'About Mark? No. Nothing.' He sighed. 'Promise me that, Liddie. You just stay clear of it. Life will just go on as normal, once I sort my own problems out. There's nothing anyone can do. Except maybe Ingram. But none of us dare tell him, do we? Yee's not the sort who lets people testify against him.' His voice was melancholy and when he smiled, Claudia wanted to cry. She cleared her throat.

'I stayed with Tony last night. He said he visited you and then he went very tense and wouldn't talk about it. What happened?' She didn't see the unexpected movement of his head rearing back, nor the anger in his eyes.

'He woke me up in the middle of the night, and I wasn't happy. Nothing else.'

There was silence for two long beats of her heart.

'I see. Well, it's late, Harry, and I'm tired. Do you want to stay the night?' She had seen his fear when he came in, the way he kept looking out into the dark. She wouldn't send him away out into it.

'I'll stay if that's all right. Maybe they haven't posted my dismissal notice yet, but I'd prefer to go back in daylight.' He gave a half-smile.

'What's that?' Claudia asked sharply.

'Dismissal from a Triad lodge. It's posted around town. Means execution generally. I haven't heard of any about as yet.' Just the odd assassin or two waiting for him in the dark, instead, he thought grimly. But he had survived it and now they would give him a reprieve. They would contact him again, give him one last chance and they all knew he would take it. He had to.

He saw the sickness in her face, the way it paled and became almost ugly, the mouth overlarge, like some gaping slash in white skin, the eyes darker than ever and shadowed with bruises. He pulled her in tightly and felt the shake in her body, tiny and almost under control but still there.

'Was there one posted about Mark?' Her voice was little more than a breath.

'No.' Harry shook his head. '*Gweilos* don't get any warning because they never really belong. They'll always be foreigners, no matter what.' She sighed deeply at those words and he knew she was wondering what she was doing there, in a place that would never really accept her, a place that had layers of deceit and cruelty beneath the light-hearted façade. She would go home soon. Soon. Lucky girl to have somewhere to go.

'Could they have followed you ... here?' She looked up at him, the fear in her eyes. For him, and for herself. He shook his head.

'No, no one followed me, I promise you that. And I don't believe Yee will do anything for a while. He's thinking, planning. Don't worry, you're safe.' He kissed her forehead, breathing in deeply, considering.

'How old are you, Liddie? Twenty-seven, now?' He felt her nod rather than saw it. 'Then come to bed and we'll pretend we're little again, giggling at night under the covers.' He smiled at her and she felt the tears well into her eyes, blurring and distorting, wishing so badly they could go back to those carefree days. But she had become an adult at seven, Harry at nine. There were no easy ways back.

'All right. But don't talk about it any more, Harry. Don't scare me any more.' He kissed her then, gently and quickly, swooping down on her as though to silence her.

'Your mother would disapprove of this, wouldn't she? She never liked me much. I can't think why,' he murmured

298

in her ear, mocking himself as much as her.

She stroked his skin and smiled. 'But my mother never had much taste. Most people agreed on that.' They laughed; smothered, intimate laughter that remembered a time when they were little together and Harry had crept from his mother's room and climbed into Claudia's bed, to whisper and play. His hand slipped up her arm, sliding beneath the robe to touch the delicate bones of her shoulder and caress the skin with long, sure fingers.

Their laughter died away, became an acutely aware silence of breath, inhaled and exhaled as they examined each other, their bodies touching, briefly, parting again.

'I dreamt about you for years – that you would come back and we would be lovers. I never thought it would happen. It was just a dream,' Harry said quietly and saw her mouth quiver, the soft curve of lips where they met fold inwards in such a revealing gesture that he was stunned. He placed his own mouth to that point, tracing the curves and folds within his tongue, tasting warm, recently soaped skin overlaid with her own particular scent and he breathed in deeply.

His fingers slipped from her shoulder to her back, stroking and gently kneading the back of the neck, strumming down lower over her shoulder blades and back up again. He kissed her throat; warm, soft movements of skin on skin and felt her respond beneath him, her head falling back on his arm, her mouth parting, the hands that had pressed against his chest, holding them apart, now sliding beneath his arm and encircling his body.

When he brushed her robe aside, it might have seemed accidental, it was so smooth and effortless. Claudia gave a shaky exhalation. He touched her breast lightly.

Before, she had had trouble seeing the boy she had once known so well in the adult Harry but suddenly, as though in a kaleidoscope that had been twisted, she slipped back into that old friendship, that old world of shared secrets and whispers, laughter and tenderness that had sustained them both through childhood. It was odd that an adult act, that as children they hadn't even known existed, could re-establish their old bond, she thought and then was caught up in Harry's arms as he carried her through to the bed, and her thoughts became muddled, mixed up in what they were doing to each other.

He stripped her robe from her gently, pausing to kiss each of her limbs as he untangled them. Claudia lay on the bed, curled slightly on her side and watched without embarrassment as Harry pulled his shirt over his head, slipped the jeans from his hips and kicked them aside along with his espadrilles. He wore no underclothes and she watched the play of shadow and light across that tautly muscled body, seeing the white gauze on his leg, wondering at it.

He turned away from her, his buttocks tight and high when he strode over to the windows and looked out. Whatever he saw reassured him and he returned to her and climbed onto the bed, gathering her into him and holding her tightly.

'It's times like this when I know I have to choose what I am. And I'm not Chinese,' he said softly, into her ear and she tried to still the way her body jerked in surprise. 'Not really. Inside, I'm a European. Like my father. I am, Liddie, aren't I?' He held her so tightly that she could not pull back and look into his face; all she heard was his appeal for reassurance and she hugged him tightly back.

Outside, the rain spattered hard against the glass and the wind grew in strength.

Chapter Twenty-Five

Sunday night

Tony Ingram led his men down a steep slope, slipping and sliding on mud and garbage, their curses muffled in the stink of sewerage, rotting vegetation and mud flats. The sampans and floating pontoons huddled down in the dark, their gangplanks ready to be lifted at a moment's notice. But the weather was in their favour, blowing and quoting hard squalls of rain now, driving all but the hardiest inside. There would be few watchers to see them pass and fewer still who would look for them down on the mud flats. Silently they pushed on.

Beyond the rain on his face and the howl of wind in his ears and the putrid smell in his nostrils, Tony was dimly aware of a feeling that he hadn't felt in years. Loss. He was sad for some reason that he couldn't fathom, a heaviness in his chest making him wonder why he bothered to do what he did, what the reward was for all this foulness? Angrily he shrugged the feeling aside, focusing his mind on the job in hand. His platoon depended on him, looked to him for guidance in what was about to become an ugly situation, and he was off woolgathering. He cursed as he stepped into deep mud and his boot was sucked almost from his foot.

'You changed your mind yet, boss?' Sergeant Chu asked mildly and Tony jerked his boot back on again and signalled to his men.

'Bring them round on both sides, the way we planned, Chu, and don't give me a hard time. How else do you think we could get this close?' They would not have dared to speak at all on a still night but in the wind and rain there was no chance of them being overheard.

'I don't think, that's not my job. You're the boss, sir.'

301

Sergeant Chu grinned and Tony couldn't help grinning back.

'Yeah, that way I'm the chump if there's nothing there, right?'

'Absolutely right, sir. See you in there.' The sergeant moved away, pointing and whispering to each of the men in turn, their movements clumsy and heavy in the mud. They moved off and Tony gathered his own two men to him and gently eased himself up beside a pontoon, slipping over the edge and waiting for the others.

He hoped his information was right and that he wasn't about to become the butt of jokes for the next week. But they so seldom got the chance to catch an initiation ceremony in progress that it was worth chancing humiliation if it turned out to be wrong. He lay waiting patiently until his men were beside him and then they all crawled forward over the wooden raft, trying not to ruffle the feathers of the many chickens in their coops or announce their presence in any other way.

It was remarkably quiet and dark, the sampans battened down against the weather, no chink of light showing in any doorway. They moved into position, surrounding the sampan with the gold-painted dragon prow, and waited, glancing down at their watches, rain streaming down their faces. Finally, Tony took a deep breath and pulled his gun from beneath his jacket, checking that the safety catch was off. He nodded tersely to the other two and tested the catch of the main hatch gently, just lifting it with his finger and pushing. It shifted slightly.

He stepped back, gave one final nod and kicked the hatch back with his foot, following it immediately with a roll feet first into the hold below. The man below, caught completely by surprise, jumped up and would have escaped out of portholes or the forward hatch if Tony's men had not poured down through every possible opening. Tony landed heavily, cannoning into someone and grappling him down into the wooden bilge, the smell of the man rising unpleasantly in his nostrils as he slithered and twisted in his hold.

302

Around him, in the confusion and shouting as men milled about, hitting into him and stepping over him, rolling and fighting like sewerage rats in the damp, sweating hold, several shots were fired. They whined past in all directions, connecting solidly with wood that splintered out in sharp daggers. Tony ducked down and held on tightly to the man he had caught, tensing as he waited for a bullet to thud into him. He heard a cry of pain near him and cursed.

The man was still struggling beneath him, wiry and slippery as he thrashed from side to side and Tony fought to hold him down and clip cufflinks around his wrists. He succeeded only after taking an elbow sharply on his cheek-bone.

Someone had kicked over a kerosene light and a small blaze started in the near dark. Tony, one hand holding his prisoner down, groped at the fire with a cloth until one of his men came and took over, beating at the flying sparks and flames, smothering it in the stinking bilge water that lapped at them, dark and vicious with age. Tony could smell the singed hair from the back of his hand and his skin felt raw. With an effort he hauled the man up into a sitting position and looked around.

Tony's men knew their job, had been trained again and again how to do just this particular task, and they had mostly rounded up the Triad members, forcing them to sit on their hands and be still. A few tussles were going on in dark corners but they were gradually brought under control, hissing and grunting with fury. Tony wiped the perspiration from his face, swaying for a moment as he straightened and his head contacted with the low deck.

He kept his gun trained on the elder of the two men who had been setting up the altar, and felt an unexpected glow of satisfaction as he glanced around. To catch an initiation ceremony in progress was rare indeed. He turned his attention back to the captives, having sensed some movement from them.

For the most part they were young men, barely out of their teens, dark-eyed and rough-looking, head thongs around their foreheads and bare-chested. Tony glanced over them, identifying the Incense master by his robes and head-dress and the grass sandal on his left foot. The man next to him, short, barrel-chested and wary, his eyes half closed as he tried to merge into the background, was almost certainly the lodge leader, the *Shan Chu*, the Big Brother. Tony watched him carefully.

The altar was a simple affair of a small incense-burning bowl filled with different banners, four oranges laid out in a pattern, three paper effigies, some wax candles and some bowls of what looked like tea to Tony. There were also pieces of red paper with symbols written on them. A tatty, tawdry affair, it gave no hint of the seriousness with which each of the initiates took it.

To them it was symbolic of their own death and resurrection, each of them being re-born as a Hung hero. The ceremony was the force that would bind them together, imposing secrecy, discipline and loyalty on each of them, even in the face of death. Tony gestured to his sergeant to take photographs.

'Anyone hurt?' Tony asked and received a couple of grunts from further back in the gloom of the hold.

'It's Ng, sir, got his hand shot up. We need to get him back to hospital as soon as possible. No other serious injuries, boss,' Sergeant Chu said and Tony gave a sigh of relief.

'Good, call for back-up, will you, corporal Ch'en? And get Fu to take Ng up to the road. We'll hold the rest here.' Tony spoke quickly in Cantonese, all of the men being required to understand the dialect even if they spoke another themselves. He saw the Triad leader watching him, his eyes almost shut as he sat quietly in the shadows. But there was a menacing feel to that stare.

'You. What's your name?' The man spat quietly into the shadows, feigning indifference.

'Sergeant, have you searched this man yet?' Tony indicated the man and the sergeant nodded. 'Have you read them their rights?' The sergeant nodded again and grinned.

'In every dialect I could think of, boss. They understand all right.'

'Right. Well, stand up.' Tony indicated the leader but the man didn't move, sitting stolidly and withdrawing into himself like a tortoise into its shell. Tony, irritated, stepped forward and leaned over the man and that was when there was a sudden flash of fire and a burning sensation in his face and he staggered back, clutching at his eyes, the pain eating into him as he clawed at his skin. Tony couldn't see anything but he felt men pushing and shoving around him, loud cries and grunts of fighting bodies, and then he felt the hard wood of the deck beneath him as the pain became unbearable, burning into him. He was not even aware when the blackness engulfed him.

Monday morning

'You really did a number on yourself, didn't you?' Claudia said from beside Tony's bed. The words didn't reveal the expression of relief on her face now that she knew he would be all right. Tony's bandaged face turned towards her, angled sharply.

'Anyone would think I did it on purpose,' he muttered darkly and she lay a hand on his and squeezed it, surprised by the way his fingers curled around hers, as though he needed the reassurance. One hand was bandaged, the skin singed and raw where it protruded from the white gauze, and there was a dark, angry bruise on his cheekbone. Her fingers hesitated over it, as though she would stroke the pain away and then withdraw.

'Quite the battered hero,' she teased lightly. 'You gave me a bad scare when I first walked in and saw you all bandaged up like a mummy. Matron nearly had to apply the smelling salts.' They both smiled and there was a moment's uncomfortable pause while they sought for something else to say.

'Who told you?' Tony managed at last.

'I rang to talk to you this morning – to apologise I guess for being so difficult yesterday – and the sergeant on duty

305

told me. I guess maybe he shouldn't have but I bullied him a bit. Are you feeling all right?' Claudia felt a shiver rack her body suddenly, remembering those few seconds of sheer terror when the sergeant on duty had stalled and evaded her questions. She shrugged it off uneasily.

'Like a fool, actually. I knew that guy was the leader and I should've been warier. But I assumed ... bad thing, that – assumption. Gets you into all sorts of trouble.' Tony's smile was embarrassed. 'It was some sort of flash powder he threw in my face. The doctors say I'm lucky not to have lost my sight. They won't take the bandages off yet, but I guess I closed my eyes just in time and they're not badly burned. That's what they say, anyway.' He was still holding her hand tightly in his and she felt it quiver, just very slightly. She wondered, if she were in a similar position, whether she could remain so calm. For someone like Tony to be blind ... it didn't bear thinking of.

'They'll be fine. The doctors know what they're doing.' She paused, trying desperately to think of something to take his mind off it. 'He got away? The leader?' Her tone was sympathetic and Tony sighed.

'Yes. And half the bloody initiates ... My men were so busy trying to see if I was still alive, they just let the bastards go. My fault.' Perhaps she ought to say something soothing, something to ease the loss, but she suspected Tony apportioned blame to himself more often than it was deserved and would not listen to sweet platitudes.

'I don't really know the details,' she said awkwardly. 'But no one's laughing about it. That's something, isn't it? And half is better than none. I hear it was pretty rough.' She saw him angle his head as though trying to see her through the bandages.

'The ones we caught won't say anything. It's who we lost that matters. I had Yee, Claudia,' he said quietly and she stilled, her hand gripping his painfully. 'You know who Yee is? How do you know that?' Although his voice was quiet, she could sense the disillusionment. She made an exasperated sound.

'Because Harry told me. He came round last night and

306

told me about this Yee fellow. The leader of the Thin Blades. The one who was using Mark as a courier and that Harry used to be mixed up with. Not that I need to tell you any of this, since you clearly already know it. Anything else?' Tony heard the curtness, the hurt behind it and softened his voice.

'Is that what you rang to talk to me about this morning?' There was apology in his tone.

'Yes.' She sighed deeply, flicking the hair back from her face as she closed her eyes. 'Everyone keeps telling me I'm the sort who doesn't want to get involved, who doesn't really care as long as it doesn't involve me. I keep telling myself that. But I guess I am involved. Mark was my brother.' Her voice grew uncertain. 'So, maybe I do care who did it and why.'

'And Harry? What does he feel?'

'He's frightened.' She sat beside Tony, holding his hand, and told him everything that Harry had said the night before. Almost everything. Tony grunted, from time to time, as though absorbing the details.

'Does that surprise you?' Claudia asked, when she finished. 'About Harry being a Triad member?'

'No. I've known for some time.'

He lay back more comfortably against the pillows and thought about all the things Claudia had not mentioned. He wondered whether Harry had stayed and then he mocked himself. What business was it of his?

'Does any of this help? Does it give you anything more to go on?' she prompted and reluctantly he let go of her hand. 'I certainly hope so, since I might have risked my neck telling you.' She gave a forced laugh that died away abruptly when he didn't laugh with her.

'It may do. Nothing dramatic and nothing immediate but we'll keep on trying. Harry obviously isn't going to come forward and testify and we don't have anything else we can prove.' His voice became intent. 'Look, I want you to stay away from it all. If Harry confides something else and you think it's really important, well, fine, pass it on. But ring me, don't come in person. And I'd rather you stayed

307

away from Harry too, if you can. He isn't safe.'

'Oh, Tony ... He's just lonely and he's hurting and he may be in danger.' And I left him once, long ago, I can't do that to him again, she added silently. 'I can't just turn my back on him.' The words were said so softly, he almost didn't hear them. He wished he hadn't heard them. How about him? Wasn't he lonely, wasn't he hurting? But he pressed the thoughts to the back of his mind.

'Then be careful, Claudia. All right? If they come after him, I don't want you in the way.'

'He says they won't but don't worry, I'll be careful.' Unable to help herself, she leaned over him and kissed his cheek, the bruise, as though it might help. 'And you too. No more heroics in the night, all right? I won't feel any better about you catching Mark's killer if you get bumped off doing so.' She forced herself to say it lightly and pressed his arm before standing to leave. 'How long will you be in here?'

'About another two days I think. Not long. Thanks for dropping by.' The tone of dismissal again, Claudia thought, biting back on the words that were about to escape from her mouth. He didn't need anything, certainly not from her. She called her farewell as she turned away.

And then she was distracted by a bustle of noise at the doors, the nurse being swept aside, an elegant woman in her early fifties or so, descending at speed on the two of them. Claudia recognised her easily.

'Tony! My poor, poor boy! What have they done to you? My God, I knew you should never join – I warned your father but would he listen? How are you, darling?' The woman swooped down on Tony, pecking at his cheek and not halting her flood of words until Tony cut across her.

'I'm fine, Ma!' He had tensed, Claudia thought, the lines around his mouth deepening. Was this the chink in Tony's armour, his weak spot, the reason he was so very wary and detached? Looking at him, Claudia knew it was so. She waited awkwardly in the silence that followed, his mother looking hurt.

'What are you doing here, Ma? Is Hamish here with you?' Tony forced himself to sound natural. Joanna glanced across at Claudia, her eyes narrowing for a moment in puzzlement.

'He's back at the hotel, Tony. I came flying the minute I heard. Are you sure your eyes are going to be all right? I could get a specialist flown in. I mean, we're only here for a few days but I'll change my booking ...'

'No! No,' Tony repeated more calmly. Claudia saw his knuckles whiten as his hand twisted in the sheet. 'I'm fine, Ma. I don't need any change of plans. I'll be out of here tomorrow, probably or maybe the next day. There's no reason to fuss. Claudia? Are you still there?' She heard the appeal in his voice, despite his attempts to suppress it.

'Yes, I'm here, Tony. Hullo, Mrs Ingram, or rather Mrs ... Um, how are you? It's been a long time.' Claudia saw the puzzlement snap into place in the older woman's eyes, wariness suddenly replacing it.

'Claudia? Not ... little Claudia? Lucille Babcock's child? Good heavens! I thought I recognised you from somewhere. What brings you here?' The clipped words and the slight hauteur in the raised eyebrows made Claudia's mouth tighten.

'Why, Tony, of course. Just like you.' An imp of malice provoked her response. She noted ruefully the flare of anger in Tony's mother's face.

'Oh? I didn't know you were friends?' After a pause into which neither Tony nor Claudia inserted clarification, Joanna added, 'In fact, I didn't even know you were still around. Didn't your mother disappear back into whatever small town she came from in the Deep South and take both you girls with her? Have you just escaped the dust and the hayseeds?' Her laugh was not amused.

'Some time ago, Mrs ... I'm sorry, I'm not really sure what your new name is now.'

'Mrs Sheridan, my dear. You were saying ...?'

'I left the dust and hayseeds some time ago. I've been in New York and San Francisco for the last nine years.' She mentioned the name of the business quarterly she wrote for and had the satisfaction of seeing Tony's mother open her eyes a fraction wider.

309

'Good heavens! A blue stocking. I can't think what you're doing around my Tony. Probably terrifying him with your brain, I should think.' She patted Tony on the shoulder and Claudia saw him stiffen.

'Thank you for your vote of confidence in me, Ma. But so far my feeble little grey cells have managed to just about understand Claudia.' It was said with amusement and acceptance that this was the way things were in their relationship but Claudia wanted to hit his mother. Perhaps Tony was mature enough to handle his mother, but she wasn't sure she was.

'What? Even with that accent?' Joanna trilled, and Claudia smiled at her.

'Even then. Jus' shows what determination can do don't it?' Claudia took Tony's hand in hers and squeezed it tightly, feeling those warm fingers grip her back. ''Bye, darlin'' she said, drawling more deeply. 'See y'all later.' She smiled sweetly up at Tony's mother. 'Gotta fly.' And with fury in her chest and a broad smile pasted to her lips, she walked off down the ward, swinging her bag as she went. She heard Tony's mothers words of dismay as she knocked the doors of the room aside and marched out.

'Tony! You can't be serious!'

And Tony laughing, long and delightedly.

Portia Hsu gestured to Claudia, slowing down her neat little convertible and forcing her way over to the corner of Ice House Lane amidst klaxon blares and shouts of disgust. She pulled to a stop and Claudia caught up with her, opening the door and climbing in with relief.

'Portia, thank God! I've been trying to get a taxi for the last half hour. Doesn't anyone ever queue in Hong Kong?' She briefly kissed the other girl's cheek as Portia thrust her way back out into the traffic with careless abandon. Portia glanced at her, seeing the pallor and the dark, bruised eyes. And the fine-boned face that Harry seemed to admire so much. Her lips compressed slightly.

'You have to learn to push more, Claudia, or you'll never make it here. How are you? I've been trying to get hold of you.' The traffic swirled down Queens Road and right into Pedder Street, Portia edging her car through the others as though it were a beaten-up panelwagon rather than her latest birthday gift, a BMW convertible. She swung her hair, dark and thick, over her shoulder, her neat face and broad forehead accentuated by the dark hair band. Soft, moth-like eyebrows and lashed framed dark eyes that glanced over at Claudia, assessing her mood, a quiver of excitement running through her. Claudia deliberately looked away, around at the traffic.

'Tony's in hospital and Harry's practically in hiding and Mark's dead,' she said flatly. 'That's how I am.' Out of the corner of her eye, she saw Portia duck back in her seat, concentrating once more on her driving.

'How's Tony then? Is he badly hurt?'

'It's just a burn.' Claudia forced herself to sound unconcerned. Tony was fine, would be fine. She was sure. And he had no room in his life for either her concern or his mother's.

'He's okay, then?'

'Yes, I guess. Better than Harry, anyway.'

'Harry'll be okay. Don't worry so much about him. He knows the score,' Portia said coolly, almost curtly, and Claudia wondered whether Portia knew something she didn't. But she sensed, basically, that Portia was right. Harry could — and would — take care of himself. He was a survivor.

'Have you seen Fish? Or Silvia?' Claudia asked.

'Fish is on a drinking binge and Silvia's going into a clinic in Macao. Her parents think it's best. You should go see her today or she'll be gone. We can go now, if you want?' Portia sensed Claudia didn't want to, not at all, but waited impatiently for her answer anyway.

'Yes, I suppose so.' Claudia looked across at Chater Gardens, at the thousands of dark heads bobbing up and down as they ate their lunches and chattered, like a flock of happy crows. She dreaded feeling Silvia's pain, having her own break through the barrier she had built up around it. The noise of Central at midday struck at her, like a physical

311

blow. Reluctantly, she asked, 'Is she going to be all right?'

Portia shook her head, flipped her hair again. 'I don't know. Silvia's always been a bit fragile and she loved Mark a lot. It's easier for you. You barely knew him.' It seemed to be said without thought or malice but Claudia flinched back in her seat, her mouth set.

'No, I barely knew him.'

Silvia lived up in Branksome, on Tregunter Path. The route took them past Mark's place and both girls turned away, purposely not looking at the crowds who still milled about in the forecourt. Police, media and sensation seekers. Portia put her foot down and the car purred steadily up Magazine Gap Road.

'Tony's mother's here. She came breezing into the hospital as though she owned it, trying to smother Tony with concern and making barbed put-downs the whole time. Just what he didn't need. Do your parents still keep in touch?' Claudia said, casting at random for something to say. Portia laughed but it was a shrill sound.

'Oh, yes, Daddy's still crazy about Joanna. Mummy pretends it never happened and that they're all just old friends but everyone knows what Joanna's like. Have you met her new husband, Hamish? He's very sweet.' She dimpled and Claudia gave a snort of amusement and shook her head.

'No. Can't say I have. Does Tony get on with him all right?' She was curious and unable to hide it. Portia glanced at her.

'He pretends to. I think maybe he even likes Hamish for himself, but he has a hard time relaxing around them. Or maybe that's just Joanna. Why?'

'I'm just trying to understand why he's so – detached, I guess. Does he ever go out with girls? He told me he doesn't have time . . .'

'He doesn't really but he also makes sure he's that way. I tried with him once.' Portia smiled tightly, seeing Claudia's surprise. 'Why, does that shock you?'

'Shock? No. I'm just surprised you admitted to it.'

Claudia shrugged. 'I'm also surprised he turned you down, quite frankly. I don't imagine that happens too often.'

'No, it doesn't!' Portia laughed. 'Tony just has too many morals for his own good. He couldn't forget that my father and Joanna had an affair.' There was a note of regret there, in Portia's voice, Claudia thought. A fleeting memory of Reginald Hsu standing talking to Joanna at Repulse Bay slid through her mind and she nodded, absently.

'Oh, I see. Yes, that would rather matter, wouldn't it?' Claudia saw that it didn't as far as Portia was concerned. 'So he doesn't have girlfriends at all?'

'Say, you're really interested, aren't you?' Portia laughed at Claudia's quick shake of her head, her frowning denial. She wasn't interested that way, just curious. But Portia was oblivious. 'Well, if you really want to know, I hear he does have girls from time to time but they're definitely the casual sorts, passing through. No one who's going to stay and spread rumours about him in his own backyard, if you see what I mean.'

'What rumours?'

'Oh, there are always rumours about the Ingrams. People are interested in what his father really does, how much money Joanna's new husband has, whether Tony is going to bust another druglord or maybe just follow in his father's footsteps. The girls too. People always seem to want to know what they're doing. They're just that sort of family.'

'And what are the theories about Bill Ingram?' Claudia was fascinated, in spite of herself, in spite of the fact that she disliked asking Portia for the information. She saw that Portia was signalling to turn right onto May Road, barely braking as they flowed across the incoming traffic and slipped between the cars. Claudia let her breath out slowly, only then realising she had been holding it.

'Intelligence,' Portia said succinctly and turned up the steep drive of Tregunter Path.

Claudia sat there, quietly mulling over the word, wondering. 'Are they going to be here long?' she asked, her thoughts jumping.

'Who? Joanna and Hamish?' Portia saw Claudia nod.

313

'Only if they change their plans and stay on because of Tony. Otherwise they're supposed to be in Singapore soon to stay with some other old friends. Say, your dad must be coming up, I guess. Is he?' Portia pulled into the forecourt of Branksome and parked neatly between a white Rolls and a gold Mercedes.

Claudia winced. 'I'm not sure. I meant to ask Tony but I got distracted ... I expect so. Dad would want to come to the funeral, at least.' She opened her door and got out, peeling the thin silk shirt-dress away from her back and rearranging the skirt into acceptable pleats. Portia wore skin-tight pink jeans and a white T-shirt, diamonds winking in her ears. Claudia glanced at her, suddenly remembering what Silvia had said the night Mark had been killed.

'Do you know anything about Mark's death, Portia? You had something to tell Harry or Mark that was urgent that night. What was it?' She turned to stare full into Portia's face, just catching the look of quick anger before it changed to a smile.

'Oh, just about Mummy's cocktail, that's all. Nothing urgent. Why?'

'Silvia said you were upset and agitated.'

'Oh, Silvia!' The laugh was dismissive. 'She gets everything wrong. No, there was nothing important.' The smile faded and dark eyes gauged Claudia, a firm chinline willing her to accept or offend.

'Whatever you say, Portia,' Claudia said casually, but she shivered as they entered the air-conditioned hall and Portia waved to the porter.

Silvia was sitting on the balcony when they entered the flat, and another girl, fair and slim with her legs crossed over tennis shorts was leaning against the railing. They both looked up as the amah gestured towards Portia and Claudia. When Silvia turned, Claudia was shocked at what forty-eight hours could do. The girl who had laughed and flirted only two nights ago was now an old woman, deep lines of pain curved into her face, her mouth tightened and

314

bitter. She looked at them with hate.

'What do you want?' The words snapped out and Claudia faltered, stood still, her mouth opening and shutting as she sought for words. Silvia gestured to her.

'No, not you, Claudia. Her. I don't want her here. Get her out!' She glanced from the amah back to Portia. 'Get out of here Portia! Get out!' Her voice rose, ending in a shriek of rage and pain and Portia turned away, flustered, motioning for Claudia to come too.

'No. You stay, Claudia. I want to talk to you. But, get *her* out of here.' And Claudia, awkward and embarrassed, led Portia to the door and apologised.

'She isn't herself. I should stay and talk to her. Come on over this evening if you'd like. Come to dinner.' Briefly she noticed the same expression of anger on Portia's face, before it disappeared and was replaced by concern.

'You be careful with Silvia. She's half off her rocker. Don't believe anything she says. This isn't the first time she's slipped a bit. Just soothe her down.'

'Yes, all right, I will. I'll see you later.' And then the Chinese girl was gone and Claudia, bewildered and increasingly wary, returned to the two girls on the balcony. The blonde watched her gravely.

'Silvia? What is it? Why didn't you want Portia here? She just came to see how you were.' Claudia sat down beside her and took her hand, noting the slackness that had come into Silvia's face now that her fury was over. Silvia shrugged.

'She could have saved Mark. That's what Silvia thinks,' the blonde girl said and watched Claudia steadily when Silvia nodded slowly.

'Portia knew. She always knows more than she should. I don't know how, but she does. But she only cared about saving Harry. Mark didn't count.'

'Knows what? About the Triads?' Claudia looked from one to the other, her stomach tightening in disbelief.

'They'll cover it up. It goes too high and no one wants to rock the boat right now. Mark was a mistake and I guess someone'll pay. They hardly ever kill Europeans. It makes

315

too much stink,' the blonde girl said evenly but Claudia saw she was angry beneath her matter-of-fact manner.

'Who are you? How do you know this?'

'Oh, I'm sorry, Liddie,' Silvia broke in, her manners taking over as though on auto-pilot. 'This is Phil. Philippa Purdey. She's an old friend of mine – and Mark's too,' she added, swallowing over the words as though to force herself to say Mark's name. 'Phil's been down in Auckland for the last month, which is why you haven't met her before.'

The girl leaned forward and held out her hand, a grim expression on her thin features. 'I got back yesterday. I'm sorry about Mark. We all are.'

Claudia nodded and shook hands, saying with difficulty, 'Yes, I wish I'd known him better.' She paused. 'But what were you saying about it going "too high" and that it was a mistake? I thought it was just a drug-related killing. How can that go "too high"?' She saw both the other girls' faces become shuttered.

Phil shrugged. 'Oh, well, Hong Kong runs on Triad-backed business. Not all of it, obviously, but a lot of the Chinese hongs, the big trading houses, started out that way and still have connections. The European ones too, come to think of it. Opium to begin with, then heroin. Drugs are big business here in the East. That's all I meant.' She had withdrawn, good sense replacing the anger that had caused such indiscretions a moment before.

'Are you from Hong Kong? Is that why you know about all this?' Claudia probed. She eased back in her chair, feeling the sun on her bare limbs but still chilled.

'I've been here about five years. My father works here and I came up and started my own business. You find out a lot about a place when you start work. Hong Kong's teetering on the brink at the moment and no one knows how long its going to last. That makes people nervous and they want to make a profit fast and get out.'

'Like Mark, you mean?' Claudia groped to make sense of what was being said.

'No. He wanted to stay. Other people. The high rollers here who want to get out before the Communists clamp down on them but who can't get their money out. People with a lot of real estate, for example,' Phil said with a curl to her lip that reminded Claudia of Portia. She felt uneasy.

'I'm going to Macao tomorrow. Did you know?' Silvia said into the silence and Claudia nodded.

'Yes, I heard. Will you stay there long?' An awkward question, Claudia realised, wishing she had bitten her tongue in time.

'As long as it takes. I don't care, it's my parents who want me to go. They're scared I'll do away with myself!' she said with a high, cracking laugh. 'But I won't. Not until I find out about Mark. Portia knows that and she's scared ... scared of me.' Her voice had become venomous and Claudia and Phil both shifted uncomfortably, the latter putting a hand on Silvia's shoulder as though to soothe her. Silvia looked down for a long moment before suddenly raising her head and glaring at Claudia.

'Harry knows too, doesn't he? He knows what's behind it all. You'd better look after him, Liddie, before they slice him up too.' But then the long, heaving sobs began again and Phil put an arm around Silvia and led her gently inside. Claudia sat, staring at her hands, in the bright sunlight.

Chapter Twenty-Six

When Claudia got home, wrung out emotionally and physically by the noise and heat and crowds, there was a note waiting for her under her door. She picked it up absent-mindedly, walking into her little house and throwing her bag across a chair. It was cool in the boat-house and the tiled floor gleamed where Dorothea had polished it and the greenery hugged in around the windows, transparent where the sun shone through it. Water lapped quietly over the boat landing and Claudia stood perfectly still, letting its soothing sound wash over her.

Finally, she looked down at the letter in her hand and turned it over and over before slitting it neatly open and spreading it out.

Dear Claudia,

Arrived this morning and am staying at the Mandarin, room 515. Tony Ingram is in hospital and you are out. Please call at once. I must know what happened to Mark.

With love, Dad

She had her own telephone now, that Fran had had installed for her that morning, and she crumpled the note in her fingers as she looked up the number for the Mandarin Hotel. She dialled and waited impatiently while they put her through.

'Hello, Dad?'

'Claudia! About time. Where've you been? I've been waiting here for hours, for Christ's sake!' There was a pause while Frank Babcock rearranged his thoughts, remembered that Claudia was his daughter. 'Look, honey, I'm sorry if I snapped but I just can't believe any of this. Is Mark really dead?' The pain was so bleak in his voice that Claudia had to squeeze her eyes shut.

'Yes, Daddy, he's dead. Oh God!' And then all the control that she had exercised so sternly for the last two days dissolved and she wept incoherently down the phone.

Frank Babcock was very much the same as she remembered, still large and bluff, a short haircut emphasising the strong jawline and thick neck. He met her in the lobby of the Mandarin, standing there staring at every young woman who passed by as though sure that must be his daughter. Claudia touched him on the arm and he turned, surprised and embarrassed that he didn't know her.

'I was the one with dark hair, Dad. Or can't you remember?' she said sharply, having seen him looking at a red-headed girl with indecision.

'Claudia! I wasn't sure, I couldn't imagine what a seven year old would look like now. How are you? You look all in.' Which he did, himself, she saw now that she was closer. His eyes were bloodshot and swollen, his skin slack around his chin. He looked ill. She nodded.

'I'm tired and a bit shaky. Can we go upstairs or something?'

'Yeah, of course. I didn't know if you wanted me to go see him, or something ...' He trailed off, his eyes tearing up and his voice beginning to disintegrate. He sniffed loudly and looked around, up at the chandeliers.

'No, it's okay, Dad. You don't have to do that. Come on, I'll explain it all once we're upstairs.' She led him gently towards the bank of elevators, angry at herself for having felt so hard done by earlier, when he didn't recognise her. Why should he? He had enough on his mind.

They talked for several hours, sitting in the cool box-like bedroom, staring out at the harbour water through shaded glass. They drank coffee but ate none of the sandwiches that her father had insisted on ordering. He sat there, as though dazed, unwilling or perhaps unable to believe Mark

319

was gone. But he hadn't seen the body, Claudia reminded herself, as she painfully went through it all again and saw him hunch into himself, folding in and packing down tight so that he became smaller and smaller. With aching distress, she watched him shrink but could not help him.

'Didn't your wife come with you?' she asked, at last, when he seemed to have finally grasped the facts and was ready to move on. His eyes were old and dead.

'No, she wanted to stay with the children. She and Mark didn't get on very well, of late. She thought it best I come alone.'

'Best for whom?' Claudia said sharply and then sighed and braked back on her anger at Joyce. She picked up the coffee pot and gestured to her father. He shook his head.

'What about your mother, Claudia?' he said, after a moment. 'I called her when I heard but she didn't know. Why didn't you tell her?' He watched her replace the pot on the tray, her face tight with distress.

She raised her hands as though to try and explain and then let them drop back to her side. She was so tired, so desperately, bone-deep weary that she could barely control her voice.

'I didn't know what to say. I didn't want to hear her deny Mark and I didn't want to hear her pain and guilt. I'm sorry, it was cowardly of me.' She looked up at her father but there was no understanding there.

'I think you should call her now. She's waiting to hear from you.' He picked up the telephone and passed it to her and she reluctantly placed the call. It rang for a long time before being answered.

'Hello?' Her mother, distant and tentative, as though waiting for and dreading the voice she knew would be there, spoke and Claudia hesitated, opened her mouth but found nothing there.

'Hello?' Sharper now.

'Mama?' The word choked out and Claudia heard the silence before her mother replied.

'Claudia? Is that you, Claudia?' The voice grew muffled, as though her hand had been placed over the receiver. 'It's her!' she said to someone. Claudia frowned over the shake in her voice.

'Yes, it's me, Mama. Look, I'm so sorry I didn't call you sooner.'

'Are you all right, Claudia? You sound bad. Is your father there with you yet?'

'Yes, Mama. He just arrived. I'm sorry about Mark, Mama . . .'

'Hush, Claudia, there's nothing for you to be sorry about. I'm the one who's sorry. I didn't want you there in the first place but I didn't think anything this bad would happen. I'm glad your father's there. You shouldn't go through all this on your own.' There was an awkward hesitation, as though her mother were forcing herself to ask. 'How did he die?'

The last question came as a painful surprise to Claudia and she paused, unsure how to answer.

'He was stabbed, Mama. Someone murdered him. He was mixed up in drugs or something. I don't really know yet.'

'Oh, Claudia, I knew something was wrong, ever since you said Mark asked you to come out there, all frantic and worried about something. I knew it! I don't know what to say . . . hold on, what?' She was listening to someone in the background and Claudia closed her eyes over the hot tears that had filled them, her mouth twisting into short sobs. She tried desperately to control them.

'Hello, Liddie? It's me, Todd. Are you all right? What's going on?' The change of voice startled Claudia and she let out a shuddering cry.

'Todd? Todd, what are you doing up at this hour?' But he was twelve now, old enough to try and help.

'I heard the phone ring. We were waiting for you to call. Are you sure you're all right?'

'Um, yes, yes, I'm okay.' Her voice had become higher as she forced back the tears. She cleared her throat and dropped an octave. 'Dad's here and we're trying to get things sorted out. We're fine, really. Is Nanna okay?'

'She's going to be fine. She's a bit upset right now but

she's more worried about you. Me too. You didn't get hurt at all? You weren't there?'

'No, no.' She said, wanting to tell him, 'but I heard it, I heard him dying in agony,' but knew there was no point, that she couldn't burden a child with that. 'Look, I have to go now, Todd. Thanks for looking after Nanna. You give her my love and a big hug for you too and I'll call in a couple of days, all right?'

'Yes, all right. Hold on ... Nanna says you have to call Joaney. It's urgent or something.'

'Joaney? Uh, okay, I will.'

'You take care, Liddie. We both send our love too, you know that, don't you?' She smiled painfully at that, at the adult tone in his voice. Little Todd, taking care of things for them. He was growing up.

'Yes, okay. 'Bye!' She rang off as he returned the farewell and slowly replaced the receiver. Her father was standing, staring out the window at the harbour below. She saw he was crying.

'Mama sent her love,' she said, awkwardly. She saw him nod.

Wednesday
The funeral was two days later. Frank Babcock hired a large junk, big enough to take the thirty or so people who turned up, and they cruised slowly out of the harbour and across the open straits to Lantau Island, scattering Mark's ashes and seeing the wind pick them up and toss them across the dark green water as the chaplain's voice was plucked away, only a few words audible. Claudia watched the grey specks fly out and disappear, her heart heavy and sullen as she looked around at the people who had come to pay their respects.

Some she knew, like Harry and Fish, Philippa Purdey, Portia Hsu, Fran and Jack Clements, Tony, looking tired and ill, just out of hospital. His father Bill Ingram was there too. Others were strangers to her but her father knew them and tried to smile and thank them for coming. Only Silvia was missing, Claudia thought. But Mark would have known how much she cared, anyway.

The official papers, death certificate and duties, had all been arranged by her father and Claudia had done her best to support him through it. But he wanted only to have it over and done with, to get away, return to his wife and new family. Claudia knew he barely thought of her and then only with guilt. A guilt he was as eager to escape as his sorrow. She shrugged and tried to be understanding.

It was a cool, windy day, the junk ploughing through the deep troughs and lurching clumsily over the peaks. Claudia, pale and salt-sprayed, glanced over at Harry, wondering if he was thinking of her, wondering, as she was, about what was to happen between them. But he continued to stare out at the green hills of Lantau as though he were there only in body, not in spirit. She was surprised he had risked coming at all, but perhaps he had sorted things out with Yee. She would have to ask him later, when they were alone. If he came. Poor Harry, he looked so pained, so ... guilty. As though he should have done something. She sighed.

She didn't see Tony watching her, his mouth tight as he saw how wretched she looked. She didn't see Fish or Tony's father, murmuring quietly to each other on the far side of the deck. Nor Phil or Portia, both angry as they stared out at the waves, glance at each other. She saw only Harry's profile, turned away.

It was a relief when they returned to port and said their stiff, formal farewells to those who had taken the trouble to come, Harry barely glancing at her before hurrying away, Tony clasping her hand in his warm one, as though trying to give her some of his strength. She had smiled awkwardly up at him, liking him so much for his tact and discretion and yet unable to sort out the muddle of Harry in her mind. He had murmured goodbye and walked away, leaving her feeling more bereft than before.

It was even more of a relief when she could say her own farewells to her father. She returned to her little boathouse and closed the door.

Only then, as she sat down with a sigh of satisfaction on her sofa, her feet tucked up beneath her, did she remember Joaney. She lifted the phone to her and dialled quickly, trying to work out the time difference in her head.

God, she missed Joaney ... and Michael, too. All of them, in fact. Maybe she should think of going back? What was there to keep her? Harry? No, he didn't need her, not really, and she sensed neither of them had found what they sought in each other's arms. The memory of each other, the fantasy they had each built up about coming together at last, had sustained them all those long years. And then they had and it had proven to be a mistake, she admitted to herself, with a painful shake of her head, nothing but a stupid, well-meant mistake. I don't love you, Harry, she thought with regret. All this time, wasted, and I don't love you. And you don't love me.

Is that why you haven't called, haven't been around? Or can't you face me, Harry? Is that it?

The dialling tone, that had been ringing endlessly, changed as Joaney finally picked up.

'Joaney?'

'Claudia? Is that really you?' she croaked and Claudia smiled to herself, knowing how bad Joaney was before midday.

'Yes, it's me. What's up? I got a message about something being urgent, but I couldn't call before now. Things have been ... difficult.' There was a long pause. 'Joaney?'

'I thought you ought to know. About Jason. He's been killed.' There was a long, howling silence down the telephone while Claudia struggled to grasp the news. He couldn't be. Not Jason too? It wasn't possible!

'When?' Her voice was hoarse.

'Last week. They're flying his body home. My parents went over.'

'But what happened?'

'He was, um, knifed or something. No one really seems to know why or how.' Claudia heard the quiver in Joaney's voice, knowing that the last time they had seen each other had been a scene of ugliness and hate. And there was no going back on that.

'Oh, Joaney, I'm so sorry. I can't, it just doesn't seem possible . . . was it a robbery, or something?'

'That's what the police thought at first, because his place was ransacked. But nothing of value was taken. It doesn't make sense!' Joaney wailed into the phone and Claudia closed her eyes, thinking that she really couldn't take any more, not now.

'Mark was killed four days ago,' she said finally and heard Joaney's gasp. She hurried through her explanations, trying to come to grips with such an unlikely, such a ghastly coincidence. But it was too much for her. She hung up on Joaney's farewells and stared at her hands in silence for a long time.

Then she rang Tony Ingram.

'You want to tell me what's going on, Dad?' Tony sat on the hard stool in front of the windows and hunched over, his elbows on his knees, his hands supporting his chin. His eyes were gritty and painful from the wind, from being out of bandages and his temper was fitful as he remembered Claudia's voice on the telephone, more wretched than he had ever heard. He watched his father fill his pipe, packing the tobacco in with his thumb and lighting it.

'In what way?'

'Mark Babcock's death. Another death, a day or so before that, in Tokyo. A Jason Hewitt? Does that ring any bells with you? He died the same way.'

Tony knew his father was being purposely obtuse when he said: 'What same way?'

'Don't mess me around, Dad. Just tell me what's going on.'

'What makes you think I know anything about this Jason, what was his name?' Bill Ingram looked up into his son's grey eyes, seeing the anger there.

'Because there's a connection between them. Mark Babcock sent Claudia a box, for safe keeping. He called it his insurance. It went missing from her apartment and the last person she remembers picking it up was Jason Hewitt. She never saw it again. And this Jason Hewitt moved to

325

Japan. You do remember Japan, don't you?' He cleared his throat, disliking the tobacco his father was using. It had a sour, musty smell to it.

'I don't deal in police matters, Tony–'

'You do if they have any overlap with what you're following. You warned me, after all, about Harry Braga and Mark Babcock. The night Mark was killed, in fact. And he was mixed up with Yee Fong Lo. I think that name probably means something to you, doesn't it? God knows I've had enough trouble in the past with your office blocking my investigations there.'

'Perhaps. But I don't know where you think this is leading, Tony.' There was a reproving tone to his father's voice that made Tony's lips tighten. The information was only ever there when his father wanted to dole it out, he thought to himself angrily.

'To a connection, Dad. Don't bluff me. You know what's going on, or you've got a good idea. What about Aidan? He took the box over to Claudia. Does he know what was in it?'

'Aidan doesn't work for me any more,' Bill replied mildly.

'Oh, come on! This is off the record, for once. If Aidan took it over, he'd have done his best to find out what was in it. Claudia said she didn't think he did because he looked disappointed and fed-up when he left. But you must have your suspicions. Was it some incriminating evidence on Yee? Something connecting him up with one of your big boys? What?'

'You seem to have an inflated idea of what my job entails, Tony.' Bill gave an uneasy laugh. 'I really can't tell you anything, I'm afraid.'

'Can't? Or won't?' Tony stood up abruptly, looking at his father coldly. 'I've never asked you anything before but there's something going on here that involves –' He broke off, unsure of what he intended to say. Unwilling to admit to feelings he was determined to ignore. Bill Ingram smiled ironically.

'Yes?'

'Don't bait me, Dad. Give me something to work on. Please!'

'I only know what I read in the papers, or the rumours I hear circulating but it seems to me that if anyone knows what's going on, it has to be Harry Braga. I'd go ask him, if I were you. Then you can tell me,' Bill said quietly and took out his lighter again, sucking hollowly on his pipe until it glowed. Tony stared at him in silence until he eventually looked up.

'Is that it?'

'Yes, I think so. Don't you?' But Tony walked out without answering.

Chapter Twenty-Seven

Late May, 1989

'You should try and enjoy life more, Claudia.' Fran sat in one of the deep wicker chairs on the terrace, looking with concern at the young girl beside her. It was over a fortnight since Mark's death, since Frank had come up and the funeral had been arranged and taken place and now Frank had gone back and still Claudia did not seem to have pulled herself out of her lethargy.

'Come out with us on the junk on Saturday. We're going over to the Frog 'n' Toad on Lamma. It'll be fun, get you away from that dreadful laptop of yours. Look at you! As pale and washed out as an office girl! You should be ashamed of yourself with all this glorious weather we've been having.' She paused when Claudia gave a wan smile.

'How's Tony? Have you seen him much?' Fran probed again but Claudia shook her head.

'Not since the funeral. I talked to him on the phone a couple of times. He's busy.'

'Jolly lucky with his eyesight. Is he scarred at all?'

Claudia tried to remember what Tony had looked like but the image wavered and washed away. He had looked grim. 'I think his skin was peeling a bit but it shouldn't scar. He'll be all right. He doesn't need or like to be fussed over.'

'Not by Joanna anyway,' Fran retorted, almost reading Claudia's mind. 'Every time she shows up, he goes back into his hard little shell. He's a nice boy and she's almost ruined him. Can't think what sort of girl could get through all that armour he's built up. Maybe someone who needs him, needs looking after.' A sideways glance at Claudia revealed nothing. 'He doesn't trust women. Such a shame.'

'He's hardly a boy at thirty-one,' Claudia replied calmly

328

but mentally she was agreeing with Fran's assessment. Almost ruined? Or already ruined? She puckered her cheek, thinking also what a shame, what a waste. But that was life, sometimes, and the kinder, the more caring a person, the more likely they were to be damaged.

'Anyone below forty is a boy to me, Claudia!' Fran laughed, a dry chuckle deep in her throat. She pushed her sunglasses up on her head, squinting out at the water. 'We'll pick you up at nine on Saturday. Bring your bathing suit.'

'Oh, but I really . . .'

'Nine. I won't hear no from you. It'll do you good.' And Fran levered herself easily out of the chair and wandered off up the garden path, plucking at some weeds or dead-heading a rose as she went. Dimly, Claudia heard the phone ringing and she returned inside, wondering if it was her editor from San Francisco. She had promised him the copy a week ago but only faxed it yesterday. He would be livid.

'Claudia? It's Phil Purdey. How are you?'

'Phil? Oh yes! Of course! Sorry, I was expecting someone else to call and you threw me. I'm fine, thanks. How are you?'

'Great. We're all wondering how you're getting on. No one's seen or heard from you since the funeral. Is there anything we can do?' We? Claudia thought? Who's we?

'No, no, I've just been working. I had a deadline. Um, how's Silvia?'

'No word. Her parents say she's better. By the way, Portia's pretty ticked off with you. Says you invited her to dinner and then weren't there when she turned up.'

'Oh! Oh, God, I'd completely forgotten. That was the night my father arrived and I went to see him at his hotel. I'll have to call Portia.'

'Um, she thinks Silvia said something that maybe influenced you. She's in a bit of a sulk.' There was a note of caution, almost warning in Phil's voice. Claudia absorbed it warily. 'So, when are we going to see you? Fish has been asking about you a bit.'

329

Claudia smiled tightly to herself. 'Fish? Really? Oh well, you can tell him I'll be at the Frog 'n' Toad on Saturday. Fran's insisting I go with them.'

'For the mud wrestling? Good, it's a fun day. We're all going to be there. Don't wear anything too nice or it'll get ruined. We're thinking of going on to Cheung Chau afterwards for dinner. Do you want to come?' Phil always sounded so connected and in control, so terribly sane, Claudia thought. Perhaps it would do her good?

'Who's "we"? Anyone I know?'

'Grief, a whole crowd of us, but I guess you only know Fish and Portia. Harry might come. He hasn't let us know yet.' There was a pause. 'And maybe Tony Ingram too. You know him, don't you? I think he's on the police team. And the usual rugby crowd, of course. We'll catch sampans across to Cheung Chau and then one of the junks home. It's easier like that.' She sounded so enthusiastic that Claudia was caught up by her words, thinking, well, everyone is going on, enjoying themselves, why should I be the only one still mourning? And then she felt guilty and found herself mentally apologising to Mark. There was an exasperated sigh from Phil.

'Look, Claudia, if it had been the other way round, if you had been killed and Mark was left, you can bet he'd come along. It wouldn't stop him missing you but he wouldn't just hole up and stop seeing people. It's unhealthy. So come, please!' she said urgently and Claudia was so startled at how easily she had been read. And Phil was right. Mark would not have grieved alone.

'All right. But I'll have to check with Fran first. It might be rude to leave them halfway through . . .'

'Fine, you check and then you can let us know on Saturday. I'll book an extra place for dinner anyway. With such a large crowd, that sort of thing never really matters. See you then. Oh! By the way,' there was a pause and Claudia had the oddest feeling that this was the whole point of Phil's phone call, that everything else had been mere camouflage. 'You know Portia has a thing about Harry, don't you?'

330

It was a throwaway remark but it fell with deep echoing reverberations. 'No, I didn't actually. Why are you telling me?' Claudia tried to sound amused and indifferent and she could sense the puzzlement down the phone.

'You haven't seen him lately?'

'No, I haven't.'

'Oh. Well, I just thought you might like to know that. Portia's father disapproves, of course, for various reasons,' there was a pause while Phil thought of elaborating on those reasons and decided against it, 'but she has a way of getting what she wants in life.'

'Good heavens, does Harry know that?' Claudia's laugh was bitter in her mouth, wishing life could be as simple as Portia seemed to think it was.

'Yes. Harry knows everything.' Phil's voice was dry.

'Like you, you mean,' Claudia retorted lightly and there was a longer pause.

'Not everything. Not quite. See you Saturday.' And then the line went dead.

There are more people per square mile in North Point than in any other place in the world. It teems with bodies, living several families to a room, rotating their bed spaces as needed, the cooking and eating done outside in the hall-ways or balconies of the huge tenement-style buildings, washing fluttering like flags from bamboo poles that climb into the sky.

Yee sat at the window of the White Pearl restaurant, slowly feeding some small, glistening Dim Sum savoury into his mouth as he listened to the man beside him tell him about the student revolt on the mainland. He raised his eyebrows meditatively when he heard that Li Peng and Zhao Ziyang were actually visiting the hunger strikers and listening to their grievances. From time to time, his nose lifted and his eyes narrowed into a shrewd smile.

Harry, reporting how the New China News Agency staff were joining the *People's Daily* in marching for press freedom, stirred the food on his plate but did not eat. He disliked the way Yee smacked his lips and murmured,

331

'Good, good. Better than expected.'

The trolley with the bamboo steamer baskets circulated by the table again and Harry paused while Yee selected another delicacy. He then continued.

'There's a rally being organised here for next Tuesday, starting somewhere down from Queensway, I'm not sure where yet. About midday so it'll get some of the lunchtime workers too. I'll let people know on my Monday night programme. And there's going to be a "Concert for Democracy in China" at the Happy Valley Racecourse on the twenty-seventh of May. I'll pass the word about that too. That's about the best I can do.' His voice was determined but Yee smiled again, shaking his head.

'No, no, that most definitely is not the best you can do, Harry. A rally against becoming part of Communist China, a concert for democracy, and the most you can do is mention them?' His voice rose and fell in cadences of question and answer. His lips pursed together. 'No. You can march in the rally, Harry, you can be there at the concert, and you can tell people you're going to do that. A lot of people listen to your programme and a lot of them respect you. If you march, if you attend the concert, they will too. You understand?' A vine-wrapped squid ball was popped less than delicately into Yee's mouth and savoured noisily.

'My name and my face will go down on the records, Yee. I'll be a marked man by 'ninety-seven. I can't do that and still stay in Hong Kong. And where else could I go without qualifications, without money?' Harry asked doggedly.

Yee shrugged. 'If we all do our work properly, there won't be any change in 'ninety-seven. You've seen and heard what the students in China are doing these last two months? They're standing up for themselves, maybe shifting the old order, maybe gaining a little more democracy. Zhao had tears in his eyes, Harry! Do you realise the significance of that?' Yee smiled merrily, a fat finger stubbing against the tablecloth, as though he were merry at some private little joke of his own.

'They're bridging the gap between the old China and the

332

new Hong Kong. And who knows, maybe there will be a change of government before we know it. So there won't be a problem for you, will there? Not in 'ninety-seven and not now. As long as you work at it hard enough. You know your other options, don't you Harry?' There was a painful silence while Harry thought and Yee ate.

'Who's backing all this, Yee? Where's the money coming from? One of the big hongs? Drug money being laundered and sent to promote a revolution? Is that it? And why you? Harry asked finally, but he wasn't surprised when Yee only smiled. Besides, he already suspected who, and as to why, that wasn't so hard to fathom when one remembered that the Triads had fled China along with Ch'iang Kai Shek's Nationalists in the face of ruthless Communist persecution. The last thing they wanted was to be under Communist rule again. It was the last thing anyone in Hong Kong wanted. But it was going to happen.

'That matter of the initiation ceremony, a couple of weeks ago,' Yee said, as though Harry had never asked a question. 'There was an informer. You don't know anything about that, do you?' His voice was low and even but Harry felt the small hairs on his neck rise and his skin contract into goose flesh. He watched Yee steadily.

'That wasn't me, Yee. How could I have known when or where such a thing was taking place? I'm not involved with the running of the lodge any more. I don't know these things.'

'No, but you could find out, if you wanted. Couldn't you? I find it an odd coincidence that Ingram was the one who led the raid.' A speck of plum sauce was removed from Yee's tie with great concentration. He glanced up, catching the surprise in Harry's eyes.

'You didn't think I knew Ingram? The son, not the father.' A smile. 'They both have been such a nuisance in the last few years, how could I not know them?' Yee shook his head at Harry's silence, his smile fading. 'The yellow-headed who so nearly, so very nearly, took me into custody, who took half of my men ... If I hadn't been quicker ... but then, that is all old news. Ingram is a problem and I know

333

how to deal with those, don't I Harry?' Yee breathed out, expelling air sharply. Harry watched him steadily, not replying with so much as a wink of his eye.

'I know you are acquainted with him, Harry. I know he paid you a visit the other night. Are you sure you didn't whisper a little tale to our good inspector?' Such a soft, amused voice but Harry swallowed over the pain in his throat.

'Why would I? I'd already received my warning. I wouldn't risk another.'

'No ... that's true. And you have seen what happens when I am betrayed. Mark was a fool. I do hope you are not.' Yee paused, seeming convinced, but Harry wasn't sure that it wasn't a game. A thread of sweat started between his shoulder blades and trickled down his back.

'Do you remember when you first came to me, an angry boy of sixteen, wanting to get away from your family, to make some money? Do you remember?' Yee continued in a nostalgic tone that Harry distrusted. He clenched his chopsticks between his fingers. Yee watched the knuckles whiten.

'Yes, of course I remember. You took me in,' Harry replied woodenly.

'That's right ... I took you in and you swore you would always do whatever I asked, always be totally loyal. And I made a man of you, taught you everything you needed to survive, taught you to think.'

Oh God, here it comes, Harry thought.

'And you repaid me by shrugging me off, by disassociating yourself from your new family, by forgetting your duties and obligations. And, because I loved you, I let you go.' Yee looked sorrowful and Harry stared at the pattern on the tablecloth, the swirls of white on white damask, the stains of sauces and food where Yee had been less than precise.

'I also must answer to people who have been good to me,' Yee continued, almost conversationally. 'And when they demand service, I give it. Like that.' He snapped his fingers sharply. 'Or I suffer an unpleasant fate. Just so, with you. When I demand service, you give it. Or my patience

334

will finally be at an end. You do not ask questions, you do not venture opinions. You give the service that is due.' His face had become stubborn, like large slabs of meat pieced together to somehow form features. He gestured with his fingers. 'Now get out of here.'

Harry pushed the bowls in front of him to one side with an angry movement and stood slowly, breathing out a long exhalation of fatigue and depression.

'You didn't let me go, Yee, not once, not ever. So let's not fool ourselves,' Harry said and there was a note to his voice that spoke of almost reaching an end. He folded his napkin and threw it down on the table before walking away.

Yee watched him steadily, dark eyes boring into his back, trying to bore their way into his thoughts. The smaller man shook his head and lit a cigarette.

And Harry, head down as he shouldered his way through the crowds to North Point station, realised that he really had only the one option left. He sighed heavily.

Lying in the sun on the upper deck of the junk, her hair tied back from her face and her body well oiled, Claudia could think of few better ways to spend a Saturday. The sea was calm and glinting in the blaze of sunshine and the junk was ably manned by a smiling crew of three. Claudia sipped at her gin and tonic and wondered if this could possibly be the same place where so much violence and deceit went on.

And she wondered just why she hadn't gone home yet. Her editor at the business journal had been understanding when she spoke to him, saying they had one article and if she wanted to wrap it up at that, she could. So just what was keeping her here? Was it because of Harry? Or was it Mark's death that still haunted her, made her determined to find out just what had happened? Or maybe, she added to herself, with the first real honesty in a long time, it was because there didn't seem much to go back for, did there?

'Oh, look!' Fran sat up, her head poised alertly beneath its deep-rimmed straw hat. 'That's the Hsus' junk, isn't it?' She pointed to a sleek white launch that was pulling ahead of them steadily, its decks crowded with young people. A hand waved and Fran waved back. Dimly, Claudia saw Portia sitting, sleek and alluring in a bikini on the top deck, talking to a man. Without having to glance twice, she knew it was Harry. Portia smiled brilliantly and flapped her scarf. Harry turned and watched their junk fade into the distance behind him without raising a hand.

'Was that Harry Braga with Portia? Good-looking young man, isn't he? I had heard rumours that they were making a pair of it, but I always thought the Hsus would put the lid on it pretty quickly. Odd that they've actually invited him along with them, isn't it?' Fran commented innocently and Claudia felt the colour flood into her cheeks.

'Why? Isn't Harry good enough being Eurasian?' she snapped.

Fran raised her glasses and looked at her steadily. 'Not for the Hsus, no, I wouldn't have thought so. They came down from Shanghai, you know. Lots and lots of money. I always thought they'd look pretty high for Portia.'

'Well, perhaps they're hedging their bets,' Claudia retorted acidly. 'A little celebrity power in case things go really wrong in 'ninety-seven. Or are they planning on running out too?' But she knew she was casting straws in the wind and Frank knew it too.

'The Hsus? I can't imagine it. Most of their money's tied up with real estate and textile mills. Hard to get their money out of that before the balloon goes up. I expect they're hoping to work out a good relationship with the Communists.' Fran sipped at her gin and tonic good humouredly, casting the occasional look over Claudia who had fallen oddly silent. Surely she wasn't in love with Harry Braga too, Fran thought with a pucker of worry? Surely not? Claudia had too much good sense for that.

But Claudia was remembering what Philippa Purdey had said, so scornfully, that day at Silvia's. Something about high-fliers who couldn't get their money out in time ...

They anchored in deep water off from Picnic Bay and were motored into the long jetty in the launch. Already the bay was dotted with junks and sailboats and there was a

336

steady trail of people moving up from the beach towards the pub. The Frog 'n' Toad was set well back from the dunes, in paddy fields, and a small path through long grass and scrubland led to it. Its rooftop awning could just be seen flapping idly in the wind above the tall sea grass.

A throng of rowdy, cheering people could be seen lining a field to the right of the pub, and as Claudia and her party drew close, onto the raised walkway, they saw that the field was filled with mud. A small grandstand had been built on the far side, backing onto light jungle, and it tottered under the weight of stout matrons and children alike. On the roof of the pub, another, slightly better dressed or perhaps more wary crowd called encouragement to the participants below. And, as Claudia peered at the mud-smeared men and women in the field, she suddenly realised she knew several of them. A man raised his hand with a grin, only his pale eyes still visible beneath the thick mud that slicked his face, hair and body. Claudia smiled broadly and waved back at Tony.

The police team were coming a strong second, she noted from the scoreboard, beaten only by the Gloating Gizzards, a rag-tag team consisting of stockbrokers, rugby players and several other professions. Claudia moved along the boards cautiously as several mud-spattered ex-contestants pressed close to her.

Fran and Jack had been delayed, chatting to friends, and she stood alone for a moment in the crowd, sensing its excitement and light-heartedness. It was good to be with people who knew nothing about her, who didn't look at her with concern or commiseration. She smiled as Tony picked up a slim young police woman for the wheelbarrow race through the mud.

'You didn't tell me you would be here,' Harry said accusingly, thrusting into a space beside her. Claudia looked up at him, seeing the deep worry in his eyes, the way he carefully looked around but saw none of the joy. His eyes were unamused by any clowning antics. 'Still trying to find out more about your dear Tony Ingram?'

'You didn't tell me, either,' she replied mildly, a slight

337

flush rising in her cheeks at his taunt. Was that Portia's doing? And what business of anyone's was it if she liked Tony. He was worth liking, even if he didn't return the feeling. Perhaps more than could be said for Harry. 'But then, I haven't spoken to you in a while, I suppose.' The neglect was unspoken but there.

'Look, I've got problems. I didn't want to involve you.' He didn't try and explain those problems and Claudia gave a half-laugh, a shake of her head. She turned back to the mud display.

'That's why you're here, hobnobbing with the Hsus, is it? Solving your problems that way?' She hadn't meant her words to sound so bitter. But they escaped her.

'Liddie, I have to find a way out of here! If you won't help me, then I'll have to go elsewhere.' The exclamation burst out, several in the crowd turning to look at the tall man, recognising him and giving each other puzzled looks. 'Come on, let's go back to the beach. I need to talk to you.' He took her arm and, reluctantly, she slipped back through the crowd and onto the beach track again. Fran smiled uncertainly when she saw Claudia with Harry.

'We're going for a swim. It's kind of hot,' Claudia said feebly and saw Fran nod and smile, her look troubled as she turned back to her friends.

They trudged through the sand, disappearing in amongst the sand dunes and Harrry pulled her off the track and between some stunted trees. They knelt on the hot sand and Claudia put a hand up to wipe the perspiration back from her face.

'Things are bad, Liddie,' Harry began at once. 'Yee's making all sorts of demands, it's getting impossible. I can't afford to do them and still stay here and I can't get away.' He paused and Claudia, seeing the fear that made his hands shake as he lit a cigarette, the cough that seemed to rack down to his lungs, reached out for his hand.

'What is it you want me to do?' she asked, wondering if perhaps Tony could help. But Harry's next words made the shimmering dunes fade into a daze of light and heat.

'You can marry me.' He looked up at her fiercely, tossing

the barely smoked cigarette aside into the sand. 'You can give me American citizenship and then I can get away. Please, Liddie! It's not so much to ask, is it?' His face was pleading, and she saw the young boy again who had begged her not to leave, the same fear and misery there in his eyes. She swallowed.

'What then?'

'Then we get away, back to America. I'll be safe there. I can get work at another radio station, set myself up. I just can't do that alone.'

'No, that's not what I meant. I wondered where you saw our – marriage – leading. Would you want to stay together or not, once you got your green card?' She felt tight in her throat, as though she had raging flu. Harry stared at her.

'What would you prefer?' He kept quite still, but his eyes looked over her head, at the line of breakers in the distance. A breeze fluttered his shirt. Claudia gave a painful smile.

'We both care about each other, Harry, as old friends. That's why I'm willing even to think about this, to help you. But you're not in love with me, are you?'

He focused back on her, the stiff mask relaxing into a smile, his eyes warming again. 'No, Liddie. No more than you are with me. I guess our longing for each other over the years was just that, nothing more.'

She nodded and smiled again, awkwardly, painfully, but with sudden relief. What had felt so odd, so strange about their relationship was that, deep down, both of them had known it was wrong. They didn't love each other. It was as simple as that. And there was nothing to stop her helping Harry except ... but no, that was just a silly dream, a crush, like the one she had had on Bo so long ago. Tony wasn't even aware of her in that way. And it was nothing she could sacrifice Harry for.

'Okay, well, if that's the only way ... the answer is yes, Harry. What else can I say?' She was equally relieved that he didn't try to kiss her or pull her into his arms. They were friends, nothing more, and it had just taken them a while to realise it, to place their old delight in each other in a different context. He sighed, nodding slowly and giving a tight smile as he looked down at his hands.

'Thank you, Liddie,' was all he said. She cleared her throat, turning as she heard voices approaching down the path. The plaintive voice of Portia could be heard clearly.

'Um, when did you want to do this, Harry?' She looked back at him. He frowned.

'Soon. I have to go to Beijing, Yee says, to cover the student uprising, give it some support, join the press there in their marches. As soon as I come back, I guess.' He smiled, relieved and Claudia forced herself to smile too.

'Tell me, what would you have done if I'd said no?' She stood up and brushed the sand from her legs.

'Portia wants me to go away with her. Somewhere, anywhere, it doesn't matter. She's tired of her father controlling everything she does.' Harry stood also. 'But she does love me.'

'I see. And does Portia have another citizenship, by any chance?' Claudia felt the smile on her face become tight as they caught sight of the crowd on the beach, Portia running in and out of the waves, laughing.

'She's trying for Canadian,' Harry replied, shortly.

'Ahh ... And what about money? How is she going to afford life without the Hsu millions?'

'She's been putting some to one side for years. She has enough.' Harry didn't want to discuss it but Claudia was curious, couldn't help the way she kept probing.

'Did Portia get to you, the night Mark was killed? Did she warn you?' She saw Harry flinch, his eyes becoming dark and impenetrable. He shook his head and turned, searching the skyline.

'Don't, Claudia. It won't do any good to dig for clues like some amateur sleuth. You don't know the score and you never will,' he said and Claudia felt the anger growing in her and she pressed him further, seeing his mouth tighten.

'How did she know, Harry? How?'

But Harry merely walked away.

Chapter Twenty-Eight

The crowd down on the beach saw Harry and waved, hailing him, and Claudia watched him walk down to them, laughing, his head thrown back as though he had no cares in the world. Then she wiped the perspiration from her forehead and headed back up the path to the pub. The heat shimmered over the sand and tall grasses, small flies whisking through the air with papery rustles. A solitary water buffalo stood in a paddy field to her left, staring mournfully at her as she passed.

For a moment, as the track dipped down into a hollow, she could imagine that she was miles from any other person, just the grass and dunes, the heat pressing in around her.

She liked solitude, empty space, and she welcomed the respite, pausing in the hollow, looking around her. There was a broken tree, just off the path in the undergrowth. It lay partially on its side, the wood weathered and smoothed and she sat down to enjoy the silence, the light breeze, the sun on her shoulders. To think about Harry and what she was about to do.

But, before long, the solitude had become oppressive, the rustling grass, the dry leaves on the few stunted trees making whispering, stealthy sounds that made her jump and look behind her. She became steadily more uneasy, and she stood carefully, inspecting the land around her. Nothing moved but she felt, if anything, more uncomfortable still. A solitary bird's cry, monotonous and harsh, repeated itself over and over. She felt a growing conviction fill her that she must move, and move fast, or it would be too late. She hesitated and then turned, hurriedly, and walked on.

A figure appeared behind her, over the lip of the hollow, and she gave a muffled cry, the fear in her making her feet suddenly pick themselves up, running forward. She turned to glance behind her, seeing the man halt suddenly, and then her headlong flight was checked abruptly, a body pressing against hers, someone who blocked the path in front of her. A cry worked its way past her locked throat and she struggled at the hands that held her.

'Claudia? Claudia, it's me, Tony!' She heard the words dimly through the roaring tide of fear that made sound seem to rush past her, and she hesitated, looking up. Tony was frowning down at her, glancing behind her at the figure. But already it was turning away, back towards the beach. Tony stood quite still, looking after it, his arms still around Claudia, his skin cool as he pressed her to him. For a moment Claudia closed her eyes, content to rest there in his arms as long as he would hold her, but then she sensed his withdrawal and stepped back herself.

'Tony, oh, look I'm sorry.' She tried to laugh it off but her throat was tight and it came out as a choked cough. 'I just got spooked, I guess. It's kind of a lonely path ...' She trailed off as she saw he was not paying attention. 'Tony?'

'Hmm? What?' Abruptly he looked down at her again, taking in the signs of fear, glancing sharply into her eyes with his own grey flecked ones darkened with concern.

'What's the matter?' Claudia asked, slowly.

'Who was that? Coming up the path behind you?' He sounded tense.

'I don't know. I just got scared for some reason. I had this crazy urge to run, and I guess I just gave into it.' She was embarrassed but less so, now that Tony seemed oddly wary himself. Her fear began to return. 'Was it someone you thought you recognised?'

'Yes. I think so.' His thoughts revolved rapidly, making him grip her hand tightly in his own and pull her along suddenly, back towards the pub. 'Come on, I think we'd be better off rejoining the others. You're okay, aren't you?' When she nodded, her face serious as she absorbed his worry, he smiled suddenly, almost tenderly at her and she

342

felt her heart become heavier still.

His pace was fast, not running but still covering the ground rapidly and Claudia kept beside him without protest. She could see the way his head was angled, tightly, the uneasiness in his eyes. For long minutes, the only sound was of their feet slapping on the hard ground and their breathing, soft and confined.

And then, coming towards them along the path, was Fish. Who also looked – tense, wary. He relaxed almost immediately as he saw them.

'Aidan!' The way Tony's breath was released, the way he suddenly smiled, spoke of greater control than Claudia had realised and she felt the pressure on her arm relax. Tony put a hand behind her, pushing her gently along, as though they were merely out for a ramble and Fish suddenly smiled, a loose, gaping smile that seemed appropriate enough for a lush but not at all for the man who had hurried towards them a few moments before.

'There you are, Tony. Your Sergeant Chu asked me to look for you. He wants to speak with you. Something's come up.' And Fish, glancing down at Claudia, gave a faint twist to his head. Tony shrugged.

'Better go see, I guess. Thanks.' It was said casually enough but he wasn't thanking Aidan for the message, Claudia thought. As though he read her mind, Tony took her arm again. 'Come on, Claudia. You better stick close for the time being. We don't want you getting lost in the crowd.' A crowd that had grown increasingly rowdy with beer and heat and that was throwing and pushing people into the mud with gleeful abandon, they noted as they approached. Again Tony smiled at her, his eyes creasing up with the sort of heady amusement that comes after great tension is released. 'With this sort of bunch around, maybe you're better off with me? At least I can slap them in gaol if they get out of hand.'

'That suits me just fine,' Claudia murmured but he didn't hear, shouldering his way through the rabblerousers and easing her after him, so that she was pressed up against him and had to fight the longing in her that wanted to tell

Harry to go to hell. To try his chances with Portia. But she couldn't do that. She had promised Harry.

They pressed on, reaching the crowd around the lower tables and then finding Chu and several other young police constables gathered in the back court of the pub. They were squatting on the rough concrete, gathered around a game of dice, laughing and snapping their fingers at each other, bottles of beer in their clenched hands. Chu glanced up and wandered over to Tony.

'Hi, boss, wondered where you'd gone,' he murmured in Cantonese, shooting looks at Claudia. Tony smiled.

'She doesn't understand. What's going on?' Tony could still feel the accelerated pulse of his heart, the way the perspiration made his shirt cling to his body, despite his having washed down only minutes before. He looked back and saw Aidan mingling in with the crowd. Claudia was watching his face carefully, trying to understand what was being said and he resisted the urge to put his arm around her, to give her a reassuring hug.

'The word's out that Yee's decided you're a problem. He's going to take care of you.' Chu flicked dark eyes towards Claudia, back to Tony. 'Any way he can,' he added and saw Tony's mouth tighten.

'His strongman's here. Back down on the path, near the beach. I thought I was mistaken at first. I hoped I was.'

'Harry Braga's down there too, I think. He went with this young lady. Saw them going off, looked like they were having a deep and meaningful conversation, if you know what I mean.' Chu kept his face bland but Claudia heard Harry's name and glanced at Tony sharply. He was looking ... pained, she thought. Chu ignored her, adding, 'He'd have recognised Yee's man, wouldn't he, boss?'

'Sure, but I doubt he'd come running to tell me. He doesn't care for me a whole lot, Chu, you know that.' Tony smiled wryly as his sergeant laughed.

'Doesn't like being woken up in the night, you mean?'

'Do any of us? Okay, Chu, keep your eyes open and tell the men. I'll be right here, in full view.' And about as vulnerable as a marked sheep in a flock with a wolf

344

prowling around, he thought. Chu sketched a brief wave and went back to his game of dice.

'What is it, Tony? I wasn't being stupid, back there, was I? There is something wrong?' Claudia plucked at Tony's arm and he turned, abstracted, to look at her.

'You went down to the beach with Harry?' He sounded neutral, as though he was merely trying to establish the facts, Claudia thought. Then why did she feel so defensive?

'Yes, we were talking but then he decided to go join Portia and some others, so I came back alone.'

'What made you run, when you saw that man on the path? Why were you so scared?' he asked suddenly, his gaze narrowing in on her, probing at her so that she felt he knew exactly what Harry had asked her and what she had answered.

'I don't know, I just, felt – panicked, I guess. Scared out of my wits. I'd felt like something was watching me, something almost evil,' she gave a shrug of awkwardness, 'and then it was there, that man.'

She saw him sigh slowly. 'That was Yee's strongman – his ... assassin, if you like.' He phrased it carefully, wondering whether she knew about Harry. Everything about Harry. And suddenly he wanted to tell her, to steer her away, to warn her. Or was that it entirely, a voice inside him mocked? Wasn't there something more?

'The one who killed Mark?' Her voice had grown high and thin, as though she needed more air. He put an arm around her shoulders, unable to help himself, pulling her in tight.

'I don't know for sure but ... probably.'

'Was he coming after me? Oh, my God! Harry's down on the beach.' The fear in her voice was painful as she clutched at him and he breathed out slowly to steady himself.

'It's okay, it's okay. He doesn't want Harry. I promise you. Besides,' his voice became hard, 'Harry can take care of himself.'

Claudia squirmed herself free of his arm.

'Why is it everyone keeps saying that, in just that tone?

345

As though . . .' she trailed off and Tony waited patiently until she had swallowed and looked up at him again, with an angry look to her face. 'Are you saying that's what Harry used to do for Yee. He was his strongman? His . . . assassin?' She licked dry lips. No, surely not. Harry couldn't kill someone, couldn't slash and hack a living person to death, like Mark had been killed. It wasn't in him. She was sure of it. 'I don't believe it.' She gave Tony a mutinous stare and he looked away, squinting into the sun for a moment, before turning back to her.

'Claudia, look.' Tony scrubbed his fingers through his short hair, searching the crowd. 'It would be better if you were to find Jack and Fran and stay with them for the rest of the day. *Close* with them,' he emphasised and Claudia breathed in sharply.

'Who is this man here for? Not Harry, you say. So . . . me? Or you?' She saw his eyes widen, read the truth there before he could hide his thoughts. 'Oh.' She felt as though her heart had decided to beat three times faster and then miss a beat, leaving her breathless and weak. 'Because you nearly arrested Yee? He thinks you're a threat?' She saw him nod curtly, his lips pressed together.

'Then why didn't that strongman come at you just then, on the path? It was lonely enough.'

'I expect he prefers an element of surprise on his side. Confronting me head on wasn't the plan.'

'I see.' She looked up into his face, trying to control the fear she felt for him. 'Tony? What are you going to do?'

'Try not to panic.' He smiled. 'It's not the first time I've been a pain in the neck to someone and they've tried to take care of me. And I'm still here.' He tried to reassure her but he could tell from her face that it was not working. 'That's the way things work out here, Claudia. But I'm not exactly alone.' He gestured to his constables. 'Chu'll keep an eye out. Don't worry.'

'And tonight, or tomorrow, or the next day? What then?' Another thought struck her. 'Was Yee's man thinking of using me as bait? Was that it?' She caught sight of Aidan signalling something and she frowned slightly, wondering . . .

346

'He would know you, he'd have seen you with Mark. I guess you were an easy mark. Which is why I'd rather you went and stayed well out of the way with Fran. It's safer for both of us that way. I don't need you being used against me,' he repeated, pointing to where Fran and Jack could be seen on the roof of the pub. Claudia sighed again.

'When is any of this going to be over, Tony?' She saw the worry in his eyes, the steadiness there that refused to be panicked, the way he even found her a smile from somewhere deep inside and she thought to herself suddenly that he was worth ten of Harry or of most of the men she knew. For his kindness, his integrity. For many reasons. But he didn't know it and wouldn't want to hear it if she told him.

'I don't know, Claudia. Soon, I hope. Just, please, stay away from me and Harry. Preferably go away somewhere, for a while. Until this is over.'

And then he pushed her quickly towards the stairs and she went without protest, knowing he was better off without her. Go away somewhere, for a while, he had said. Stay away from me, go away. But where? And then the thought sprang into her mind, and she drew in a deep breath, half of exhilaration, half of fear.

Beijing
Thursday, 1 June, 1989
Claudia had the short wave radio turned up as she knelt on her small balcony, staring out at the haze-filled day, out at the people who flocked along the streets below, their movements quick and tense. The commentator's voice sounded agitated as he reported on the fear in Beijing that had been building all day, about the tanks of the 27th army that were massing on the outskirts of the city, the rumours that were flying that Li Peng intended to put an end to the students' revolt. Claudia wiped her hair back from her face, hot and flushed, and she squatted on her haunches and listened to the news, jotting down notes and impressions on her pad as she did so.

For a moment her stomach fluttered uncertainly,

347

wondering whether she were being foolish in staying on. What if it did turn nasty? Was she putting herself in danger by being there? Should she get out now, while she still could?

But her editor had been thrilled with the idea that she come and since she was there in Hong Kong at their expense and they had been so understanding about the single article she had sent so far, she didn't really feel she could leave yet. Besides, most of the foreign press had news crews still there. Harry was there. She had been listening to his report every evening for the last four days. Surely the most that might happen would be a crackdown, rubber bullets, tear gas and a lot of arrests. Foreign press would be expelled. There was nothing to be frightened of.

But still, she was frightened. The exhilaration that had gripped her for the last few days was beginning to slide, reluctantly, as the situation deteriorated. Where, before, she had happily patrolled the streets, taking in the situation for herself, she now was wary and listened more and more to her radio. She sighed and carried the radio inside and set it firmly against a pillar.

There was nothing to prevent her going outside. Nothing except her own nerves, she realised, and knew, suddenly, just what Harry was going through, would continue to go through if she didn't help him. It helped resolve the uncomfortable to-ing and fro-ing she had been doing in her mind, the uneasiness she felt about just what sort of man Harry really was. It didn't really matter, she thought, looking around her. What he needed was an escape. She would marry him, help him out of this mess. It was the least she could do.

And then her thoughts returned, as they had repeatedly over the last few days, to Tony and she frowned, worrying about him, his safety. It was like a spiral, her fear edging up and up as she fretted her way through one problem after another, the situation there, Harry, Tony ... when would any of it end?

She wandered through into the bathroom and washed her hands in the sink, scrubbing at the dirt that had embedded itself beneath her nails. Political swings trigger economic ones, she told herself firmly, looking at herself in the mirror, at the pale, bruised eyes that watched her back. And that was her job, reporting on economic issues. Forget the rest for the moment, there's nothing you can do there. Concentrate on your job.

Outside, she heard a backfire and had to force herself not to jump. There was nothing to worry about, not yet. And she needed to be out there to see it for herself.

So, why had her interpreter suddenly not appeared that morning, as planned? Why had he looked so unsure yesterday, when she asked what the people were saying about the tanks, about the army? She wiped her face with a towel and threw it down again. Come on, Claudia, she jeered at the face in the mirror. What's happened to the intrepid journalist you thought you were, always tracking down your lead, getting your story? But those were just big businesses she had been stalking, a cowardly little voice inside her protested, and she knew little or nothing about what it took to be a war correspondent. And that was what it was looking like to her out there. War.

So now's the time to learn, she goaded herself, pushing the hair back out of her face. Stop being a coward and go on out there. Confront something for a change, don't just run away. She grimaced at her reflection. Oh hell, why not?

Hong Kong
Friday, 2 June
Tony was tired of looking over his shoulder, of shying at shadows and noises. If Yee was trying to wear him down, he was doing a good job. It was a week since he had been warned and nothing had happened or been noted, despite the vigilance of his men and of himself. And there was nothing they could pin on Yee if he didn't make some move soon. Tony sighed in frustration and slammed his desk drawer shut.

It was late and he was supposed to be on day shift at the moment. Time to go home and catch up on some of the sleep he had wasted lying awake, staring into the darkened corners of his room, listening for the footsteps that he would never hear anyway. Yee's man would be too good for that.

He called goodnight to the desk sergeant, laughing at the ribbing he received about going out alone, and stepped out into the warm night air. If Yee wanted him, he would choose his time and place and there was nothing Tony could do about it. But it didn't prevent the uncomfortable tingling in his back as he leaned over to unlock his car door, nor the sudden swooping of his stomach and accelerated pulse as a cat delved in amongst bins and knocked a lid over to clatter into the street. He jerked his car door open and climbed in, slamming the door after him.

He drove fast, wanting to be home, to put an end to this day. Christ, he was tired. His eyes blurred with fatigue so that the lights of Wanchai melted together, long, silver, green and red ribbons of light. Red! He slammed on his brakes, his tyres leaving rubber on the surface of the road as he skidded to a halt. An old man, sleeping in a doorway, raised his head, peering in at him suspiciously and Tony forced himself to breathe normally, to blink himself wide awake. There was no one else along the road, just the old man. He fought the temptation to put his foot down again, to accelerate away from those peering eyes.

He beat a tune out with his fingers on the steering wheel, glancing up at the traffic lights. Come on, come on! He was never normally impatient but he couldn't explain the nervousness that seemed to pulse through him. He glanced in his rear-view mirror as another car drew up slowly from behind, easing into the outside lane beside him. A Toyota, the windows down, furry dice dangling from the mirror. A Chinese radio station blared out into the night.

Tony turned, the street light glinting on his fair hair as he looked over to the right, at the car. His eyes widened, grey and staring, as he saw the arm raised, the gun lining up, taking aim.

As the window exploded above him, he threw himself to one side, heavy, thumping sounds punching into the air above his head. Go! Go! His mind screamed at him and he pressed his foot to the accelerator, leaping the car forward, throwing it into second and risking a look up, over the windscreen, his breath coming in quick jerks of fear and anger.

There was another explosion, from behind him and through the windscreen and he fought the wheel over sharply to the left, taking the corner too fast and mounting the pavement before overcorrecting back again. He fish-tailed on the wet, slick road, dragging his head around to look behind him.

The car following him missed the turn and kept going and suddenly, as quickly as it had begun, it was over. He was alone on the street, breathing heavily, the car moving too fast. He braked lightly, seeing the slick wet left by street stalls, closed for the night, and tried not to skid, the silence rushing at him. There was still nothing behind him. Nothing.

His breath was coming in ragged spurts as he slowed the car to a crawl, looking forward to where the lane ended. Nothing. The wind blew in through the shattered windows and he felt a wetness along his cheek. Gingerly he put his hand up and then examined the blood on his fingers. A cut from flying glass, he decided, and swept the rest of the glass from the seat onto the floor of the car.

Was this Yee's idea of a night's entertainment? Intimidation, terror ... Tony gazed out into the quiet lane, sitting there quietly until he was in control again. He now knew what fear was all about, how Yee used it to debilitate, to debase, and he felt stupid that he had allowed it, had waited for Yee to make the move. He was suddenly blindingly angry at being played so deftly.

After a few moments he drove on again, but not towards his flat as he had intended before. Instead, he drove towards Old Peak Road. Time to take Yee's game back to him, he thought savagely, and who else knew what was going on but good ole Bill Ingram? Except that this time his father was going to do a little more explaining. Wasn't he?

351

The red banners furled and snapped in the wind, streaming out their gilt characters, cries for freedom, for democracy, cries of defiance as the tanks lined the square in front of The Great Hall of the People and the students marched out and climbed up the monument to the heroes of the revolution so that the news cameras could see them better. Down Changan Avenue, near the Jianguo Hotel, Harry paused in amazement, caught, like those around him, by the sight of a lone man in a white shirt standing in front of a column of tanks. He waved a cloth, and then stood there, perfectly still. The tanks came to a halt.

You fool, Harry thought. Oh God, you fool. But the man continued to stand there until Harry couldn't bear it any longer and had to turn away. He spoke into his mini recorder, glancing speculatively at the crowd around him, and then moved on uneasily and fast down the avenue towards Tian'anmen Square.

It was growing late by the time he found the bicycle he had left chained to a railing and freed it from the fifty or so others that had miraculously appeared around it. He was hungry, tired, and out of cassette tapes. He would return to his hotel for an hour or so before doing his evening report.

The night was heavy with heat, hanging there limply, the breeze dying down to a whisper, unable to blow the gathering clouds away. Harry pedalled along Nanchizi Road, slipping amongst the thinning traffic, sensing the tightening tension around him. He wished he were a thousand miles away, ten thousand, far away from the fear and anger he saw in the old people's faces, far away from the exhilaration and hope he saw there on the young people's faces. It was all going to come down around their ears, he knew. He could feel it.

By nine, he reached the hotel and, carrying his bicycle up into the lobby with him, for fear of not being able to find it later should he need transport fast, he reached the front desk. And there, rising uncertainly from a chair in the foyer, was a girl in black jeans, a white shirt, looking tired and strained, like him. Claudia.

'For God's sake, what are you doing here?' He was white with anger and she flinched at that anger, sensing he was nearing the edge.

'I've been here since Tuesday, Harry.' She looked at him quietly. 'My editor wanted some first hand copy. I've been out there,' she waved to the streets, the impending storm, 'all day. I thought maybe I could tag along with you this evening.' The way his hands tightened on the bicycle was unnerving.

'No,' he said. Just that. No argument.

She closed her eyes for a moment and breathed in deeply before looking back at him.

'I know it's bad, Harry, but I'm here now and I might as well report on what I see. I am going out there tonight and I'd rather not go out there entirely alone. It's your choice.'

'And I'd rather you didn't go out at all. I think you should stay put in your hotel and wait and see what the 27th army decides to do. Claudia, I don't want to go out there either, but I have to. You don't.' He hefted the bike onto his shoulder and walked towards the elevators, ignoring the angry gesticulations of the hotel porter. Upending the bike, he pushed it in to the elevator and waited for Claudia to join him.

'I have to see what happens, Harry. I don't want to look back, twenty years from now and say, yes, that was the turning point but I didn't see it, even though I was right there in Beijing, because I was too scared to go out and look.' She waited for the elevator doors to slide shut and heard Harry make an unexpected sound behind her.

'Don't be such a little fool. This isn't anything to do with heroics. It's downright stupidity, all of it.' He saw her turn and look at him, slowly up and down, and he almost flushed. His voice became gentler. 'I don't want you getting hurt. You're my ticket out of here, Liddie, and I can't afford to have anything happen to you.' She saw he was smiling but there was no amusement either in his words or his eyes. A deep feeling of loss filled her. Where had her Harry gone, what had happened to make him like this? She couldn't begin to guess.

'Then you'd better look after me while we're out there, hadn't you, Harry?' She forced a smile back. 'Because you can't stop me.'

They arrived back in the square around 11 p.m. and saw immediately that matters were rising to a head. The students were sitting in rows, hand in hand, staring at the soldiers who were now idly fingering their rifles, staring back with hard, anxious faces. Harry drilled Claudia in what to do, about never getting herself in a position from which she couldn't run, about staying on the edge of the crowd, about staying with him. But still he was frightened for her. For both of them.

They milled along the eastern side of the square, near Changan Avenue and the Beijing Hotel where he had told her to go in case of trouble, stopping to ask questions, to try and understand what was happening. People said the tanks were there to protect them against Li Peng, others said the rest of the army was coming to their aid against the 27th, still others said the army and police were being given drugs, told crazy things about infection and treason, that there would be death that night but the students would prevail.

But when death came, it was so unexpected that neither Harry nor Claudia moved fast enough. There was suddenly the sound of machine-gun fire crackling through the air and Claudia was swept to one side by the crowd thrusting forward to see what was happening. She lost Harry in an instant.

Ahead of her she could make out dimly, through the writhing throng of heads, a line of students forming up in front of the soldiers. And then there was more machine-gun fire and they were falling, and another line of students was getting up but she couldn't hear the firing now for the screams and cries that filled the air.

She looked around desperately, searching for Harry's face in the sea of milling people, crying out his name. When the tanks began to move forward, she panicked along with everyone else, running, plunging into the crowd as they thrust and buffeted against her, screams and smoke filling the night air.

354

There was gunfire from all directions now and she didn't know which way to run, spinning around and being pulled down flat by a man with glasses as the gunfire swept over them. She tried to rise but he pushed her back down again, screaming at her, his mouth snarling up and filled with spittle. Beneath her she felt wet and she raised the palm of her hand, finding it red, slick with blood.

She couldn't see Harry anywhere but the man suddenly pulled her to her feet and along after him, glancing over his shoulder with terror. Claudia looked back and saw a tank running over a woman, crunching her beneath its massive treads, the sound of her head like a bell chiming hollowly as it was crushed. She turned around and ran then, losing the man who had pushed her along, seeing the corner of the square and the police and soldiers there, hundreds, thousands of them, shoving and hitting the people with sticks and fists, beating them along, faster, out of the way.

People with blood covering their faces, their shirts, were falling, being trampled beneath their feet, but the soldiers urged them on with bayonets and Claudia, terrified and unable to think, ran with them.

From somewhere, rocks and branches were being hurled and she saw a group of protesters ripping the shirt off a young soldier, pulling at his hair, kicking and spitting on him. He was rescued by another group of police moving in and the protestors ran, raging and crying along the street. Those with bikes were flying down the road, screaming at those ahead of them and Claudia knew what they were saying, though she spoke no Chinese. They were screaming about the army, the army was coming.

She saw an intersection coming up and realised she was on Changan Avenue again, and that the hotel must be near there. But there were police lining the sides of the street, pushing and shoving people along, not letting them through. She ran on and on, darting down side streets when the crowd flowed that way, back out of alleys, running away from the smoke and the gunfire and the death of Tian'anmen Square.

Eventually, exhausted and dazed, she leaned against a

355

building, looking around her and seeing unfamiliar streets, quieter and darker now. Limping, her shoes lost and her feet cut and bleeding, she walked on until she reached a guardpost. A US marine stood there, his face pale and gaunt in the light. In the air, the faint crackling of gunfire could still be heard.

'Where am I? Where can I find shelter?' she called, and the guard hesitated, walking forward to peer at her, then to take her arm as he helped her around the checkpoint.

'This is the Jianguomenwai compound.' His voice was Southern and infinitely reassuring after the screaming terror of the night. 'You're safe here. This is where the diplomats and foreigners live. They won't come here.' The words eased her fear and she straightened up, looking about her as though in a daze.

'Are you with one of the news crews, lady?' he asked but she shook her head.

The marine watched her in silence, looking at the blood on her shirt, her hands, the way she stared out into the night in dread. Then he spoke quickly into a walkie talkie.

'I lost Harry,' she said softly, turning to look at him. 'He's still out there. Can't you do something? Please?'

But the marine was pushing her gently to one side, out of the way, and then moving forward to raise the barrier. He saluted smartly, his eyes directed centre front, not listening to her at all, not listening about Harry.

And then she turned as a car glided under the barrier, glossy black in the lights, shining brightly. In the back she saw, for a moment, as it slid by her, a dark-haired man in a suit, his grey skin smooth and well shaved, his dark eyes noting her and looking away. She stared after him, opening her mouth, screaming.

'Fish! Fish!' Trailing off to mutter weakly, 'Oh, you bastard, Fish!' until the night seemed to be spinning around her, twisting the lights into flashing stars and the car seemed to fall into that blackness.

Chapter Twenty-Nine

Hong Kong
7 June

Claudia re-read what she had written on her laptop computer, idly feeling the bruises along her cheekbones as she sat, leaning on her hand.

'Is this the end of an era as the reformist China of the 1980s, whose trade with foreign corporations over the last decade has committed $25 billion in joint venture enterprises, now looks set to undo that economic liberalisation with its hardline reaction against democratic reform? Or, despite the devastating crackdown of Tian'anmen Square, will China still seek to woo foreign investment once the dust clouds have settled and the screams have faded from our ears?' She sighed and erased the page, staring out instead at the flat shimmer of the bay.

'Am I disturbing you? Do you want me to leave?' Tony looked up from where he had been reading the paper. It was his day off and he had sensed she didn't want to be alone, had sensed the need in her ever since he had met her off the flight from Beijing. She was fragile, bruised both mentally and physically, and he knew she needed someone there for her. He wanted to be there, if she would let him.

'No, no, it's not that.' She gave him a wan smile, looking at his face and seeing the concern and the quiet strength that wanted to help. It was reassuring having Tony around, like a warm blanket against the cold. She could grow used to feeling this safe, she thought, and then hushed the idea. 'I just don't know how to write about economic triggers and the damage that rising inflation will do, when all I can remember is their screams and the bodies falling everywhere.' She shook her head. 'I can't see how Harry could have survived that. I don't know how I did. It's been three days now, Tony, and there's been no word.'

He saw the pain in her face. 'I know. But there's a lot of confusion over there at the moment. You're lucky we got you home so fast.' He could have told her there had been reports that the wounded had been dragged out of the hospitals and loaded onto trains and taken away somewhere. Perhaps killed. But he didn't think she was ready to hear it yet. And, despite everything, he didn't believe Harry was dead.

They were both silent, contemplating the horror and unable to bring themselves truly to believe in it. Outside, in the streets of Hong Kong, grief and fear could be seen on every face, black ribbons fluttering from car antennae, a black banner draped across the Bank of China building site, demanding 'Blood for Blood'.

The stock market had dropped 22 per cent of its value on the Monday after the massacre and there was a run on mainland Chinese banks. Property prices were predicted to be dropping between 10 to 20 per cent over the next few months. And there was nowhere for them to go.

'Tony, what was Fish doing over there? What does he really do? I'm not talking about that news editing nonsense. I mean, *really*.' She stressed the last word and the ease between them died, Tony glancing up at her, his face strained. She saw him finger the strip of sticking plaster across his cheek.

'Was he there?' he asked, a small frown on his forehead. 'Are you sure?' But he knew, even before she confirmed it, that Aidan had been there. So his father had lied to him about that. It came as no surprise. Everyone was busy trying to cover up, his father along with the best of them.

'Oh yes, I'm totally sure.'

'Well, perhaps the same as you were, or Harry? Gathering news.'

'Gathering heads, more like. He was in an official, diplomatic car. Not out on the streets getting the story.'

'Well, Aidan has his own sources. You know he used to work as a civil servant?' He sounded hesitant, hating the prevarications, to her, of all people.

'Civil servant? Now isn't that a handy catch-all.' Claudia looked at Tony steadily. There was a long moment of silence and Claudia began to wonder if he would answer at all.

'There are some things that are best not delved into too deeply,' he said unexpectedly and Claudia gave him a startled look.

'Do you really believe that, Tony? I'd never have thought it. I could hear Harry saying that, or maybe your father . . .' She gave him a look that was tired and disillusioned and he knew how she felt. He had been asking the same questions for so long, he had just about given up any hope of really knowing what was going on. But there was a lot he had read between the lines when he had spoken to his father last, and even more that he had guessed.

'And if I were to tell you what I think, would you print that?' He nodded towards her laptop. 'Or discuss it with other people? Would you tell them it was what I thought happened?' His voice had a warning note to it that Claudia absorbed in silence.

'No. I just want to *know*,' she said finally. He breathed in deeply, looking down at his hands clasped together as he sat hunched over them.

'This is all – hypothetical, you know. No facts, no names. Just, theory. Possibility.' When she nodded, he looked at her for a long moment, forcing himself to open up, to trust her. She read it in his eyes. 'All right then, about fifteen years ago, when it became obvious which way things were going to go here, a particularly ambitious criminal came to power. He realised, along with quite a few other people, that when Hong Kong reverted to Chinese rule, a number of things were likely to change. Crime for a start. Triads would not be welcome.

'Another figure, a very wealthy land and textile owner, also realised he would not be able to get his fortune out in time. It occurred to both these men that the best thing they could do was make sure the Chinese never took over. The rich Taipan met with the Triad leader and they made a connection. Drug dealing escalated and the money was laundered through legitimate outlets. Are you still with me?' Tony asked and Claudia nodded, watching him steadily.

'Good.' He smiled briefly. 'Well, the Taipan had connections on the mainland also. He knew a man there, a politician who was also ambitious, who also wanted to see a change take place with himself at the head of it all. And so a certain percentage of that laundered drug money began to find its way into this politician's pocket and he began to prepare for a revolution. A democratic one, if possible.

'And all might have been well and good, except that this minor character, a junkie who did some courier work for the Triad leader, stumbled on one of their meetings and he took a photograph.' He paused as he saw Claudia's eyes fly open, her mouth part in shock.

'That's right.' Tony nodded in confirmation. 'And when this courier realised who the men in the photograph were, he was scared and sent the photograph away to his sister. Unfortunately, another minor character, with few scruples, stole the photograph from the sister and took it with him out to Japan. Eventually, he figured out who the men were and he tried to blackmail the Triad leader, the Taipan – and, I would guess, the British Government.'

'Why the Government?' Claudia broke in.

'Because he realised that they would either pay to find out what was going on,' Tony rubbed his hands together slowly, as his voice became tentative, 'or they would pay to hush it up because they already knew what was going on.'

'Because . . . oh, dear God. And the blackmailer?' Claudia sat back, looking pale. She saw Tony look into her face, trying to read her thoughts and she swallowed over the tightness in her throat. 'Go on.'

'Now, exactly what happened next is unclear. Most probably, the Triad leader sent someone to kill this blackmailer and retrieve the photograph.' I'd like to believe that, to be sure it was Yee, Tony thought. But he wasn't, entirely. 'He also looked around and decided that it must have been either the courier or perhaps another man, an ex-master of the lodge, who had taken the photograph. And so the Triad leader ordered both of them to be killed.' Tony's voice was gentle but Claudia had to blink the fierce, stinging tears away. He halted and she shook her head.

'I'm all right. Go on.'

'The courier died, but the ex-member survived the attack.'

360

Claudia remembered the bandage on Harry's leg with sudden precision. 'And then the Taipan stepped in, ordering the ex-member to be spared. He was useful in promoting the revolution, gathering support, and ... he was the Taipan's daughter's lover. And she had great influence where her father was concerned.' Claudia's head had flown up and she gazed at Tony with angry, reddened eyes. He returned her gaze steadily and she breathed out slowly, acknowledging the truth.

'What then?'

'I suspect that the British Government realised just what was going on, having had a source for some years through the ex-member of the lodge. And while they didn't particularly like the Triad leader or the Taipan or the way they were funding the revolution, they nevertheless were happy to see it happen. And so they blocked certain police investigations,' Tony's voice had become grim, 'and they quietly helped in the funding of that particular politician's ambitions. They even welcomed the idea of a backlash against the democratic reform, believing, mistakenly, that the carnage would provoke such anger in the Chinese people that the government would be swept away entirely. Such things were happening in Europe. Why not in China?

'But they overestimated the Chinese people's ability and instead the ambitious politician suddenly disappeared and the Republican Government is strongly back in power. Which means that the Triad leader is no longer useful and neither is the Taipan. And they will be thrown to the wolves.' Tony smiled quietly at the thought.

'And Fish? I mean, a certain ex-civil servant?'

'He was, I think, always employed by the government and he was – is – useful in gathering information. And in disseminating it.'

'In China?' Claudia asked and Tony gave a pained smile.

'Anywhere it's necessary, I would think.'

'And the Triad ex-member? What will happen to him, if he returns?' She saw Tony give a quick shrug.

'Nothing. As long as we put the Triad leader away before then. Otherwise I wouldn't give him very long odds. But you might like to know that Portia Hsu had gone away, according to her mother, to spend some time in Vancouver. And the airline reported there were two tickets booked by Miss Hsu. I don't know any more than that, but, it's interesting, don't you think?' He saw her face tighten, her mouth pressing quickly together.

'Will you put Yee away, Tony? Can you do that? Do you have enough evidence to convict him?' He noticed her slip, in naming names but did not correct her. He was tired of silly games.

'Yes, finally. A lot of information I've tried for before, but been blocked on, will now become available. I wouldn't be surprised if he were to be picked up any day now.' And Tony thought of the folder of information against Yee that his father had finally handed over. Information supplied by Harry and passed on through Aidan. It was Harry's only chance of staying alive, his father had said, and he had made the choice only after Yee had pushed him too far. As Yee had pushed Tony too far.

He shrugged. 'The only thing we still have to do is link the Triad leader with the Taipan. And, somehow, I don't think that'll be that easy. He's no fool.'

He stood up and went to stand in front of the windows, staring out at the island opposite and the rush of dark water between, trying not to wonder at the silence in the room. But he couldn't help it. Was Claudia making choices now, deciding where she intended to go, when? He forced himself to be still, to damp down the loss he would feel if she left, to prepare himself for the emptiness that would, inevitably, be there for some time. He would have liked to have known her better. More than better.

He heard, rather than saw, her come and stand beside him, his breathing tight and constricted. 'What about you, Tony? Are you safe now?'

'I will be very soon. Yee's too busy right now trying to think of a way out of his hole to come after me. And I'll get him first.' He glanced at her, smiled a complicated sort of smile and she nodded, almost sadly.

'You enjoy your work, don't you? There's nothing else for you, is there? No time, no room for anything else.' She saw him pause in confusion.

'I could always try and make room, if . . .' he paused, unable to say it. Claudia frowned.

362

'If, what?'

'First, tell me something. Are you still in love with Harry?' He saw her eyes dart up to his in surprise, her mouth part with laughter. Almost immediately that changed, and she frowned again.

'No, no, I don't think I ever was. It was just this big fantasy both of us built up about each other and when we actually came together, we realised there was nothing there. Not for us.' She picked her way thoughtfully through her emotions. 'I still care about Harry but I don't trust him, I don't feel safe with him, and I don't really want him in my life. I hope he is with Portia. It'd be nice if he got a break, finally.' Her voice was musing, and she would have moved out through the window, onto the terrace if Tony hadn't put a hand on her arm, turning her towards him.

He couldn't conceal the relief, the way his own mouth curved up into a wide smile and she flushed, looking down and away.

'I know maybe this isn't the right time, but I don't want you just going off somewhere, not knowing there are other options.' He paused, his voice growing quieter still. 'So I suppose, I was wondering, if there's any way you might grow fond of me, in time?' He didn't press for more, was as quiet and gentle as he had always been with her and Claudia felt her admiration for him grow again. She wondered why she had never felt like this with any of the other men she had thought she was in love with? Never felt warm and safe and cherished. Never felt respect – such an old-fashioned, dated notion, but for her it was important.

'Oh, Tony, I'm more than fond of you already! Don't you know that? But I ... I'm scared,' she floundered over her explanation, desperate for him to understand. 'I've had pretty appalling luck with men most of my life and I don't even know whether that was due to me or to them. Maybe I'm useless at relationships, I don't know.' She smiled awkwardly. 'Tony, I don't want to make any promises and then end up hurting you – or me.' She gazed at him carefully, seeing the dark flecked eyes so clear, like washed granite. I don't want to lose you, Tony. I don't, she thought, but instead she said, 'But I'd like to try. If that's enough for you? For now.' He touched her cheek gently with his thumb, stroking the bones lightly.

When he leaned forward and softly brushed his lips over hers, she was reminded of that first night after Mark's death, when he had lain on the bed beside her and so much might have happened if they had let it. He tasted warm and fresh and she pressed herself against him, so that when they parted they both smiled and laughed slightly.

'It's okay, Claudia. I know how you feel and I think we both need to take this carefully and slowly. Neither of us has had a lot of success in the past.' His eyes were clear and tender as he shrugged. 'I guess I can settle for a little right now.' Maybe that way I'll get it all, one day, he added to himself. He felt the warmth beneath his thumb of her skin, the way she put a hand up to cup his hand to her cheek.

'Oh, Tony . . . I don't know what I'd do without you.' She saw the grey flecks in his eyes darken, the small lines around his eyes crease up and she wondered how she could have missed Tony beside the glamour of Harry. Fool's gold.

'Can you convince your editor to let you stay a while longer?'

'Yes, I think so, once I get this article off to him. And I thought I might have another go at that bestseller, some time soon. I feel like I might have something to say this time.'

'About China?'

'That too.' She smiled and rested her head against his chest with a sigh.

When Tony got home, he sniffed the air, smelling the sour, musty aroma of tobacco smoke and narrowing his eyes. But there was no one there. Pinned beneath the black and white photograph of three children there was another photograph. Tony plucked it from the wall with careful fingers, standing, staring at it for a long time. A note had been attached to it, in his father's handwriting.

'Pandora's box,' it said. 'Full of surprises.' The photograph showed three men in conversation.

Yee Fong Lo was there with a mainland China politician whose features Tony recognised well, and beside them both was a very clear likeness of Reginald Hsu.

Tony smiled quietly to himself.